Diane Janes was born and grew up in Birmingham. In between marrying and raising children, she worked in a variety of jobs until eventually giving up work to write full-time. This resulted in two shortlistings for the CWA Debut Dagger award. Diane has lived in Cumbria for the past twenty years and when not writing or lecturing she enjoys travelling and watching tennis.

Also by Diane Janes

The Pull of the Moon

Why Don't You Come For Me?

Diane Janes

Constable • London

Constable & Robinson Ltd
3 The Lanchesters
162 Fulham Palace Road
London W6 9ER
www.constablerobinson.com

First published in the UK by Constable,
an imprint of Constable & Robinson, 2011

This paperback edition published by Constable, 2011

A copy of the British Library Cataloguing in Publication
Data is available from the British Library

ISBN 978-1-84901-596-7

Printed and bound in the UK

1 3 5 7 9 10 8 6 4 2

CHAPTER ONE

Harry half walked, half ran up the lane. All-out running made the torch beam swing wildly from side to side, but when he slowed down to see where he was going, the night-time sounds crowded in on him and his own footsteps echoed in mocking pursuit. When an owl hooted somewhere close by, he all but dropped the torch. It was the sort of thing his parents went on about all the time, these so-called joys of the countryside, banging on whenever they heard a woodpecker or sighted a deer, and going into ecstasies that time a badger scurried across the road. Every school holiday it was the same, coming up to 'the cottage' as they called it, when he would much rather stay in Heswall with his mates. If they had to have a second home, why couldn't it be in the Algarve with a swimming pool, like his uncle John's villa, instead of bloody Cumbria, where it rained nine days out of every ten? And if they had to come to Cumbria, then why not the touristy bit, rather than a miles-from-anywhere hamlet, with the stupid name of Easter Bridge, where there was *nothing to do*? At least you could hire rowing boats in Bowness Bay, but they hardly ever went anywhere like that. Bowness wasn't 'the *real* Lake District', his dad said, although the shop selling thirty-six different flavours of ice cream seemed pretty darned real to Harry, and a damn sight more interesting than Easter Bridge, which consisted of fewer than a dozen houses, strung out along a little-frequented lane, which

Leabharlanna Poiblí Chathair Bhaile Átha Cliath
Dublin City Public Libraries

wasn't even within a mile of a lake. Lake District – pah!

He thought it must be even worse for Sean, who was stuck here all the time, the only kid in the place when Harry and his younger sister Charlotte weren't there. The parents had been really pleased when he told them that Sean had invited him round to play computer games. They seemed to imagine that it signalled some kind of rite of passage – acceptance by the locals – becoming part of the community. Their disappointment on learning that Sean's family were incomers had been palpable.

Anyway, Sean's company had been a godsend this half-term, getting him out of several boring walks, to say nothing of evenings playing Monopoly and Jenga en famille. It was quite a laugh hanging out with Sean, who had the new *Grand Theft Auto*, which Harry's own parents had refused him on grounds of its violent content, but tonight had been their last night together, because after a week at the cottage it was time to go home.

It had been right at the end of the evening when Sean had come out with it. Harry had been sounding off about Easter Bridge, and how it must be the dullest place on earth, when Sean looked up from the shelf where he was taking out a DVD and asked, 'What would you say if I told you there was a murderer living in Easter Bridge?'

Harry had restrained himself from the temptation to respond, 'I'd say you were a dickhead, who is absolutely full of it,' because, after all, Sean was not one of his mates from home, but still something of an unknown quantity. He was a recent acquaintance, and some eighteen months older than Harry, to say nothing of being his only lifeline from all those 'Let's-climb-Hellvelyn' initiatives that his parents categorized as good clean family fun. So Harry had bitten back his instinctive response and said instead, 'No. You're kidding me?' At which Sean just fixed him with a look which said he wasn't.

'How do you know?' Now Harry stopped to think about it, that wasn't the most obvious question.

'Oh, I know. I've got proof. I'll show you some time – maybe when you're next up here. I don't want to put anything on Hotmail. It's not secure.'

'We might not be coming back until the Easter holidays.'

'Next time,' said Sean. He turned back to the shelf containing the DVDs. It was a gesture of dismissal.

Harry knew he was being toyed with, but the digital clock already stood at 10.05 p.m. and his return time had been specified as 10 p.m. (It was a point of honour to be a little late – to demonstrate disregard, but not such outright disobedience that the parents could claim they had been worried about him.)

'OK then. See you.' Harry tried to make it sound as if he didn't much care whether Sean told him more about this supposed murderer or not. But now he wondered as he hurried along – had Sean been winding him up? It was easy to imagine anything, out here in the dark, with the wind making the trees creak and sending whispers through last year's dried-up beech leaves. Surely he must be bullshitting. A story to scare the kid up from the south?

Harry reached the gate of his parents' cottage, almost wrenching it off in his hurry, then letting it go with a bang once he was safely through. If either of them said anything, he could say the wind caught it.

Jo looked up from her book when she heard Sean descending the stairs. 'Has Harry gone?' she called into the hall.

Sean appeared in the doorway, his expression contemptuous. 'Didn't you hear the door?'

Since she had obviously heard Sean on the stairs, it was pointless to deny that she had also heard Harry. She had intended the question to be the opening gambit in a friendly conversation; to afford Sean an opportunity to tell her something about what he and Harry had been getting up to in his room for hours on end, but the initiative had already stalled.

'If you heard him go, why ask?' His tone was unmistakably sarcastic.

She managed a reasonably neutral tone in return. 'Please don't be rude, Sean. I was only making conversation. It's what normal people do.'

He shot straight back: 'Are you saying I'm not normal?'

'Of course not . . .' She paused, about to add something else, but he stalked off in the direction of the kitchen, leaving Jo feeling that she had just lost another round of a contest in which she wanted no part. For a moment she considered following to remonstrate with him, but she decided to let it go.

'It's difficult being a stepmother,' people had assured her. 'You have to work things out gradually.' She tried very hard, for Marcus's sake, but in the six months since Sean had come to live with them, the relationship between herself and her stepson had not improved. Sean hardly spoke to her unless he had to, and she found the prolonged silences between them a strain. Sean had the ability to render silence hostile in a way she could not easily explain to Marcus, who appeared oblivious to it.

When she and Marcus first got together, there had been no suggestion that Sean might become part of the package. Marcus had been divorced for years, and although a model absent father, maintaining contact, sending presents, periodically appearing to provide trips and treats, he had never expected his son would want to live anywhere but with his ex-wife. All this had changed with the arrival of a new man in her life. 'I don't like him,' Sean told his father. 'Mum doesn't have time for me any more, not now she's expecting another baby. Why can't I come and live with you?'

'It won't be for ever,' Marcus had said to Jo. 'He's fourteen now. He'll be eighteen and off to uni before we know it.'

She had assured him that she did not mind. She knew that with a partner came the baggage of their past relationships – and Marcus had always been the most understanding man in the world when it came to that. She had tried to make allowances for the fact that she and Sean hardly knew one another. She did everything she could think of to welcome him: spent money hand over fist redecorating his room, involving him, letting him choose whatever he wanted to have in it. She endeavoured to provide the food he liked at mealtimes, to be supportive when it came to starting his new school. She even covertly studied books about how to be a good step-parent, but none of the advice seemed to work. Was it just a teenage-boy thing? Maybe it was teenagers in general, she thought. Everyone said teenagers were difficult. Her only real experience of teenagers was being one herself, and that had been a long time ago.

She was not used to having teenagers – or even children in general – around. Her eyes strayed to the stainless-steel photo frame which stood in a prominent position on the pine dresser. A head-and-shoulders shot of a blonde toddler, snapped against a backdrop of garden flowers. A happy little face, looking straight into the camera. Lauren's smiling eyes met hers. 'I love you, Mummy,' they said.

Sometimes Lauren reproached her in dreams. *Where are you? Why don't you come for me?* Sometimes, even now –

getting on for nine years after it happened, Jo would still wake suddenly, thinking she heard a child's cry. For a split second the wind in the trees outside the bedroom window would sound like the sea as it surged up the shingle beach and Jo would picture the buggy, suspended among the brambles which grew on a rocky outcrop, a dozen or so feet below the cliff top. Sometimes she called out, clutching at the empty air beyond the bedclothes, imagining she saw the child, falling, falling, tumbling head over heels in a long, slow-motion descent past the off-white chalk: the tiny figure in its scarlet t-shirt and sky-blue dungarees, bright against the dull backdrop like a splash of paint flung at a prepared canvas. She always woke before Lauren hit the ground. Shuddering in the darkness, Jo would remind herself that Lauren had not plummeted to her death. Nothing had been recovered from among the smooth, clean stones. There had been no sign of a child's body. The summer tides never reached the foot of the cliffs. Only the empty pushchair had been found, crazily tilted among the bushes, leaning at an angle potent with false suggestion.

There had been pictures of the empty pushchair in many of the papers, photographs taken from far below with a telescopic lens. One appeared under the headline WHERE IS BABY LAUREN? It was the question everyone had asked a million times. Lauren – where was Lauren? At each of the news conferences, Jo had vowed to go on searching. 'I will never give up hope.'

'Never give up.' She had spoken those words a thousand times – sometimes standing in Lauren's empty bedroom, where only a gaggle of abandoned toys remained to hear her. But never is a very long time. Someone else occupied the bedroom now. Someone else played in the pocket-handker-chief garden, where Lauren had taken her first faltering steps.

On the day when the toys were finally packaged up, that room, that house vacated, Jo had comforted herself with the thought that Lauren would be far too old for those things now. She would need new toys when she came home, toys more appropriate to her age group. Other people tiptoed around the issue of the baby toys, saying – if they spoke of it at all – that this long-overdue act of disposal was a positive step, a way of moving forward. They didn't seem to understand that moving forward inevitably meant leaving something – or someone – behind. As the timescale lengthened until it was reckoned in years, Jo did sometimes forget. Gradually she had learned that respite *could* only be found in forgetting.

Marcus had helped, of course. To love and to be loved, that was the nearest thing to a cure for everything. So first had come the tonic of Marcus's love, and then the idea of turning their mutual interests into a business – the all-encompassing project that had become M. H. Tours. The irony was that when she and Marcus had begun M. H. Tours, it had been with the idea of working together. In the early days, they had jointly accompanied nearly all the tours, only working separately as the business expanded and they offered more itineraries to cater for increasing demand. People tended to assume that the name M. H. Tours had been chosen because of Marcus's initials, but in reality it started as a private joke – Magical History as opposed to Magical Mystery – a company which provided holidays in various parts of the UK for groups and individuals with a passion for history. It was squarely aimed at the top end of the market, with some tours themed to specific periods or events – Battlefields of the Wars of the Roses, or Monastic Life in Medieval England. Some were based around the lives of famous people: there was a Mary Queen of Scots tour, one featuring Richard III and another which majored on Brunel. The company had their own luxury midi-coaches, which transported guests between carefully chosen accommodations. As well as British travellers, there was a big market among the Americans and Japanese, and the business had blossomed even further since M. H. Tours had gone into partnership with Flights of Fantasy Ltd, a similar company to their own, specializing in holidays themed to Lake Country writers such as Beatrix Potter, Arthur Ransome and William Wordsworth. The timing of their amalgamation with Flights of Fantasy had proved unexpectedly opportune, not only in its potential for further expansion, but also in that it provided a fresh source of experienced specialist guides at the very time when Sean's arrival necessitated Marcus and Jo taking turns to stay at home.

In spite of the difficulties child care presented to a couple whose working life had hitherto been spent largely on the road, she fully accepted that Marcus had a duty to his son and that she in turn had a duty to Marcus. Unfortunately, these new arrangements not only contrived to leave her alone with the boy for days at a stretch, but also ensured that periods at home with Marcus were invariably shared by Sean. She soon realized that unless she set aside a great many Sean-related grievances, a lot of their time together as a couple would be dominated by her problems with Marcus's son.

Being away with M. H. Tours had been a way to immerse herself and to forget – the surest anaesthetic for a pain which was otherwise too great to bear. The waves of guilt that followed each period of forgetfulness were a terrible side-effect, but like a cancer sufferer enduring chemotherapy, Jo had come to realize that without recourse to the antidote, she simply could not go on living. Like a painful amputation, the agony became less acute; one adapted, got used to living with a part of oneself gone. Sometimes she wondered if her new life had helped her to forget too well, so that as time went by she almost welcomed the return of the pain. Sometimes the harder it hurt the better she felt, because remembrance was payment. And she must never forget – not that there was much chance she or the world at large ever would – that it was she who was to blame. It had been she who had left their sleeping child unguarded.

Such a *nice* day. A sunny day, holidaymakers strolling around in summer clothes, everything gaudy and bright, like a scene in a child's picture book: the sort which has a happy ending. It had not begun like a story where some devil steals away the golden-haired child. The village street was busy with people (so busy with people, and yet no one saw a thing), just ordinary people having a day out (were they all blind?). Dom had slipped into the little chemist's shop to replace his forgotten razor. He had come away on holiday without it, left it sitting on the bathroom windowsill at home. 'I'll catch you up,' he said.

She had only walked on a matter of yards, drawn to take a closer look at The Shell Shop. She had scarcely expected such an old-fashioned seaside emporium would still exist. The proprietors had expanded their operation on to the pavement, setting up tables out front which were covered in shells for sale, tables placed too close together to allow for the passage of a pushchair. She had only slipped inside for a moment. For a long time afterwards she could not even remember why. 'Did you want to look at something?' the policewoman kept on asking. 'Was there something you wanted to buy?' As if she would want to buy some piece of old tat made from shells, for heaven's sake. But if not, then why – why – had she left Lauren alone?

The shop had a coloured awning which extended right out over the pavement with 'The Shell Shop' spelled out in huge letters across the blue and white stripes, the words faded by five seasons of sunshine. Hooks had been driven into the outer edge of the awning, and from these were suspended strings of shells, ropes of shells, shells fashioned into wind chimes, shells made into dangling objects reminiscent of an Australian bushman's hat. There were shells which shifted in the breeze, clattering uneasily against one another like unwieldy strings of giant worry beads. Every spare inch of window space was filled with objects adorned with shells. Useless, tacky souvenirs which screened anyone inside the shop from what was happening on the pavement outside, where Lauren was sleeping in her pushchair.

She remembered fingering a mouse on skis – the whole thing made from shells – contemplating it as a joke present for some friends (remembering this only much, much later – far too late to convince the police that this had been her original motive for entering the shop). She didn't buy anything. Mere minutes had passed between her entering and emerging from the shop. On her way out she had to wait while a fat woman momentarily blocked the doorway, then threaded her way between a table stacked with sea urchins and another covered with the polished vacated homes of a hundred queen scallops, before she could get back to Lauren. The empty space on the pavement stopped her dead. A pair of feet had moved into the space where Lauren's buggy should have been. A pair of feet in open-toed sandals, which belonged to a man wearing a pair of brown shorts. He was picking up items from the display, showing them to a disinterested teenage daughter. Jo stared at him, all but shoved him away, as if by removing him she could recapture what she ought to be seeing there.

A solution presented itself in a rush of anger. Dom must have pushed Lauren further up the street, not thinking of the fright he would give her when she emerged from the shop and found Lauren was gone. Then she saw him approaching. The smile as he caught sight of her died in an instant. Her expression and the absence of the pushchair told him everything. It was then that she began to scream.

CHAPTER TWO

Jo made sure that Sean set out for the school bus in good time on Monday morning. A little cloud of guilt descended on her as she watched him slouching away from the house. Did all parents' hearts gladden to see the back of their offspring at the resumption of each new term? She called a goodbye from the doorstep, but when he did not turn she let the arm she had lifted in farewell fall back to her side.

Was this the answer to all those prayers, all that yearning to have a child in the house? She had often imagined how life would be when Lauren was restored to her. She had even tried to kid herself that if she took proper care of Sean, maybe the Fates would see what a good mother she could be – given the opportunity – and then Lauren could come home. Of course, life did not work like that, but at least if she lavished enough love on Sean and was seen to take good care of him, then maybe people would stop thinking . . .

She was rinsing a bottle at the sink when she caught sight of the Phantom Jogger. That was what Marcus had nick-named him, because when he first started to pass the house on a daily basis, a grey shadow in his faded jogging bottoms and pale t-shirt, they could not imagine where he had come from. Although their house, aptly named The Hideaway, was partly screened by trees, from the kitchen window it was just possible to see a short stretch of the lane where it began its descent to the little stone bridge from which the hamlet took its name. Jo watched the Phantom Jogger as he steadily covered the ground, striding out easily, looking neither to right nor left, until he went out of sight where the lane bent sharply to avoid an outcrop of rock. Although his identity had initially been a mystery, within a week of his first appearance, Maisie Perry, who passed for the next best thing to a town crier in Easter Bridge, had informed them that the daily jogger was the latest tenant of High Gilpin.

High Gilpin belonged to a family called Tunnock, but was often let on short leases to people who were working on temporary contracts, or needed a base while looking for a permanent home in the area. It was generally considered that if any place was calculated to put you off country living, it was High Gilpin, a one-time working farm, which stood in an isolated spot at the end of an unmade track, a good half-mile or so from the next nearest habitation. After heavy rain, ice or snow the track was impassable to any but four-wheel drives, and the house was completely off the radar of delivery vans or taxi firms. Easter Bridge might be the best part of ten miles from the nearest shop, but at least you had a handful of neighbours to whom you could turn *in extremis*. When the power line blew down and the lights went out at High Gilpin, you were on your own.

When Jo had finished with the milk bottle and dealt with the rest of the recycling, she crossed the hall and went into the room they called the office, in order to check emails. There was a new message in from Nerys, sent from an internet café on the other side of the world – a couple of chatty paragraphs in which Jo could hear her friend's voice outlining her latest adventures in New Zealand.

She missed having Nerys readily available at the end of the phone. Not that she begrudged the trip for a moment. If anyone had earned their midlife gap year it was Nerys, who had survived redundancy, divorce and a brush with cancer. 'There's a million and one reasons why every woman knows all the words to "I Will Survive",' Nerys once said.

Resolute, grounded Nerys, whose friendship had stood the test of time, someone with whom she had managed to stay in close touch, even after moving north with Marcus. When Nerys fell ill, Jo had made frequent trips down to visit her, both in hospital and at home. It had been during one of these that Nerys had announced, 'I've decided when this is all over, I'm going travelling. I'm going to see the world.'

At the time the prognosis had seemed so dire, Jo could only wonder at Nerys's determination – no ifs, or buts, she *was* going to go travelling. That conversation had been four years ago, but it had taken time for Nerys to get well again, and almost as long to formulate her plans and put them into action. 'I've been taking lessons from my nephews and nieces,' she told Jo. 'The thing to do is bum a bed from anyone you can claim the slightest link with: third cousins once removed, long-lost colleagues, friends of friends. All the kids do it – they're quite shameless, and I'm getting good myself. I've even managed to trace a girl I used to know at school whose family emigrated to New Zealand. Turns out she lives near Snells Beach, which isn't far from Auckland, and she's offered to put me up for a couple of nights.'

About a week before she left, Nerys held a going-away party. Marcus had been tied up with work, but Jo travelled down to be there. It was great to be part of the send-off, yet at the same time she had experienced a faint sense of misgiving. There was something so final about a going-away party. It made you feel as if you might never see the person again. Nerys must have picked up on this, because when she gave Jo a farewell embrace, she said with attempted gravity: 'You do know that I might not be coming back?'

'What do you mean? Of course you'll be coming back.'

'Not if I meet a millionaire and he takes a fancy to me. An oil tycoon would do nicely. And, of course, if I'm discovered on some beach in California and they want to put me in the movies . . .'

'Well, don't forget that if you do land the lead in a remake of *Gone with the Wind*, I want to be the first to hear about it.'

'Absolutely. I expect Spielberg has got broadband in his mansion – and if not, there's sure to be an internet café just down the road.'

To date, Nerys's emails had made no mention of millionaires or film directors, but she had been swimming with dolphins, hiking on the Tereziana Trail and photographed in front of the Taj Mahal . . . *Maybe not as slim as Diana, but much funnier . . . you should get some tours organized in India. Can't you come up with a Kipling link?* Without a set itinerary, she had overstayed her time everywhere and arrived in New Zealand at least six weeks later than originally anticipated, so it was no surprise to read this morning: *I'm hoping to extend the trip. It sounds as if my tenants would be happy to stay at least another six months, and my money is lasting really well. Everyone is so hospitable, and won't let me pay for anything.*

'I miss you,' Jo said aloud. 'Don't stay away too long.' She hit the reply key and began to type. *That would be fantastic. It's so great that everyone is giving you such a lovely welcome.*

She did not have much news to offer in return for Nerys's lively description of the Takapu gannet colony. Spats with Sean and what she thought of Sebastian Faulks's latest novel were rather small beer by comparison, and seemed to emphasize an increasingly large gap in her life. Before the amalgamation with Flights of Fantasy, she had been much more involved with the day-to-day running of the business. At the inception of M. H. Tours they had employed an extremely capable woman called Moira, who had driven out from Ulverston four days a week to work in the little office at The Hideaway, but Moira eventually decided that her elderly mother needed her more than Jo and Marcus did, and after Moira there had been a succession of short-term staff, some better than others, until the company eventually acquired proper offices in Kirkby Lonsdale, with two full-time women, both of whom seemed more than adequate to the task. The location of the company's offices had been chosen for its proximity to the home of Melissa Timpson, one-time proprietor of Flights of Fantasy and now their business partner, which meant that when Melissa was not guiding tours herself, she was nicely placed to keep an eye on things.

These new premises were a good forty-five minutes' drive from Easter Bridge, but as Marcus said, with phones and email what did that matter? It was undoubtedly far easier to recruit good staff to work in the little market town than it was to persuade them to drive out into the countryside, and besides which, the room they used as an office at The Hideaway was not large enough to allow for expansion.

When she and Marcus had originally agreed to take it in turns to stay at home, Jo assumed that during her periods as the parent 'off-tour', she would go into the office at Kirkby Lonsdale while Sean was at school, but though she had initially tried to establish this routine, she soon began to feel surplus to requirements. Sally and Janice ostensibly went out of their way to make her welcome, but on volunteering to check the drivers' hours, she would be greeted by, 'Oh, Melissa went through them yesterday.' A suggestion that she might relieve them of inputting some invoices would be met with the smiling reassurance that Janice had them all completely up to date – and the statements too. When the telephones rang, she was always just too late picking them up. The business which she had coaxed gently into life, nurtured like a baby and helped totter to its feet, was all grown-up and doing very nicely without her. She consoled herself with the thought that she and Marcus had not begun M. H. Tours so that they could sit in an office, shuffling papers. She still went out regularly with the tours, and after all, that was the heart and soul of the enterprise.

Thus Jo had fallen out of the habit of going into the office, using her new-found leisure to catch up with long-postponed household jobs, initially luxuriating in the chance to watch a film or read a book during the day. Marcus certainly had no problem filling the days when it was his turn at home – not with satellite television beaming cricket and rugby from around the globe virtually twenty-four/seven. Which was not to say that he did not put time in on the business too. Somehow his visits to the office seemed to be more productive. Jo had seen the way Sally and Janice visibly brightened as he swept in, full of easy charm, always ready with an amusing anecdote about something which had happened on a tour. He didn't need to justify himself with offers to help out – his mere presence had a positive impact on staff morale. He also managed to research and work out new itineraries, often in collaboration with Melissa, whose days at home seemed to coincide with his quite frequently, so that when Jo got home after a week with a coach load of Richard III enthusiasts, she would find Marcus brimming with their latest ideas. She tried to stifle any feelings of exclusion because she didn't want to dampen his enthusiasm, and on the odd occasion when she had grumbled that at one time he would have talked through the new Daphne du

Maurier tour with her rather than Melissa, Marcus simply could not see her problem. What difference did it make who came up with the ideas, or who worked on what particular aspects of the business? The three of them worked as a team now. It did not matter which particular permutation of staff was involved, so long as they got the job done well.

Jo attempted to compete with some suggestions of her own, but somehow her ideas were never so inspired or so workable as the schemes which Melissa and Marcus dreamed up in her absence – in spite of her having an abundance of thinking time. That wasn't a good thing, either. For the past few years a large part of her survival mechanism had relied on not thinking too much, keeping busy, always having something immediate to think about, something to do. In the past few months there had been terrible stories in the news about young girls being kidnapped and kept prisoner for years, used as sex slaves, never seeing daylight. It could send you mad, dwelling on stories like that.

As an antidote to having too much time on her hands, she had recently taken up sketching. She had not done any 'art' since school, but it was one of those things she had always yearned to have a go at. She told herself that she might eventually buy some watercolours, then maybe enrol in a class, although the peripatetic nature of her work made any regular weekly commitment impractical. She was disinclined to sign up for any of the painting days which were always being advertised, in case everyone else turned out to be an experienced artist and she looked ridiculous. Instead she began to work alone, almost secretively. At first she arranged groups of objects in the house, rather as they had done in art class at school, but soon she was venturing beyond the house, trying to capture trees, buildings and the natural features of the landscape, then figures covertly observed from a distance as they ate their picnic lunches. All of these were infinitely more satisfying than a trio of oranges in a bowl. She knew she was improving, but was shy of showing her work to anyone – even Marcus, who teased her gently about her 'secret sketches' whenever he caught sight of the drawing book lying about. Going out to draw had become a regular routine. On days when the weather permitted, she packed her sketch pad and pencils into a rucksack, together with a flask of raspberry tea and her mat to sit on, before heading out in search of a subject.

After a whole week of being at home with Sean, she badly needed to escape the house. It was a cold day, but dry and bright – ideal weather so long as she wrapped up warmly. Her walking boots sounded loudly on the tarmac as she headed north away from the old stone bridge. The Hideaway stood at one extreme of the hamlet, a modern house set back from the road. A much older building stood a few yards further north on the opposite side of the lane. There had been no blacksmith at The Old Forge in living memory, but according to Sean, who had a penchant for the macabre, the house was haunted by the ghost of a drunkard who had burned to death after falling into the blacksmith's fire. Sean said he got the story from someone at school, and although Jo regarded all this with considerable scepticism, she had always thought there was something creepy about the place, even before Sean related his dubious tale.

More recently The Old Forge had been home to Mr and Mrs Pearson, but the latter was long dead and old Mr Pearson had eventually gone into a nursing home, leaving the house unoccupied for almost a year. About a month before Christmas, news had reached them of Mr Pearson's death, and in January a house-clearance firm had removed all contents save the greying curtains at the windows. Soon after that, a black and yellow 'For Sale' board had appeared, nailed to the rotting front gatepost. The property particulars described The Old Forge as 'an investment opportunity', although Marcus said 'money pit' might be a better term. Very little had been done to the place since the Pearsons moved in at the end of the 1960s, but in spite of the obvious drawbacks, there had been a good deal of initial interest. Glimpses of the estate agent's silver BMW were a frequent event, and it was not long before a red 'Sold' sign was fixed to each side of the yellow and black board.

Jo glanced at The Old Forge as she passed. The place had been empty for more than a year, but she often felt as if there was still someone inside the house, watching. Even as she ridiculed the notion, she found herself reluctant to look up at the windows, lest she glimpse a pale face there in confirmation of her fears. Subconsciously she quickened pace, hurrying past much as Harry had done a couple of nights before.

The next building was an old farmhouse, now a holiday let and currently unoccupied. For practical purposes this was The Hideaway's next-door neighbour, although it was too far away to have much impact on them unless occupied by exceptionally noisy visitors. They occasionally caught a whiff of barbecuing, if the wind was in the right direction, and once discovered a woman exploring their garden, her justification arising from the townie notion of a 'right to roam' anywhere she liked, once she got into the countryside.

Across the lane from the farmhouse was Honeysuckle Cottage, a seldom-occupied second home, and a few yards beyond Honeysuckle Cottage lay Throstles, home to Maisie and Fred Perry. (After more than half a century of jokes about cheap Wimbledon tickets, the unfortunate man's smile was wearing a little thin.) The Perrys were a retired couple with a passion for gardening. When not fulfilling their duties at Holehird Gardens, where they were both enthusiastic members of the Lakeland Horticultural Society, they were tending their own plot with such assiduous devotion that in summer their bungalow was almost obscured by the fecundity of the garden. Marcus was convinced that the real motive for Maisie's constant presence in the garden was the insight it gave her into other people's business, privately theorizing that the principal attraction of Throstles for Maisie lay not so much in the generous size of its garden but its position on the bend, from whence the gateway to every other property in the lane was visible, affording Maisie a virtually uninterrupted view of all her neighbours' comings and goings.

As Jo approached the Perrys' gate, she caught sight of Maisie emptying some peelings into a compost bin near her kitchen door. There was no chance of escape because Maisie looked up at just the wrong moment, waved a hand in greeting then made purposefully for the gate. Maisie did not bother with any 'how are you' preliminaries – a sure sign that she had some news worth sharing.

'Have you heard who's bought The Old Forge?' She scarcely waited long enough for Jo to shake her head before continuing: 'Well, as you know, I had heard a rumour that it was going to a builder. There was some talk of planning permission and I said to George, "They'll be putting in to knock it down and start again. We'll have no peace if that goes ahead." My friend up at Holehird has been driven mad this past year, what with the alterations her new neighbours are having done – noisy jack hammers and mud everywhere.' Maisie paused to take a breath. 'But apparently it isn't a builder who got it in the end. Definitely a private buyer – a widow with a daughter – and she plans to live here all the time.'

'I expect they'll still need to have a lot of work done,' said Jo. 'It hasn't had anything done to it for years. Is the daughter grown-up?'

'No. Just a youngster of thirteen or fourteen, so I heard. That would be nice for your stepson, wouldn't it – another young person? I saw Harry going up and down last week. What a shame he and his sister aren't here all the time. It makes for a proper little community, having children around the place, the way things used to be in the old days.'

Jo didn't want to get into a discussion about second homes and vanished communities. It was one of Maisie's pet topics, although Jo was not entirely sure what kind of community Maisie imagined had ever existed at Easter Bridge. It had never been large enough to call itself a village. There had never been a school or a shop here – if anything, the small settlement had expanded in recent times thanks to an enterprising local farmer selling off building plots before the inception of stricter regulations imposed by the National Park Authority. Fortunately, Maisie showed no inclination to mount her soap box and Jo managed to escape after a brief exchange about the weather, crossing the opening where the track led up to High Gilpin, then heading steadily up the hill.

The next two buildings on Maisie's side of the road were extremely incongruous in the context of a Cumbrian hamlet. The first of them, Ingledene, was a double-fronted Victorian house, complete with bay windows and streaky-bacon brickwork, which would not have looked out of place in a London suburb. It had been built to house a minister for the matching chapel next door, both structures dating back to the last decade of the nineteenth century, when the farmer at High Gilpin, having found religion in a big way, financed the erection of both buildings in the expectation of a New Jerusalem arising in the valley.

Folk history had it that the family from High Gilpin and their minister held services in splendid isolation, with even their immediate neighbours declining to join them in the new oak pews. After a short life as an active place of worship the chapel had enjoyed a chequered history, eventually becoming an art gallery, which was currently run by Brian and Shelley, who lived in bohemian disorder at Ingledene.

Jo got on well with Shelley, and quite often dropped into the gallery for a chat when she thought Brian was not around. Something about Brian had always unnerved her. He was a well-known local artist whose work commanded four-figure sums, a great bear of a man, known for his intensely held opinions and very short fuse. It was rumoured that he once took such violent exception to the views expressed by an art critic at a Royal Academy Summer Exhibition that he punched the man in the jaw and was prosecuted for common assault. Another reason for her eschewing the local art classes was that Brian sometimes taught them. Shelley was an artist too, but she was far less commercially successful – or volatile – than Brian.

The gallery was still in darkness as Jo passed. Shelley and Brian did not generally open for business until about eleven. There was not much passing trade – they relied on people who were serious about art, Shelley had once explained; people who came out of their way specially, because the gallery had a high reputation and only hung work which represented the very best of local artists.

Local artists . . . It suddenly occurred to Jo that it might be possible to build a tour around artists associated with Cumbria. She did not know much about famous local painters, apart from Ruskin and Collingwood, who featured in their existing literary tours, but maybe this was something she could talk to Shelley about – not Brian, who she thought sure to be contemptuous and dismissive of the whole idea.

A few yards beyond the gallery she reached the last dwelling in Easter Bridge, The Hollies, a barn conversion now the country retreat of Harry's family. She knew that they had returned south on Saturday, and guessed that the place would probably sit empty for several weeks now. Maisie Perry was wont to cluck about this, but Jo tended to be more realistic: it was not merely house prices which put a house like The Hollies beyond the reach of a family on a modest income. There was no work nearby, no shops, no local school, no viable public transport – unless you counted the twice-daily school bus. Ordinary life in a place like this was too expensive for any family on a low income. Living out here required at the minimum a well-maintained car for every working adult in the household. Food shopping had to be carefully thought through and involved a round trip of almost twenty miles – with cheaper supermarkets all but double the distance. Television reception was only available to those who could afford a satellite dish. In Jo's opinion, the so-called scourge of second homes and holiday cottages was often what prevented tiny hamlets like this from falling into the semi-dereliction of rural poverty.

A hundred yards or so past The Hollies, she negotiated the squeeze style at the side of the lane and began to climb a steep footpath through the trees. Apart from a nearby robin, it was exceptionally quiet; no cars passing along the lane, no voices floating up from the gardens. There was a timelessness up here: it might have been tomorrow already, or a hundred years ago. It was very damp among the trees. Mosses and lichens were misted with winter moisture. In places water oozed up from beneath the carpet of fallen leaves, forming puddles around the soles of her boots, deep enough to flick muddy water on to her thick woollen socks when she lifted her feet.

It was a fairly stiff climb at the beginning, and after a few minutes of steady walking, the path turned rocky, becoming a stream in places, with a hundred miniature waterfalls each singing their own distinctive tune. When the path eventually emerged on to the open moor, the change was abrupt, the contrast almost startling after the close intimacy of the trees. From here Jo headed north-west, until the Coniston range loomed into view, impossibly large, making you wonder how it could have hidden itself behind a small ridge for so long.

When she reached a group of large flat stones, an imperfect circle which looked as if it had been set out there on purpose for a meeting, she dragged her mat out of the rucksack, sat down and prepared herself to draw, securing the sides of her sketch book with bulldog clips to prevent the light breeze from interfering with her endeavours.

You could lose yourself in drawing. That was one of the great things about it: if you really focused on what you were doing, there was no room to think about anything else. And whenever Jo attempted to capture the landscape on paper, she always saw things that she had never noticed before – a tiny thread of water marking its course downhill; the shadows which darkened the side of Brown Pike. It was a different way of looking – a new way of seeing.

This total concentration did not always work entirely to her advantage. Left to their own devices some of her thoughts – a subversive group which operated to an agenda of their own – had a nasty habit of bursting to the forefront of her mind when she was least expecting them. Thus, after she had been working steadily for a time, she abruptly became aware of Sean's voice in her head, repeating the question he had put to her on Saturday night: 'Are you saying I'm not normal?'

It was a horrible accusation – something she would never say to a child. A memory returned, sharp as a shard of freshly broken glass: Jane Hill's tenth birthday party – the pointing fingers and staring faces. Some of the mothers – not her own mother, of course; her own mother had not been there – other people's mothers ranged around her, tall as houses, all crowding into the Hills' kitchen, where they had taken her to be out of sight of the other children. Staring at her, their faces curious or anxious in varying degrees, whispering among themselves, someone saying in a low voice which she was not supposed to hear: 'She's not normal.'

One of them tried to give her a hug, but she had torn herself away, backing into the corner until the intervention of the draining board prevented further retreat; all the time that horrible music going on and on, the children's voices half drowning it out with their shrieking now that the party games had resumed in the front room, while in the kitchen all those other mothers kept on staring at her.

With a determined effort, she focused her attention back on her sketch of the hills, but as soon as she did so she gave a little cry. She had ruined it – doodling in the bottom right-hand corner of the page when her mind was somewhere else. She pulled out her rubber and attacked the intrusion savagely, not stopping until the fat face topped by an old-fashioned policeman's helmet had completely disappeared. Perhaps if she drew some rocks in the foreground it would cover the smudge.

She worked at the drawing steadily for some time before looking up again. Clouds of a similar hue to the marks left by her rubber had begun to appear from behind the ridge above Torver. If she did not pack up and begin the return journey, there was a strong possibility she would get wet. It was always quicker going home – downhill all the way, for one thing. She saw no one as she hurried along the lane under the darkening sky. Everywhere looked barren at this time of year, before the daffodils brought a splash of colour to the roadside verges. There was a lot of grey in Cumbria, she reflected: stone buildings under slate roofs, walls instead of hedges.

When she opened the front door she saw that the postman had called in her absence. The face on the home-made picture postcard looked up at her from the mat. A chubby face surrounded by blonde hair, trusting blue eyes, pink baby mouth parted in a smile. She reached for the card with trembling fingers, turning it over to read the words printed on the reverse, although she had already guessed what the message would be, because she knew it off by heart: *I still have her.*

CHAPTER THREE

The enormous success of M. H. Tours was due in no small part to the influence of its co-founder, Marcus Handley. From the outset the company prided itself on providing a very personal service, and Marcus excelled in creating a sense that every possible thing was being done to ensure each traveller's individual enjoyment and well-being. He exuded approach-ability, with no question too obscure or too trivial for the application of his undivided attention. He knew instinctively which of their – predominantly female – clientele would respond well to intellectual flattery, and which to gentle flirtation. Women liked Marcus, and men respected him. His long, thin face and shoulder-length curling locks, often held back by a pair of glasses perched atop his head in the fashion of an Alice band, gave him a scholarly appearance. He stood well over six feet tall, and was slim enough to make jeans work with an open-neck shirt and smart jacket. There was a comforting solidity about Marcus Handley which made people feel they could rely on him. He was the sort of man who, when helping you into the lifeboats, would still have found time for a pleasant word to everyone, remaining completely calm even as the liner was sinking beneath his feet.

This easy bonhomie required a level of concentrated effort, seldom suspected by participants of the tours he escorted. Marcus maintained his focus from the moment he appeared in the hotel foyer shortly before breakfast, until he switched off just before falling into bed at the end of each day, having often sat conversing in the bar until well beyond midnight. This attention to detail, which some might have defined as obsessive, Marcus merely deemed professional. Melissa, Jo and their other guides endeavoured to offer a comparable service, but Marcus did it best.

It was an absolute given that he and Jo did not interrupt each other's working day with anything short of a major emergency, which was why her calling him on the mobile about the arrival of the postcard was so annoying. He understood that she was upset – of course he did – but the arrival of the card did not represent something about which he could, at that precise moment, do anything at all. And distressing as it was, they had been here before: it was not the first of its kind and nor, he supposed, would it be the last.

Marcus accounted himself an exceptionally patient man, who had always done his best to consider the feelings of others. He invariably approached issues pertaining to Lauren with the utmost sensitivity, but surely Jo could see that the arrival of the card – albeit unpleasant – did not constitute the kind of major emergency which licensed her to phone him at this most inopportune of moments, just when he was addressing his little group of Brontë devotees prior to their entering that literary Holy of Holies, the parsonage at Haworth.

The Brontë tour was not one of his favourites. Melissa generally escorted the Brontë tours, or else they were undertaken by Jenny, one of their part-time guides, who was a retired lecturer in English Literature. But Jenny's daughter was about to produce a grandchild, Melissa was already committed to a week with some American women's group who wanted to know all about Vita Sackville-West, and Jo had never accompanied the tour and didn't know the material well enough, which was how he found himself standing in the Pennine drizzle, clutching a golf umbrella in one hand and a copy of *Wuthering Heights* in the other, when his mobile struck up with the *William Tell Overture*.

His immediate and obvious instinct was to anticipate bad news about his mother, but no – it was Jo, expecting him to indulge in a completely inappropriate conversation. Inappropriate because it never did to distract a group who had become utterly immersed in the theme of the trip. Conversations suggestive of a private life were off limits – whatever life he had beyond Charlotte, Emily, Branwell and the rest of their unfortunate family was something which belonged to an entirely separate world.

What kind of conversation about the card did Jo imagine he could possibly have with her, in the middle of a working day, during which he was never out of earshot of his charges? Any mention of 'take it to the police' would plummet his audience straight back into the twenty-first century and have them frantic with curiosity. They were all ladies of a certain age, hungry for second-hand excitement. 'Is everything all right, Marcus?' they would ask, voices a treacly mixture of solicitude and curiosity. Even if he employed a more ambiguous phrase, such as 'We will have to talk about it later', he risked a rumour running round the party that there was a problem of some kind, perhaps with the hotel they were heading for in Scarborough. Whispers of that kind, even when they subsequently proved to be incorrect, ruffled the surface of the smooth organization on which he prided himself; nothing but the view across the valley must be allowed to distract the ladies from their lunch in the Jane Eyre Tea Rooms.

So when Jo babbled out the reason for her call, Marcus

said in the most casual voice he could muster, 'I'm afraid you have caught me at a very bad moment. I'm just about to lead our party into the Brontë parsonage.'

Jo had babbled some more and begun to cry, but Marcus, still wearing an expression of benevolent amusement, while pressing the phone painfully hard against his ear to prevent the smallest sound from reaching the ladies standing nearest, waited until she paused for breath, then said, 'Yes, of course. Why don't we talk about it some other time?' He rang off, and ostentatiously switched off his phone before replacing it in his jacket pocket, then turned back to the group with an apologetic smile. 'The marvels of modern communication. A friend who didn't know my schedule. So sorry, everyone – now back to the parsonage . . . When the family first arrived in 1820 . . .'

Naturally the episode *had* upset him, in spite of his apparent lack of concern. He might be cross with Jo for calling, but he did not like to think of her alone and upset. As his charges dispersed around the parsonage, exclaiming – as first-time visitors inevitably did – on the smallness of the interior, Marcus's concentration ebbed in the face of a guilty sensation that he had let Jo down.

He wondered if she would contact the police straight away, and wished there had been a way of telling her to wait until he got home, because then at least he could give her some moral support. On the last occasion when they had taken a missive of this kind to the police, events had taken a rather unaccountable turn. He had been invited into an interview room by a CID man – a young chap full of false friendliness, accompanied by a stony-faced female colleague who, so far as Marcus could remember, had never uttered a word the whole time.

Just somewhere a bit more private to wait, the young

policeman said, while Jo went in a separate room through the formalities of making a statement about receiving the card. Marcus had felt uneasy, but was uncertain how to refuse – and even more uncertain of what might be construed from a refusal. It had not been an interrogation – hardly even an interview – but after chatting in pretty general terms for a few minutes, the CID man had suddenly asked Marcus whether it had ever occurred to him that his wife might be sending the cards to herself.

'And why on earth should she do that?' Marcus asked, barely able to disguise his annoyance.

'I don't know, sir.' The guy was very smooth. 'To draw attention to herself, maybe? Perhaps to get some sympathy?'

'And what particular aspect of my wife's situation do you imagine she might want to get sympathy about, apart from the fact that her child was abducted some years ago and has never been seen since?' Marcus's voice was heavy with sarcasm. 'Give me one good reason for suspecting that these communications aren't either the genuine article or the work of a hoaxer. Better still, give me one good reason for suspecting that my wife is behind them.'

The policeman's expression remained neutral, but he was watching Marcus closely and, to his intense embarrassment, Marcus could feel not only that his face had reddened, but also that he had started to sweat. He could see why the police were sceptical about the postcards. Every major enquiry attracted its dedicated loonies. There was nothing whatsoever about the cards to indicate that they were genuine, and no forensic clues which might have led to the apprehension of the sender. Until then the postmarks had mostly been illegible, but one of the early ones had been posted within easy driving distance of where they lived, and the most recent card had been posted in London, on a date when Jo herself happened to be there – a coincidence which they had remarked upon themselves.

'Kidnappers don't usually bother to communicate unless they're asking for a ransom.' The policeman's voice was completely without emotion. 'Then there's the address. Your wife has moved about quite a bit since it happened; changed her name, too – but these cards have kept on coming.'

'It can't be that difficult to keep tabs on someone, if you put your mind to it. My wife has never been in hiding.'

'Seems like a lot of trouble to go to, just for a hoax. Can't quite see the point, can you?'

'Some people are weird,' Marcus said, as if pronouncing on a subject in which he was well versed. 'They will go to all sorts of lengths just to feel they are involved in a case that's in the headlines. Some even confess to murders they haven't committed, for crying out loud.'

In his heart of hearts he knew it wasn't the same thing. Walking into a police station and confessing meant a lot of detectives dancing attendance and maybe your name in the papers. The thrill factor in sending anonymous letters about something currently in the news was harder to fathom, but maybe it gave you a sense of involvement, when you saw the story in the headlines: someone who continued to send things, years after the initial press furore was over . . . well, that was possibly unprecedented.

That was the trouble; it had gone on for years and years. He realized now that this was something he had not properly anticipated when he and Jo first got together. He had been drawn by her very vulnerability, fired with a genuine desire to take that fractured life and rebuild it. While he had recognized this as a long-term commitment, perhaps he had not fully understood its open-ended nature, that it could never be over until Jo knew one way or the other what had happened to Lauren – and maybe not even then. Between them they had found the means to accommodate this void in her life. She had thrown herself into the business with a single-minded enthusiasm second only to his own, and with no new leads and nothing further that could be done, the tragedy of Lauren's disappearance had sometimes lain dormant for months at a time; but then something would happen to provoke the memories. It often began with the arrival of one of these wretched cards. Always the same thing – a scanned photograph of Lauren – the one which had appeared on every front page; the smiling blonde toddler in a sundress, with a glimpse of the sea sparkling behind her. Always the same message on the back, printed in Times New Roman, those same four words: *I still have her.*

At the conclusion of the Brontë trip Marcus drove straight to Manchester, where he found his mother much the same. His sister Sandra was much the same too, resentful and monosyllabic, not understanding – or maybe not wanting to understand – how difficult it was for him to get down to visit his mother on a regular basis, with a business to run and responsibilities at home. He usually managed to drive from the hospital to Easter Bridge without a break, but the traffic was so bad that he stopped at the services for an indifferent cup of tea and an overpriced sandwich. The knowledge that when he got home he would have to unpack and repack, in readiness to leave again the following day, did not encourage him to linger. He had often done tours back to back when the schedule demanded it, but he was feeling particularly tired tonight. At least he would have some back-up over the next few days. He and Melissa were managing the next one together – it was a one-off package, tailored to a group of English Civil War enthusiasts and their wives. While he led the men around various battlefields, Melissa would be taking their spouses on a round of galleries, antiques shops and various other upmarket retail opportunities, with visits to a chocolate maker and a stately home thrown in.

It had been raining all the way from Manchester, but when he turned off the M6 it became torrential. As he negotiated the winding lanes, great sheets of water flew up every time the car encountered one of the miniature lakes which had spread themselves across the tarmac. He was dog-tired, but the knowledge that he was nearly home lifted his spirits.

He had spoken to Jo the night before from the privacy of his Scarborough hotel room, by which time she had seemed much calmer, the initial upset of the card's arrival behind her – touchingly contrite, in fact, about the interruption she had forced upon him in Haworth, and appearing to agree when he said that the card was just another cruel hoax like all the others.

As he rounded the bend above the bridge, the lights of the house became visible through the trees. Another few seconds and he was turning into the drive. When he switched the engine off the rain seemed to pour onto the car roof with renewed vigour, water cascading down the windscreen unchecked, obscuring the lighted house, turning everything into a watery blur. No one appeared to open the front door for him, so he had to juggle his bags and keys, fumbling for the lock as the rain plastered down his hair.

'Anyone home?' he called from the hall.

'In here.' It was a tone which made his heart sink. In spite of their relatively upbeat conversation the night before, things were obviously worse than he had thought. He felt an intense weariness pressing him down.

The voice had come from the sitting room. Marcus entered and attempted to muster a cheerful expression. 'What's up?', adding as he caught sight of Jo's look of acute distress, 'Has there been a call from the hospital?'

She stared up at him. 'It would have been – is – Lauren's birthday.'

'Oh, I see.'

'You'd forgotten.' She slumped back into the chair, absently twisting her wedding ring between her right thumb and forefinger, while tears began a parallel descent down each cheek.

Although exasperated, Marcus was invariably moved by her beauty. The newly shed tears made her look impossibly young and vulnerable. 'I'm sorry.' He advanced to embrace her, but when she stayed wooden in his arms he withdrew, repeating his apology but this time adding with a hint of reproof, 'I've just driven all the way back from Manchester. Sometimes the living have to take precedence over the dead.'

An arctic chill instantly enveloped him. It had slipped out so easily – the great unsayable. Even so, he felt she could have offered him something, at least asked after his mother, but she resorted instead to noisy sobs, between which she gasped out, 'She's not dead. She's not dead.' It reminded him of when he was a little boy, sitting between his sister and his mother in the theatre at a performance of *Peter Pan*, with the whole audience shouting out, 'I do believe in fairies', and Tinkerbell miraculously restored to life.

'My darling Jo.' He put a hand on her shoulder, which seemed to calm her.

'I've been in touch with the local police about the card, and they're going to contact Devon and Cornwall,' she said. 'The policeman was so nice – I explained it all to him and he seemed quite hopeful. He said they'll probably analyse it. There are so many new tests now . . . DNA . . .'

He gave her shoulder another squeeze before withdrawing his hand, saying nothing. She had clearly spoken with an officer who was unfamiliar with the case, unaware that the cards had never afforded any forensic clues whatsoever. By the time the police got hold of them, they had always been handled by too many other people, while the cards themselves could have been produced by anyone who had a computer equipped with a couple of standard programmes and a colour printer.

'They might even find Lauren's DNA on it – if he still has her somewhere – if she's still alive . . .'

'Jo, I do understand that this has hit you hard, especially coming so close to today of all days, but you know we've been through all this before, and nothing has ever come of it. I realize it's easy for me to say, but you have to try to put it out of your mind.'

For a second she appeared to be on the point of arguing, but she sighed instead and reached for a tissue from the box on the table, wiping her face while he nodded encouragement. Aiming for a return to normality, he asked, 'What time are we going to eat?'

She looked startled, as if eating was an alien concept which had never entered her head. 'I haven't got anything planned. Sean had a pizza.'

Marcus tried to stifle his annoyance. Useless to shout at her, ask her if she realized how tired and hungry he was, after being on the road for hours, with an interval sitting beside his mother's bed. Better to come up with a practical solution. Dredging deep, he forced himself to be patient. 'Would you like me to cook something?'

'No, of course not,' she said quickly. 'I'll cook. I'll do anything you like. Just say – whatever you want.'

Marcus considered this. What he wanted was to come home to a welcoming smile and the smell of a hearty casserole simmering in the kitchen. To a laid table and the offer of a gin and tonic. To a woman who asked after his mother and made an overt gesture of affection. Eventually he said, 'Anything that's quick.'

Her attempt to make amends took the form of a hearty pasta dish involving mushrooms, bacon and a generous slug of red wine. To his relief, there was no further mention of Lauren or the card while they were eating. Instead, Jo made an effort to bring him up to date on various items of interest.

'I've had another email from Nerys – she's loving New Zealand. Oh, and I met Maisie in the lane yesterday. She says The Old Forge is definitely sold. To a woman, apparently. According to Maisie, she's a widow with a teenage daughter, and she plans to live there all the time.'

'How on earth does Maisie know all that?'

'You know Maisie – she's the *News of the World*.'

'Whoever has bought it will have their work cut out. Nothing has been done to that place for years.'

'Oh yes, and I nearly forgot to tell you: Melissa rang. She wants you to ring her.'

He couldn't keep the impatience out of his voice. 'Why didn't you tell me as soon as I got in? It might be something important.'

'I'm sure it can't be,' she snapped back. 'If it was anything important, it would surely have been something she could share with me. I am a partner in the business too, you know.'

'Oh, don't be so silly, Jo. It's probably something she wants to discuss with me about tomorrow's run.' He abandoned the last few twists of fusilli on his plate and scraped back his chair. 'I'll ring her from the office. I might need to check on something in there.'

She watched him go in silence, then stood up to collect the plates, muttering as she carried them across to scrape into the waste, 'Obviously *I* couldn't be trusted to give you a message.'

The part-full bag of fusilli was still standing open on the work surface and she caught it a glancing blow with her elbow as she reached across for the pan. The pasta spilled out of the bag, streaming across the slate floor of the kitchen, pattering against her feet, with some of the green and orange spirals rolling right across the room until they were brought up short by the bases of the kitchen units.

Sean chose this moment to enter the kitchen. He scrunched through the scattered pasta, ignoring it as effectively as he ignored his stepmother. It would never have been like this with Lauren. Lauren would have loved her. Sean would never love her, not least because he had a mother of his own. Marcus loved her, or at least . . . she wondered about the conversation he was having with Melissa. They should never have gone into partnership with Melissa – smooth, smart Melissa, so full of charm and wit and cleverness. Then she remembered Lauren again, and the two trains of thought collided. Did Melissa know about Lauren? Not unless Marcus had told her. People up here didn't know. Of course, they would probably remember the story of little Lauren Ashton, who had disappeared in the summer of 1998 – you could hardly fail to know about it, it had been all over the newspapers and television for weeks after it happened – but although people round here might remember the case, they did not know that she was Lauren's mother.

It was a long time ago now, so people didn't whisper any more or point her out in the street, but she knew how easily that could change. The local police would be discreet. Nothing had ever been said publicly about the postcards. If the press got wind of them, someone would make a story out of it and her life would become public property again in an instant.

The very thought of it made her recoil, as if already

assailed by the flashbulbs. She shuddered at a particular memory of a woman who had confronted herself and Dominic, as they walked through a shopping precinct. 'Everyone knows you did it.' Those were the words: loud, so that other passers-by could hear. Then a forceful launch of spittle; the humiliation of wiping it off, gripping Dom's arm as they walked on, pretending not to notice the stares which burned them, hot as branding irons. They might as well have had the words *Child Killer* stamped across their foreheads, the way people looked.

Sean slammed a drawer, making her jump. Pulling herself back to the here and now, she attempted contact. 'Your dad's home.'

'I know.'

'What's that you're making?'

'Nothing.'

They could both see that it was a peanut-butter sandwich. 'Take no notice,' that was inevitably Marcus's advice. 'All fourteen-year-old boys are impossible.'

But surely that couldn't be true. And what did that mean, exactly – impossible? Where did the weird posters on his wall and the locked cupboard in the boy's room fit in to 'impossible'? Was the cupboard full of drugs? Porn? It wasn't really big enough to hold much drink.

Sean recrossed the kitchen to get a plate, crunching some more fusilli underfoot as he went by.

'Sean!' she remonstrated.

'What?' He didn't bother to play innocent, didn't even turn to look at her.

There are a thousand and one reasons why women know all the words to 'I Will Survive' – and one of them was in the room with her right now. I am a strong person. I have rebuilt my life more than once, and I am not going to be intimidated

40

by a child. She took a deep breath. 'Don't make any more mess. Get a dustpan and clean this up, please.'

'I didn't spill it.'

'No, but you've made it worse by walking through it twice on purpose, so you can jolly well clean it up.'

There was a long pause, during which she wondered if he was about to tread the route of outright defiance, but after making an elaborate show of putting away the peanut butter, he took the pan and brush from the cupboard, not meeting her eye. She wondered if this small victory would make things better or worse in the long run.

Marcus left the house again at just after six the next morning. Jo got up to see him off, but their parting hug was lukewarm. It was still dark outside, but she waited at the front door, shivering in her dressing gown, until the car turned into the lane. The bulb must have been in the hall fitting for a long time, because its stale glow seemed to deepen the shadows around her eyes when she glanced in the mirror. 'Eyes like a startled fawn,' Marcus had once described them. She wasn't sure if it was meant as a compliment or not.

She contemplated returning to bed, but as she wasn't sleepy she turned aside into the office instead, where she began to google for information on artists with associations to the Lake District. A new project was good. It was what she needed to help her forget about the postcard, because in her heart she knew that Marcus was right in what he said. The postcards had never brought them any closer to a resolution – they just jabbed at a raw wound.

She had not mentioned her idea for another tour to Marcus, because he would be sure to say something to Melissa and she wanted to retain sole ownership of the idea for a while. Incorporating a visit to Brantwood would be a given, and of course there was Friars Crag and the Lodore Falls. Plenty of artists had drawn inspiration from the area, but could you make a really good tour out of it? Where had Turner, Constable or Burne-Jones actually stayed? Clients loved to sleep in locations which had links to the subjects – even if the buildings in question had been altered beyond recognition. She would have to do a lot of proper research in due course, but the internet was always a good starting point – even if you discovered later on that half the stuff posted on there was wrong!

Jo worked steadily through the morning, scribbling notes as she went, breaking off only to chivvy Sean out to school, shower and dress herself and consume a breakfast banana. At about midday she walked briskly through the drizzle to the Old Chapel Gallery, where she was relieved to find Shelley alone, leafing through a stack of prints on the pine table, which doubled as a counter and a desk.

'You're not too busy for a chat, are you?'

'Not at all. Glad to be diverted, actually. Can I get you a coffee?' Shelley rose to relieve her visitor of a damp cagoule before pouring them both mugs of coffee from the jug on the hot plate. When Jo began to explain her ideas for a new tour, Shelley mostly listened in silence, only nodding or putting in an occasional word.

'It would need a lot more work,' Jo concluded. 'None of our current guides has a fine-arts background – but I could really see this being a winner. I'd like to include some stuff about lesser-known artists – the ones who seem to have been influential at the time, but aren't exactly household names now. Apparently there was this guy called Thomas Girtin, who died when he was only twenty-six or twenty-seven, but his paintings were really important. I'd never heard of him until this morning.'

'Why just stick with the eighteenth and nineteenth centuries?' asked Shelley. 'If you're going to talk about Collingwood and the start of the Lake Artists, you could bring the whole thing up to date. If you run these tours during the summer months, why not throw in a visit to the Lake Artists Exhibition in Grasmere?'

'Shelley, you're a genius. That would be a marvellous way of structuring it. I was worried about not having enough indoor venues to visit – famous landscapes are all very well, but the age group we cater for can't all manage to tramp up Castle Crag. Maybe we could bring them here, too. You specialize in the best contemporary local work.'

Shelley laughed. 'Even if they don't buy anything, I suppose they might tell their friends about us.'

'Have you got any books I could borrow, to help me get started?'

'Probably more than you've got houseroom for. I'll sort some out and bring them down later. It's no good me saying I can put my hand on them straight away. You know what it's like in our house – books four deep everywhere.'

Shelley was as good as her word, arriving at The Hideaway later that afternoon with such a weight of books that she had travelled the few hundred yards by car. Jo helped her carry in a dozen or so volumes – 'Just for starters,' Shelley said – which she left Shelley to arrange in piles on the sitting-room floor, while she made some tea. (Shelley invariably declined Jo's coffee as inferior to the brew she fermented in the gallery.)

It was only when Jo carried the mugs in that she finally noticed the large bruise forming above Shelley's left cheekbone, which had certainly not been there that morning. 'Whatever have you done to yourself?'

'I was reaching a book down and another one fell on me.

43

It was a great thick book of essays – goodness knows what they're about. I don't think Brian will ever read them. It's just another of his must-haves from a second-hand bookshop.'

'Oh no! I feel sort of responsible.'

'Don't be silly. It wasn't your fault – I should look what I'm doing. What's Marcus up to this week? Is it still the Brontës?'

'That one finished yesterday. He's doing battlefields for the next four days.'

Shelley sipped her tea. 'I always thought the Brontës were a massive bore myself. We were made to read *Wuthering Heights* at school, and quite frankly I didn't get it. Give me Jilly Cooper any day of the week.' This observation took them in a pleasantly literary direction until Shelley asked, as she put her empty mug on the side table, 'How's Marcus's mother, by the way?'

Jo sighed. 'She's still the same. It's just a matter of how long she lasts, really.'

'Poor Marcus. We'll all have to go through this in the next few years I suppose. My parents are pretty good for their age, but they aren't getting any younger.' When Jo said nothing, Shelley, sensing that she had somehow hit a wrong note, asked rather awkwardly: 'Are your parents still alive?'

'No, they're both dead.'

'Sorry, I didn't know that. You're very young to have lost both parents.'

'I'm thirty-nine,' Jo snapped. 'I don't suppose it's that unusual.'

'Of course not.' Shelley cast around desperately for some other subject. Most people were prepared to bore for England once they got started with their families, but it was obvious from Jo's voice that this was an off-limits area.

44

It was Jo who broke the short silence. 'Have you heard about The Old Forge?' she asked.

'Yes, Maisie told me.'

'Naturally!'

They both laughed, but Shelley could sense that the discord she had inadvertently sounded was still ringing out faintly around the room, and Jo made no protest when she said that she must get back to the gallery.

After seeing Shelley out, Jo returned to the sitting room, where she selected the first book from the nearest pile. For some reason the illustration on the front reminded her of a children's story in which people could step into pictures and explore them at will, seeing beyond what the artist had actually painted. If you stepped into this bucolic landscape, she thought, you would probably need to watch out for cow pats. She peered at the grass in the foreground for evidence of realism, but the image seemed to have faded, its place taken by a set of wooden garage doors, one of which stood ajar. She only had to reach for the handle in order to pull one of the doors wide open and see what was inside. She recoiled from the thought, and fought to refocus on the book in her lap, noting that it must have spent a long time on a shelf which caught the sun, because the spine had faded from the rich red of the front and rear dust jackets to a muddy brown. The scene chosen for the front cover, of cattle grazing peacefully in an idealized cow-pat-less landscape, was surrounded by a border of this deep blood red. Jo tried hard to concentrate on the cream and brown cows against their backdrop of woodland and sky, but the grassy meadow kept turning into the park across the street from William Street School, viewed through two sets of metal railings: the tall ones, which surrounded the park itself, and a smaller set, which had been erected on the edge of the nearest pavement

– the kind of waist-high railings which were placed at every school gate to prevent pupils from running straight out into the road.

When the bell sounded at half past three, all the infants came swarming out of that gate to where their mothers were waiting, some grouped on the pavement, some in nearby parked cars, some with shopping bags, or pushchairs containing younger brothers and sisters. She looked up into the faces of all these mothers: even down among their feet for a sign of the familiar scuffed trainers, but her mother was not there. Gradually the other children and their mothers thinned out, until it was possible to see right up and down the road: to know that her mother was not approaching from either direction. Left alone, she pressed her back against the wall which ran all around the school's perimeter, until she could feel the rough brickwork through her thin clothes.

At ten minutes to four the juniors were let out of another gate, which stood a few yards further along the road. Some of them were met by grown-ups too, but none of these adults noticed her: something or someone always screened her from their potential concern. A couple of bigger girls did stop and tried to talk to her, but when she refused to answer they continued on their way. Some bigger boys came and pinched the belt out of her mac: they tossed it around for a while, then threw it in the gutter and ran off. She was frightened by the big boys, but she ignored them, pretended they were not there, even when they came close and shouted something at her. She knew she would be in trouble about the belt, but although she could see where it lay, she could not bring herself to cross the pavement and retrieve it. The pavement looked so wide, the park a million miles away. She liked the swings in the park, but she was not allowed to cross the road alone, so she stood with her back pressed hard against the brickwork and wondered why her mother didn't come.

Jo shook herself back to the present, and hastily discarded her first choice of book in favour of another. She wished Shelley had not mentioned her parents. It was not Shelley's fault, of course. If she had known what happened, she would never have asked the question.

CHAPTER FOUR

'So,' Melissa said, 'it's agreed that we drop Lawrence from next year's itinerary, and replace him with Daphne du Maurier.'

Jo said nothing. It was yet another of those decisions which Marcus and Melissa had effectively made already, during the course of their joint excursion the week before. Just like the decision to hold this meeting in Melissa's sitting room – 'much more comfortable than the office' Melissa purred – where they were now planning the programme of tours to be advertised for the following year.

'I've been thinking about that hotel in Fowey,' Marcus said. 'I know it's a long way to go, but we've always inspected the hotels personally before using them. I think one of us should go down.'

'I'm sure you're right,' Melissa nodded. 'But who can fit it in? It has to be done before the material goes out – any changes from the advertised itinerary always shake customer confidence.'

'I could do it,' Jo said. Some Cornish sunshine would be a welcome change to the persistent Cumbrian drizzle. She had just begun to imagine herself looking out across a rocky headland when Marcus cut across the vision.

'It ought to be me, as I'm the one who'll be accompanying the tour.'

Jo was about to say that she couldn't see what difference

it made: hadn't Marcus said only the other day that it was a team effort, in which it did not matter who did what? Melissa chimed in first with: 'I think you're right, darling. It puts you on familiar ground when you get there.' Melissa addressed everyone as 'darling'. It was one of the things which ground Jo's gears.

Marcus was already thumbing through his diary. 'I can see a possible window in a couple of weeks,' he said.

'Hold on . . .' Jo began, knowing perfectly well that the 'window' in question could only be during a period when they were scheduled to be at home together. A Vesuvial warmth of indignation was rising within her. If Marcus hopped off down to Cornwall, that inevitably left her alone with Sean, and she could not help thinking that in volunteering himself for the Cornwall trip, Marcus was taking another of his favourite maxims, 'what's yours is mine', rather too much for granted. Step-parenting was hard work, and if anyone needed a break in Cornwall, it was not Marcus. Rather than say anything which hinted at marital disharmony in front of Melissa, she kept her eyes fixed on him, awaiting the moment when he registered her expression of mute protest and passed the Cornwall trip along, but once Marcus had finished jotting in his diary, he returned his full attention to their hostess without so much as glancing Jo's way, thereby ratcheting up her annoyance by several more notches.

'Just going back to the scheduling –' Melissa paused to drag the chart across the floor, so that they could all see it better. She was sitting on the carpet, at just the right angle for Marcus to see down the front of her top. 'I see we've got Jo on a back-to-back here . . .' she indicated the block of dates with her pen, 'when there's no need, because I can take over Mary Queen of Scots in the Lowlands.'

'No!' Jo almost shouted. 'I always do Mary Queen of Scots.'

'Not always,' Marcus began.

'Yes – always.'

'But it means disembarking the American Plantagenet Society at Manchester Airport, then driving all the way to Newcastle to meet the coach at four o'clock.'

'I'll have plenty of time,' Jo said. 'The airport drop is early morning, and my car will be there already.'

'But why on earth stretch yourself like that in the middle of a busy season?' Melissa protested. 'I'll be available, and I can do a perfectly good job on old MQS.'

That's another thing, thought Jo. I hate the way she abbreviates things and Marcus picks up on it and copies her. 'But I *want* to do it. I have a special affinity with Mary Queen of Scots.' She saw Melissa raise her eyebrows in Marcus's direction and instantly regretted her words.

'Sorry, darling, I didn't realize that.' The amusement in Melissa's voice was evident. 'Perhaps we could rejig the schedule so that someone else takes care of the Richard III groupies.' She pretended to consider for a moment. 'Of course, if Marcus stayed home with Sean instead of . . . no, no, that won't work. Who else could we call on to take care of Richard III for us?'

'There's no need to call on anyone,' Marcus broke in impatiently. 'It's perfectly obvious that you should take the MQS tour in place of Jo. There's no need to bugger up the whole schedule just so that Jo can have a monopoly on MQS. Besides,' he turned to Jo, 'you shouldn't go wearing yourself out by doing a back-to-back when there's no need. We get so little time at home together, and this way it gives us an extra three days.'

Jo was about to say that he hadn't worried about that when

he volunteered to inspect the hotel in Cornwall, but she remembered just in time that whichever of them made the trip, they would not be at home together, and said nothing. She understood the logic in what they were proposing, and she didn't want to make a bigger fool of herself than she already had. And no wonder Melissa had reacted as she did, because clients who claimed to enjoy a particularly strong affinity with the subjects of the tours were regarded with a mixture of caution, bordering on carefully concealed contempt. Someone who turned out to be a complete obsessive could become a nuisance, spoiling the atmosphere by competing with other members of the party about who was the most knowledgeable, or else boring them to tears with long stories about being 'in touch' with long-deceased writers or royalty. None of which altered the fact that Jo could not help but feel a special bond with the tragic queen, whose life had been scarred by circumstances mostly not of her making. Poor Mary, who had been steadily deprived of almost everyone who was dear to her, including the child snatched from her when he was just a baby, after which she had never seen him again.

'You know, darling,' Marcus said as they drove away from Melissa's house, 'you were being rather difficult over that scheduling. Melissa is extremely good about the fact that one of us always has to be at home now because of Sean. I do wish you would try to go with the flow a bit more.'

'Go with the flow,' Jo repeated. 'What's that supposed to mean? Is it Marcus-and-Melissa speak for "do as you're told"?'

'Of course not.'

'Because it looks to me as if the two of you are running things now, and I simply have to go along with everything you decide.'

'That's just silly . . .'

'No, it isn't. You two plan a Daphne du Maurier tour and it goes straight into the list. I suggest Lake District Artists . . .'

'Which is a great idea,' Marcus cut in, 'but it needs more work. How can we include it when you haven't got a definite itinerary? We can put it into the programme in 2011, when you've had time to formulate it properly.'

'*And* Melissa has taken my Mary Queen of Scots tour.'

'Now you're just being childish. We have to do what's best for the clients, and you won't be at your best if you've just driven hell for leather from Manchester to Newcastle. We all have to accept the strictures that scheduling sometimes imposes. That occasionally means guiding a tour we're not so keen on, or giving up one of our favourites to someone else.'

'I do wish you wouldn't talk to me as if I were a ten-year-old.'

'Don't act like one, then.'

It was rare for them to bicker. Jo had been on the point of taking issue with him over the Cornwall trip, but she thought better of it, and they continued the journey in silence, arriving just as the school bus deposited Sean at the place where the lane forked towards Satterthwaite, thereby saving him a ten-minute walk in the rain. In spite of this, he did not appear particularly pleased to see them, climbing into the car with no more than a sullen grunt, which might have been 'Hi', and banging his school bag on to the seat beside him.

As soon as they reached the house Sean went straight up to his bedroom, while Jo followed Marcus into the kitchen. 'Why does he have to be so rude?' she demanded.

'Please don't start,' Marcus said. 'It's been a heavy day. Anyway, he wasn't rude – not really. Kids hate being quizzed about what they've done at school.'

'I wasn't quizzing him; I was just trying to make conversation.'·

'Maybe you should just leave him alone.'

'So it's me that's wrong, as usual.'

'Oh, for goodness' sake, Jo, cut the kid some slack, why don't you? It can't be easy for him, having to move into a completely new environment . . .'

'As if I didn't know all about that.'

Marcus faced her wearily. 'This isn't about what you have had to deal with in the past. This is about Sean and *his* life, and what he is having to deal with. Everything isn't always about you.'

He left her standing in the kitchen, feeling crushed. She sank down onto a chair, momentarily defeated by the curious humiliations of the day, but after a minute or two she pulled herself together, stood up again and began to prepare the bolognese sauce for the lasagne. Whenever she paused in the act of chopping the onions, she could hear the drone of the television in the sitting room, and from somewhere above her head came the persistent thudding of Sean's CDs. Fainter still was the patter of rain on the windows. It was already almost dark outside; the low clouds had brought with them a premature dusk. Just another normal family evening. She would make them a good dinner and get everything back on an even keel. Afterwards maybe they could persuade Sean to stay downstairs for a game of Balderdash – he had enjoyed that last time they all played.

She was just getting carried away with this vision of family fun and laughter, when she heard Sean padding into the kitchen behind her. When she glanced round she saw that he had already changed out of his school uniform and was wearing ripped jeans, worn low enough on the hip to expose a ruff of blue-grey boxer shorts when he bent to look in the cupboard where they kept the crisps. Since Marcus's latest advice on Sean-handling was not to attempt conversation at all, she ignored him for the time being, focusing instead on the ingredients in the pan, stirring in the tomato purée and oregano, as if she did not know he was there.

Of course she could empathize with his being transplanted into new surroundings. It had been worse for her, she thought. At least it had been Sean's choice to come and live here with his father. He was not having to get used to foster-parents, or live in a house he had never set eyes on, before being dumped there without warning. She pulled herself back to the present. What had Marcus said? Everything isn't always about you? Well, no, of course it wasn't . . . It was only natural for Marcus to take Sean's part . . . It was a big adjustment for them all . . . And of course Marcus was trying to win Sean over, so that they could establish a normal loving home life out of unnatural circumstances. She went on stirring the sauce, which had begun to bubble. Why did tomato mixtures always spatter so much?

She crossed from the hob to the fridge and began to collect the ingredients for the béchamel sauce, but there was a gap on the shelf where the cheese should have been. Glancing across to where Sean had abandoned the breadboard, a knife and an open jar of Branston pickle, a few crumbs of cheese told their own story. He had eaten it – the best part of half a pound of cheese – gone.

She took the stairs two at a time and erupted into his bedroom without knocking. He had been sitting on the edge of the bed with his back to the door, but as she entered the room he turned in alarm and in a single movement had slammed shut the door of the cupboard which stood on the floor by his bed.

'What have you got there?' she demanded, the missing cheese entirely forgotten.

'Nothing.'

'Don't give me that. What have you got in the cupboard?'

'Private stuff. You're supposed to knock before you come in here. Get out of my room – go on, get out!' He stood up, grabbing the nearest missile to hand, which happened to be a size-nine trainer, hurling it at her with sufficient force that she had to step backwards in order to avoid being hit in the face. He took advantage of this partial retreat to lunge forward and shut the door. Jo had no intention of indulging in a door-pushing contest with a fourteen-year-old. It was time to summon reinforcements.

Marcus heard her running downstairs and emerged to meet her in the hall, his face anxious.

'Marcus, you need to do something. Sean has got a knife in his room.'

A crinkle appeared between Marcus's eyebrows. He regarded his wife uncertainly, rather as he might peer at a mathematics problem which had so far eluded him.

'He's been keeping it in the old cupboard he brought back from that car-boot sale. The locked cupboard at the side of his bed.' It was as much as Jo could do not to grab Marcus's arm and drag him physically up the stairs. Why did he just go on standing there, looking like that, not saying anything? 'I went into his room just now and saw him with it.'

'What sort of knife?'

'A big one. Like a hunting knife. A dreadful-looking thing.'

'Are you sure?'

'Of course I'm sure! What do you take me for? I went in without knocking and caught him sitting on the bed, looking at this knife.'

'I thought we agreed not to go into his room without knocking? He might have been getting changed or something.'

'He was already changed,' Jo almost shouted. 'I think we're getting off the point here, which is about the knife in Sean's bedroom, not the accepted etiquette for families with teenage boys. Are you going to come upstairs and do something about this or not?'

For an awful moment, Jo actually thought he was going to opt for 'not'. Marcus certainly hesitated before following her upstairs. At Sean's door, she stood to one side while he tapped on the panels.

'What?' Sean's voice emerged from within, the usual blend of belligerent boredom.

'I'd like to come in and have a word.'

'OK.'

Sean was reclining on his bed with his laptop alongside him, logged into MySpace. He reached for the remote and muted the CD player, as if to facilitate conversation.

Marcus took a deep breath. 'Sean, do you have a knife in here?'

Sean affected to look puzzled. 'Mmm – yeah – I think so.' He raised himself to a sitting position, swinging his feet on to the carpet before gesturing theatrically at the remnants of the previous night's beans on toast supper, among which lay a knife and fork. 'Should've brought them downstairs – sorry.'

'I don't mean that kind of knife,' said Marcus, patiently.

'We're talking about the knife I saw you with a minute ago,' Jo interrupted. 'The knife you've got locked in that cupboard.'

Sean stared at her blankly. 'What knife?'

'I think it would be a good idea if you let us see what you've got in the cupboard,' Marcus said.

Sean looked uncomfortable. 'There's nothing in there. Just some private stuff. There isn't any knife.'

'All the same, I'd like you to open it up please.' It was the voice Marcus used if ever there was a problem with one of the hotels. It was excessively polite, but brooked no opposition.

With an air of reluctance, Sean went to his wardrobe and felt around among the shoes he kept in the bottom of it, withdrawing a small key which he used to unlock the cupboard – no bigger than a bathroom cabinet – which stood on the floor by his bed. With another resentful glance at his father, he stood back to reveal the contents: three magazines, which judging from the uppermost cover, had all derived from the top shelf of the newsagents. 'Satisfied?' he spat at Jo, before slamming the cupboard shut and turning the key in the lock.

'He's moved it,' Jo said. 'He must have moved it while I went downstairs.'

'I don't know what she's talking about,' Sean protested. 'She came busting in here, going on about stuff in my cupboard. She's not supposed to come in here without knocking . . .'

'Sean.' Marcus silenced his son with a look. 'Do you have a knife anywhere in this room – apart from the one on the plate?'

The boy met his father's eye, unflinching. 'No, Dad.'

Marcus was already walking away. Jo followed him, remonstrating angrily even as Sean took advantage of their departure to shut himself back inside and turn the music up. 'You can't just let him get away with this. A kid his age shouldn't have a knife like that. If you search his room . . .'

Marcus stopped dead at the foot of the stairs and faced her. 'I am not going to search anyone's room. Do you want him to feel like he's living in Stalag 97? You've been very wound up lately, and you could well have seen something else and imagined it was a knife. I mean, honestly, where do you think a boy of his age is going to get hold of something like that?

And now you've cornered me into humiliating him, by forcing him to show us his pathetic little stash of dirty magazines. Or is that what you were up to all along? Scoring points because we had a row earlier on?'

'I don't try to score points, and we didn't have a row – just words.'

'It's perfectly healthy for boys his age to have a few things like that lying around,' Marcus continued, 'and I don't want you to start making him feel uncomfortable about it. In fact, that's exactly the sort of reason why you ought to knock before you go into his room.'

'I saw him with a knife,' Jo began, but Marcus held up his hand, the gesture subduing her into silence as effectively as if he wielded a physical force.

'Sean has given me his word that there isn't a knife. Use your common sense, Jo. There's no earthly reason why he would be likely to have one. We don't live in the sort of area where a kid might think he needed to acquire a knife for self-defence. How good a look did you get at this so-called knife?'

'I just saw it for a second. As soon as I opened the door, he shoved it into the cupboard. I honestly thought it was a knife.'

'Thought?'

'I saw it.'

'A minute ago you only thought.'

'I'm going to make the dinner,' Jo said. 'This isn't getting us anywhere. By the way,' she added as an afterthought, 'it'll be spag bol rather than lasagne, because Sean's just eaten the last of the cheese.' She caught sight of Marcus's expression as he turned into the sitting room, and wished she had not mentioned the cheese. It just sounded like another petty jab in her stepson's direction.

CHAPTER FIVE

Jo's first real opportunity to search Sean's bedroom did not come for more than a week. First she was away for four nights leading In the Footsteps of Wordsworth, and when she got back, either Sean or Marcus always seemed to be in the house. Only when Marcus left to take care of Border Raids and Battles, and Sean had gone to school, did she have the house to herself.

She was still annoyed with Marcus about the Cornwall trip, but in the interests of avoiding further accusations that she was being self-centred, she had decided to bide her time. Once she had shown Marcus that he had been wrong about the knife, she would be in a far stronger position to raise the issue of who should go down to inspect the hotel in Fowey. Her plan was to locate and confiscate the knife, keeping it somewhere safe from Sean until she could lay the evidence of its existence before Marcus on his return. She assumed that it would be back in the cupboard by now, so it was merely a question of finding the key.

She was not surprised when a thorough search in and among the shoes in the bottom of the wardrobe drew a blank. Never mind – she had all day if that was what it took. For the next ninety minutes she undertook a fingertip search of which any undercover agent might have been proud, taking great care to replace everything exactly where she found it. Trouser pockets, CD cases, the furthest corners of shelves, under the mattress, inside the pillow slips and duvet cover, she probed every possible place, gathering dust from along the top of the doorframe, even feeling along the hems of the curtains, but as she worked her way round the room, it was with the ever-increasing conviction that Sean must have taken the most obvious precaution of all. He had taken the key with him.

When she had tried every possible hidey-hole, she knelt in front of the cupboard and investigated it more closely. It appeared to be homemade, perhaps the result of some long-forgotten woodwork class. At some stage in its history a coat of gloss paint had been applied, which had faded to the shade of cream left too long in the fridge. There was a narrow gap between the door and body of the cupboard and Jo found that by pushing repeatedly against the door she could make it rattle. If only the hinges had been on the outside, she could have unscrewed them. Damn it, he was not going to beat her! She marched out to the garage, returning with a torch and a large screwdriver. When she shone the beam of the torch up and down the crack, she could make out the dark rectangle of the lock – one small metal obstruction which stood between herself and the contents of the cupboard. She slid the point of the screwdriver into the gap at a point just below the lock and began to lever her improvised jemmy against the frame. The first two or three attempts resulted in no more than a series of ugly marks on the paintwork. At the fourth attempt, the screwdriver jerked out of the crack and she narrowly missed gouging a lump out of her cheek. She tried a slower, steadier pressure, until with an elongated creak of protest, the door finally gave way, a jagged split appearing in the wood from the edge nearest the lock to a point just above the lower hinge. Although the tough little lock held firm, enough of the door could be moved aside to see that the cupboard's contents were unchanged since Sean had reluctantly displayed them a week before.

Jo sat back on her heels, completely at a loss. Maybe he took the knife with him to school. For a moment she thought of ringing to suggest they search his belongings, but then she thought of what Marcus would say if she ended up getting Sean expelled – which could well be the penalty for bringing an offensive weapon on to the premises. Then again, what if she rang the school and her hunch turned out to be wrong? He might have sold it on to someone else by now. Marcus would be just as furious, the whole episode put down to her overactive imagination again.

There had been a couple of occasions in the past when she had got things very wrong, and she could see now that it had probably been a mistake to confide these episodes in Marcus because they naturally reduced the likelihood of him accepting everything she told him at face value. The worst of these had occurred four years ago, when she followed a woman in a car – the impulse of an instant – because there was a little girl in the back, a little girl who had looked just the right age . . .

She stared afresh at the mess she had made of the cupboard door. The irony of her earlier cautious search was not lost on her; she might as well have turned the place upside down, because there was no way she could pretend the cupboard had met with some accidental injury while she was cleaning the room. Cold fingers of doubt encircled her neck and crept over her scalp. Without the justification of a newly dis-covered knife, the cupboard simply appeared to have suffered a violent attack from a random maniac. She saw the screw-driver in her hand with fresh eyes. Suddenly she wanted to put as much distance as possible between herself and the cupboard and screwdriver.

She retreated downstairs, noting that the post had been delivered, probably at the very moment she had been breaking into the cupboard, since she had not heard the letterbox. She collected the cluster of envelopes as she passed, flipping through them to see if there was anything interesting. Halfway down the pile she encountered a couple of envelopes addressed to Shelley and Brian, which had somehow found their way among The Hideaway's post.

The misdirected mail provided her with a welcome excuse to depart the scene of the crime. She would walk into Grizedale and find something to draw, dropping off the stray letters on her way. In less than five minutes she was striding along the lane, resolutely ignoring the threat of rain in the sky ahead. She had intended to drop into the gallery and hand the letters over in person, but when she got there she found the lights were out and the 'closed' sign still displayed, so she backtracked to Ingledene where she opened the wrought-iron gate, advanced up the path and climbed the trio of steps to the front door.

As she gained the top step she was met with the sound of loud, angry voices. With no passing traffic, sound penetrated the wood as easily as if she had been in the next room. It was awkward, but it was too late to go back now. If someone happened to see her, she would still have the letters in her hand, so it would be obvious that she had overheard them quarrelling and was trying to slip away. At the same time she was reluctant to open the letterbox, because the feuding parties might be standing in sight of the door and realize she was there.

She tried the flap with a fingertip but it did not move. It must be held in place with a taught spring - the sort of letterbox which would make a loud noise unless handled very cautiously. She pushed a little harder, levering the flap upwards as slowly and quietly as she could, almost letting go in fright when an angry roar erupted from Brian, in which she could make out the words, 'Oh, no you won't.'

'Let me go, you bastard!'

Who would have imagined that gentle Shelley could conjure up such a harridan shriek? Jo fed the letters in and heard them flop on to the encaustic tiles a spilt second before there was a crash of something heavy hitting the floor. Jo let the flap go with a snap. The occupants were making so much noise they probably wouldn't hear it. She tried not to be in too obvious a hurry to reach the gate – much better to pretend she had not heard anything.

Pretending – always pretending that there was nothing wrong. That's what I'm doing now, she thought. I do it all the time, pretending that there is nothing wrong between me and Marcus; pretending that I can cope with Sean; pretending that I'm not thinking about what happened to Lauren, every minute of every day.

She wondered where Marcus was just at that moment. Some itineraries she knew well enough to place him almost to the minute, but Border Raids and Battles was a new addition to their repertoire, so she was not familiar with it. More to the point, where was Melissa? Melissa could so easily join up with Marcus on those nights when she was not booked to be away with a tour herself. Man-eating Melissa, who had already worked her way through two husbands. Not that you could condemn a woman just for being married twice – she had been married twice herself – but Melissa, with her fake fingernails and her two divorces, why, why, why had they ever thought it was a good idea to go into business with Melissa?

There had been room for two firms offering a similar kind of thing: plenty of customers to go round, in fact, and even if there had not been, you didn't have to jump into bed with your competitors, figuratively or literally. It was not as if she had any definite proof, except that Marcus seemed to have changed recently. He had once been her rock: the one person in the world she could always turn to, the one person who would always be on her side. It did not feel like that any more. When they were at home together they skirted around one another, as if each were afraid of too close an encounter, lest they find in the other what they already feared to be there.

When it began to rain Jo drew up her hood and carried on walking. It was too wet to draw, but she did not want to return to the house, where Sean's cupboard stood fatally wounded in his bedroom. Her boots sounded out a steady rhythm against the tarmac, although she wasn't sure where she was going any more. It was like the day after Lauren disappeared, when she and Dom had joined the search, carrying on long after the weather turned against them, refusing to stop when everyone advised them to; continuing to look because there was nothing to do *except* go on looking. Scouring the countryside, yet hardly knowing what they were looking for, because it was perfectly obvious that Lauren had not wandered off into the fields on her own. Someone had taken her. Someone had wheeled the pushchair down the street towards the sea, then turned aside into the public gardens and from there up on to the cliff path, where they had tossed the buggy – but not Lauren, thank heaven, not Lauren herself – over the edge of the cliff.

Where was Lauren taken after that? In place of the valley bottom, misty with rain, Jo pictured the cliff path, following the shape of the land where it rose in imitation of a round-topped rolling wave, the path sometimes wide enough to walk two abreast, sometimes narrowing to single file, hemmed in by the gorse which grew there in abundance. She pictured the

64

abductor, a shadowy figure carrying Lauren along the path, further and further away from the village street, which was already alive with rumours of a missing child. Jo began to walk faster in tandem with the figure in her mind, her boots splashing in the puddles, her breath coming harder and harder, but although the figure on the path did not appear to hurry, even encumbered as it was with a child, she could make no ground upon it. The path twisted out of sight and the figure vanished with it. From somewhere down the years, she could hear the voice of a child, fearful, uncertain: 'Why didn't you come for me?'

She realized that she was gasping for breath, all but running along the road. She slowed to a steady walk, conscious of the cold perspiration which was running down her back, making her shirt feel damp inside her anorak. It was not Lauren who had asked that question. Lauren had been too young to talk properly when she was taken away. Jo had never heard her speaking in sentences. The voice belonged to that other little girl, standing uncertainly at the kerbside, behind the railings which guarded the William Street School infants' gate, waiting for what had seemed like an eternity, until someone came to collect her. A car screeching to a halt, the result of last-minute arrangements cobbled together in a hurry, to take care of her until 'things were sorted out'. That had been the first time they had taken Mum away to the hospital – when she had come home a few days later. Not like the last time. The vision of the wooden garage doors had been growing in her mind, but she pushed it away. 'No,' she said aloud. She did not want to go back there.

With a start she realized that she had almost reached Satterthwaite. In her hurry to leave the house she had forgotten to make up her usual flask, but she was briefly cheered by the thought that when she got to the Eagle and

Child she could go inside and have a coffee. Alas, when she reached the pub she found it was closed. There was nowhere else to get a warm drink until you reached the Grizedale Visitor Centre, which was at least another mile and a half along the road.

'This is crazy,' Jo said to herself. *Crazy.* For a second she caught sight of her reflection in the wing mirror of a parked car. Did she look like her mother, or didn't she? She had never been able to make up her mind. She turned around and began to trudge back towards Easter Bridge. The rain was in her face now, and blinded her whenever she lifted her head. The Lake Artists Tour – she would focus on that. Maybe when she got back to the gallery the lights would be on and Shelley would be inside, her quarrel with Brian over. They could talk about the tour together, over mugs of hot, bitter coffee. Shelley had appeared enthusiastic about the idea, and now it occurred to Jo that maybe Shelley might like to guide it. The company needed knowledgeable people who were good communicators and passionate about their subject; people who were happy to take on an occasional specialist assignment. She suspected that Shelley was quite often short of money. She hardly ever seemed to buy herself any new clothes, and never had her hair done. Luckily she was a petite natural blonde, who could look marvellous simply by pinning up her hair, putting on a flowing Indian cotton dress and big earrings.

When she eventually drew level with the gallery it was still in darkness – which was very odd, because they were not usually closed on Wednesdays. As she passed beyond the gallery and reached the wall which marked the frontage of Ingledene, she heard a couple of car doors slam in relatively quick succession, and then a car engine coming to life. Brian and Shelley's estate car shot out from the parking place behind the house, swerving so violently into the lane that it narrowly missed the wall on the opposite side of the road. Brian was in the driving seat, but there was no sign of Shelley.

Jo hesitated at the gate, but then thought better of it. Shelley might be upset after their row, and it was not as if she and Jo were close enough to have a heart-to-heart about a marital contretemps, so Jo walked on towards The Hideaway, while the sound of the speeding car faded into the steady whisper of the rain.

As she walked through their ever-open gates, she noticed that someone had put a seashell on top of one of the gateposts – some passing walker probably, perhaps a child. She wondered absently how long it had been there without her noticing.

Her heart sank when she entered the house. She was dreading the inevitable confrontation when Sean came home. He would notice the cupboard immediately, and flare up. She spent some time rehearsing an argument to the effect that had he not been so duplicitous about the knife, she would not have been forced to take matters into her own hands, but she knew that without hard proof of the knife's existence, it was a difficult line to pursue. As the afternoon drew on, she began to watch the lane for signs of his approach. She saw their local farmer, David Tyson, trundle past on his tractor, and later Brian's car returning, before Sean finally came into view.

She greeted him normally when he came into the house, received the usual grunt in reply, then positioned herself just inside the kitchen doorway, listening as his dragging footsteps mounted the stairs, fully expecting him to come pounding down again seconds later, but to her surprise, there was no immediate outburst of adolescent fury. Instead he stayed in his room until she called him down for dinner.

'Now for it,' she thought, but Sean was quiet throughout the meal, almost subdued. Even when his stepmother offered him an opportunity to unleash invective, asking him if there was anything the matter, he only said, 'No, nothing,' if anything in a marginally more polite tone than usual.

There was no accounting for teenage boys, she thought. Sean was normally red hot on the issue of his privacy, and this was the first occasion he had genuine cause for complaint. After he left for school the next morning, she slipped up to his room, where she found the vandalized cupboard and its contents just as she had left them the day before. He had not even bothered to push the broken part of the door back into place. It was as if he was pretending not to have noticed.

It began to rain again at about nine o'clock in the morning, which precluded any possibility of an escape with her sketch book, so she washed the kitchen floor, then tidied up in the office for a while, although there was not much for her to do.

It had been so different in the early days of M. H. Tours, when she and Marcus had done almost everything themselves. It had been her first real job since being forced to give up work when Lauren went missing. She had been on a fortnight's holiday when it happened, and this had extended into compassionate leave, then sick leave and finally they had to let her go. The company had made her redundant on health grounds – nervous exhaustion, the doctor had written on the certificate, or something like that.

Eventually, when her financial situation had become pretty desperate, when there seemed nothing else she could actively do to look for Lauren, and when she no longer cried every day, she had tried to go back to work, but it had been impossible to get another job. All the application forms asked 'Reason for leaving last employment', so an explanation was unavoidable. Employers did not like the idea of nervous illness, although quite a lot of people invited her for interview, probably just to get a look at her – see what she was like in the flesh – since none of them offered her a post. One or two had actively probed into areas which seemed unconnected with the job. Never mind her qualifications, or how up to date her IT skills were; what did she think had happened to her daughter? Their curiosity was always wrapped up in affected concern. 'That must have been a terrible time for you . . . I wonder, did they ever find anything . . .?'

Intrusive questions. The things everyone wanted to know. She and Dominic had achieved a horrible form of celebrity, which drew false friends like wasps to a jam pot. People they had hardly known before it happened now appeared in the newspapers, talking about them, making things up. Complete strangers approached them in the street and hundreds of people wrote letters – all of which they opened in the hope that, sooner or later, one of them might contain news of their daughter. But the communications which were not completely mad either said terrible things about herself and Dom, or else came from would-be hangers-on, people who wanted to be your 'friend', just so that they could satisfy their curiosity about you. It was just the same with people you met. They wanted to talk to you and weigh you up, so that they could tell their friends all about you, what they had made of you and how it affected their take on the case.

Marcus had not been like that. Although he undoubtedly knew from the very first exactly who she was, and even if he hadn't realized straight away, someone would have been quick to tell him. By the time she met Marcus, her confidence was at rock bottom. If Nerys had not dragged her along to an open meeting of the local history society called 'Who *Really*

Killed the Princes in the Tower?' they might never have met at all.

Even her marriage to Marcus had attracted adverse attention. The local paper got hold of the story, described Marcus as 'a businessman' and made a point of mentioning that Jo had previously been claiming benefits. They made her sound like a gold-digger. An old anger surged at the thought of it. She must stop dwelling on the past. Why not pop some of the books she had finished looking at back to Shelley? And while she was down at the gallery, she could sound Shelley out about becoming a guide when her new tour got off the ground.

Jo double-wrapped the books against the rain, encasing half a dozen volumes inside one tightly folded plastic carrier bag, which she then placed inside another before setting out. The lights inside the gallery were on, but when she looked through the glass panels in the top half of the door, there was no one sitting at the desk-cum-table. She pushed the door open and stepped inside, calling out, 'Anyone at home?'

Brian stepped out from behind one of the display panels, his face darkening to a frown at the sight of her. Brian was a big man, not quite as tall as Marcus, but much broader. He had wavy black hair which was going grey at the sides and matching bushy eyebrows, which made him look fearsome when he glowered.

'Oh . . . hi.' Jo hovered just inside the door, trying not to drip anywhere except the rope-weave door mat. 'I've brought back some of the books Shelley lent me.'

'Just drop them by the door.'

Brian was often curt to the point of rudeness. Jo did as she was told, noticing the way the rain ran off the yellow and white plastic bag on to the pine floor. 'Is Shelley around?'

she ventured. 'Only there was something I wanted to have a chat with her about.'

'She's not here.'

'Is she in the house? I could come back later if she's busy.'

'When I said she is not here,' Brian appeared to be on the edge of losing his temper, although Jo could not see what possible reason she had given him for doing so, 'it means she is not here, full stop. Not in the house, not in the gallery, not hiding in the garden shed, not here *at all*.'

'Oh, I see.' Something made her pursue the issue. That faint sense of unease she had experienced on overhearing noises through the front door of Ingledene had returned with a vengeance. 'What time do you think she will be back?'

Brian hesitated. He half turned away, as if his attention had just been caught by a bold abstract piece in green and red oils. 'She won't be back. She's gone for good.' He turned his back and stalked down to the far end of the gallery, where he was hidden from her by a couple of display panels.

Jo stood dripping on to the mat for a minute or two longer, but when Brian failed to reappear – he must have known she was still there; there was a little bell above the gallery door which tinkled when anyone let themselves in or out – she stepped back into the rain. It seemed unaccountable that Shelley would just leave. They might not have been bosom pals, but Jo knew enough of her neighbour to know how much she cared about the gallery and, indeed, how loyal she was to Brian, in spite of his difficult nature. As she walked home a jumble of ideas competed in her mind. How long had it been between her hearing Shelley in the house and seeing Brian drive away? And if Brian had been using the car alone, how could Shelley – and presumably most of her belongings – have been spirited away? Unless Brian had driven her somewhere, then driven back again, the car could not have returned by itself. She suddenly remembered the afternoon when Shelley had originally loaned her the books: Shelley had said the bruise on the side of her face had been caused by a book falling on her. Brian was a great bear of a man, whereas Shelley looked as if a puff of wind could knock her flat. *Let me go, you bastard!* Then that awful crash, like a piece of furniture going over.

CHAPTER SIX

Marcus had barely been home from Border Raids and Battles for eighteen hours before he waved Jo off to lead an Arthur Ransome tour. The success of every trip was hugely dependent on what each individual guide brought to it, and in a business which relied heavily on personal recommendations and repeat bookings, it was vital that standards never slipped. He would never know how well the tour had actually gone unless she made such a hash of it that there were letters of complaint – but something in her demeanour made him uneasy. Once you lost confidence in a member of the team, you were walking on quicksand. He experienced a sinking feeling as he watched her drive away.

Last night, tired from the journey, he had almost lost patience with her over some nonsense about the gallery people; another little incident which had contributed to the unspoken tension which existed between them lately. He knew that a lot of it related to his son's arrival in the household, and on the one hand he did feel guilty that she had to spend so much time at home taking care of Sean. He would gladly have done the same for her if the situation had been reversed, but that did not alter the feeling that he owed her, whereas in the past it had always been the other way around. Even so, he thought most people would have classified him as a more than normally considerate spouse. Taking on a woman like Jo would have been too much for a lot of men –

in fact, there had been times in their five-and-a-half-year marriage when he had found it pretty taxing himself. There were so many minefields to avoid – tiptoeing around all the things he must never say. Familiar patterns of speech were denied him, everyday expressions completely out of bounds. No 'You must be mad to say a thing like that'; not even in the face of the latest fantasy – that one of their neighbours might have done away with his wife.

It was crazy, of course. Only Jo would imagine the worst, having merely overheard a domestic argument, following which one of the parties had walked out. But of course 'crazy', like 'bonkers', 'barmy' and 'doolally', was also among the words he must not use, all as verboten as implying that Lauren might be dead – although privately Marcus was more than ninety per cent convinced that this was so. He could understand – of course he could – why Jo could never bring herself to accept this, even if in her heart of hearts she must know that abducted children almost never come home.

He had never imagined that marriage to someone as traumatized as Jo would be plain sailing. They had been through some bumpy patches before, and the arrival of a 'Lauren postcard', bearing the usual cruel message, was often a trigger. Jo inevitably erred towards the belief that they were genuine, although there was nothing about the cards to specifically indicate that. On the contrary, they always featured the same old photograph, which had been in the public domain since Lauren's disappearance. The picture had clearly been obtained from a newspaper, whereas a genuine kidnapper might have given them something more – a photograph of Lauren which had been taken after she was abducted, a lock of hair, or a voice recording perhaps.

'Not if they were clever,' Jo argued. 'Not if they didn't want us to track them down.'

He had not disputed the point, although he couldn't see anything particularly clever in sending the cards. If the kidnapper didn't want to be found out, why draw attention to himself in any way at all?

Missing children always attracted the loony brigade. Just weeks ago there had been something in the papers about a case in the USA. A man had come forward claiming to be one and the same person as a two-year-old boy who had been kidnapped back in 1955, but DNA tests had disproved the theory.

Marcus could well imagine the agony of the family involved. Could you resurrect a familial relationship after more than half a century – or even after a decade? Suppose Lauren were to be miraculously found? She would be a stranger now. It would be horribly complicated, much more so than Sean's coming to live with them had been. At least he had always maintained regular contact with Sean; even when they lived in different parts of the country, they had enjoyed a regular relationship which gave them something to build on now. He had been surprised when Sean expressed the desire to live with him; he'd told himself that the odd feeling of victory in being chosen over his ex-wife had scarcely come into it. Not that Sean's arrival had made for an easy situation, involving as it did a complete rethink on both work and domestic fronts. A few teething troubles were inevitable.

Marcus's ruminations were abruptly interrupted by his son appearing in the doorway.

'Has she gone?'

Marcus was about to remonstrate that Jo had a name, but Sean's anxious expression stopped him in his tracks and he nodded instead.

'Can you come upstairs, Dad? I've got something to show you.'

Confronted with the broken cupboard door, Marcus forced

himself to stifle his anger. Flying off the handle would not help things now.

'I just came home from school and found it.'

'And she didn't mention anything about it? Say it was an accident, or tell you how it happened?'

'No. She just seemed a bit weirder than usual. Anyway, I don't think it was an accident, do you?'

'Look, Sean . . .' Marcus paused, momentarily at a loss for words. 'I'm really sorry about this. I . . . we'll buy you another cupboard, one you can lock. It's only fair. And of course I'll talk to Jo about it when she gets home.' He was going to tack on a platitude to the effect that it could have been an accident, but he knew that was ridiculous. He felt as if Jo had humiliated him – left him with no recourse but to admit that the woman he had taken for his wife was capable of such irrational behaviour.

In the meantime, Jo had driven to Kendal for her rendezvous with the coach. All the drivers who worked for M. H. Tours were good, but Clive was one of the best: calm, resolutely cheerful and adept at turning the coach in seemingly impossible places. They left the garage spot on time. When there were no passengers on board, Clive liked listening to the radio, so after a brief chat about the health of his wife and his cat, on whom he doted in almost equal measure, he tuned in to Radio 2 while Jo watched the familiar landmarks go by.

There were pick-up points at Manchester Airport and Preston, and according to her manifest, the party would include Americans, Australians, Canadians and some British clients, so it would be quite a mixed bag. When they passed the service station at Forton, she took out her folder of notes to check through the itinerary again, although she already knew it by heart. Marcus's parting 'You will be all right,

76

won't you?' echoed in her ears. Of course she would be all right. She knew what she was doing. She had led dozens of tours over the past four years, and she wasn't about to let him down. She might not be as decorative as Melissa, but she knew her stuff.

Yet in recalling Marcus's parting words, she was suddenly assailed by doubts. Suppose she messed it up. A vision grew in her mind, of herself standing in The Square at Cartmel, quailing before a semicircle of faces and being quite unable to summon up the year in which Arthur Ransome had first holidayed there.

Steady the Buffs. That had been something her foster-father used to say. She had never heard anyone use the expression until he did, and hadn't really known what it meant. The other kids probably didn't either. There had been two other children while she was there. Jake, the one who had lived for football, might even have made it as a professional if he had not been so clearly heading off the rails. Jake was forever running away, financing his train journeys with petty thefts which brought him continually to the attention of the police. 'Why do you keep doing it?' the foster-parents had asked. 'Aren't you happy here?' But Jake hadn't been able to tell them why. He didn't appear to know himself.

Then there had been Robbie, little thin Robbie, who chewed the sleeve of his jumper and scarcely said a word. She had tried to be kind to Robbie and make a friend of Jake, even though it had been shaming to become part of such a household of flotsam and jetsam – a place to which 'problem' children were consigned, in the hope that Ma and Pa Allisson could sort them out. She attempted to convince the kids at her temporary school that she was staying with relatives, but everyone in the neighbourhood knew the Allissons fostered.

It marked you out as different. When people laughed at

Robbie, he just dipped his head and started chewing the neck of his jumper, or the collar of his shirt. No one laughed at Jake – not unless they wanted to be duffed up in the playground after school. Jo herself had tried not to attract undue attention. She learned not to say too much in class – to appear neither overly smart or stupid – and she never wet herself like Robbie, so there wasn't much laughing and outright pointing. But she was careful, always on her guard, always pretending. She never let anyone see how much she minded, ignoring the occasional whispering and pointing. Even the mothers did it. She saw one of them once, pointing her out after school. Too much pointing and too much attention – it had been the story of her life. It was the supreme irony that she and Marcus ended up buying a house called The Hideaway.

She thought it would be easier when they let her go back home and return to her old school, but when she got back it seemed that everyone knew about Mum. Whereas before they had merely glanced sideways at Mum's tatty trainers, the outsize home-made jogging bottoms, or the flower she sometimes wore in her hair, now there was a new recognition in their eyes. It tainted Jo much in the way that being part of a foster-family had done. People felt sorry for her. Obvious acts of kindness stung as much as overt expressions of pity.

And they watched *her*, too. Where once they had merely thought her unfortunate to have a mother who was 'a bit odd', now they kept an eye on her, ready to rescue their own children from an unsuitable friendship at the first manifestation of any unusual behaviour. At the same time they tried to be nice, making a point of including her in other people's parties, never guessing how much Jo dreaded the arrival of such invitations. Party attendance meant buying a present, which was bad news if Mum happened to be in a funny mood. The present-buying for Jane Hill's party had gone OK. There had been no repetition of the episode with the cream crackers wrapped in newspaper. Mum had managed a box of chocolates, coupled with an appropriate card and wrapping paper with clowns on it. There hadn't been any trouble about ironing Jo's party frock, and Mum had walked her as far as the Hills' front gate.

Everything had been fine until they turned on the music for Pass the Parcel, and that hideous song 'The Laughing Policeman' had begun. By the first chorus Jo had begun to shake, and the longer the forced laughter echoed around the room, the more she had sobbed, until one of the mothers stopped the music and another of them conducted her into the kitchen. She might have been OK after that, but as soon as she had been taken out of the room the game resumed and with it the song, so that the maniacal laughter filled her head again and it was all she could do not to scream.

She still hated that song. Mercifully it was seldom played these days, but back then it had been a regular request on *Junior Choice*. Children were supposed to find it funny, although she had never been able to understand why anyone would think an exhibition of demented laughter was amusing.

The radio had always been on at home when she was a little girl. Mum often joined in with the songs – which could be a good or a bad thing, depending on her mood. Sometimes she danced while she sang, holding out her hands for Jo to join in. They would career around the room together, weaving between the armchairs or circling the coffee table – those had been the good times.

Mum had only once joined in with 'The Laughing Policeman' – just the laughing, not the lyrics – a high, unnatural laugh, which she carried on with, even after the song was finished. Jo had been frightened then. She had known something was going to happen. Mum had gone on laughing and laughing, drowning out the voice of the disc jockey, forcing the laughter out of her throat, growing hoarse with the effort, on and on across the opening of the next record, 'Ah ha ha ha ha ha ha ha ha ha ha ha ha,' wrenching open the cutlery drawer, clattering among the knives, bringing one of them down again and again on to the wooden draining board, until it finally stuck there; at which point Mum had stopped laughing, collapsed on to her knees and started to cry, slapping her hands ineffectually against the cupboard doors.

Jo had watched from the doorway, too scared to approach, her mouth silently forming the words, 'Stop. Please stop it.' She had been in middle infants then – Miss Simms's class – it had been around the time Mum had first failed to pick her up from school.

The episode had stayed with her all that time, from middle infants to top juniors and beyond. She could never bear to listen to that song. If she heard it announced, she would snap off the radio before it began. Mum didn't like her messing with the radio, but an unspoken understanding appeared to exist between them when it came to 'The Laughing Policeman'.

'I don't like that one,' Jo would say, and her mother would just nod or say, 'Oh, all right then.'

People said afterwards that something should have been done. Why had no one helped them? Why hadn't her mother been given treatment, supervision, proper support? People were always clever after the event. The doctor had prescribed tablets, but Mum didn't like taking them. She was supposed to go to a clinic, but she hardly ever turned up.

'They think I'm barmy,' she said. 'Well, I'm not.'

Jo had lived with a sense of her mother's difference for as long as she could remember. She knew her mum was not the same as the other mums. She didn't look the same. She always stayed on the periphery, mostly walking to and from school on her own, not pairing up to talk to the other mothers – although she sometimes talked to herself – not joining in the chat with the woman in the corner shop. But Jane Hill's party had been the first time anyone had openly suggested that Jo herself might be different.

'Not normal,' one of the other mums had said, watching from a vantage point beyond the kitchen door, from where she assumed Jo could not hear her. 'Like mother, like daughter,' whispered another.

It was a suggestion which had haunted her ever since.

When Lauren disappeared, the press never made the connection. Different name, different place. A long time had passed, and her mother's case had never been high-profile; just a brief flurry of local headlines and no subsequent trial to resurrect interest, the defendant being unfit to plead.

Local people did not easily forget, but Jo had moved right away as soon as she was old enough to do so. Even when she married Dominic, his family had not known any details. The official line was that her parents were dead and she didn't like to talk about it. Dom knew, of course. She told him when they were first going out. He said it was tragic. It just made him love her all the more, he said. But all the same, he had decided not to tell his mother. She could be very old-fashioned about things like mental illness.

Those first years with Dom had been a new beginning. They had been the best years – even if admitting that to herself was disloyal to Marcus – because there had been no shadows then. She had escaped the past, forgotten . . . well, perhaps not forgotten, but been able not to remember. They had been like any other young couple, setting up home, getting married, having a baby. It had been joyful. It had been *normal*.

No one had pointed her out any more, as the girl whose mother had murdered her father.

CHAPTER SEVEN

They used the Linthwaite for their Arthur Ransome tours because the food, service and views of Windermere never failed to impress the pickiest of clients. Although the hotel was within a few miles of home, there was no question of Jo slipping away for a night with Marcus: being on hand to mix with clients was very much part of the service. Instead, she undertook a minimal amount of unpacking, then rushed her shower in order to be first down to the lounge, so that any solo member of the party who came down early would be greeted by a familiar face.

When she got downstairs, however, she found the three adjoining rooms which made up the lounge at the Linthwaite were all empty, with only the crackle of the open fires for company. She normally stuck to slimline tonic before dinner, but when the waiter approached, temptation overcame her and she asked for a glass of red. He brought her a large one, which she cradled in both hands, watching the undulating reflection of the fire in the copper-coloured coal scuttle which sat on the nearest hearth, and wishing that she had risked a quick phone call to Marcus after all. It would have been good to exchange a few words, and in the process reassure him that everything was going well.

With no one to engage her attention, her mind began to wander. Shelley and Brian usually drank red. Wine was one of those things Brian knew about. She remembered Shelley saying, half in jest, that Brian was a wine snob. It had been on New Year's Day, when Fred and Maisie Perry invited all the neighbours round for lunchtime drinks. Jo had been standing next to Shelley when Brian wrinkled his nose at the glass of cheap Chilean plonk he had been given.

She was worried about Shelley, but did not know what she ought to do. Two days after her visit to return the first lot of Shelley's books, she had been on her way out to do some drawing when she caught sight of Brian emerging from Ingledene. He had his head down, and didn't notice her until he was out of the garden gate and coming towards her along the lane. She had opened her mouth to greet him as normal, but instead of acknowledging her, he had turned abruptly aside on to the track which led to High Gilpin. It wasn't a public footpath, and the Phantom Jogger's tenancy had come to an end a fortnight before, so she couldn't imagine why Brian would be going up there. Had he avoided her on purpose, guessing she was suspicious?

She had waited for Marcus to get home before explaining about Shelley, but when she sought his advice he had been no help at all, merely ridiculing her concerns. 'People have rows and walk out all the time,' he said. Actually he had reacted rather strangely, almost as if *he* was angry with *her*; although a few minutes later he had added in a much kinder voice, 'It's understandable that you always think the worst.'

Lately, Marcus was often irritable with her. That seemingly boundless tolerance and patience which he had always exhibited in the past turned out to have limits after all. It worried her, this change in him. He had always been so gentle and supportive, willing to listen, endlessly kind. Was it just the stress of his mother's illness? Or maybe having Sean around? Or had he fallen out of love with her? She had been watching him closely at the itinerary planning meeting. He was always so nice to Melissa, laughing at her jokes, agreeing with her ideas. Of course, Marcus was like that with most people. That was his way of charming them into doing what he wanted – a softening-up process, which began by his appearing to agree with them. Maybe it was no more than that with Melissa.

She brought the glass to her lips and drank deeply, scarcely aware of what she was doing. She could not bear it if Marcus deserted her. If she was absolutely honest with herself, she had never really loved him in the way she had loved Dominic, but that did not mean she did not love him *enough* – and moreover, she needed him. Melissa did not need Marcus. Melissa would just make a plaything of him, until she was ready to move on to the next man; whereas she, Jo, would always be faithful. Faithful unto death. No – that had been the set of promises she had made to Dom, when they were married in church. What had she and Marcus said to one another on their wedding day? It had been a secular event in a small hotel, with just a few close friends and relatives. Nerys had read an Elizabeth Barrett Browning sonnet, and for music they had John Dowland's 'Come away, come sweet love', but she was alarmed to discover that she could no longer remember exactly what form of words she and Marcus had said to one another. It was only five years ago, but it had already gone, washed down the sink along with so many other memories, some good, some bad.

It's understandable that you always think the worst.

Well, yes, why wouldn't she? Dom had once said something along similar lines, on a day which had been much longer ago than that second wedding ceremony, but his words, and the expression on his face as he spoke them – that particular memory had clung on, evaded the tide of red wine and tears, so that she could still see the look in his eyes, desperate, almost fearful. *How much bad luck can you have in a single life?*

He didn't really mean bad luck. Bad luck is when your number doesn't come up in the raffle, or you've just missed the bus. He meant horrible things; the kind of hideous events which don't intrude into most people's lives at all. That was why it was possible to believe that Brian had killed Shelley in a fit of temper and then pretended she had gone away – because lightning did strike twice. It struck the same people again and again and again, and although everybody hopes for a happy ending, not all of us get one.

Jo's thoughts were interrupted by the sound of voices from the hall, but when she looked up she found that the women entering the lounge were not members of her own party, but two young women, one fair and one dark, who made a faint nod of acknowledgement in Jo's direction before seating themselves on a striped sofa at the window end of the room. They had already equipped themselves with glasses of wine from the bar, and continued the conversation they had begun there without pause. Jo had spent enough time in hotel lounges to become adept at guessing the reason behind visitors' stays: the lone businessman or woman, the couple on a romantic break, the fag ends of a wedding party, scrutinizing the prices in the bar and wishing their friends' nuptials had been booked at a more affordable venue. She guessed that these two were girlfriends, taking a break from families or careers. She did not set out to overhear them, but the room was too quiet not to do so.

'I'd forgotten how tiny they are,' the brunette was saying. 'Her little feet were lost up the legs of her babygrow.'

'They grow so fast,' said the blonde. 'The first-size clothes only fit them for a week or two.'

'Those tiny little fingers . . . and all that hair when she was born.'

'Brandon looked as bald as his grandpa, but he wasn't really. His head was covered in hair, but it was so fine and pale you couldn't see it.'

'And they have a lovely smell,' the brunette eulogized. 'You know, I'd have laughed if anyone had said that to me before I had Cassie. But I used to press my face against her hair and just smell her.'

They all smell unique, Jo wanted to say. I read it somewhere. Someone somewhere did experiments with mothers and their new babies. They found out that mothers could pick out the garments their own babies had been wearing, just by the smell.

'I'd forgotten the smell,' said the blonde. 'You know, before I had Brandon, I used to think all babies looked alike – at least, they did to me . . .'

And to me, Jo added, silently. I know what you're going to say next – and it was the same with me, just the same.

'. . . but once I'd got him, I would have been able to pick him out from a thousand other babies.'

'Your own baby looks completely different to anyone else's,' her friend agreed. 'There must be some sort of primitive mechanism going on. You know, some sort of instinct.'

And surely you must go on knowing them. Even if you haven't seen them for years, you would still recognize your own child. There would be something about them – there would have to be something . . . The tight band of pain around her chest took her by surprise. A constriction of grief so fierce and unexpected that for a moment she feared some actual physical illness had overtaken her. She put her empty wine glass on the low table beside the chair, before getting to her feet. The two women on the striped sofa were facing out towards the view and paid her no heed, but Mrs Tanner and Mrs Cohen from the tour glanced at her as she passed them in the hall. She forced herself to nod in their direction and, rather than run the risk of meeting other members of her group on the main stairs, she fled into the ladies' cloakroom. It smelled of perfumed handwash and pot pourri, refreshed daily. There were stacks of individually folded white towels, daintily sized for single use. A huge vase of fresh flowers stood on the marble counter, neatly placed between the inset oval basins. The flowers were reflected again and again in the mirrors all around the room, so that there appeared to be dozens of vases in front of her, behind her, all around her. It reminded her of a game she and her mother had sometimes played when she was very little, in which they angled the moveable side mirrors of her mother's dressing table until they reflected dozens of faces which seemed to people the whole bedroom, all of them looking like herself and her mother, all of them pulling the same faces, mocking them.

She grabbed the edge of the counter as if to steady herself. She must not cry. If her make-up got smudged, there would be no chance of escaping upstairs to repair it without being seen. She ran cold water into one of the basins, splashing some on to her wrists, then cupping some to her mouth. Using one of the pristine towels to dry herself, she watched the last of the water gurgle down the plughole. *More memories gone*. She would have forgotten this in a few days' time. The women talking on the sofa, the heady sensation of too much wine. She had been a fool to gulp down a whole glass on an empty stomach.

Now that the water had stopped running, she was aware of a faint hum; the electric lights, perhaps, or a discreet fan. She smoothed her hair and checked herself in the mirrors, front, side and rear views. It was like being in a dressing room backstage. She had that same sense of being about to participate in something which was not quite real; getting herself into character, moulding herself into the part she was to play. In a moment or two she would emerge as Jo Handley, a director of M. H. Tours (in association with Flights of Fantasy) Ltd. Calm, clear-headed, professional to her fingertips: someone who would sit down to a dinner she did not want, delivering lines about Arthur Ransome in response to appropriate cues.

At around the same moment Jo was emerging from the ladies' cloakroom in the Linthwaite Hotel, Harry was vigorously working the knocker at the front door of The Hideaway. It was Marcus who admitted him, necessitating a fidgety exchange of pleasantries in the hall, before he was free to mount the stairs and tap at Sean's bedroom door. Sean appeared gratifyingly pleased to see him, which reassured Harry that the coming days would bring plenty of remission from 'family fun' back at The Hollies.

For the first hour of his visit, Harry managed to subdue his curiosity, hoping that the matter uppermost in his mind would be raised spontaneously by Sean, but when the minute hand had begun another circuit round the face of his watch, and the older boy had still made no reference to their parting conversation at the end of half-term, Harry cautiously broached the subject himself.

'You know that stuff you were saying last time?'

'What stuff?'

Sean sounded genuinely innocent but Harry proceeded carefully, still wary of a wind-up. 'That story about there being a murderer in Easter Bridge.'

'That – oh, yeah.'

'You were kidding me, right?'

'Deadly serious.'

'So, who is it?'

Sean hesitated. For a split second his eyes darted in the direction of the bedroom door, as if afraid of an unseen listener out on the landing. 'Let me show you something,' he said. He brought his laptop on to the bed and positioned it so that they could both see the screen. Harry watched while Sean woke the machine, then located a file identified only by a series of apparently random letters and numbers, like a code. 'I started hunting around on the net,' Sean said. 'There was loads of stuff about it. I've downloaded quite a bit.'

The file seemed to take an age to open. When it eventually did, the front page of a newspaper appeared onscreen: a block of text on the left and a picture on the right, which unrolled downwards like a slow-reveal picture question on a TV quiz show.

'It's a kid,' said Harry. 'A missing kid.'

'Not just any kid. Ever noticed that photo on the dresser in our living room?'

'No,' said Harry. 'I've hardly ever been in there.'

'Well, it's the same kid.'

'Hunt Continues for Baby Lauren,' Harry read aloud.

'They never found the body,' Sean said. 'So they couldn't charge anyone. Now look at this.' He moved the cursor, shrinking the first image and clicking on another item, which opened a different newspaper article.

'Tragic Sequel in Lauren Mystery,' Harry read aloud again. 'Father's body found on beach. So?'

'It's her, you idiot. My dad's wife. Don't you recognize her?'

Harry looked back at the woman in the picture, then stared at Sean.

'First her daughter, then her husband,' Sean said.

'Jeez . . .' Harry made a whistling sound. 'Hang on, though – you said it was murder.'

'Look,' Sean was putting up yet another page of newsprint, 'there's loads more. You have to put everything together to work it out. I knew about the kid. Dad told me ages ago, so I wouldn't upset her by asking about the girl in the picture – like I would be interested in some baby picture. The official story is that she was kidnapped from outside a shop, but no one saw anything. No witnesses. Only the parents' word for it that the kid had ever been outside the shop in the first place. They found the empty buggy chucked over the cliffs, but they never found the kid's body – so *officially* she's still a missing person. Then a couple of years later, some people found the dad's body on the beach, pretty much near the same place. Again, there's no witnesses. Some people think he chucked himself off the cliffs, some that he fell – but if you look at the evidence, the most likely thing is that she pushed him off.'

Harry opened his mouth, then shut it again. 'How is that the most likely thing?' he asked at last.

'I've googled it. It's all there in the papers, what everyone said, because there had to be an inquest – that's what they do when someone dies and it's suspicious. The two of them were staying at a caravan site, near where their daughter was supposed to have disappeared. Some people saw them set off together, but when she came back to the caravan she was on her own. Said her shoe strap had snapped, so she'd come back while he walked on. As if . . .' he finished scornfully.

'But the kid in the buggy – surely someone must have seen –'

'They appealed for witnesses, but no one saw anything. The first thing anyone seems to remember is her screaming out that her baby had been stolen, but who's to say the baby was outside the shop in the first place?'

'Why would she do it?'

'Because she's a nutter. She belongs in the bin. I'm telling you, she's not just one sandwich short of a picnic, she's missing the pork pie and the crisps as well.'

Harry was visibly struggling to take it all in. 'She always seems all right,' he said, doubtfully.

'All right? Let me show you "all right".' Sean pointed to the smashed cupboard door. 'She did that while I was out at school. Does that look "all right"?'

Harry conceded that it was not the kind of thing his own mother would do. Up until now, he had still been able to think the whole thing a kind of game. A putting together of two and two, the sum of which made an exciting five – something you could accept without entirely *believing* it. The splintered wreck of the door was far more solid and immediate than a bunch of images on the net. It was there in the room with them, thrusting him abruptly into a real world of murderous stepmothers who wrecked your things and pushed people off cliffs.

'What about your dad?'

'What about him?'

'Does he know about all this stuff?'

'He must do. He knows about the kid disappearing because he told me about it. He must know that her first husband's dead.'

'Doesn't he suspect? I mean . . . it's like she's the black widow, or something.'

'I don't know. I don't think he could have realized how strange she was to start with, but he must have noticed by now. He tries to make excuses for her when she's being weirder than usual.'

'You wouldn't marry someone if you thought they'd murdered people.'

'You think, Genius?'

'So he must believe what she's told him about it.'

'Yeah.'

'What are you going to do?'

'How do you mean?'

'About her?'

'It's a waiting game. One day she'll flip and do something really extreme, and then maybe Dad'll get the message and get rid of her. And in the meantime, if she goes for me or Dad . . . well, I've got a few tricks up my sleeve, too.'

CHAPTER EIGHT

Jo had been looking forward to getting home, not least because she and Marcus had tickets to hear the Manchester Camerata in Ulverston that night. It was a rare treat for a night at home together to coincide with a concert date, so it was aggravating to be slowed down by the ever-present road-works on the M6, then delayed by an accident just after Junction 34. When she phoned Marcus on her mobile to explain that she was going to be late and they should go ahead and eat without her, he sounded rather cool, but then lateness always wound Marcus up – punctuality was one of the ten commandments by which he ran his life.

'Hello,' she called from the front door, dumping her bags on the hall floor and following the sound of their voices into the kitchen, where she approached Marcus for a homecoming kiss, which he appeared accidentally to avoid by turning to put something back in the fridge. Sean studiously ignored her greeting.

Slightly thrown by this chilly welcome, but attributing it to Marcus's displeasure at her lateness, Jo continued cheerfully, 'Sorry I got held up, but it will only take me two ticks to have a quick shower and get changed. We won't be late for the concert.'

She was surprised when he followed her up to their bed-room, not saying a word until he had closed the door behind them. 'Sean showed me what you did to his cupboard.'

She was caught completely off guard. The truth was that she had forgotten all about the episode with the cupboard, partly because it suited her to do so, and partly because once several days had gone by without Sean making any reference to it, she thought he had let it go. It had not occurred to her that he would merely wait his opportunity to snitch to Marcus when she wasn't around.

'I was trying to find the knife.' She could see her own expression reflected in the mirror doors of the wardrobe, shifty and unmistakably embarrassed at being caught out.

'But you didn't find a knife, did you?' Marcus's voice was a shade louder than it needed to be. He sounded both exasperated and angry. 'Basically, you hunted through his room and smashed your way into his cupboard, after I had specifically said we shouldn't search his room.'

There was no real evidence that she had searched the room, but it seemed pointless to deny it. 'I was sure I saw a knife.'

There was a brief silence while the phrase drifted around the room, pathetic as a half deflated balloon waiting to be kicked aside. This is how it was between my father and my mother, she thought. He not wanting to make a direct challenge, not wanting to say outright that she *was* imagining things. A shudder ran down her spine – a sensation that her mother had been wont to describe as a goose walking over your grave.

'Sean was very upset.' Marcus began to speak in an oddly controlled voice. 'He doesn't understand why you smashed his cupboard up. I think . . .' again the pause was unbearably long '. . . I think he was a bit scared. It's not a normal thing to do, going into someone's room and smashing their things. He's not used to anything – anything so violent.'

'I'm not violent.'

'You know what I mean.'

She stood beside the bed, frozen in the act of removing her sweater, suddenly afraid of what Marcus might say next: that there was no knife and never had been, that Brian had not harmed Shelley, that no unseen stalker had dogged her movements for years, mocking her with picture postcards of her vanished baby daughter. She wanted to say that she had changed her mind about the concert, and didn't want to attend – that she suddenly had the strangest sense of foreboding about it. However, Marcus might interpret that as sulking or deliberate spite – or worse, as madness. There. She had allowed herself to think the word.

Marcus was still standing with his back against the bedroom door, almost as if he was expecting her to make a run for it and was ready to stop her. 'You need to get ready,' he said. 'Otherwise we are going to be late.'

She nodded, dragging the sweater over her head, then fumbling with the hook of her skirt, while he continued to stand there watching her. She felt as if his scrutiny went deeper than her outward appearance, that he was examining things she could not see herself.

Eventually she said, 'I shouldn't have broken into his cupboard. It was just that I was so sure . . . Only now I'm not. I only got a glimpse – maybe he was looking at one of those magazines and the light caught the page when he shoved it out of the way.'

'I think you should apologize to Sean,' he said quietly. 'Even if you can't explain to him why you did it.'

'Would you still have asked me to apologize if I'd found a knife in his cupboard?' she flashed back.

'But you didn't.'

There was another silence while she peeled off her tights.

'I didn't smash the cupboard up on purpose. I know that it

looks pretty violent, but I just levered the door open and it split. It looks worse than it is.'

'It's broken,' he said. 'How can that be better or worse?' He walked out of the room before she could reply.

It was an uneasy drive down to Ulverston. She asked about his mother, he asked about the tour, but Jo felt that the issue of the knife travelled with them as surely as if it was lying on the dashboard, its shiny blade caught every so often in the headlights of passing cars. It *was* possible that she had been wrong. Mistaking an innocent object for a firearm had led to people being shot before now.

It had begun to drizzle, so they hurried up the hill from the car park, she clinging to Marcus's arm as they sheltered beneath his big umbrella, partly as a matter of form, partly in order to keep up. Past the Laurel and Hardy statue and into the Coronation Hall, where the booking office doubled up with Tourist Information, showing their tickets to the dinner-jacketed stewards on duty at the front doors.

They had seats in the balcony because Marcus preferred the acoustics up there. Although Jo had been raised on pop music, she always enjoyed the Camerata, and the music seemed extraordinarily beautiful that night, a programme of Elgar and Vaughan Williams. At the end of the first half, when they joined the crowd shuffling down to the bar for interval drinks, she knew that both their spirits had been lifted: she returned Marcus's smile, and he squeezed her hand. As they entered the bar she caught sight of Maisie Perry, down at the other end of the room. 'Look,' she said. 'There's Fred and Maisie. If we had known they were coming, we could have offered them a lift.'

The Perrys had seen them in the same instant, and Maisie began weaving her way towards them, her progress considerably impeded by people moving in all directions, many carrying a glass in each hand, everyone trying to negotiate a path around the clumps of people who had chosen a spot to stand in and were now impervious to all other human traffic.

'Marcus, Jo – how lucky to see you here. Now I'll be able to introduce you to our new neighbour, Mrs Iceton – the lady who has bought The Old Forge.' Maisie waved an explanatory arm to where Fred was in conversation with a woman who had her back towards them.

As they followed her through the crowd, Jo turned to Marcus. 'Surely someone hasn't moved in there already.'

'A removal van came, the day you went away.'

'Goodness, but it's crowded tonight,' Maisie prattled as she shepherded them across the room. 'Still, that's a good thing, isn't it? To see the concert so well supported. We're very lucky to get the Camerata coming to the Coro, I always say.' She ended her monologue with a flourish: 'Gilda, meet some more of your new neighbours, Jo and Marcus.'

Only then did the strange woman turn and face them for the first time. It had been twenty-five years, but Jo knew Gilda instantly. She swallowed hard. Marcus was already shaking hands, ever ready with some pleasantry suitable to the occasion.

'And this is Jo.' Maisie was enjoying her role as introducer-in-chief.

'I believe we've already met.' Gilda's smile was bright, but when Jo automatically extended her hand, the one she received in return was like a dead thing.

'I don't think so,' said Jo, trying to meet the other woman squarely in the eye. 'Or if we have, then I'm afraid I don't remember you.'

'Oh, I don't think you can have come across Jo, yet,' Maisie chipped in helpfully. 'She has been away on one of their tours, until this evening. I think I already mentioned to you that Marcus and Jo run a company which specializes in historical and literary tours – such an interesting way to earn a living. You'll have to get them to tell you all about it.'

Jo was too flustered to experience her usual level of irritation at the way Maisie was evidently au fait with all her movements. She was aware of Gilda regarding her discomfiture with cool amusement, while Maisie continued to chatter, oblivious to any possible tension. 'What a coincidence, finding that half of Easter Bridge is here this evening.'

'That's not so very difficult,' suggested Marcus. 'Given the total population of Easter Bridge.'

'I see the Wheatons are back at The Hollies,' Maisie went on. 'It's their second home,' she explained for Gilda's benefit. 'They have a boy and a girl, which might be nice for your daughter, when she's at home. Gilda has a daughter at boarding school.' She tossed this snippet of information in the direction of Jo and Marcus, barely pausing for breath before adding something about Brian and Shelley often coming to the Ulverston concerts too.

Jo turned swiftly to Maisie. 'I haven't seen anything of Shelley lately, have you?' The words almost ended in a squeak as Marcus surreptitiously grasped her hand and dug his fingernails into her palm, while politely asking Gilda, 'Your daughter will be home for the holidays at the moment, I suppose?'

'No, I was hoping she would be, but she's been invited to stay with a schoolfriend for a few days, and yesterday she rang to say that there's some sort of party at this friend's house on Saturday, so can she stay on until after the week-end.' Gilda punctuated her monologue with the exasperated sigh of a parent who can hardly keep up with their offspring's social life. 'Then they are going to drive her up to Helmsley, where she's due to spend the last week of the holidays with my cousin Carole. She always has Becky over in the holidays – Carole is our closest relative, and they're very fond of one another, so in the end I've arranged to go across and see Becky *there*, before she goes back to school.'

'I expect it's fallen in very well, keeping her out of the way while you get straightened up after the move,' Maisie said. 'Moving is such a hectic time, although I expect she's dying to see your new home together.'

Without giving Gilda the opportunity to confirm or deny this, Maisie turned to ask Fred something about the second half of the programme. Jo felt Gilda's eyes on her again. It made her feel as if she were standing under a hot, bright spotlight. Maisie continued chattering to Fred and Marcus about Thomas Tallis. Fred was saying something about a piece which had first been performed in Gloucester Cathedral, but Jo wasn't listening properly. She had to escape from the heat and dazzle. She edged away from the group, excusing herself with something about going to the ladies'.

As she hurried down to the ground floor, she realized it was becoming a theme, running away to hide in the toilets. She would have to grow up – in fact, that was the solution – she *was* a grown-up, and the uncomfortable memories which Gilda represented belonged to an another time – a time when she had been no more than a child. She had left all that behind now, and Gilda or no Gilda, she wasn't going to resurrect it.

The crowd in the bar was thinning by the time she returned. A lot of people had already made their way back to their seats, and the little group from Easter Bridge appeared to be on the point of dispersing. Gilda was facing the opposite way, which gave Jo the chance to take a long, hard look at her new neighbour. Her hair was as lank as it had always been, although these days it was streaked with grey, and she still wore it scraped back into a plastic hair clip which might have come from Woolworth's. Her trousers were ill fitting and not quite long enough, revealing pale blue ankle socks and flat lace-ups, the ensemble topped off with a strange knitted jacket, possibly courtesy of Oxfam. In twenty-first century Ulverston, where any eccentrically dressed bag lady might just turn out to be a moneyed recycling fanatic, it was impossible to make completely objective judgements based on fashion considerations alone, but in Gilda's case, Jo detected the natural successors to the old-fashioned pleated skirts and hand-knitted cardies which had singled Gilda out as 'different' at school, before the girl even opened her mouth.

Jo reminded herself firmly that nothing which had happened in the past could possibly matter now, although if Gilda was going to live just across the road, she would presumably have to come to some accommodation with her. She decided the safest line to take would be amnesia. She would claim to have pretty much forgotten everything about Gilda – after all, a great deal of water had passed under the bridge since then.

The playing in the second half was sublime, but Jo struggled to focus on the remainder of the programme. She kept experiencing the irrational sensation that Gilda was watching her from somewhere in the semi-darkened hall, though when the lights came up and she scanned the applauding crowd in the balcony, and then the departing concert-goers on the stairs and in the street outside, there was no sign of their new neighbour. Not that she was allowed to forget her.

'What's the deal with you and the weird woman?' Marcus asked as they headed back to the car, sheltered again by the big umbrella.

Weird – that was exactly it, she thought. Gilda had always been a bit weird. 'We were at senior school together, in the same class. Her name was Gilda Stafford then.'

'Why did you pretend not to recognize her?'

'It's awkward – complicated.'

'Why?'

Jo hesitated. They had reached the big roundabout at the bottom of the hill, and had to pause for a couple of passing cars before they could cross the road. The pavements reflected cold and wet in the street lights. It was quiet enough to hear their footfalls when there wasn't any passing traffic. 'It's something I'd much rather not talk about. Something I'm rather ashamed of, if you want to know the truth.'

Marcus said nothing, leaving a long silence during which he clearly expected her to elucidate further, but she said nothing as they crossed the car park and climbed into the car. After starting the engine, he said, 'If this woman is going to live just across the road and there's something – or was something – between the two of you, don't you think it might be better if you told me?'

'It's nothing really. It's all in the past. You know – just schoolgirl stuff.'

'No, I don't know.' He reached across to increase the heat on the windscreen, which was starting to mist up. 'I think you'd better tell me about it. If it's something trivial, then you're right, it doesn't matter. If it *is* something important, then I ought to know.'

Jo hesitated. It was obvious that his curiosity was aroused and he wasn't going to drop it. 'OK. When I started at St Catherine's, everyone else had been there for a couple of years and already made their friends. I was a very lonely, very scared new girl. I fell in with the first people who offered to be friends with me and I became part of their . . . crowd. All

101

I wanted was to fit in and be accepted. You can understand that, can't you?'

'Of course,' said Marcus, but his tone was cautious rather than warm.

'We – they – were quite a tough crowd. You know, the sort of girls who are always a bit cheeky to the teachers, always on the edge of any trouble. We used to dare one another to do stupid things. We even did a bit of shoplifting, not because we wanted or needed the things we took, but just to prove we could get away with it. I knew it was wrong and I was petrified that I'd get caught, but I did it because the others did it, and if you didn't keep up, you'd be out . . .'

'Of the gang,' Marcus finished for her. He sounded like a vicar who has just found a fag end in the collection plate.

'And no one else wanted to be my friend. I'd had such a hard time at my other schools, always being pointed out, always being made to feel different. People calling things out, or just whispering behind your back.' She paused, but Marcus continued to focus on the road ahead, giving her no sign.

'So instead of being a victim, you joined the bullies,' he said quietly.

'Gilda Stafford brought trouble on herself!' Jo exclaimed. 'She used to bring this rag doll thing to school and talk to it. One time she pretended to do voodoo, you know – sticking pins into a plasticine figure. It was supposed to put a curse on Colleen Hudd – she was sort of the leader of our group. As you said yourself, Gilda's weird.'

'I didn't mean weird in that sense. She's got a slightly odd appearance, that's all.'

'She's always had what you call an "odd appearance", and it wasn't just the way she looked. While the rest of us were listening to Duran Duran and watching *The Outsiders*, she was talking to a bloody rag doll. Is it any wonder the other kids took a rise out of her? If it hadn't been us, it would have been someone else.'

'But it *was* you.'

'For crying out loud, Marcus, don't sound so judgemental. I don't suppose anyone's led an absolutely blameless youth, not even you.'

'I never bullied anyone.'

'I never really did anything to her. I wasn't one of the ringleaders, I just tagged along and let things happen because I was too much of a coward to go against people like Colleen. It's easy to look back now and say that I should have spoken out. Believe me, I'm not proud of it.'

'What did you do to her, exactly?'

'Really Marcus, this is ridiculous. I honestly don't remember anything specific. It was something which happened at school – it went on for a couple of years, then Gilda left.'

'Because you bullied her?'

'Not me! I told you, I was just a bystander. I don't suppose Gilda differentiated between us, but in my case it was just a question of hanging around with the wrong people. And I'm sure there were other reasons for her leaving, too.'

'Really? Such as?'

'Oh, I don't know. You're making it all sound important, and it really wasn't. I don't know exactly why she left – I don't know everything there is to know about Gilda Stafford, or whatever her name is now.'

Jo huddled back against the seat. They had long since left the main road; dripping hedges and dry-stone walls appeared for a few seconds in the headlights, approaching fast before dropping away into the blackness again as soon as the car was past. The steady hush-hush of the wipers, the faint glow of the lights on the dashboard and the hum of the air-con, all contrived to give the impression of security, but Jo knew it was an illusion. Sooner or later you always had to go out and confront the dark again. She considered pointing out to Marcus that Gilda had survived; she had evidently married and produced a child, and what was more, she still had *her* child – but she decided against it. Better to say nothing more. To live in the moment of the car journey, where everything appeared superficially safe and warm.

Next morning, keen to avoid any possibility of making an apology to Sean with Marcus looking on, Jo feigned sleep until Marcus was almost ready to leave for another round of castles and abbeys. When she finally drifted downstairs in her dressing gown, safe in the knowledge that there had been no sound from Sean's room to suggest his imminent appearance, she was relieved to find Marcus in a much more equitable mood.

'It looks like a nice day.' His greeting was cheerful, and he kissed her on top of the head.

'Yes. I thought I might go out and do some drawing later on. Any idea if Sean has plans?'

'He didn't mention anything specific, but I expect he'll be hanging out with Harry. The two of them have been pretty inseparable these past few days.'

'I'm going to do some more work on the Artists in the Lakes idea, while you're away.'

'We'll need to come up with a better handle than that. Artists in the Lakes is too vague. It doesn't say enough.'

'I know, but the title is often the last thing we come up with. I'm sure I'll think of something better, when I've got the format clearer in my mind.'

'We should ask Melissa – she's always full of good ideas.'

Jo turned away, so that he would not see her face.

'You know,' he said, 'you shouldn't let that business with the woman at The Old Forge worry you. Kids say and do all sorts of daft things – sticks and stones and all that – she probably doesn't remember anything about it. She was chatting in a perfectly ordinary, pleasant way last night. And if she does remember, she's hardly going to make a thing of it – she's probably as embarrassed by it all as you are.'

In the office, Jo found an email had come in from the other side of the world, bringing her up to date on Nerys's latest adventures and asking, among other things, how it was going with Sean. Putting a mental picture of the damaged cupboard firmly to the back of her mind, Jo typed: *Sean-wise, things are about the same. It's very hard to build a relationship with someone who makes me feel as if I am wearing my wicked stepmother badge and riding my broomstick the whole time. Marcus falls over backwards to be fair to Sean, and sometimes he gets caught between the two of us, but I know we'll manage to work things out eventually.*

Sean had still not emerged by the time she had showered, dressed and sent her email, so she left him a note on the table in the hall to say she would be back in time to do his lunch. As she turned to close the front door, she noticed that the seashell she had last seen on the gatepost a few days before had been moved to the front step, where it now sat alongside the old-fashioned boot scraper. Presumably Sean or Marcus had put it there, although she could not imagine why.

When she reached the end of the drive, she was half inclined to turn right and head down towards the bridge, where some daffodils growing near the beck might provide an easy subject. Whichever way she chose, she could not go very far because she did not want to leave Sean alone for too long. Besides which, there was a backlog of jobs in the house which required her attention. It occurred to her that she had never drawn the cluster of buildings at High Gilpin, and since the house was currently without a tenant, now was as good an opportunity as any. She told herself that any interest in High Gilpin had nothing at all to do with seeing Brian go up there a few days before.

The track leading to High Gilpin initially ran through an open field, crossing first a cattle grid and then a concrete culvert which carried a tributary of the main beck down towards the bridge. After this it proceeded steadily uphill, heading for a gap in the wall, where once upon a time there might have been a field gate. From this point it was possible to see a couple of chimney pots above the trees, providing you knew just where to look for them, but the rest of the house and buildings remained hidden behind the shelter belt until you were almost on top of them.

The farmhouse itself was painted white, but the cluster of buildings which had once housed livestock and farm machinery were the original unfaced local stone. By the time Jo reached the point where the rough track became a concrete drive, the sun had gone behind a cloud, rendering the buildings dark and uninviting. She followed the drive along the side of the house to where the outbuildings formed a kind of courtyard at the rear of the property, stopping short at the back corner of the house, when the yard came into full view and she recognized Shelley and Brian's estate car standing with its boot open alongside the barn which now served as a garage. The barn doors were shut, but the door to an adjoining outbuilding stood ajar, its padlock dangling from the hasp with a key still in it.

Jo swallowed so hard that she almost choked. Although she had seen Brian heading this way a few days before, the last thing she had expected was to find him here, doing something in the sheds at High Gilpin. Of course, it could be something perfectly legitimate – he had obtained a key from somewhere after all – but on balance, it would surely be better if she slipped away without Brian seeing her. Then another idea arrived hard on the heels of the first: that if Brian had access to the sheds at High Gilpin, maybe she ought to find out what he was up to. No, no. That was silly, melodramatic. Much better to get out of it, before Brian came out into the yard and saw her hanging about, but her heart seemed to have jumped up into her throat and her legs refused to obey her. And suppose she started to walk back and Brian overtook her on the track? There was nowhere but the house she could have been. He might think she had seen something. Stupid, stupid. There was nothing to see.

At that moment Brian appeared in the doorway, both arms occupied with a lump of something swathed in black plastic. He took it round to the back of the car and placed it inside, seemingly oblivious to her presence. Jo continued to stand rooted to the spot, watching as Brian returned to the outbuilding. Faint sounds came from within, suggestive of large boards or planks of wood being moved around, before Brian emerged again after a moment or two, loaded down with another object, longer and narrower than the first, but similarly shrouded in plastic. Had he really failed to notice her, or was he for some reason pretending she wasn't there? This time he slammed the rear hatch closed and went back to lock the outhouse door.

If he had not seen her already, he certainly couldn't avoid doing so once he got into the vehicle and drove it through the gap in which she was currently standing. She forced her legs into action, darting back along the side of the house. She would never make it into the trees before the car overtook her, but the small patch of garden at the front offered few possibilities for concealment. In desperation, she crouched down beside a large plastic water butt, which stood halfway between the corner of the house and the parlour window. It would at least shield her as Brian drove by – she would be fine as long as he didn't bother to look in his driving mirror – and surely he would keep his eyes fixed on the track ahead, because there was no reason to check the rear-view mirror up here. The blood was pounding in her ears, and she stayed with her back pressed hard against the farmhouse wall until long after she had seen the car disappear behind the trees, and could no longer hear its engine in the distance.

Her mother had sometimes hidden from people. When Jo had been very little she had treated it like a game of hide and seek, but later on she understood that it was not a game. She stood up and made her way back along the track, any desire to draw the buildings forgotten. She forced herself to walk so hard that her breath came in gasps, once or twice almost breaking into a run in her desire to put as much distance between herself and High Gilpin as possible.

On the doorstep of The Hideaway she stooped to pick up the shell. Now that she looked at it properly, she wasn't sure whether it was the same shell that had been on the gatepost or not. She took it into the kitchen and put it on the shelf where they kept the recipe books, intending to ask Sean or Marcus where it had come from. The whole episode at High Gilpin had already taken on a kind of unreality. She decided that on the whole it would be better not to mention anything about it to Marcus.

CHAPTER NINE

Although his mother liked to read P. D. James and his father watched detective shows on TV, Harry had never been much interested in murder mysteries before. This was different, of course, not least because it was not a game. During the first week of the holidays he pored over Sean's accumulated files of information. Together they interrogated the internet afresh, discovering a number of crime forums and blogspots which freely discussed the case. *Yeah, she did it*, ran one posting. *The whole story is just too many coincidences.*

Harry suggested that if they tried hard enough, they might come up with the one conclusive piece of evidence everyone else had missed, but Sean was less than convinced by the idea. If hard evidence had been available, he said, the police would have arrested his stepmother years ago. She was too clever for them – even if she often looked and acted so dumb. His own strategy was more concerned with observing their suspect for signs that she was about to kill again. As he pointed out to Harry, she had recently been behaving more oddly than usual. The other day she had asked him, a propos of nothing at all, whether he had put a seashell on the front doorstep. The way she held the shell out to him on the palm of her hand reminded him of the way a mad bloke on the bus in Manchester had once offered him a glass marble, claiming it was a sweet.

In the face of his newly acquired knowledge, Harry was

taking no chances either. He carried a heavy torch with him when walking between The Hideaway and The Hollies, even though he didn't really need it now that the nights were lighter. In the privacy of his bedroom, he had practised swinging it towards the head of an imaginary assailant; an overarm movement for someone in front of him, a reverse underarm swing if anyone came at him from behind. The law allowed you to use 'reasonable force' to defend yourself. Sean had looked into the question on the net.

Although Harry had been happy to play Watson to Sean's Master Detective, their investigation quickly began to run out of steam. Soon their searches merely came up against sites they had visited before. Even hits which appeared to be fresh were only repetitions of things they had read elsewhere, and after a few days the case began to lose some of its fascination.

On the second Tuesday of the holidays, Harry's mother developed a violent toothache, which meant making an appointment with an Ulverston dentist. John and Suzanne Wheaton had never left their children alone at the cottage before, but after some discussion it was agreed that while John drove Suzanne to the dentist, Harry and Charlotte would remain at The Hollies, with Sean to keep them company. In the run-up to their departure, Mrs Wheaton issued numerous strictures and appeared less than reassured by Harry's irritable protest: 'We're not going to burn the house down, you know. It's not like we're going to say "Ooh, Mum and Dad are out, let's all play with matches!"'

However, even she had to admit that when they left the cottage there did not appear to be anything to worry about. Harry, Charlotte and Sean were all reclining in various attitudes on the sofas in the sitting room, watching a DVD of an old *Superman* movie. (After years of resistance, television and DVDs had been allowed to infiltrate the Wheatons' 'simple holiday home' – not least because Mrs Wheaton was fed up with missing *Desperate Housewives*.) Little did she realize that as soon as the car was safely out of sight, the Man of Steel had been spewed out of the player in favour of a horror movie, in which a crazed serial killer stalked a party of teenagers who were holed up in an isolated country house. It was not a particularly plausible plot, and the two boys mocked it ceaselessly until Sean eventually said, 'I've got a better one than this, at home. Have you seen *The Terror at French Creek*?'

Ten-year-old Charlotte piped up: 'Mum won't like us watching that.'

'Shut up, short-stack,' said Harry. 'You wait here while we go up to Sean's for some better merchandise.'

'You're not supposed to leave me on my own,' Charlotte protested.

'So? Who's going to tell Mum and Dad?'

'Not me,' said his sister, quickly.

They left her sitting in front of the television, from which the latest victim's screams were ringing out in stereo. With her brother gone, Charlotte considered the fact that although Harry had threatened her with serious penalties if she muted, paused, turned off or otherwise interfered with the DVD, he had not said anything about staying in the room with it. She knew that it was a stupid film really, but now the cast had been whittled down to one girl, left all alone in the house with the killer somewhere close to hand, the tension was almost unbearable. Charlotte could not decide which was worse: to stay in the room with the film, or to wait in another room, from which she would undoubtedly still be able to hear the sound effects and that awful music, which always told you when something horrible was about to happen. Maybe she could lock herself in the loo until the boys came back. Then she thought about the faulty bolt, which Dad was always going to screw in more firmly, but never actually got round to fixing. He said it didn't really matter, because it was only family, and you could always call out and say it was occupied. Much good that would do you, when a maniac with a chain-saw came barging in.

The two boys slouched into The Hideaway just as Jo appeared from the kitchen with a shopping bag on her arm. 'Hello,' she said. 'Where's Charlotte? I thought you weren't supposed to leave her on her own.'

'We've just come to fetch something,' Sean said, not making eye contact.

'Charlie's OK on her own for a few minutes,' said Harry. 'She's not a baby.'

'No, of course not,' said Jo, half wondering if she ought to interfere, teetering as usual on the tightrope between responsible adult and heavy-handed step-parent. 'You haven't forgotten I'm going to Booths for some shopping?'

'No,' Sean shouted impatiently from halfway up the stairs. 'You already told me at least three times. I've got my key.'

Up in the bedroom, Sean could not immediately locate the promised DVD. While he hunted through his collection, Harry fidgeted with some Warhammer figures which stood on the bookshelves.

Somewhere below them, the doorbell rang.

'Ignore it,' Sean said. 'It won't be for me and *she's* gone out.'

Harry instinctively glanced towards the window, but Sean's room faced into the trees at the back of the house. Sean had just finished leafing through his wallets of DVDs when the bell rang again – someone was keeping their finger on it far longer than was normal or polite. The sound cut off abruptly when the pressure was removed.

'It'll be a delivery man.' Sean's tone registered weary resignation. 'That film's not here, anyway. I must have lent it to someone or swapped it. Let's go down.'

They ambled downstairs in no great hurry, but there was no *We tried to deliver* card on the mat, nor any shadow on the half-glazed front door to indicate that someone was still waiting.

'I didn't hear anyone drive off, did you?'

'Bloody hell. It's like in the film, where there's no one at the door, and then one of them goes outside and gets grabbed.'

'Bollocks,' said Sean, but he opened the front door with elaborate caution. There was no one in sight, and nothing to indicate that anyone had called. The two boys stood in the hall, half serious, half laughing.

'Do you think she's really gone?' Harry asked.

'Who?'

'Your stepmother.'

'I don't know. You can't always hear the car from my room because of the double glazing. But why would she want to lure us outside? She's got her own key – she can come in and get us any time.'

'That might not fit in with her plan.'

Sean let the front door close. 'We can check the garage, just to make sure her car's not in there.'

They approached the door at the other end of the hall as if expecting something to spring out at them, but nothing did. The key was on their side of the lock, but when Sean reached for it Harry whispered, 'Suppose she's waiting on the other side?'

'I'll get a weapon.' Sean tiptoed to the cupboard under the stairs and returned with a length of rigid grey plastic tube, which normally formed part of the vacuum cleaner. It was only a lark, after all.

'What are you going to do?' asked Harry. 'Suck her to death?'

Sean worked the key silently in the lock before flinging open the door, but the garage stood silent and empty.

'Delivery guy, after all,' Sean said.

As he swung round from the garage door, he misjudged the length of plastic tube in his hand and it caught against Jo's sketch book, which had been left on the hall table. The pad somersaulted on to the floor, landing face down and open.

Harry, who was nearest and unencumbered, bent down to pick it up, turning it over as he did. A low whistle escaped his lips. 'Take a look at this.'

Sean came to stand beside him.

'Whose book is it?' asked Harry.

'Hers.'

'It's like – porn.'

'Definitely rated eighteen,' agreed Sean. 'But it's not really porn, is it? It's torture – three different ways of putting someone to death. I know who it is, too.'

'You mean, she's drawn a real person?'

'It's Melissa Timpson.' When Harry looked blank, he added, 'She's in the business, with Dad and Jo.'

'Do you think she's planning ways of killing this Melissa woman?'

'Well, that's what it looks like.'

'Should we tell someone?'

Sean thought for a moment. 'We'd have to take the book away and show it to them – then she would know it was us. Better just put it back. Flatten that corner down, where it got creased against the floor. That's it – now put it exactly where it was.'

Harry positioned the book carefully. 'I'm not sure which way up it was,' he said.

'She probably wouldn't remember herself. It's not like she's expecting us to look at it. No one ever does. It's her private stuff – her secret sketch book, my dad calls it.'

'Doesn't he wonder why it's a secret?'

'I don't think so.'

'Shouldn't we look and see if there are pictures of anyone else in there?'

Sean hesitated. If she had gone to Booths, then she wouldn't be back for ages. 'You're right.' He relinquished the vacuum-cleaner hose and flicked through the pages, but although there were a few oddities among some of the drawings, apart from the page at which the book had fallen open, there was only one other which contained a troubling image; nor was this a scene of violence. It was the back view of a woman looking into a mirror. The figure itself and even the frame of the mirror had been drawn in great detail, but the face reflected in the mirror was blank.

'That's creepy,' said Harry. 'Do you think she hasn't finished it, or is it like that on purpose?'

'I don't know.' Sean stared at the drawing for a moment or two before he snapped the book shut and replaced it on the table. 'Come on. Let's go.'

'We could sneak up on Charlie,' Harry suggested, when they had gone a couple of yards down the drive. 'She'll wet herself after seeing that DVD.'

Although he knew it was childish, Sean was perfectly willing to enter into the spirit of the thing. The idea lightened their mood considerably, and they traversed the lane with a level of stealth that would have impressed an SAS recruiter, keeping low behind walls and sprinting across openings, finally arriving slightly breathless alongside the front door of The Hollies, where they flattened themselves against the wall while Harry slid the Yale into the lock and opened the door by inches. They crept into the small square hall, eased the front door closed behind them, then on a nod from Harry they crashed into the sitting room, where the blood-curdling screams intended to terrify Charlotte died on their lips. She was not there. The only sound or movement in the room came from the flat-screen TV, where the titles of the horror movie were scrolling steadily upwards against a background of grim orchestral music. For a moment they stood looking at one another, feeling somewhat foolish.

His sister could easily have gone up to her room or been playing a hiding-and-jumping-out game of her own, but something in the stillness of the house immediately troubled Harry. 'Charles,' he shouted. 'Charlie. Midget Features. Come out, wherever you are.' When this brought no response, he added, 'Don't piss about with me, Charles, or you'll be sorry.'

Still nothing.

Unnerved by the silence, Harry marched systematically through the house yelling for his sister to reveal herself, while throwing open doors to cupboards scarcely big enough to conceal a well-fed cat, let alone a ten-year-old girl. Sean stood in the hall, watching and listening as the search progressed upstairs. It wasn't his sister, but he had been made partly responsible because in the general scheme of the arrangements it had been assumed that he – the oldest of the trio – would stay on the premises until Harry's parents came back.

Harry's face appeared at the top of the stairs. 'She's not here.'

'You're kidding. She has to be somewhere. Have you tried the garden?'

'There's nowhere to hide. You can see it all from here.'

It was true. The Hollies sat in a small, easily maintained

plot. There was a patch of mossy lawn broken up with a few knee-high dwarf conifers and a bird table. There were no outbuildings, and the family parked their Subaru on a patch of gravel at the side.

'Has she ever pulled anything like this before?'

'Never. She's scared of her own shadow. She wouldn't go off on her own.'

'Well, she has.'

'Not by herself,' Harry repeated. 'Can't you see what's happened? *She's* taken her – your stepmother. She's the only person who knew Charlotte was here on her own.'

Sean had never heard Harry use his sister's given name before. They stood staring at one another, each waiting for the other to say something. At that moment they caught the sound of a car pulling on to the gravel.

'Shit,' said Harry. 'Shit, shit, *shit*.'

John and Suzanne Wheaton were no more or less intuitive than the next couple, but the moment they opened the front door and caught sight of the two boys' faces, they knew that something was very wrong. In the garbled moments which followed, with everyone talking across everyone else, two things became clear to John. First, that his daughter was missing, second, that the boys were not telling all they knew. His wife, words muffled by a frozen mouth, said they should call the police. There was no landline at the cottage, and mobile reception was far from good; the best place to get a reliable signal was out on the parking area, but at the front door he hesitated. Although he was filled with the cold terror of a parent whose child is unaccounted for, John Wheaton did not want to make a fool of himself with the police.

'Let's go through this again,' he said, as calmly as he could. 'You two went down to Sean's house, leaving Charlotte here watching the television.' At this point he had to raise his hand to silence his wife before continuing. 'You were only gone about five minutes, but when you came back, Charlotte was missing. You've searched the house, but nowhere else.'

'Where else would she be?' interrupted his wife. 'She wouldn't go wandering off by herself. Charlotte doesn't do that sort of thing.'

'You didn't see anyone else about?' He focused his gaze squarely on Harry, who hesitated and glanced at Sean. 'You weren't playing some sort of game with your sister? Something that went wrong? You have to tell me the truth *now*, Harry. It's very important. Whatever has happened, you have to tell me before the police get here. Has something happened to Charlotte? I know there's something you're not telling me.'

'It's about Sean's stepmother,' Harry blurted out. 'We think she might have taken her.'

'What are you talking about?' his mother all but screamed. 'What do you mean?'

'She knew Charlotte was here on her own because she met us going into Sean's house. Then she went out, and when we got back here, Charlotte had gone.' Harry looked desperately from one parent to the other. 'She's done it before. She's killed people before.'

His father grabbed him by the shoulders and brought his face close to Harry's, squinting directly into his eyes and smelling his breath. 'Have you been drinking, or sniffing something?'

'No!' Harry wrenched himself away. 'Tell them, Sean.'

Sean felt their eyes burning into him. 'It's true,' he almost choked on the words. 'She killed a little girl – years ago – nobody knows.' He felt as if he was going to cry. Letting it all out brought a strange mixture of shame and relief.

'Oh my God! John, call the police.' Mrs Wheaton took a step backwards and leaned against the wall for support. She put her hand to her mouth, but her sobs escaped anyway. Harry stared at her, white-faced. Sean had to scrub the sleeve of his sweatshirt across his eyes.

At that moment there was a discreet tap on the door. John Wheaton was nearest, and flung it open to reveal Charlotte standing sheepishly on the step, next to a woman in a pilled body warmer and a shabby, dung-coloured skirt, the hem of which was coming down on one side. Her greying hair was escaping from where it was loosely tied at the back of her head.

'I saw your car go past, so I've brought Charlotte home. I didn't want you to be worried, but –' she looked from face to face. 'I fear I may have been a little tardy.'

As his wife grabbed Charlotte to her, John stared at the stranger in confusion. 'Who are you?' he asked.

'I'm sorry, I should have explained better. I'm Gilda Iceton.' She extended a hand, which he took automatically, finding it soft and cold in his momentary grasp. 'From The Old Forge. I happened to be looking out this afternoon when I saw your daughter passing my house, looking rather distressed. Apparently she was nervous waiting here by herself, so she followed the boys up to The Hideaway, but when they didn't answer the doorbell she ran back here. Unfortunately, she had forgotten to put the door on the catch and found herself locked out. She was on her way back along the lane again, not knowing what to do next, when I saw her. I could see there was something wrong – I have a little girl of my own – so I went out to see if I could help, and we decided the best thing would be for Charlotte to come in and wait with me until we saw your car coming back. She said you had driven into Ulverston, so I knew you would have to pass my

119

house on your way home. I hadn't realized that the boys were back here; I didn't see them go past.'

'Thank you.' John Wheaton was recovering fast. 'Of course you did exactly the right thing in not leaving Charlotte to wander up and down the lane on her own.'

'Although we were very frightened when we got back and couldn't find her,' Suzanne added with a hint of reproof, all the time holding Charlotte to her tightly, as if she thought someone might attempt to steal her away.

'I was going to pop a note through the door to let you know where she was, but I'm afraid you beat me to it because I stopped to give Charlotte a drink and a biscuit first.'

'She's got a funny stone cat called Timmy, who sits by the fire,' Charlotte piped up, somewhat reassured to find that she did not appear to be in any trouble. 'It's life-size, and it's got eyes made out of a different kind of stone, so it seems like it's really looking at you.'

John Wheaton was wondering whether they ought to ask their new neighbour inside. Although she had tried to do the right thing by Charlotte, there was something about her which didn't incline him to further their acquaintance.

'When her daughter, Becky, comes home, I'm going to be invited round to play,' Charlotte announced.

'My daughter is staying with relatives over in Yorkshire,' Gilda explained. 'She boards at St Aelfric's, but when she's next here I'm sure she would like to meet Charlotte.'

A daughter at boarding school. Well, that gave out a rather different signal to the jumble-sale wardrobe, Suzanne thought. People in the country were so funny, of course, and sometimes had quite different standards to people in town. Maybe they should invite this Gilda Iceton and her husband – assuming she had one – over for a drink one evening. At the moment, however, there were pressing matters to be raised with Harry, so she was relieved when Gilda declined her half-hearted invitation to come in.

The front door was hardly closed before everyone's full attention returned to Sean and Harry, who were standing sheepishly at the foot of the stairs. 'You', said John Wheaton, glowering at his son, 'have got a lot of explaining to do. And as for you, Sean, you had better go home. You can assume that Harry is grounded, and not receiving visitors until you hear otherwise.'

CHAPTER TEN

Jo felt vaguely uneasy as she made her way round Booths supermarket. She was convinced that Harry and Sean were up to something, and was still wondering whether she ought to have dealt more firmly with the issue of Harry's sister being left at home on her own. Distracted by these thoughts, she almost collided with Brian when she turned her trolley into the chiller aisle. He had a basket over his arm, into which he was just placing a tub of coleslaw. When he appeared to ignore her, she said, 'Good afternoon, Brian,' in a pointed way.

'Oh – sorry. Didn't see it was you for a minute. I was miles away.' He would have walked away, but Jo had allowed her trolley to drift sideways as if by accident, so that he could not move on without walking right round it.

'How are you?' she asked, in a voice which was far too brittle.

'About the same as usual. Yourself?'

'I'm fine. How's the gallery?'

'Still standing. Busy, in fact, so I must crack on.'

'Of course.' She still did not move out of his way. He was a big man, intimidating face to face, and his irritation was palpable, but they were in the middle of a supermarket – what could he possibly do to her? 'I want to get in touch with Shelley,' she said. 'Is there a phone number where I can contact her?'

'I really can't help you – but if you're such mates, then I'm surprised she hasn't been in touch with you already, telling you the same sob-story she's been telling all her other friends.' Brian's sarcastic smile wilted her. 'And by the way, the Tunnocks don't like people trespassing up at High Gilpin, particularly when there isn't a tenant in res.' He gave the end of her trolley an impatient shove in order to extricate himself, then stalked away without another word.

Jo's face burned. She lingered in the dairy section for what she hoped was long enough to avoid bumping into Brian at the checkouts. He must have seen her hiding behind the water butt. Somewhere in the back of her mind a laughing policeman mocked her mercilessly.

Back at home, she discovered Sean watching TV in his bedroom, but there was no sign of Harry. She wondered if they had fallen out, but decided it was better not to enquire. When Marcus arrived home in time for them to eat together, Sean joined them at the table, taciturn as usual, but more subdued than surly. He withdrew upstairs again as soon as the meal was over, leaving herself and Marcus to spend the rest of the evening listening to the concert on Classic FM.

Marcus seemed to have forgotten his previous annoyance with her, but they found little to say to one another, and when they made love that night, the act was accompanied by a curious air of detachment. She knew that some men fantasized about being with other women, and that this supposedly did not mean they loved their wives any less; but all the same, the thought that he might be imagining himself with Melissa was unbearable. Afterwards, as they lay side by side in bed, she asked: 'Do you think men find Melissa very attractive?'

'Do you actually mean, do *I* find Melissa attractive?'

'I meant men in general, but as you're the only man here,

123

I suppose it's got to be your opinion on behalf of the rest.'

She had spoken lightly, and he answered in similar vein. 'Speaking for the entire, red-blooded, macho bunch of us, I'd guess the answer is yes – although not half so attractive as we'd all find you, of course.'

'Be serious – I wasn't fishing.'

'I am being serious. Why do you ask, anyway?'

'Oh, I was just thinking about the differences between what women might think men find attractive and what they actually do find attractive.'

'I see what you mean. Well, I would say that Melissa is glamorous in an obvious way, but you are beautiful. Glamour is carefully acquired, but beauty is the genuine article and can't be faked.'

'Sometimes you say the loveliest things.'

When he reached out and drew her closer, she nestled securely into the crook of his arm.

Down at The Hollies, Harry lay miserably awake long after everyone else's lights were out. From somewhere nearby a tawny owl was annoying him with its persistent *ke-wick, ke-wick*. He would like to wring the neck of that owl – to say nothing of the neck of his little sister, whose fault everything was. The latter half of his day had been dominated by inter-rogation after interrogation, and telling-off after telling-off, but none of it was his fault, he thought bitterly. If Charlie had only done as she was told and waited in the house, then she would still have been here when he and Sean got back. They could have whipped that DVD out of the machine and replaced it with some childish Disney rubbish as soon as they heard the car; his parents would never have been any the wiser.

And that whole business about Sean's stepmother – he had

certainly been dragged over the coals for that! He half wished that Sean had never told him anything about his stepmother, although that was Charles's fault too, because if only she had arrived home a couple of minutes sooner, none of that stuff about the stepmother would ever have come out. Once Sean had been sent home, the parents had wanted to know all about it, so that bit by bit Harry had been forced to reveal what he knew and how he knew it.

Much to his surprise, he discovered that his parents already knew a lot about the case, although not that baby Lauren's mother was living just along the road. They remembered seeing it on the news, although their take on the situation was very different to most of the internet bloggers. According to his mother, saying that Joanne Handley had harmed her own child was 'an extremely cruel and very silly thing to say. And I don't suppose Sean really believes any of it,' she went on. 'I expect he was just feeling cross with her about something and said it to be spiteful, and to make the whole thing into an exciting game for you.'

'Except that this is something very serious and not a game at all.' His father took up the role of prosecutor-in-chief. 'It is very wrong to snoop about on the internet, downloading material about someone you know.'

'Imagine how that poor woman would feel, if she knew what you were saying about her. Don't you think she has suffered enough?' You could always count on his mother to play up the emotional angle.

His father majored on different aspects of the matter. 'You ought to know by now that you can't believe half of what you see on the internet. As for repeating allegations like that, well, perhaps you don't realize that this is a very serious matter. It's slander, Harry. Do you know what that means?'

Harry did know. He had to repeat for them, again and

again, that he had never discussed anything about Sean's stepmother with anyone other than Sean. All manner of promises had been exacted from him regarding what kind of material he would and would not be accessing on the net, or for that matter watching on TV or via any other medium in the future. In the meantime, he was grounded for the rest of the holidays, and likely to be under far too close surveillance to get his own back on Charles for quite a while – although he had already managed to shoot her a couple of looks on the sly, to let her know she had it coming.

In the end, his parents had gone on at him for so long he hardly knew what he did or didn't believe about Sean's stepmother, although on one point at least he was sure they were wrong. For some reason they were both adamant that Sean could not possibly believe her guilty of harming anyone. Well, they had not seen the intensity of Sean's expression when he talked about how dangerous she was, nor did they know about the weird stuff she had drawn in her book. Harry had not breathed a word about that – his parents might think they knew everything, but they didn't – a point from which he derived a curious satisfaction.

The wind had risen during the evening, so that long after Marcus had fallen asleep, Jo was aware of it buffeting through the trees, occasionally picking up small objects and tossing them against something more solid. Sometimes there would be a bigger gust, a sound like a giant intake of breath which rattled the plastic air vent on the bathroom wall, making the slats scrape one against another like fingernails against a window pane. A sensation that something was not right began to grow in Jo's mind. It was akin to the prickly feeling of being watched, like knowing that there was someone standing just behind you, except that this seemed to

126

encompass the whole house. It was as if someone was outside among the trees, watching the house as it slept.

Taking great care not to disturb Marcus, Jo slid sideways until she reached the edge of the bed and could twist herself into a sitting position while barely moving the duvet. The bedroom was dark, but three steps took her across to the door where she could reach out to locate her dressing gown on its hook and feel for the door handle. Out on the landing where a plug-in night light glowed, she paused to push her arms into the sleeves of her dressing gown and knot the cord around her. Without the night light, the stairs would have been inky black.

She crept downstairs to the kitchen. Just as she entered the room, the security light at that side of the house illuminated the garden like a prolonged lightning strike, revealing a world of startled pot plants, with the winter jasmine clinging panic-stricken to the wall, the whole picture criss-crossed by a black gyrating mesh of shadows formed by the wind-blown shrubs and trees. The security lights were not infrequently set off by the roe deer which regularly ambled through, but there was no sign of them or any other likely trigger.

She slipped across the hall to look through the sitting-room window. Here the curtains had been drawn, and she had to twitch one aside to look out. The front of their plot was partially illuminated by the security light at the side of the house. The line between light and dark ran along a perfect diagonal, starting at the right-hand corner of the house and extending towards the gate, here and there interrupted by shadows marking the position of the larger shrubs, huge shadowy shape-shifters which swayed uncertainly in the wind. Beyond this patch of light everything was blackness except for a single yellow bulb, which Jo identified at once with the one over the front door of The Old Forge. It appeared to be flickering, but she knew that was just an illusion caused by the constant movement of the intervening trees.

She wondered what Gilda Iceton was doing up at this hour. Then it occurred to her that since there appeared to be no other lights on, Gilda might have left it on by mistake; it was easily done when going out to fetch some logs for the fire. She knew that there was still an open fire at The Old Forge, because she had seen smoke rising from the chimney.

Although there had been no direct contact between herself and her new neighbour since the night of the concert, Jo was uneasily aware of her: the arrivals and departures of Gilda's old blue Volvo, the occasional presence of washing hung out to dry all served to remind her that Gilda was living just across the lane, and that although she might prefer never to set eyes on her again, another encounter was all but inevitable. She had pretty much succeeded in forgetting all about certain episodes in her adolescence, until confronted by the sight of Gilda at the Coronation Hall. Nor was her problem with Gilda confined to the awkwardness and embarrassment of some long past foolishness catching up with her. Gilda almost certainly knew not just about her childhood, but probably about Lauren too. Easter Bridge had seemed the perfect place in which to escape the past, but it did not matter where she went – it was never long before that echoing cry of 'Coming, ready or not' rang out.

The security light faded, leaving her staring into the darkness at that single point of flickering light at the far side of the lane. So far as she knew, Gilda had done no work on The Old Forge prior to moving in. It still looked dingy and depressing from the outside, and its windows continued to stare aggressively as passers-by, with more than a suggestion that unseen watchers stood just out of sight, screened behind the grubby panes. With so much property available at the moment it was hard to fathom why anyone would choose that house, but presumably Gilda saw some sort of potential in it. Maisie's fears of a massive building project might yet come to fruition because, now she came to think about it, Gilda's parents had been fairly well off – enough money, anyway, to take their daughter out of a state school and pay for private education. And it looked as though Gilda must be pretty comfortable financially: it wasn't every widow approaching forty who could afford boarding school and a house in the Lakes, and yet had no obvious regular day job. It could be that Gilda had big ideas for The Old Forge, and the wherewithal to put them into effect.

Even so, the idea of living in The Old Forge made Jo shudder. She remembered Sean's story of the ghostly former occupant of Gilda's new abode. The blacksmith, who had perished there in an agony of fire – some saying he had fallen drunk into the blaze, others that his bitter-tongued wife had pushed him from behind. Did violent death really leave an invisible footprint in the air? She became aware of a familiar set of wooden double doors taking shape in her mind. Shivering, she let the curtain fall back into place and turned smartly towards the kitchen, thinking that she might as well make herself a cup of tea, now that she was downstairs.

Without the security light, it was very dark in the kitchen. Her fingers found the switch by the door and a bar of spot-lights sprang to life. The sensation of some watchful presence outside persisted, so she approached the window to pull down the blind. The interior lights were reflected back at her, rendering almost everything outside blacker than black, but as she reached for the blind cord Jo drew back with an audible gasp. Just visible on the other side of the pane, balanced on the sloping white window sill, was another seashell.

She raced back upstairs. 'Marcus, Marcus!' She shook him

awake. 'Come down, quickly. There's been someone in the garden.'

'What? What the – an intruder, do you mean?'

He followed her downstairs, shovelling his arms into his paisley dressing gown and tying it as he went, relying on the night light as she had done, rather than bothering to switch on anything else. 'Are they still out there?'

'I don't know.' Jo had run ahead, into the kitchen. 'But look at this.' She pointed to the window as Marcus appeared in the doorway.

'I can't see a thing out there,' he said. 'You'll have to turn these lights off.'

'No, no! You won't see it if you do. Look – here – it's on the window sill.'

Marcus stood in silence for a moment, taking it in.

'As I came into the kitchen, the security light came on. Whoever put the shell there must have set it off.'

'Jo, what are you talking about? Did you actually see anyone?'

'No . . . but the shell –'

'A shell?'

'It's the third time. The first one was down by the gate; then I found one on the doorstep about a week ago. It's a sign.'

'What on earth are you talking about?'

'Lauren was taken from outside The Shell Shop. That's what this is all about – I didn't realize before, but now I'm sure of it.'

'Did you actually see or hear anyone?'

'No.'

'But if this person had tripped the security light, then you would have seen them come up to the kitchen window, wouldn't you?'

'No. You see, after the light came on I went into the sitting room, because I thought the person watching the house might be at the front.'

'*What* person watching the house?'

'It . . . it was this feeling I had. That was really why I came down in the first place.'

'Because you had a feeling?'

'Yes. And then there was a light on at The Old Forge. Maybe Gilda had heard something, too.'

'But you said you didn't hear anything.'

'Not exactly, no.'

'Jo, I think you need to go back to bed and get some sleep. We can talk about this in the morning.'

'You don't believe me, do you?'

'About what? I certainly believe that there's a seashell on the kitchen window sill, and that you think someone just crept up to the house and put it there.'

'But *you* don't believe anyone was here.'

'I don't know what to believe. Please will you come back to bed?' He reached out and placed a protective hand on her shoulder.

There had been times in her life when such a gesture from Marcus had the power to put a great deal right, but at that precise moment it just seemed to symbolize everything that was wrong and she had to resist the urge to shrug it off.

CHAPTER ELEVEN

The only real point of agreement between Marcus and Jo concerning the shells was that it would be pointless taking them to the police. Marcus was convinced that they had arrived courtesy of Sean and Harry. 'It will be some sort of game,' he said. 'A shell on the doorstep means see you at mine, a shell on the window sill . . .'

'But I asked Sean about the shell on the doorstep and he said he didn't know anything about it.'

'Well, of course he did. No point in having a secret sign if you don't keep it a secret.'

'Harry wouldn't have come round here in the early hours.'

'Couldn't it have been there for a while?'

'No, it wasn't. It was in plain view of anyone using the sink. I washed some mugs out just before I came to bed, and I didn't see it then.'

'You might not have noticed it.'

'I'm sure I would. And what about my feeling that someone was prowling around? Something made the security light go on.'

'It was very windy last night. That sometimes sets it off – when something gets blown across the sensor. Maybe the wind blew the shell there.'

'Where on earth from? We're miles from the coast.'

But Marcus would not concede that there was any particular significance in the appearance of the shells, and eventually refused to indulge in any further speculation about their arrival. Even Jo had to admit that they were not the sort of shells found on sale in The Shell Shop, where all the stock had been polished specimens suitable for display. The shells left outside The Hideaway were just ordinary shells, collected straight from a beach. The one which had appeared on the window sill was a cockle shell – she had looked it up – whereas the one she picked up on the doorstep was a carpet shell. The original shell seen by the gatepost had vanished by now, perhaps purloined by a passer-by, or accidentally knocked into the long grass which grew at the side of the road. After Marcus had lost interest, she hid the remaining shells in one of her bedroom drawers, where they sat like a couple of tiny conspirators, sharing the secret of Lauren's whereabouts. For surely their arrival *must* be a sign of some kind – a message from the person who had Lauren.

In the following days, in her mind she went over and over the episode of the third shell's arrival. She was sure she would have seen it if it had been there any earlier. It was true that the security light might have been triggered by the natural disturbances of a windy night. Passing bats or owls could set it off too; but you could not get away from the fact that whenever the shells had arrived, they could not have got there by accident. Someone had put them there, someone who had come on foot, almost certainly after dark, probably having left a car parked well out of sight, in some gateway much further down the lane. Or maybe the shells had been put there by someone much closer to hand. The light above the door of The Old Forge was suggestive; although when Marcus asked her if she could honestly imagine their new neighbour creeping along the side of the house at dead of night and carefully depositing a shell on the window sill, she had to admit that it was not a very likely scenario.

'Think about it, Jo. It's the fag end of the holidays and the kids are getting bored, so they've come up with some sort of signalling game. It's the kind of thing kids do. You remember how when we first discussed Sean's coming here, and you said you wanted to make a loving home for him, well, this is what having kids around is all about. Letting them have their own space and not getting uptight if they have one or two secrets.'

Jo thought that if Sean had any secrets, they might be rather less innocent than a seashell code with Harry, but decided it was not the moment to say so. It was all very well, Marcus prodding her about how she had set out to build a good relationship with Sean: there had been nothing wrong with her intentions, but somehow things always went awry. It seemed to her, as she sat alone in the kitchen, that lately *everything* was going wrong: her ongoing problems with Sean, the disappearance of Shelley and her awkward encounters with Brian, to say nothing of the uneasy knowledge that the one person from her schooldays – well, no . . . if she was honest, one of several people from her schooldays – that she would rather not ever have set eyes on again, was now living just across the road.

Gilda's knowledge made her vulnerable to the very gossip and scrutiny she had come here to avoid. Rather than anaesthetizing her against curiosity, past exposure had scoured her raw. People staring, whispering, photographers shouting, 'Joanne! Joanne! Look this way.' Her solicitor telling her after Dominic's death, 'Don't hide your face – people think it's a sign of a guilty conscience.' The same solicitor reading a statement on her behalf, things she couldn't remember whether she had said or not. Reporters camped outside the house. Dominic's family not sitting with her at the inquest, not even looking at her, freezing her out.

134

It wasn't my fault. How could I have done anything to make it different?

Then the bleak, dark loneliness of life without him. The desire to follow him only tempered by the thought of Lauren. Someone had to be there for Lauren when she came home. Part of the trouble was that Dom had not been able to believe in Lauren's coming home, not in the same way she had done. He went through the motions with her, the public appeals and the trips back to Devon, asking people, showing photographs, a desperate dispiriting quest for answers, not welcomed by the locals, who said these constant reminders about what had happened to Lauren were bad for tourism because families with young children were staying away. Surely people ought to have understood that they had to do something? They had to keep on looking. What did it matter about a few less cream teas being sold, or a few empty beds in B and Bs, compared with finding out what had happened to their daughter?

Things might have been different if she could have had another child. They began to try about six months after Lauren disappeared, not to replace her, but to keep their family going. They spent a long time agonizing before Jo stopped taking the pill. She had been less keen than Dom; surely if Lauren came home to find a new baby, that would make her adjustment back to family life all the harder. But Dominic had wanted to go ahead, and their GP said he thought it would be 'a positive thing'. But it never was. The tests were always negative, and mostly there was evidence of her failure to conceive before they got as far as needing a test. Dom found this particularly hard to cope with. They never spoke about whose fault it was, but as every month brought fresh disappointment, the uncertainty about why she did not conceive formed up with all the other miseries and

135

circled them like a group of angry seagulls, screaming and dive-bombing their prey.

When the inquest was over, Dominic's sister made a statement to the press. 'My brother could not bear the loss of his daughter. Our family will never get over this terrible tragedy.' They had not invited Jo to stand alongside them. They blamed me, she thought. Perhaps they even believed what others had suggested – that she had pushed Dom over the edge, figuratively or literally.

She had to give evidence at the inquest. Fortunately she had it all clear in her head at the time. It only became confused later. Now when she thought of his death, she remembered rain pelting down on the roof of the caravan, a clap of thunder making the van shake while forked lightning tore across the sky, turning the white caps of the waves in the bay to silver, while she sat alone wondering why he didn't come back. The trouble was, she knew it had not been like that. It was dry and sunny when they set out for their walk. They would not have gone if it had been pouring with rain, and it had still been dry when those people found his body on the beach.

Memory wasn't always reliable, particularly when it was something you didn't really want to remember but were forced to go over again and again – or maybe something you wanted to believe had happened differently to the way it actually did.

She realized that the coffee mug she had been cradling was empty and grown cold in her hands. As she stood up and carried it across to the sink, she automatically glanced out of the kitchen window and stopped dead. The edge of the wood between their garden and the beck was carpeted with wild garlic, but the shadow she might or might not have seen was further away than that, deeper into the trees where the line of sight was obscured by low branches and undergrowth. For a moment or two she thought she must have been mistaken, but then she made out the dark silhouette of a figure, watching and waiting. A public footpath ran through the woodland, but it was lower down the slope, out of sight of the garden, nearer to the beck. Anyone standing in that position could only have got there by straying well off the path.

She watched for a moment longer, then ran to the kitchen door and out across the grass. There was no fence to formalize the boundary of their plot, nothing to prevent her from plunging headlong into the trees, heedless of the wet bracken which saturated her jeans before she had gone ten yards. She tried to keep her eyes on the figure, but she had to keep glancing down to check her footing and within seconds of entering the wood she had lost sight of her quarry. 'Hey,' she shouted. 'Wait. Who are you? What do you want?'

The rain had painted the tree trunks black. Everything was damp and dripping, the wet canopy of leaves creating an unnatural gloom under the leaden sky. 'Come out,' she shouted. 'Come out and let me see who you are.'

She stopped running and stood still. She must be within a few feet of where the figure had been, and anyone trying to escape must surely make some kind of noise and give themselves away. She waited and listened, her breath coming in quick short gasps, but the wood was alive with nothing but the sound of water. A branch directly above her head chose that moment to deposit a shower of raindrops on her head. Great damp splotches appeared on her shirt. She looked around for some sign that this had been the place – any indication that someone had been standing there just a moment before, but there was nothing.

Looking back, she could see the kitchen window surrounded by a frame of pale green leaves. It looked a long way away, and panic rose abruptly within her. There was no one inside the house, and even if there had been, they would not hear her if she shouted. She turned back the way she had come, tripping over bramble cables and catching her hand on a stinging nettle in her hurry. Whatever had possessed her to come racing out here, without so much as her mobile phone to summon help? It came to her that she was making so much noise in her headlong flight that it would mask any sound of pursuit if there was one, but stopping to listen was the last thing she intended to do. *This is bad*, she thought. *I'm within sight of my own home and I'm afraid.*

She regained the kitchen door and all but fell inside, locking it behind her. She considered calling the police, but reason intercepted her. There was no one to be seen now, and the prowler had been within twenty-five yards of a right of way. She returned to the kitchen window, standing well back into the room, where she thought she could not be seen from any distance, but then she saw that it had begun to rain again, falling in hard straight lines, blanking out everything beyond the edge of the garden. She transferred her attention inside: her hands, hair, shoes and clothing were all wet to some degree.

As she climbed the stairs to change, it occurred to her for the first time how vulnerable she was when Marcus was away. In the past she had never been afraid of staying by herself at The Hideaway, but that was before she had acquired an intermittent feeling of being watched. She could hardly count on Sean to defend her, even when he was here. Apart from the fact that he was only a kid, by the time he had finished arguing with her about whether or not he intended to come out of his room, she would probably be dead already.

She knew it would be useless to try telling Marcus about the figure in the wood. He would only say that she had imagined it. Now that she was upstairs, she decided to pack for the trip she was due to lead in Yorkshire. Focusing on her packing would give her something else to think about.

Jo was two days into the From Herriot to Heartbeat tour when she picked up a text to say that Melissa was unwell, so could she take charge of Mary Queen of Scots in the Lowlands after all. When she called Marcus later, he explained that Melissa had a nasty cold, and that since Jo had previously been keen to conduct the tours back to back, they assumed she would be willing to cover.

Jo had never liked the Herriot to Heartbeat tour. It was an itinerary they had inherited from Flights of Fantasy, and although it was theoretically themed to books and authors, in reality it was just a trip around the various television locations which had been used in the two long-running series – a distinctly lowbrow excursion, which attracted a very different kind of customer to their regular clientele. She always did her best to raise the level, but it was hard to see this turn of duty as much more than babysitting a group of gossipy old ladies. As a result, Jo was not in the best of spirits when she took the call from Marcus, and felt sorely tempted to remind him that it was one thing to do back-to-back tours when you had prepared for them in advance, and quite another to be washing your underwear in the hotel handbasin as you went along. She half wondered if Melissa was behind the suggestion that she take over, hoping to make it look as if she made a fuss when she was taken off the tour, then another fuss when she was reinstated. Well, if that was the game, it would not work. She would rise above it. Far worse things had happened: clients with suspected heart attacks; getting stuck in a motorway jam for three hours; a mismatched hotel booking which temporarily left a party with nowhere to lay their heads. Coping with the unexpected was all part of the job.

At least the group bound for Scotland were likely to be an improvement on the current lot, who chattered and fidgeted and fussed about loo stops like a group of schoolkids. The Mary Queen of Scots tour invariably attracted knowledgeable enthusiasts, the kind of people who listened attentively when called to order, not just a bunch of old ladies looking for a convivial coach trip. Moreover, she always looked forward to staying at Borthwick Castle, which was their first overnight stop. The candlelit dinners at Borthwick were superb, and afterwards the group would be taken on a guided tour of the building, before hearing the usual ghost stories over a wee dram in front of the roaring fire. It always made for a great start, and the prospect cheered her.

There was an inauspicious beginning at Newcastle Airport, where some of the luggage went temporarily astray, and it took all Jo's charm and tact to keep everyone reasonably happy while the problem was sorted out. The subsequent journey north was marred by rain, but this had eased away by the time they reached Crichton and left the coach to undertake the short walk to the castle. Jo had already memorized names and matched them with faces – it was always important to make clients feel that you recognized each of them personally from the outset. Mr Radley fell into step with her and began to explain in detail why his wife had wanted them to come on the tour. He himself was not interested in 'the Scottish queen', being an aficionado of model railways, but 'the wife comes with me, and I go with her . . . you see, the thing about being married . . .' Jo recognized a familiar type in Mr Radley: someone not interested in the subject matter, who would none the less enjoy monopolizing the guide given half a chance. She managed to extricate herself with one of her brightest smiles, on the pretext of making sure that Mrs Van Halsen, who had begun to lag behind, was doing OK. Mrs Van Halsen greeted her with a complaint. Had she realized walking was involved on this first day, she would have travelled in different shoes. Jo coupled sympathy with an assurance that it was not much further. No matter that the full itinerary had been provided, together with advice about suitable footwear in bold, there was always someone who had not read it properly.

A first glimpse of Borthwick from the coach windows drew the usual appreciative gasps, but when the party gathered for pre-dinner drinks in the great hall, it soon became clear that not everyone was happy. Mrs Van Halsen grumbled that there were too many stairs to get to and from her room. Jo tried to lighten the mood with a quip about medieval architects not providing elevators, but another member of the party joined in to say that they regretted not asking for a room on a lower floor. Discontent spreads quickly. Someone else noted that it had begun to rain again, and Jo had to come up with something quickly before the entire party fell into moaning mode. Dinner should have cheered them up, but just as it seemed that even Mrs Van Halsen was thawing, Mrs Barber, who had earlier jumped on the too-many-stairs bandwagon, now sent back her beef, claiming that it was inedible. Since the food at Borthwick Castle was inevitably wonderful, Jo strongly suspected that it was simply a case of the meat not being cooked to Mrs Barber's liking, but Mrs Barber's prolonged dissatisfaction about the 'inedible beef' cast a pall over the entire meal. When the post-dinner tour of the castle was offered, there were uncharacteristic numbers of queries about how many stairs would be involved.

Once the party had broken up just after eleven, Jo slipped outside the main door, switched on her mobile, managed to get a signal and phoned home. She was surprised when Sean answered.

'Dad's not here.'

'Well, where is he?' She expected Sean to say, 'in the bath', 'out in the garage', or something of that sort, so 'Manchester' took her aback.

'You're not there on your own, are you?'

'Yes, but he said he won't be late.'

'It's eleven o'clock.'

'So?' asked Sean, insolently.

'We don't normally leave you alone overnight.'

'He won't be gone overnight.'

'Is your grandmother very poorly?'

'She's always poorly.'

'I mean, is she worse?'

'I don't know.'

They had reached an impasse. After a moment's silence, Sean said, 'Can I go now?'

'Yes – OK. Tell him I rang.'

She wasn't sure if Sean had heard the last bit or not. The phone went dead while she was still speaking; possibly they had lost the signal, or maybe Sean had rung off.

She felt exhausted as she began the long climb back to her bedroom in the north tower, which seemed double the distance she remembered from previous visits. For once she found herself in sympathy with the claims that there were too many stairs. She knew that she should have ended her conversation with Sean on a better note, perhaps with some expression of affection; at the very least a little gesture in the direction of the motherly: 'Take care of yourself,' or 'Don't answer the door to anyone.' Not that there ever were any unexpected callers after dark. Easter Bridge was too far off the beaten track for door-to-door salesmen or even carol

142

singers at Christmas – although someone had come to leave the shell. It was never far from her thoughts, that shell – all three of them, in fact – at least two too many to have blown there by accident.

She had not expected Marcus to be in Manchester. Perhaps his mother was finally dying and his sister had made the 'come now' phone call. It was strange, though, that he had not said something to Sean about it, even if only in preparation for the news he might be bringing home. She managed to get an intermittent signal beside the window in her bedroom, but when she tried Marcus's mobile he did not answer – which he wouldn't, not if he was driving. She left her own phone switched on, periodically climbing out of bed and holding it up to the window, but by midnight Marcus had not returned her call. She was torn between ringing home again – which might wake him up, if he had fallen straight into bed after a long journey – and not ringing, which made it look as if she did not care how his mother was. She sat with the tartan bedcover huddled up to her chin, her mind a whirlpool of uncertainty. He *might* have tried to ring her, but the phone reception was uncertain because of the thickness of the walls, and she didn't like leaving her room at night to locate a better signal. The spiral staircases and cavernous rooms, although well lit, were unwelcoming at this hour. It took stout nerves to ramble around the castle on your own.

She fought against it, but another idea, darker than his mother's death, was growing. Suppose Marcus had not gone to Manchester after all? How would Sean know where his father was headed, once the car had turned out of the drive and sped south across the bridge? She pictured Melissa's sitting room with its soft lighting, a fire in the hearth and Melissa reclining among the scatter cushions. Red wine poured into a pair of lantern-sized goblets, Marcus offering

143

her a tissue, making a joke about her so-called 'cold'. It made her feel sick to think of it, but she couldn't get rid of the thought. Marcus did not need to stay all night in Kirkby Lonsdale, so Sean need never suspect a thing. He knew that Borthwick was usually a late night, so he would not have expected her to phone.

When she finally fell asleep, it was to a dream of Melissa and Marcus, grappling naked on a huge bed, which was for some reason covered in red shiny plastic. Melissa kept scoring her painted nails into Marcus's back, so hard that they left a pattern like Chinese characters scratched into his flesh. It must be hurting him, Jo thought, but he gave no sign of it; did not flinch or cry out. It was then that she noticed the tableau was silent, like watching television with the mute on. *That's because it's only a dream*, said a voice in her head. *It isn't real – you only have to wake up and it will be all over*. But somehow she could not rouse herself. The two of them went on thrashing about, Marcus thrusting and thrusting and Melissa covering his back in hieroglyphics, while the plastic melted from the heat of their bodies and turned into a huge bath of scarlet emulsion paint, on which the pair of them floated effortlessly, unaware of anything except the act in which they were engaged. *You see*, said the voice, *it's ridiculous; no one could float like that. It's just a dream. If it was real they would be drowning in the paint by now*. That was it: of course. That was the other way of stopping it. If she couldn't wake up, then maybe she could cross the room and push them under. Hold them down in the paint; that would do it.

One minute she was watching from a few feet away, and the next she was leaning right over them. She wasn't entirely sure how she got there, but now that she was standing above them it was easy to press down on Marcus's back so that they both

144

disappeared into the paint. There was no more resistance than when she pushed her undies into a basin of water. Her hands and arms went in up to the elbow, but they didn't feel cold or wet. Marcus and Melissa must have sunk to the bottom, because she couldn't feel them either. The momentary relief at having stopped them was overtaken by the horror at what she had done. And in the bath of paint a face was reflected back at her – not her own, but her mother's.

Her scream woke her. She lay there in a panic, wondering if she had really cried out, and if so, whether it had been loud enough for anyone to have heard her. The rooms were well spread around the building and the walls thick, and maybe the sound, which had been so loud in her own mind, had only been part of the dream. She was afraid to relax straight back into sleep lest the dream returned, and when she felt that it was safe to settle down again, sleep eluded her. She eventually fell into a fitful doze from which she awoke feeling jaded at around seven. Before breakfast, she took her phone out into the grounds to maximize the signal and managed to get through to Marcus. Her first question naturally concerned his mother.

'She's much the same.'

'Then why on earth did Sandra phone for you?'

'She didn't.'

'But if Sandra didn't phone for you, why did you go down specially, leaving Sean by himself?'

'I didn't go specially. I told you I was going ages ago, and Sean wouldn't have been on his own if you hadn't taken this extra trip. I didn't want to ring Sandra and cry off – you know what she's like, forever complaining that I don't do my share when it comes to visiting.'

'How is Melissa's cold?' She switched tack, half hoping, half fearing to catch him off guard.

145

'She was a lot better yesterday.'

'So you saw her yesterday.'

'When I called in to the office there were some papers for her, so I dropped them off.'

For a split second she almost asked him: are you having an affair with Melissa? Instead she let him ask if the tour was going well, to which she answered in the affirmative – the only safe response when there was even a remote possibility of a client suddenly appearing from behind a buttress. She might have been a colleague reporting back, she thought. Why didn't they talk properly any more?

The Day Two schedule was tight, so it was always a relief to find that everyone had appeared in good time for breakfast, although Jo soon realized that the party were not in universally good spirits. Mrs Barber of the 'inedible beef' was now grumbling that their room had not lived up to expectations. 'I think it's very pricey, for what it is.'

Jo was desperate to divert the conversation before Mrs Barber turned the collective enthusiasm dial down to zero, but by dire mischance she had ended up sitting next to Mr Radley, the miniature-railway man, who was intent on explaining something called block signalling to her. She was simultaneously aware that at the far end of the table Mrs Bennett-Wilding and Miss McClintock, sisters travelling together from Australia who had hitherto given no trouble at all, now appeared to be upset because Mrs Bennett-Wilding had mislaid a bracelet, given to her by her late husband. Miss McClintock was trying to establish where it had last been seen, appealing to the other guests to corroborate that her sister had been wearing it the night before during dinner.

'If it was a valuable bracelet, I'd ask to have the staff questioned,' suggested Mrs Barber.

Jo did her best, making enquiries with reception, even

joining the sisters in another fruitless search of their room. A member of staff was despatched to check the route of the previous night's tour of the building, but with no result. In vain did the management assure Mrs Bennett-Wilding that if the hotel found the bracelet, they would send it on.

'You might have packed it, by mistake,' Jo suggested as gently as she could, but Mrs Bennett-Wilding vehemently denied the possibility and continued to dart around the room, lifting bedding, opening and closing drawers. 'I'm afraid we do need to be downstairs now,' Jo reminded them. 'I'll see you at the coach in a couple of minutes,' she added from the door.

The day had started dry but soft, misty rain began to fall as the party's luggage was loaded into the bus. Jo paused in the car park to point out the window from which it was believed that Mary Stuart had made her escape in 1567, and then stood at the door of the coach to see them all aboard, but with everyone seated in readiness for departure, there was still no sign of the Australian sisters. The schedule was already slipping, and Jo's hopes that the two women would appear of their own volition had not been realized, so there was clearly nothing to be done but go and fetch them. Fit as she was, Jo's heart rate quickened and her calves began to ache as she tackled the spiral stairs. When she finally arrived at their bedroom door she found it locked, and no amount of knocking raised a reply. As she made her way through the apparently deserted lower floors, she gave vent to some unladylike expressions under her breath, meeting no one until she got back to the coach, where she found the two women already installed in their seats. It appeared that the sisters had descended by an alternative route, Mrs Bennett-Wilding hoping in vain to discover her bracelet in some area of the castle which she had visited the day before.

'And now Phil has gone to see if he could find *you*, to tell you the Australian ladies are here,' the wife of the model-railway enthusiast said in a tone of accusation.

Jo felt like screaming. If only Mr Radley had minded his own business and stayed in his seat, the party could have been on its way. Instead she had an increasingly impatient group of people sitting on the coach and had to decide whether to return to the building, thereby risking the possibility that Mr Radley would give her the slip as effectively as had the Australians, or whether to wait him out in the car park. While she was hesitating, the man in question appeared at the castle entrance and made his unhurried approach to the bus.

'*There* you are.' He addressed Jo as one might a naughty five-year-old. 'I knew I'd got you cornered, because I took the precaution of stationing two of the waitresses at each of the main staircases.' He spoke as one whose quick thinking had saved the day.

Jo managed to muster a warm smile. 'Thank you. But for future reference, if anyone else goes missing, it would be better if everyone waits on the bus and we don't send a second search party out to look for the first.'

'Well, let's hope you don't manage to lose anyone else, eh?' Mr Radley was not to be easily demoted from his role as the older, wiser man, resolving a situation where others had failed.

It was still raining when the coach reached Dunbar. The wind had risen, so that the group had to wrestle to keep their umbrellas slanting in the right direction, while they stared across the windswept harbour at the tumbled remnants of the once great fortress and Jo gamely brought to life the story of Mary's various journeys there: the dramatic ride through the night with Darnley, and the subsequent Dunbar excursions with Bothwell. There was more to see further up the coast at

Tantallon, where the remaining façade perched on the cliff tops for all the world like a two-dimensional stage set. Tantallon did not have the same importance in the story as Dunbar or Hermitage, but like Crichton, where they had paused the day before, it was an atmospheric ruin, and the Queen of Scots was known to have been there.

The rain had eased, but a chilly wind still whipped across the car park as Jo ushered her group towards the entrance. She had talked them through Tantallon en route, and by cutting down the amount of time there, she still hoped to get them back on track. The unseasonable weather would help too; who would want to linger at an exposed coastal ruin on a day like this? Sure enough, they were all back at the coach with time to spare. As Jo stood at the front wearing a fixed smile, while mentally checking their numbers (M. H. Tour guides never marched up and down the bus, counting heads like schoolteachers) she was aware of Clive slipping out of the driver's seat into the car park. On reaching the correct tally of eighteen, she glanced over her shoulder and saw him beckon. She joined him outside before asking, 'What's up?'

'The warning light that tells me the rear luggage compartment is open has come on. Can you give me a minute to check it?'

'Of course.' She followed him round to the rear of the vehicle. Surely nothing else could possibly go wrong today. Clive opened and shut the hatch a couple of times, but there did not appear to be anything amiss.

'There's probably a fault with the electrics,' he said. 'It seems secure enough. Nothing to worry about.'

'Thank goodness. Someone's luggage falling out is all I need right now. Let's get the show on the road again, shall we?'

As the bus pulled away, she switched on the microphone

and gave them a brief cheery spiel about how soon they would all be sitting down to lunch. Another shower had begun to hit the windows, but it was warm and dry inside. She switched off the mic and relaxed. She was dreadfully tired, but she must not let herself doze, however tempting it seemed just then. As she leaned her head back against the rest, the sixth sense of an experienced guide abruptly kicked in. A murmur of disquiet reached her ears, followed seconds later by Mr Radley, asking in the voice of one taking command: 'Is Mrs Van Halsen on the bus? Has anyone seen the American lady with the orange rain hat?'

Jo unfastened her seatbelt and stood up. Mrs Van Halsen had been occupying a double seat, three rows back on the right, which was now vacant. How could that even be possible? 'I counted,' Jo said, under her breath. 'I know I counted.'

'I saw her getting off the bus, back at the last stop.' It was one of the Australian sisters who spoke.

'When?' asked Jo.

'When you and the driver went off together. Maybe she was popping to the ladies'. I thought she must have got back on again without my noticing. I can't see her from here, when she's sitting in her seat.'

Jo bit back the desire to yell: 'Why didn't anyone speak up before?' It wasn't their fault, it was hers. She should have double-checked before they set off. But who would have anticipated a member of the party getting off the bus at such a moment, or that no one else would speak up until they had driven away without her?

Clive had already found somewhere to turn the bus around, without needing to be told. Jo resumed her seat, eyes front, as if they might spot Mrs Van Halsen hurrying along the road in hot pursuit. Excited chatter had broken out behind her.

'I didn't realize . . . I just thought she must have changed seats . . .' 'You say she got off again? I didn't see her, but of course I was taking a last look out of the window at the castle . . .' 'Fancy leaving someone behind . . .' 'Poor woman, she won't know what to do . . .'

Mrs Van Halsen was not amused. She had been seized with a last-minute desire to purchase some engraved goblets from the little gift shop, she said. It had never occurred to her that the bus would set off without her. 'Heaven knows, we have had so many delays today that I hardly thought another tiny one would make any difference, although it seems you were not willing to hold the coach for a moment or two, so that *I* could make *my* purchase.' All Jo's apologies could not make it right, and Mr Radley did not improve the collective mood with his hearty: 'And there was me this morning, saying we'd better try not to lose anyone else.'

When they arrived at the lunch stop, Jo managed to seat herself as far away from Mrs Van Halsen as possible, but occasional snatches of conversation floated down to where she was sitting. 'Disgraceful . . . left standing in the rain . . .' 'A shambles . . . one thing after another . . .'

'Don't worry dear,' said Miss Watt, a long-retired schoolmistress, who had taken the chair opposite Jo. 'I'm sure the sensible ones know that it wasn't your fault.' She patted Jo's hand in a well-meaning gesture of comfort.

At this point a shriek emanated from Mrs Barber. 'A bug! There's a bug in my food!' Jo arrived at Mrs Barber's shoulder at the same moment as the waiter, to find Mrs Barber indicating a small black object in the juice of her Florida cocktail.

'Ees not a bug, madame. Ees mint – a leaf of mint – tiny piece gone black. I fetch you another.'

Mrs Barber was neither convinced nor mollified. She

insisted that she wanted nothing else. 'It's turned me up,' she said. 'I can't eat anything after that. First the meat last night, and now this . . .'

'It really was just a little piece of blackened leaf,' Jo tried but failed to assure the Barbers. 'Mint goes like that very quickly, if it gets crushed and left in the juice. It's poor presentation, I agree . . .'

'The food was supposed to be one of the high points of the tour,' Mr Barber interrupted. 'There have only been three meals so far, and my wife hasn't been able to eat two of them.'

Jo's head was beginning to thud. As soon as the opportunity arose, she covertly extracted some Paracetamol from her bag and took them with a few sips of water. She could not remember a party who had been such hard work for a very long time – and the thing was that she should not have had to be dealing with them – Melissa should have got this bunch, not her. The thought made her irrationally angry, so that her head thumped harder than before.

She was conscious that her delivery on the approach to Edinburgh had begun to sound flat, like the reluctant reader in an English class called upon to go through a well-known passage in a set book, and she sensed an air of dejection about the group when they disembarked into a mist of fine rain at their first stop in the city. Her announcement that the amount of free time available for souvenir shopping would now be shorter than anticipated met with a rumble of discontent.

In the early days of M. H. Tours, she had been carried along by the buzz of it all. They had prided themselves on offering something special: any problems they encountered along the way were merely challenges to be overcome and turning round a client like Mrs Barber was all in a day's work. Key to it all was the pleasure of sharing knowledge, faces lighting up as your passion for the subject brought it to life for them; but today she found herself wondering what on earth was the point. What did it matter if Bothwell had wooed Mary, as the romantic novelists would have it, or raped her as historians thought more likely? It was all one and the same now, because they were both dead and buried these past four hundred and some odd years. The possibility that she no longer cared hit her hard. She was like the adolescent who suddenly doubts her own belief in God, and yet is still helping to run the Sunday School. Without the belief, without the enthusiasm, she not only felt that she was a sham, but wondered if the whole group did not sense it, too. She urgently wanted to escape from them all for a few hours – even the earnest, note-taking Mr and Mrs Hart and the kindly Miss Watt – unable to face any more conversations about Mary, Darnley, Bothwell, John Knox and the whole long-dead crew of them. As they assembled in the Edinburgh drizzle, waiting to gain admission to the Palace of Holyroodhouse, she imagined herself saying, 'Look, you go on in and buy a guide book. Have a ball. You won't believe the size of that alcove where Mary was sitting with Rizzio, when the rebels came to kill him. No, really – you'll enjoy it all the more if I'm not there to put a damper on proceedings. Me? Oh I'll be getting the next train south. I've seen it all before, you see. I'm done with Mary Queen of Scots, or MQS as my husband's lover calls her. Yes – it is a bit irrelevant, isn't it – who MQS was sleeping with, when your husband's fooling around? Anyway, so long. Have a good trip.'

In reality, she shepherded them inside, saying all the right things like a well-programmed mechanical doll, pretending, always pretending. Why do we care about the past, she wondered – not our own past, but other people's? She had first discovered Mary Queen of Scots via some faded Pan paperbacks which sat on Ma Allisson's bookshelves. The cover illustrations had caught her eye: velvet-clad heroines, complete with eye shadow and mascara and knowing, twentieth-century faces. The stories had been an escape route from reality, and even if Jean Plaidy's version of history had been highly romanticized, the books had still served as a first step on the road to a real interest in the Tudor period and beyond.

Other people's lives, however terrible they happened to be, could still provide a good antidote to the bad things which were happening in our own. At least, she had thought so until now. Today in chilly, dour Edinburgh, it was as if the spell had been broken; maybe it was the wreckage of her own life which required attention. Did Mary Queen of Scots matter? Did M. H. Tours? Surely what really mattered was finding Lauren.

At this point another voice – it sounded very like Marcus – intruded to ask just how she proposed to pay the mortgage or settle up for the groceries, without the steady income generated by the business. Moreover, it asked, what did she think she could actually do to find Lauren? Searches, the police, media appeals, none of it had worked.

She was so tired. Once they got to the hotel, she would have to lie down, snatch a nap, try to shake off her headache. Mrs Van Halsen loomed up beside her. 'I thought I should tell you that I intend to lodge a formal complaint. Thanks to your mismanagement, we will not have a full opportunity to enjoy the retail experience that is Edinburgh.' She pronounced it *opportoonity* and *Edinburrow*. Mrs Van Halsen stalked away again without giving Jo time to respond. From somewhere behind her she could hear the familiar voice of a miniature-railway engineer assuring another unseen person that you should never set off without making sure everyone was on board the coach. 'Beginner's mistake,' he said.

Jo was so preoccupied that she almost fell over the child's buggy. A small blonde girl, muffled up in a pale pink jacket, with imitation pink fur around the hood. 'Why didn't you come for me?'

Jo stepped back abruptly and burst into tears. Various members of the party surrounded her at once, faces anxious, voices asking her what was wrong. She had to excuse herself as swiftly as possible, promising to meet them at the exit. As she hurried away, she caught sight of Mrs Van Halsen's contemptuous expression. She had given way to emotion – marked herself down as an amateur. It was the final loss of face.

It was cold in the ladies' toilets, and the floor tiles looked damp and dirty after being repeatedly traversed by wet footwear. The expression of the woman who looked out at her from the mirror had a familiar, haunted look: a look which might always be there if it were not carefully hidden behind a mask. She would have given anything not to return and face the party, but she regained her self-possession and forced herself back into part. She would make a success of this bloody tour if it killed her.

When she rejoined the group she apologized profusely, inventing a lie about some news of family illness; thinking all the time how furious Marcus would have been. *I had to tell them something*, she responded angrily to the voice in her head.

It was considerably less simple to deal with the man in person.

We felt deeply sorry for your guide, who did very well, when having to cope with a family tragedy.

155

'Family tragedy? What bloody family tragedy?' Marcus waved the customer satisfaction form at her, much as an irate householder might wave his torn *Daily Mail* at the paper boy.

'I got a bit upset. I had to tell them something. You know what people are like – you hint at something and they invent the rest for themselves.'

'Why did you have to tell them anything?'

'I told you.' Jo's tone was defensive. 'I got a bit upset.'

'Why? What do you mean, upset?'

'If you would just stop shouting at me for one minute . . . I started to cry.'

Marcus stared at her. 'You started to cry,' he repeated. 'Just like that? Out of the blue?'

'I couldn't help it. So I just said I'd had some upsetting news. I never said tragedy, I'm sure I didn't.'

'Golden Rule Number One,' said Marcus. 'Nothing gets in the way of the subject matter, unless the clients themselves introduce it. If you're on an MQS tour, the topic is MQS, later medieval architecture, Scottish society in the sixteenth century, maybe even the suppression of Catholicism. It is not our private lives: yours, mine, or anyone else's. You know that.'

'But it didn't spoil the tour for them,' Jo interrupted. 'The form says "your guide did very well . . ."'

'No, she did not,' Marcus shouted. 'You gave a below-par performance, which these people forgave because they thought you'd suffered a bereavement. And it wasn't just one adverse comment. There were problems mentioned across the board – hold-ups, itinerary issues, food at the hotel . . .'

'There was nothing wrong with the food. You know some people are professional complainers.'

'It's your job to smooth things over.'

'Don't tell me my job, please. I know my job.' She was

156

overcome by the absurd sensation that she was in the midst of an interview with her head teacher, or had been transformed into a very junior member of staff, carpeted by the MD.

'And at Tantallon, you managed to leave someone behind. There were only eighteen of them, for goodness' sake. Checking the numbers is a basic, an absolute given.'

'It was a fluke. I had checked, but . . .'

'Satisfied customers are our bread and butter. We can't afford to have a bunch of people telling their friends we didn't measure up to the company promise. You must have known you'd messed up because you never said a word about any of this stuff when you got home.'

Jo stayed silent, knowing only too well that this was true. There was a long pause while Marcus appeared to be wrestling with his own thoughts and inclinations. Eventually he took a deep breath and said, 'You'll have to hand your tours over to other guides. We'll reschedule –'

'No,' Jo cried. 'That's unfair. You can't punish me for something one old crone has written on her comment form!'

'Old crone? Is that how you think of our clients? How many other things have gone wrong lately that you have forgotten to mention?'

'None of what happened was my fault.'

'Leaving people behind? Bursting into tears? How is that anyone's fault but yours?'

'Hang on a minute. I'm a partner in the firm. You can't just order me off the tours, as if I was some inexperienced nobody. Surely there has to be a proper discussion about this, with me getting a chance to have my say.'

'You mean a partners' meeting? You, me and Melissa?'

One look at his face was enough. 'Oh my God! You've discussed it with her already – you have, haven't you?'

'She was the first person to read the forms. She drew it to my attention.'

'And the two of you made a decision without even consulting me.'

'Melissa knows you haven't had a recent bereavement. What on earth did you expect me to say?'

'I expect you to take my side.'

'It isn't a question of taking sides. We have to do what is right for the business. Times are tough economically. We can't afford dissatisfied customers – not even slightly dissatisfied customers. If it had been Melissa, you would have been the first to say that she had to be replaced – temporarily.'

'Temporarily?'

'Until you sort your problems out.'

'My biggest problem is that my daughter went missing ten years, nine months and two days ago. How do you and Melissa propose I solve that?'

'That's not the problem I'm referring to. I think you need to see a doctor.'

Jo shook her head, so that the tears which had welled up in her eyes zigzagged wildly across her cheeks.

'Maybe some counselling might help,' Marcus continued. 'But you can't go on like this – we can't go on like this.'

'Like what?' She struggled with her tears, making a monumental effort to steady her voice as she asked, 'Marcus, are you having an affair with Melissa?'

'Like that,' said Marcus, as he turned to leave the room.

CHAPTER TWELVE

Are you having an affair with Melissa? Whatever had possessed her to say such a thing? Why had she even allowed herself to think it? 'I was angry and upset,' she told Marcus. 'Imagine how you would feel if someone told you that you were off the tours, just like that.' Although he had forgiven – or at least appeared to forgive – the implication that she thought he was having an affair ('It's insulting, Jo, to both me and Melissa'), he was unmoving on the question of the tours. 'It was one slip-up,' she pleaded, although in her heart she knew it was more than that. Somehow she had to get back on to the tours, had to persuade Marcus that she was fine. If they forced her to stay at home with Sean the whole time, she really would go crazy.

Persuading Marcus that 'her problems were being sorted out' meant at the very least meeting him halfway, so she agreed to make an appointment to see their family doctor, taking care that it fell on a day when Marcus could not possibly attend. To Dr Hillier she presented her problem as occasional migraine-type headaches, and destroyed the prescription he issued instead of cashing it in.

'How did it go?' Marcus asked, when he returned home next day. 'Did he suggest a referral?'

'A referral for what?'

'For anything? Did you ask him about counselling?'

'I've already told you', said Jo wearily, 'that I don't want

159

counselling. Talking things through with some fat ex-social worker is about as much good as a chocolate teapot. I'm up to my eyeballs in counselling, and going over and over things can only help so much.'

'So what did he suggest?'

'He said a bit of a break from work might be a good thing – just for a while. Rest and recuperate, that sort of idea . . .' She waved an arm, as if encompassing a whole variety of restorative activity to which she couldn't quite put a name.

'I wish you had let me go with you.'

'Marcus, I am perfectly capable of going to see the doctor by myself, and I don't see what difference your being there would have made.' It was such a big fib that she had to look down and flick an imaginary crumb from her lap, in order to avoid his eyes.

'So he didn't prescribe anything?'

'No. Not least because, unlike you and Melissa, he didn't think there was anything wrong with me! Quite honestly, I think he only said the stuff about rest and recuperation to humour me. I think if I'd been in a job which called for him to write a sick note, he might have thought twice about issuing one and asked me if I wasn't swinging the lead.'

'So what exactly did you tell him? Did he examine you?'

'Physically, you mean? Blood pressure?'

'That sort of thing.'

'Yes – he did all the usual sort of things.'

'And what did you tell him – about why you were there?'

'For goodness' sake, Marcus! Must you subject me to the third degree? Can't we just drop this? You've got your way. You and Melissa have rescheduled everything for the next three months even though, according to Dr Hillier, there's nothing much wrong that a couple of weeks off work won't put right. In the meantime you get to travel all over the country doing the job you love, while I stay here, keeping house and looking after your son.'

'You could think of it more positively,' Marcus said. 'Think how much reading you'll be able to catch up on. And maybe you could do a bit more work on those new tours – so you still feel involved.' His tone was conciliatory, ignoring the jibe about Sean. Recently he had started asking to speak to Sean, as well as to her, whenever he called home. Sean always pointedly carried the phone off into another room, so that Jo could not hear what was being said. She had half begun to wonder if Marcus was not using Sean to keep an eye on her: 'How does she seem today?' 'Well, Dad, she's not done anything weird so far.'

Fortunately neither Sean nor Marcus had been there to see a little scene played out on Booths' car park, the day before her appointment with Dr Hillier. Walking back to her car with a trolley-load of shopping, she had almost cannoned into Brian coming the other way. Neither had been paying proper attention to their surroundings, and each had seen the other too late to take evasive action.

Brian had greeted her gruffly, made the inevitable remark 'we must stop meeting like this', and asked how she was, although Jo suspected this was less out of friendliness than because the position of her trolley made it almost impossible to ignore her. Last time she'd had him pinned against the dips and boxed salads; this time his route was blocked by parked cars, a concrete bollard and a flowering cherry tree.

'I'm very well, thank you.' She made a point of looking him directly in the eyes, so that he could see she was not going to be intimidated. Several times since returning from Scotland she had again experienced the strong sensation that the house was being watched. She had half suspected Brian, and briefly considered suggesting to Marcus that they install a security camera, but that would surely lead to accusations of paranoia, so she had not pursued the idea.

'I was wondering what you were doing that day, when I saw you up at High Gilpin,' she said. He could not fail to pick up the note of accusation in her tone. She would show him that she was not afraid to ask awkward questions.

For a moment Brian looked so puzzled that anyone who had not known better might have thought he had no idea to what occasion she referred. Then he said: 'I was moving some pieces of sculpture. I rent some storage space up there from the Tunnocks. Anything else you'd like to know?'

Jo refused to be deflected by his sarcasm. 'Yes, actually. I would like to know where Shelley is. There's something I want to ask her.'

'Then I suggest you drop in at the gallery – she was there when I left.' Now it was his turn to hold her in remorseless eye contact.

'But . . . you told me Shelley had gone away.'

'And now she's come back again.'

She had spluttered something, then, about being sorry or glad, or at any rate a combination of words which completely betrayed her embarrassment and confusion. Brian, unsurprisingly, had said nothing to help put her at her ease.

When she told Marcus that Shelley had returned home, he made a point of not being surprised, which stopped just short of saying 'I told you so'.

In fact, she really did have things she wanted to ask Shelley about, particularly the Pre-Raphaelites, because the BBC had been advertising a forthcoming series about them and there was nothing like a TV tie-in to raise interest and awareness in a subject, but she dreaded the possibility that Brian might have told Shelley about their encounters at Booths, or worse still, how oddly she had behaved up at High Gilpin. Shelley

162

would at best think her daffy and at worst, completely bonkers. Looking back now, the whole business made her feel both stupid and curiously ashamed of herself. Marcus had been right about her overreacting, and as well as being more than slightly annoying, this only served to encourage him in his sense that he was right about everything else, too. On the one hand she felt too embarrassed to drop in on Shelley, but on the other, she knew that the longer she left it the more awkward it would become.

Without the tour schedules to keep her busy, she had been spending more time than ever working with her sketch book, mostly out of doors. She had done a series of pen and ink drawings of sheep against a mountain background, which she thought as good as some little notelets she had seen on sale in Greenodd Post Office. There were other elements of her growing portfolio which she liked less, such as the fat-faced policemen, seashells and similar alien objects, which she sometimes spotted insouciantly lurking in the corners of landscapes, unconsciously pencilled into places where they did not belong.

There had been no other signs and portents since the arrival of the third shell. Every day she checked around the house, scanning the doorsteps and window sills, falling eagerly upon the mail. She studied the belt of woodland from the kitchen window several times a day, but although she sometimes thought she caught sight of a watcher standing among the trees, if she stared long enough it always transformed into a tree trunk, or a patch of shadow. Some days she felt as if she was inhabiting a world in which the edges of reality were blurring, like watercolours running into one another, except that she knew the shells were real. It was a rare day when she did not take them out of her drawer and slide her fingertips over them, committing every nuance of their texture to

163

memory, as if more intimate knowledge would ultimately help her crack their code. She was sure that something else must happen soon.

She was careful not to say anything to Marcus about this sense of anticipation, instead allowing him to believe that she was working assiduously on the Lake Artists Tour and endeavouring to appear keen to discuss all other aspects of the business at every opportunity, an activity for which Marcus had never needed any encouragement. His conversation was peppered with: 'Melissa says this,' or 'Melissa says that,' or 'Melissa's had a great idea.' She just adopted a fixed smile and said nothing. As if she couldn't see that he was besotted with bloody Melissa. When he was not there, she actively tried not to think about the business, which in turn meant that she did not have to think about Melissa. Mostly she thought about Lauren. She had begun to think of her in a more positive, less painful way; to visualize her as the girl she would be now, a girl who would be coming home . . . soon.

Being at home enabled her to catch up on a variety of jobs, and during the May half-term, she decided it was the turn of the kitchen cupboards to get a thorough overhaul and clean. She started one morning with the wall cupboard nearest the kitchen door, unloading its contents on to the work surface so that she could wipe out the interior. The house was very quiet. She had not bothered to switch on the radio, and there was no sound from upstairs, where she assumed Sean was still in bed, although it was approaching noon.

As she rinsed her cleaning cloth at the sink, she pondered yet again how the shells had arrived on the doorstep and the window sill. Had someone crept along the lane with them, keeping low behind the walls, scurrying from one bit of cover to another? Probably nothing so obviously furtive than that.

Around here it was not unusual to encounter walkers at any hour, sometimes even late at night. Several footpaths converged on Easter Bridge, since foot traffic down the ages had always needed to avail itself of the crossing. Dressing as a hiker would be the perfect cover for moving about on the public roads because no one looked twice so long as you had the regulation boots and rucksack. If anyone had happened to pass in a vehicle, or even look out of their window, the sight of someone striding along the road in hiking gear was just about as unremarkable as you could get – and it would take less than a minute to sneak down the drive to the house and back. You would have to be extremely unlucky to get spotted. It was not a comfortable thought, the idea of a shadowy figure creeping into the garden, then sliding away again, melting back into the Lakeland scenery. In an instant they would be an ordinary, anonymous person again, someone she might pass by without a second glance – they knowing perfectly well who she was, but she not recognizing them.

This image of a backpacker trekking up from the bridge changed into that of a young girl strolling along in the sunshine. A girl of roughly twelve years old, with long blonde hair – Lauren – Lauren as she would look now, walking up from the bridge . . . coming home. Jo's eyes followed the vision up the lane. It disappeared now and again. behind the trees and shrubs, which were still pale with the spring colours which came late to the Lake District. Once or twice Jo thought she had lost it, but the figure kept on coming nearer, its progress steady and unhurried, just as it would be in real life.

Without realizing it, Jo began to grip the edge of the sink for support. It was really her. Lauren was walking up the lane, heading for The Hideaway just as surely as if she knew exactly where she had to come. Although her knees were all but giving way, she managed to run outside on to the drive. She tried to shout, but nothing came. Seemingly unaware of her, the girl continued to approach in the same unhurried way, like a ghost which inhabits its own parallel arc of time and place, seen by but unseeing of the living.

'Lauren!' Jo reached the gateway just as the girl drew level. 'Lauren,' she repeated, holding out her hands.

The girl shied like a startled foal, removing tiny headphones from her ears as she edged away. Jo was momentarily aware of a crackle of music, cut off as the girl's fingers found the switch of something hidden under her jacket. She spoke warily, all the time keeping her eyes firmly fixed on Jo. 'Sorry – did you want something? Are you OK?' The voice was polite but nervous, slightly plummy.

Jo stared at the apparition. The sense of fairy-tale unreality which had carried her thus far was ebbing away.

'Is there a problem?' Gilda Iceton's words swept down the lane like an audible storm warning. Jo automatically turned at the sound, to find that Gilda had appeared in the gateway of The Old Forge. Jo noticed for the first time that Gilda's voice was quite plummy too.

'I think this lady might be ill.' The girl sidestepped neatly, putting herself further from Jo and closer to Gilda, who was now advancing in swift strides.

'You go into the house, Becky. I'll take care of Mrs Handley.' It was a tone which, while not unkind, brooked no argument. As the girl headed up the lane, Gilda stepped nearer to Jo and spoke in a voice too low for the girl to hear. 'You leave my daughter alone. I don't want you anywhere near her. How dare you think you can try to terrorize her, the way you and your friends terrorized me.'

'I wasn't – I didn't . . .'

Gilda had already taken Jo's arm and begun to lead her

166

towards The Hideaway. To any onlooker she might have appeared to be helping an unsteady neighbour back home, but it was an iron grip, the strength of which was not only surprising but painful, too.

'Leave us alone,' Gilda hissed in her ear. 'Do you understand me? Just leave us alone.' She steered Jo right back up the drive, only loosing her hold when they reached the kitchen door. Jo automatically reached up and rubbed her arm, which continued to throb as if Gilda's fingers were still clamped into it. 'Hurt you, have I?' Gilda seemed to tower over her. Jo had forgotten how lanky Gilda had been at school; there she had been a thin, daddy-long-legs kind of figure, gangly-limbed, with a running style all of her own. She was carrying a good deal more weight now. 'If you ever do anything to upset Becky, I swear I'll hurt you so badly you may never recover.'

Jo opened her mouth to protest, but Gilda stalked away before she could say a word. When Jo called after her the other woman took no notice.

Gilda's daughter. The girl was Gilda's daughter. Wave after wave of disappointment swept over her. She stood outside the door for several minutes, rubbing her arm where Gilda had held her and gulping for air. If only Gilda had let her explain. Dear God, it was not as if she would have done the girl any harm. Surely even Gilda could see the difference between the kind of things one might get drawn into as a teenager and the kind of things one was capable of as an adult.

When she eventually re-entered the house, she had to sit at the kitchen table for a long time, trying to recover from the shaky feeling Gilda had engendered in her. Although she told herself that she had merely been confronted by the natural wrath of a mother protecting her young, there was something else she could not quantify. Perhaps it was no more than a primitive instinct telling her that people who appear different may be dangerous, an old, irrational prejudice against someone whose outward appearance is not quite right.

While she was still sitting at the table, Sean ambled downstairs and made straight for the fridge. If we live here long enough, Jo thought, he will erode a track: bedroom to fridge, then back to bedroom.

'Good morning,' she said, summoning an effort. 'I'm just making tea.' She would have preferred coffee, but she knew he didn't drink it. 'Would you like a cup?'

'Yeah – thanks.' His tone was cautious.

'It's a much better day, quite warm outside. Have you got any plans?'

'I might go down to Harry's later on.'

She allowed a pause to develop before saying casually, 'I see the new girl who lives at The Old Forge is home for the holidays.'

'Yeah. Her name's Becky. She's been playing with Charlie.'

At any other time Jo would probably have derived pleasure from such a breakthrough. Sean volunteering information in a conversational way without having it forced out of him was a red-letter event; but this morning she felt only frustration. It was evident that Sean had been aware of the girl who lived across the lane for a couple of days. If he had only said something about it earlier, she would have been alerted to the girl's presence and much less likely to have made such a catastrophic error.

'If you go to Harry's,' she said, 'be sure to lock up after yourself and take a key. I might be going out later on.'

'OK.' Sean paused to examine the items she had removed from the cupboard, picking through them one by one. 'Why is all this stuff out?'

'I'm cleaning the cupboard.'

She was beset by the awful suspicion that he was reporting back to Marcus: 'Nothing abnormal observed today, except that she'd taken everything out of a kitchen cupboard. She said she was cleaning, but I didn't see any signs of it.'

After pouring the tea, she made haste to resume her spring-cleaning activities – dreadful, this idea of being under surveillance. However, once Sean had taken his bowl of Weetabix and mug of tea, she quickly wiped and dried the shelves and replaced the contents any old how, deciding that the time had come to cut and run. When she had changed into her outdoor clothes, she called out from the landing to tell Sean she was going and heard a muffled 'OK' in return. As she laced her boots, she noticed that her fingers were still trembling. She badly needed fresh air and some sun on her face, but in order to gain the fells, she would have to walk right through Easter Bridge, passing all the other houses, including The Old Forge, en route.

She set out briskly enough to make her heart rate quicken, looking neither to right nor left, trying to ignore the sensation which came from the certain knowledge that she was being observed – maybe by the ghosts in The Old Forge, or maybe by Gilda Iceton herself. Or perhaps by Sean, keeping a covert watch from an upstairs window, preparing his report on her movements for his father. Most certainly by Maisie Perry, if she was at home; possibly by the family who had rented the old farmhouse for the week, exhibiting their holidaymakers' curiosity about the people who lived in the village, or perhaps even by Shelley and Brian, from the windows of the gallery. As she approached The Hollies, she saw Harry's mother in the act of placing a knotted carrier bag into the wheelie bin. Harry's mother had always been friendly, generally going out of her way to say 'hello', but Jo felt that she could not face a chat with anyone just at the moment, so she focused her eyes straight ahead to avoid seeing the other woman.

In the end, she did not go up on to the fells. She had been on the point of taking her favourite path up through the woods when she saw some of Mr Tyson's highland cattle grazing in a field not far along the road, and she decided to sketch them instead. She stood at the stout wooden field gate, resting her drawing book on the top bar. One of the beasts obliged her by approaching to see what she was doing, giving her the benefit of its full-faced curiosity, coming so near that she could see the texture of its rough ginger fringe and tough pale horns. The big eyes stared at her unblinking while she struggled to capture the creature's appeal, without falling into the traps marked cute or cartoonesque. When the beast eventually decided that she was not of any interest and moved off to resume feeding, she began to sketch the other animals, all of them presenting at slightly different angles and attitudes. Finally she roughed in the line of the hedgerow on the far side of the field, thinking that when she sat down with it at home, she might try to incorporate all these various elements into a composite drawing.

She had come without her watch, but she guessed it must be well beyond lunchtime when she turned for home. She had just reached the Old Chapel Gallery when she caught sight of Shelley, who was just emerging from Ingledene.

'Hi.' Shelley waved a hand. 'Long time no see. Are you coming in for a coffee?'

In truth, Jo was still shaken from the events of the morning and would much rather have gone straight home, but Shelley's invitation was the perfect way to get over an awkward hurdle, and a refusal was open to misinterpretation, so she agreed at once, waiting at the door of the gallery while Shelley unlocked it and preceded her inside.

'Brian's down in Barrow for the day,' Shelley said. 'So I'm holding the fort alone. The trouble is that I forgot Bri was going out and started some tea breads for the freezer, so I've just had to pop back and turn the oven off. How's your Lake Artists project coming on?'

Jo was grateful to accept the prompt, noting that Shelley seemed keen to gloss over her recent absence and pick up where they had left off. She accepted a mug of Shelley's bitter brew and began to outline some of her queries and ideas. When she mentioned the Pre-Raphaelites, Shelley said: 'I've got just the thing for you. It's a leaflet about all the places in Cumbria with Pre-Raphaelite stained glass – there's a woman in South Lakes who's an expert on it, and she's produced this handout. I know I can put my hand straight on it; I only saw it the other day when I was hunting for something else. I'll go and fetch it now. If anyone comes in, make sure they buy something nice and pricey – I could use the pennies for the meter.'

While Shelley was gone, Jo sipped her coffee and looked at the nearest paintings. There was an exquisite representation of a red squirrel in oils, hung alongside another by the same artist of a snowy owl, both precise and detailed as photographs, but with the depth and beauty which a mere camera could never achieve. These were in complete contrast to the huge canvas on the facing panel, which appeared to have been slashed about with browns and greens. Jo had little or no knowledge of abstract art, but she did know that Brian would not have hung anything he did not consider very good, and from where she sat, she could see that the price tag read £2,850. She supposed that an occasional collector making a purchase of that magnitude once in a while would help keep 'the meter' going for some time.

When Shelley came back, she was carrying not only the

171

promised leaflet, but also three large books. 'These might come in useful. This one is the book about Ruskin that I couldn't find when I looked last time, and these others will give you a bit more background on the Pre-Raphaelites, since you seem to be branching further in that direction. It would give you a chance to put in a nice bit of scandal too, with Ruskin, Millais and darling Effie.'

'It certainly spices up the human interest,' Jo laughed.

'I should have brought you some sort of bag. They're a bit awkward to carry, and this one's got a cover which keeps slipping about.'

'There's plenty of room in my rucksack. I've only got my sketch pad and some waterproofs.' Jo unfastened the rucksack as she was speaking and unpacked her sketch book on to the edge of the table, while she opened the drawstring wide enough to accommodate the largest of the volumes.

'How's the drawing coming along?'

'I think I'm improving.' For a moment Jo considered asking Shelley's opinion of her sheep and cattle, but it seemed presumptuous when Shelley was a proper artist who sold her pictures.

'You should join the Art Society. I keep on telling you that's the way to bring yourself on.'

'I'm really not good enough.'

'Rubbish – that's what everyone thinks. The Art Society accepts anyone who's keen – and you are keen – yes, you are. You're always heading off out to draw something. You'd gain so much from it, and what have you got to lose?'

'I'll think about it.' Jo was lifting the last of the three books into her rucksack. She imagined Brian, towering over her, making some cutting remarks about her efforts with a paint-brush. She had always been wary of Brian, and now it was even worse.

Shelley might almost have read her mind. 'Brian's a marvellous teacher, you know. He would bring you on no end if you enrolled for one of his painting days.'

'No thanks.' The words were out before she could stop them – way too emphatic. The awkwardness was palpable, but she couldn't find the words to put things right. 'I mean . . . it would be difficult. And – and I'm just not ready.'

'Your choice, of course,' said Shelley. She shrugged and half turned away, as if her attention had been caught by something which needed rearrangement on the table.

'Thanks for the books.'

'No probs. Hang on to them for as long as you need them.' Shelley didn't look up.

She knows, Jo thought, she knows what I thought about Brian. 'See you,' she said, as brightly as she could.

'Yeah, see you later,' said Shelley.

CHAPTER THIRTEEN

'I've been doing some thinking', said Jo, 'while you've been away, and I was wondering whether we should consider moving away from here, making a fresh start.'

Dinner was over. Sean had returned to his room, but Marcus and Jo had lingered at the kitchen table, finishing off a bottle of wine. She had spoken tentatively, her eyes cast down on the place where her dinner plate had recently been, but now that she looked up to see how Marcus would react, she suddenly noticed how tired he seemed.

'This was our fresh start. A new place, a new enterprise. This is it, Jo. You can't just run away and start again every few years.'

'I just think that maybe we'd all be happier somewhere else.'

'Moving is a huge expense. We can't afford to extend our mortgage, then there's the business and Sean's school.'

'It would be better for Sean if we didn't live right out in the country like this. If he was nearer his school, living in a bigger community, where there were more young people . . . He's had Harry this week, but Harry's family went home yesterday and there isn't anyone else of his own age for miles.'

'But he's just got started at his new school, and anyway, he always knows he can ask us for a lift to anywhere he wants to go. That's how kids in the country manage – they travel by car between each other's houses.'

'He never wants to go anywhere. In fact, I don't believe he has made any new friends – so it wouldn't matter much if he did change school.'

'Give him a chance; he's only just settling in. Friendships don't always happen overnight. It definitely wouldn't do his education any good to have another move.'

'Well, maybe he wouldn't need to change school. There must be other places to live in the school catchment area.'

'I don't get it.' Marcus changed tack. 'What is it that you suddenly don't like about living here? You used to love it. What's changed?'

Jo hesitated. She didn't want to tell him about the constant feeling of unseen eyes watching the house, and she certainly couldn't tell him about the unfortunate episode with Gilda Iceton and her daughter. 'It's very isolated out here,' she began tentatively. 'You don't notice when you're away a lot, but it's different now that I'm here all the time. In other places I've had friends living nearby.'

'You liked the peace and quiet, you always said. You could always make a bit more effort – join something – get to know a few people. And what about Shelley? I thought the two of you got on well . . .'

The telephone saved her by trilling insistently at just the right moment. She stood up and lifted the phone from its cradle. 'Hello?'

'Hello – is that Joanne?'

'Yes, it is.'

'It's Monica here – Aunty Beryl's daughter. I've got some bad news, I'm afraid.'

'Oh dear,' Jo braced herself. 'What's happened?'

'Well – inevitable really – but Aunty Joan has died. I expect you knew that she's been poorly for some time.'

As Jo hunted up some appropriate expression of sympathy

for Monica, a mixture of emotions rose within her. Aunty Joan had been one of her mother's aunts, the one who had never married, to whom Jo had been despatched a couple of times between periods with foster-parents and other relatives. Aunty Joan had lived in a small, terraced house in Accrington, which she had originally shared with and then inherited from her mother. The bedrooms had been full of strange old furniture, cavernous wardrobes, the interiors of which smelled like mothballs. When everyone else had long since gone over to duvets, Aunty Joan's spare bed was still made up with starchy white sheets, ton-weight woollen blankets and a shiny, purplish-red quilted counterpane over the top.

Jo would have loved to live permanently with Aunty Joan, who bought cream cakes from the baker's shop to eat after Saturday tea and a block of fruit and nut to share on Sunday evenings, but it had been impossible: Aunty Joan was a shop manageress, who did not get home until six o'clock in the evenings and had to work on Saturdays. That would have made Jo a latch-key kid, and the authorities didn't like that; although Jo could have told them that lots of people managed perfectly well in similar situations, and besides which, there were far worse things for a kid to be.

Mum's other aunt, Beryl, could not have Jo either, because she already had her own daughters, Monica and Verity, in bunk beds and her mother-in-law sleeping in the little back bedroom. So in the end Jo had gone to live with Grandma Molesly, who had taken her out of duty because no one else would or could: and because, as she said to her sisters, what would people think, if you let your granddaughter go into care? Jo had barely kept in touch with the rest of the family since Grandma Molesly died, but now she asked Monica for the funeral arrangements and jotted them down, promising to be there if she could.

'My Aunt Joan has died,' she told Marcus when she came off the phone. He had risen from the table, quietly tidying up in the background, while she talked to Monica. 'Her funeral's on Wednesday. I think I should go.'

'Come and sit down.' Marcus was already moving into the hall. 'I've got your glass. Remind me again how Aunt Joan fits in.'

'Aunt Joan and Aunt Beryl were my grandmother's sisters, so really they're my great-aunts, but because they were a lot younger than my grandmother – not much older than my mum – they seemed more like *my* aunts. Joan was the one who never got married – Monica is one of Beryl's daughters. Beryl was the younger of the two and she's still alive.' She paused for breath.

'OK, Joan and Beryl were actually your mother's aunts – so was the grandmother you went to live with their sister?'

'Yes – that was Grandma Molesly. She was their much older sister.'

'Your mother's mother.'

'If she *was* my mother's mother.'

'What do you mean?'

'I must have told you. She used to say that she didn't think my mother was her daughter at all, and that maybe she had been given the wrong baby in the nursing home. I'm not sure if she said it because she wanted to distance herself from Mum and the way she turned out, or whether she really believed it. But whenever she was really annoyed over something I'd done, she would say, "But then you're not really my granddaughter," because of course if there had been a mix-up and my mother was swapped at birth, then I wouldn't be her blood relative either.'

'That's an awful thing to say to a child.'

'But think what it must have felt like for her, too. All the

177

horror of the murder, those years of embarrassment, having a daughter who wasn't quite right, then having me there like a great cuckoo in the nest, a constant reminder. She was too old to cope with a teenager in the best of circumstances, and those circumstances certainly weren't the best.'

'It's still inexcusable. She shouldn't have taken it out on you – her grandchild.'

'But she wasn't sure if I *was* her grandchild. That's the point. These days she would probably have asked for a DNA test. Anyway, let's not talk about it any more.'

Marcus put on some music and began to tell her how the latest tour had gone. There was no more talk of Grandma Molesly, but when they retired to bed and Marcus had switched out the light, Jo was free to remember her again. Except that she found she could not – her grandmother had become no more than a series of faded snapshots in her mind. Grandma in her chair behind the evening paper, Grandma calling sharply from the kitchen, 'Tea's ready', or 'Wipe your feet'. Grandma with her back to the kitchen, stirring something on the stove. Aunty Joan's face was clearer, her eye shadow an overly bright blue, her lips shiny pink with lipstick and her nails always done in a matching shade; even then the makings of a double chin. If only they had let her stay with Aunty Joan. She wouldn't have ended up at St Catherine's if she had lived with Aunty Joan, whose house in Accrington was served by an entirely different set of schools. She would have been thrown into completely different company and never become involved in baiting Gilda Stafford. In fact, she would never have heard of Gilda until she moved in across the road. With no history between them, the situation in the lane the other day could have been easily resolved.

Not only might her school life have been different, but it

followed that the rest of her life would have been different too. Lots of things might or might not have happened. Just one decision on the part of some case worker or committee – her entire future had hung on that moment and they had gone the wrong way. Or maybe not. Perhaps the path had been set in stone much earlier than that.

She thought about her own mother's childhood. Could you take it back that far? What was it that had made her turn out the way she did? There had never been anything odd about the other members of the family. Beryl's and Joan's lives were steeped in ordinariness. Had Grandma Molesly been right about the nursing home? Perhaps she *had* been given the wrong baby – a child who brought a taint of bad blood into the family. Perhaps the mother of this other child had deliberately exchanged her baby for Grandma Molesly's. Maybe this woman had stood over the cots in the hospital nursery, looking down on the sleeping mite who would one day become Jo's mother, guessed at what was to come and taken her chance on a better outcome, a child forged from a safer set of genes. *Bad blood* – that was what they used to call it, when Grandma Molesly was still a girl. These days people pretended to know better, to embrace more modern ideas about the nature of mental illness, but deep down the old ideas were still strong. 'Like mother, like daughter', that's what people said – not when Grandma Molesly had been a girl, but when she herself had been, barely thirty years ago. Once something really bad happened, no one ever looked at a family in quite the same way. We might pay public lip service to the theories of psychiatrists and their ilk, but our old instinctive senses kick in, once suspicions are aroused.

And even when things did not go so catastrophically wrong as they had in her own mother's case, it did you no good to have eccentric-looking parents. That had been halfway to

179

explaining Gilda's problems. Her parents had been old enough to be her grandparents, and their ideas were rooted in the 1950s and early 1960s. They had dressed her in hand-knitted berets and cardigans, cut her hair clumsily at home, kitted her out in pleated skirts and knee socks when everyone else wore trousers. They encouraged her to keep apart, to despise modern music, to be ignorant of any kind of popular culture to the point where, like an elderly judge or university don, she thought dubbing was something with which to treat football boots, if she thought of it at all.

Jo understood how important it was not to be different: she had battled against it all through childhood, endeavouring to look and behave like everyone else, even in the face of Mum's persistent oddities; trying to keep her mother as invisible as possible at school events, never inviting the other children back home. But some things you can't conceal. The familiar wooden doors loomed ahead of her. The paint was peeling in places, and one of the doors caught at the bottom. It needed to be taken off, sanded down and rehung, but somehow it never got done so it always scraped across the ground when it was opened.

Her mother used to annoy her father by calling it the lean-to. 'You can't call it a garage,' she said, 'because you don't keep a car in it.'

He almost never argued with her, certainly not about household terminology: he just kept on calling it the garage, while she continued to call it the lean-to. Jo trod a narrow line, depending on who she was talking to, trying not to antagonize either of them. It was not that her father would have become annoyed if she had said 'lean-to', in the way that her mother might have done if she had said 'garage'; he might not even have corrected her, but his eyes would have implied betrayal.

In a way, of course, her mother had been right. The car was always parked on the drive, or more often on the remnants of the worn grass verge between the road and the pavement, because it was a nuisance having to squeeze between the car and the line of rose bushes which separated their narrow drive from the small front lawn. The garage itself was too full of other things to fit a car inside. The lawnmower lived in there, standing next to her father's seldom-used workbench, which had forks, spades, a big old crowbar and an axe propped up against it; the washing machine stood against one wall, where it was convenient for the side door which opened directly into their small square kitchen.

Dad's car had been parked on the verge *that* day, when she came home from school. She would have seen it as she walked up the road. She must have known then that there was something wrong because it should not have been there. It was a Thursday, so Dad should have been at work.

She always entered the house through the garage. She didn't have a front-door key, but the garage doors were left unlocked in the daytime. She had never really liked going through the garage. It was always dark in there, and the light switch was right inside, next to the kitchen door, so on a winter afternoon you had to run the gauntlet blindfold. Once, she tripped over a broom handle which had fallen across the part where you walked, coming down hard, scraping her hands and knees on the concrete floor. Even in summer the light which came through the lone pane of glass in the door to the back garden was barely enough to penetrate the shadows. Apart from a narrow space on one side which was left clear to walk through, the interior was a jumble of cardboard boxes, with here a pile of discarded light fittings draped with an old curtain, and there a clumsily reeled stack of garden hose, which tilted crazily atop a broken kitchen chair waiting to startle the unwary by overbalancing and slithering to the floor like an outsize green python. If the kitchen door happened to be open that would let in a bit more light, but otherwise the garage was a place to traverse as quickly as possible, lest some bogey man grabbed at you from out of the gloom.

But not that day – not when she had stood outside the garage door for what must have been the last time. That day it had all happened in slow motion, starting with the age it took her to pluck up enough courage to put her hand on the door. In her mind's eye the garage door stood just ajar. That must have been a warning signal, too. The doors were always kept shut, in case the wind blew them back on their hinges and they slammed. Mum screamed if that happened. Sudden loud noises alarmed her, and she must not be alarmed.

Reach up for the door handle – she had just turned twelve, but she could not have been very tall, not if the handle seemed high up. It was cool to her touch; the sun had gone from the front of the house by late afternoon, leaving the garage doors in shadow.

Pull the door towards you . . . nothing to see at first. It was September, a bright day outside, your eyes have to get accustomed. But then you see. You see his feet first. His feet are nearest to you, and for a split second you think he's lying down to do something, maybe trying to fix the washing machine, which must have broken down again. But it isn't the washing machine. It isn't the washing machine which has leaked all over the floor; it's your father's blood, and there is the axe which spilled it lying on the concrete floor beside his head, showing you how it was done – and although you've never seen a dead body before, you know without a shadow of a doubt that you're looking at one now.

The kitchen door is open a crack, and Mum must be inside.

You have to find Mum. You don't know how this terrible thing has happened in the garage, or why your father came to be lying on the floor with his blood splattered from the pile of old newspapers stacked on the redundant television stand, to the front of the washing machine beside the kitchen door, where it has trickled down in pale, uneven stripes. What you do know is that it is around 4.30 p.m. on a Thursday afternoon, and that means Mum will be somewhere in the house.

So you step around him, very carefully, not touching anything, not treading in anything, almost having to jump over him, in order to reach the kitchen step because he takes up most of the space – much more lying down than he used to standing up. This will be a feature of the coming days: the way until he died Dad took up so little space that people had almost stopped noticing him, whereas Mum, of course, had always managed to be noticeable.

It's so quiet in the kitchen that you can only hear two things: the tick of the clock and a fly, buzzing against the window, frantically bashing against the glass until more by luck than judgement it finds the open top light and is abruptly gone. You don't want to break the silence, so you don't call out. Mum doesn't like it when you shout; although, of course, she doesn't like it if you take her by surprise either, which she calls creeping up on her, even though you didn't mean to.

The door between the kitchen and the hall is half closed, but the door handle has dried blood on it. Hook your fingers around the side of the door and open it that way. Mum isn't in the living room, although there's evidence of her presence, a puzzle book open at an incomplete Word Search, a pencil with a very frayed piece of string tied around one end, a plate on the coffee table containing a half-eaten sandwich and surrounded by toast crumbs from some earlier snack. There's also a mug with some tea left in the bottom. The remaining liquid looks pale against the tannin-stained interior. The door to the front room is open, but there's too much junk in there for anyone to be inside, unless they are hiding – and Mum hasn't done that for ages.

Then you turn the corner and see her sitting on the stairs. She's got the pills and the sherry bottle beside her, but she hasn't managed to kill herself because the stupid, stupid, stupid woman never managed to get anything right.

CHAPTER FOURTEEN

Aunty Joan's funeral took place at the local crematorium. It was a standard one-size-fits-all Church of England service taken by a priest who had never met the deceased, but managed to get all the names right by referring to his notes. The singing of 'The Lord is my Shepherd' was greatly enhanced by the presence of several ladies with whom Aunty Joan had once upon a time sung in a choir, and the coffin went out to the strains of 'Que Sera Sera', which had apparently been her favourite song. There was little obvious emotion: Aunty Beryl was seen to wipe her eyes a couple of times, but the general ambience was one of calm acceptance. Joan had been unwell for some time; it wasn't a shock. There was no grieving partner or children, and everyone said it was a blessing that she hadn't suffered.

Jo had approached the occasion with some trepidation, but the cluster of black-clad figures, standing on the pavement outside cousin Monica's house (chosen for its convenient proximity to both Aunt Joan's sheltered-housing complex and the crem), had greeted her warmly, Aunt Beryl enveloping her in a warm hug and Monica planting a kiss on her cheek before saying that they had saved her a place in one of the funeral limousines.

During her journey south down the motorway, Jo had built herself up to expect a much cooler reception. Was she not the daughter of the evil changeling who had brought so much shame and distress to the family all those years ago? Of course, if Grandma Molesly had been right, then she was not really their relative at all. She didn't look much like them, although family resemblances between cousins were not always strong. And if she was not of their blood, then neither was Lauren. She wondered if her mother had been aware of the doubts cast upon her parentage when she was growing up. Lauren too must be growing up in alien soil. Jo had generally taken the repeated message *I still have her* as a taunt, but just occasionally she wondered whether the abductor's motive in sending it was a misguided attempt at reassurance, letting her know that her daughter was still alive and well and safe. The seashells might simply be more of the same, a secret code meant only for her – except that she could not decipher it.

It was possible that Lauren never even suspected she did not belong with these people. Suppose she was happy where she was, and did not want to leave. The idea of Lauren loving her captors more than herself was heartbreaking. In her oft-replayed vision of Lauren's eventual homecoming, the scene always ended with the child running into her arms, but lately this version of events was sometimes rudely interrupted by another, in which a girl who looked very much like Gilda's daughter shied away from her, as from a stranger. So many years had gone by. Lauren would recall nothing now of the monkey mobile which once hung above her cot, the musical box with the dancing bears, the home-baked biscuits in the kitchen . . . and her mother's face.

Suppose she *was* better off with this other family. At least with them, she would never have to know about the mad grandmother, the tainted blood she carried in her veins. Were there circumstances in which it would be to Lauren's advantage, if she – Jo – were to give her up? Although not religious, Jo had prayed many times after Lauren disappeared. Sometimes she had promised God that providing He made sure no harm came to Lauren, He could if He wished take Jo instead, by whatever terrible means He chose to devise. In the long silences which followed, Jo had been forced to conclude that God was not up for trade-offs. What was it she had once read? *God always answers prayers, but sometimes the answer is no*.

Maybe this was the deal. She would have to give Lauren up in exchange for the knowledge that she was safe and happy. Lauren might very well benefit, said the treacherous devil's advocate in her head, from not growing up in the shadow of her dubious genetic inheritance.

'No!' Jo startled herself by speaking aloud. How could any child-stealer be a better parent than she was? How could anyone who would kidnap a child possibly be suitable to raise one? A person capable of such a dreadful act must be unbalanced, dangerous. She noticed that she was getting too near to the car in front, eased back a little and tried to concentrate on the road.

'It's always better for a child to be with its own mother,' she said as she steered the car into the centre lane, to overtake a slow-moving motorhome.

'Always?' asked the devil's advocate, slyly tossing snapshots of her own mother on to the table like a louche poker dealer.

And now she was in Accrington, back in the bosom of what was left of her mother's family. She could not recognize any of Aunt Beryl's grandchildren, all of them in their late teens and early twenties, who raided the buffet table in Monica's dining room then stuck together in a corner, the boys with their borrowed black ties loosened, the girls – who must surely have compared wardrobe notes beforehand –

187

pretty much uniform, right down to their carefully applied eyeliner.

'We haven't seen you for ages,' Monica was saying. 'You and your husband run a travel agency now, don't you?'

'A tour company,' Jo corrected. 'We run specialist coach tours, themed to famous people and historical events.'

'That must be interesting. Do you get to go on these tours yourself?'

I used to, Jo thought sadly. Aloud she said, 'I'm one of the guides.'

'That must be great. Do you hear that, Mum? Joanne gets to travel round on these tours they run. Mind, I don't suppose it's much of a holiday for you,'

Jo confirmed that it was not.

'Excuse me,' Monica said. 'I think the choir ladies are on their way. I must just say goodbye and thank them for coming.'

Jo found herself temporarily alone with Beryl. An adjacent armchair had just become vacant, and Jo sank down beside her aunt. It was now or never.

'Aunty Beryl, you remember what Grandma Molesly used to say, about Mum not really being her daughter?'

Her aunt did not appear to be taken aback by Jo's abrupt enquiry. 'Of course I do – she said it often enough.' There was something comforting about Beryl's no-nonsense, Lancashire voice, with its matter-of-fact conveyance of information.

'Do you think she really believed it?'

Beryl pursed her lips in momentary consideration. It made the wrinkles around her mouth more pronounced. 'Do you know, in the end I think she did. It started off as a bit of a joke, because your mother had these hazel eyes – well, not hazel exactly – more of a flecky grey really, although your grandmother always had it that they were hazel. Anyway, there was no one else in the family with eyes quite like them. Mind you, we never knew much about Dad's family, with him coming from such a long way off. There were a lot of his side we never met at all, and he was dead by the time your mother was born, so we never got to hear his opinion. Then, of course, me and your Aunty Joan were blondes whereas your mother's hair was a browny colour, and she was always skinny whereas we were on the plump side even as little 'uns.' She paused to glance down at her ample bosom, before continuing: 'Your grandma would look at your mother and say she wasn't one of us at all, you know, joking like. I'm sure that's how it started, but later on, after your mother began having her problems, well, your grandmother couldn't seem to understand that it was an illness – that it might happen to anybody. Perhaps she worried that people would blame her – I blame those doctors myself – saying these things are all to do with what happened to people in their childhoods. We went all through the war as children, and it didn't do us any harm. Anyway, after . . . it happened, I think your grandmother just wanted to believe it was as she had said all along – that your mother wasn't really hers. I used to get annoyed with her. "How can you deny your own flesh and blood?" I'd say, but your grandma was a hard woman, God rest her – and once she'd made her mind up, there was no shifting her.'

'I think I can understand where she was coming from – at least, a little bit,' Jo said. 'Everyone always drums it into you that you have to love your family, even when they're not doing very lovable things. Children are supposed to love their parents, and parents are supposed to love their children, but suppose you just can't? When I was little, I sometimes used to wish I could have someone different for my mother,

189

someone who was more like the other mothers, I suppose. But then I used to feel that even thinking something like that was very wicked and that I must be a very bad person. Other times, I used to just wonder why it was so unfair – you know, what had I done to deserve a mother who was so different from all the others?'

'In your case, pet, it wasn't a wicked thought, it was an understandable one.'

The kindness in Beryl's voice encouraged Jo to go much further than she would normally have done. 'After she killed my dad, I really began to hate her. I felt bad about it sometimes, but how are you supposed to go on loving one parent when they have murdered the other parent?'

Beryl brought her bent fingers down to rest on top of Jo's slim ones. The sympathetic pressure stimulated Jo to continue. 'I was thinking about it the other night. I mean, how can anyone expect a child to get over that? Walking into the garage one day after school, and finding your father dead on the floor?'

'But luvvie, you didn't find him.' For the first time in their conversation, Beryl registered surprise. 'It was a neighbour what found him.'

'It was me. I came home from school and found him on the garage floor.'

'No, love. I know for sure that isn't right, because it was me and your Uncle Geoff who came to fetch you out of school.'

'I thought that was the other time – when I was very little and I waited and waited outside the school, because Mum had been taken to hospital after she cut her wrists.'

'We came that time as well. No, it was definitely a neighbour, a man who lived a few doors down, who found your father. This chap hadn't gone to work that day because

190

he couldn't get his car to start and he was standing outside his house, waiting for the AA to turn up, when he heard a commotion – shouting and screaming and what not. He thought there must be something up, so he went to your house and knocked the front door. When no one answered, he noticed the garage door was ajar, so he opened it. I think he just meant to shout through and ask if everything was all right, but of course as soon as he opened that door he saw your father.'

'What happened then?'

'Well, so far as I remember – we had to sit through it all at the inquest, of course – this neighbour, Radcliffe or Ratcliffe his name was, he ran back home and phoned the police.'

'And what about Mum?'

'She was in the house the whole time. I think the police must have found her. She'd taken some tablets, but they got her to the hospital in time and pumped her stomach.'

'So I wasn't there at all?'

'No – and to my knowledge you never went back there. We went and got all your things, your Aunty Joan and I, once the police would let us in to take stuff.'

'I thought I found him. That's how I've remembered it for years and years.'

'You must have heard people talking about it.' Aunt Beryl did not appear to think there was anything extraordinary in writing yourself into scenes in which you had taken no part. 'Folk will talk in front of children, even when they shouldn't. And your Grandma Molesly would have been no help. I wanted to take you in myself, but we didn't have the room, with Geoff's mother needing nursing and us in that little house in Longfellow Road. Your Aunty Joan would have had you, but they wouldn't let her, her being a maiden lady and having to be out at work full-time.'

Monica rejoined them. 'Have you had much rain up in the Lakes?' she asked. 'It always seems to rain when we go up there.'

'The weather hasn't been very good so far this year,' Jo said, but while she indulged in inconsequential chit-chat with Monica, her mind was already racing elsewhere.

False Memory Syndrome. Construction. Confabulation. She found them all on Google when she got home.

False Memory Syndrome: a condition in which a person's identity and interpersonal relationships are centred on a memory of a traumatic experience which is objectively false, but which the person strongly believes to be true.

Construction: when an event is mistakenly recalled which only accords with the gist of what happened, because a person has acquired memories from a combination of internally and externally derived sources, subconsciously adapting or adding to the story, to make it more consistent.

Confabulation: the spontaneous narrative reporting of events that never happened. A falsification of memory occurring from organically derived amnesia.

None of the definitions seemed to be an exact fit, although all of them were close. At first she had wondered if her aunt was the one who had got it all wrong, because her own memory had always seemed so solid – but the more she went over it, the more sense Beryl's version seemed to make. Beryl placed the episode in the morning, which was far more logical because that would mean the attack had taken place between her leaving for school and her father leaving for work a few minutes later; so that unlike her own version, there was no mystery about her father's being unexpectedly home in the afternoon. Then there was what she now recognized as the dreamlike quality of her memory; the way she had hopped – almost flown – over her father's body to

192

gain entry to the kitchen. Would she really have gone into the house without a word or a second thought? Wouldn't she have shouted, or screamed, or run for help, instinctively shying away from such a horrible sight, rather than skipping over it? In her version she approached the garage doors with trepidation, as if in her heart of hearts she already knew what she was about to find. Similarly, during the search for her mother and her eventual discovery on the stairs, she was like a cold, dispassionate onlooker, not a hysterical child who has just seen her father's butchered body. Moreover, she had no recollection of phoning the police or fetching a neighbour, which was strange when the rest of it had always seemed so crystal-clear. The memory finished with her standing over her mother, as if it was the final frame at the end of a reel of film and, try as she might, she could not locate the next reel.

No. She was as confident as she could be that Aunty Beryl's version was the right one. Although her own memory of the event still seemed as solid as ever, she knew that it was not real. Not, she told herself, that there was anything abnormal about the tricks her mind had played. The information about False Memory Syndrome and Confabulation might be full of references to psychologists, but it was clear that you did not have to be ill to fabricate a few memories. Perfectly normal people did it all the time. One control group after another, asked to relate a story they had been told a short time before, invariably adapted it with omissions and embellishments. There was even something called the 'Lost in the Mall' technique, in which a group of adult volunteers were told a purportedly true story by another family member, of their being lost in a shopping mall at the age of five or six years old. At least a quarter of the people fed this story not only claimed to be able to remember this entirely fictional event, but many provided additional details which they had not been told in the first place. Everyone – or at least a high proportion of people – was suggestible.

Yet at the same time it was frightening. How many of her accumulated memories were real, and how many fantasy? If you could not rely on one memory, what did it say about all the others? It was like going into an exam on your life, but discovering on the way in that you had been revising from the wrong textbook.

CHAPTER FIFTEEN

Another postcard arrived in June. After weeks of dull, chilly weather punctuated by regular downpours, the 'barbecue summer' predicted by the Met Office had finally arrived with a vengeance. Jo was taking advantage of the unaccustomed sunshine to cut the grass and drag some weeds out of the flower beds, so she happened to be in the garden when the postman arrived. She saw the van draw up in the gateway and went to meet him.

'Another nice day,' he said, as he handed her the little pile of letters.

She carried them over to the wooden bench beside the sundial, which had been her gift to Marcus on his fortieth birthday. The postcard was the second item down the pile, a standard plain white card with the address printed directly onto it in Times New Roman, and Jo recognized it immediately for what it was. The postman's demeanour on handing it over had not conveyed the slightest suggestion that he was aware of bringing anything out of the ordinary, but then she assumed that he did not understand the significance of the card or notice anything exceptional about it. She turned it over, expecting to find the same old picture of Lauren printed on the other side – and so it was – but this time it was not the same old words. Jo stood up without realizing that she had done so, then sat down hard again on the garden bench, staring at the card in disbelief. For almost eleven years she had been reading the words *I still have her.* This time the statement had been replaced with a question. *Do you still want her?*

She continued to stare at the card for a long time. The taunt of a cruel hoaxer? Or was this something else? Of course she still wanted Lauren, of course she did! But how was she supposed to reply?

In the past, she had always taken the cards straight to the police, but not this time, she thought. It was not as if they had ever managed to obtain a single clue from any of the cards – and anyway, this one was special. The message marked a new turn in her relationship with Lauren's captors, the words potent with the suggestion that things were moving forward, that something was going to happen. She was being asked a question, and there had to be some way of responding, but in the meantime she would tell no one about the card.

She stood up again, steadying herself with a hand on the sundial. What about Marcus? She knew that deceiving him was wrong, but if she told him about the card, he might insist she hand it over to the police. He was not due home for hours, but all the same she took the card straight upstairs and hid it in the drawer where she kept the shells. Didn't this latest development vindicate her faith in the shells, which she had always interpreted as the precursor to something else? Moreover, when she opened the drawer and saw the shells sitting inside, she was suddenly seized with a solution. She could not send a message using shells, but the garden was full of stones, and they would make a perfectly good substitute. After positioning the postcard so that Lauren's picture would look up at her whenever she opened the drawer, Jo went down to the garden and began to gather stones, which she spread across the newly cut lawn, sorting them into different sizes, shapes and colours as she went.

She gradually realized that it would take a lot more stones

than she had initially envisaged. As the day wore on her collection extended to include everything from modestly sized pebbles to large lumps of brick and slate. Once or twice she made a foray out into the lane, so that she could look back into the garden and view her handiwork work from a distance. Neither the heat nor the fact that she had skipped lunch distracted her from her objective. When Sean came home from school she was still working with a kind of frantic energy, filling in the gaps with smaller stones, adding and removing others in a bid to neaten the edges and make the letters clearer.

She had seen him coming up the lane and called across from the lawn: 'Sean – can you see what it says?'

Sean was sufficiently nonplussed that for a moment he couldn't say anything at all. Eventually, he said, 'It says "YES".'

He continued to stand out in the road for a moment or two, as if waiting for permission to move on, but when Jo said nothing further, he turned in at the gate and walked up the drive. As he drew level with her, Jo smiled at him. 'It's a modern sculpture, giving a positive message,' she said.

'OK.' Sean's tone mimicked the asylum keeper, humouring an inmate who has just hoisted a chair above his head. 'Whatever.' He continued on his way into the house.

The modern sculpture explanation was less readily acceptable to Marcus. It was dark when he got back from the hospital visit he had tacked on to the end of Tennyson Trails, but he saw the stones next morning, when he strolled into the garden with his mug of coffee after breakfast.

'Has Sean done that?' he asked Jo, who had followed him outside.

'Of course not. Since when did Sean do anything to help in the garden? It was me.'

'You?'

'Me.'

Marcus approached the newly arrived message on his lawn with caution, as if he thought it might conceal a basking adder or two. 'What's it for?'

'It's a modern sculpture. A positive, life-affirming message.'

Marcus circled the stones, perhaps thinking that all would become clearer if he viewed them the right way up. 'Is this something out of a self-help book?'

'No. You know I don't read self-help books – and there's no need to be sarcastic.'

'I wasn't. Just exactly what are you saying yes to?'

'To life . . . the universe. Everything. I'm being positive, looking forward, as you have consistently told me I should.'

'Don't you think people will find it a little bit strange? I mean, did you have to put it right here, facing the lane? Couldn't you have it round at the back where you can still see it, but every passing car can't?'

'It wouldn't work there.'

'Why not?'

She had not anticipated this line of questioning. Sensing her hesitation, Marcus repeated the question, but Jo could only mumble that the sculpture had to be just where it was, facing into the lane.

'Are you planning any other sculptures on the lawn, because I really think we ought to discuss it first. You wouldn't be too pleased if I popped down to the garden centre, came back with a concrete Venus de Milo and stuck it right in front of the house, now would you?'

'There won't be anything else. This was just spontaneous – positive. I thought you'd approve.'

'Well I don't. I don't like the idea of people goggling over the wall into our garden. Next thing you know, some joker will join in with a message of their own and you'll wake up to find graffiti sprayed on to a tree, or some tacky home-made banner tied on the gates.'

'That's ridiculous,' Jo said, although she knew that it probably wasn't because there were some people who looked on the Lakes as a great big holiday camp, where stag and hen parties could wander around in fancy dress doing all kinds of stupid things – although that sort of crowd seldom found their way out as far as places like Easter Bridge.

'Can I suggest you move it, darling? I'm totally on board with the spirit of the thing; being positive, embracing all life has to offer and that sort of stuff, but I'm sure you can express it in other ways – and if it has to be a sculpture, then please let's put it somewhere a little less prominent.'

'No. I can't move it. It took me all day.'

'Perhaps I could help you.' Marcus was employing his painfully patient voice. 'If we moved the letters one at a time, I'm sure it would be far –'

'No! It has to be here. It won't work otherwise. There's no point having it round the back.'

'Jo – what is going on? This isn't a sculpture, is it? This is a message.' When she would not meet his eye he continued: 'Is this anything to do with that woman at The Old Forge? You've had a thing about her ever since she moved in.'

'No, it's not her.' She hesitated. If she couldn't trust Marcus, who could she trust? Reluctantly she said, 'Wait here and I'll show you something.'

Marcus waited for her in the garden, standing well away from the disputed word. He took another sip of coffee and noticed that it was getting cold. When he saw her returning with a postcard in her hand, his heart sank.

'You see,' she said, thrusting it at him. 'It's a new message. I have to answer it.'

'How can you possibly do that? You don't know who is sending these things, or where they come from.'

'The person who sent this is the same person who left the shells in the garden. It's someone who knows exactly where we are – someone who comes to look at the house.'

In spite of himself, Marcus had to suppress a shudder at the thought of someone watching them. He took the postcard and read it, before turning it over several times, scrutinizing it front and back.

'How long have you had this? Why didn't you take it to the police?'

'What's the point? They always say there isn't anything they can do.'

'There's no postmark.'

'So? It must have missed the franking machine.'

'How did it get here?'

'The postman delivered it. He handed it to me with the other letters. I was out here when he came.'

'OK.' Marcus was silent, remembering the voice of that rather noxious young policeman. *Has it ever occurred to you that your wife might be sending the cards to herself?* Aloud he said, 'Why didn't you tell me about the card?'

'I was going to.'

'No, you weren't. You only told me when I threatened to remove your so-called sculpture.'

When Jo said nothing, he balanced his half-empty cup on the arm of the garden bench, before placing his hands one on each of her shoulders. 'We'll leave the stones where they are, for now – but only on condition that you get some help. I want you to have some counselling, at the very least.'

'No.' She ducked away, stepping back to be out of his reach. 'I don't need that sort of help. I'm not mad, Marcus. I'm not my mother.'

'I never said you were, but—'

'No, no, no!' She put her hands over her ears and turned away. 'I'm not going down that road, and you can't make me.'

He tried to approach her again, arms outstretched, expression conciliatory, but she ran into the house, collapsing into the chair nearest the sitting-room door. To her relief, he did not follow her. For one awful moment she thought he might have set about dismantling her stones there and then, but when she slipped across to look out of the window she saw that he was sitting on the garden bench with his back to the house. It had been a mistake, she thought, to show him the postcard. What had an old boss of hers been fond of asking people? 'Are you part of the problem, or part of the solution?' Where he had once bolstered her confidence, Marcus now undermined her: he had deprived her of meaningful activity and left her stranded. You can be lost so easily, once you don't know who you are, or where you are going. 'And what about you?' asked the devil who rode on her shoulder. 'Are you part of the solution?' 'I can be . . . I won't sink under it all . . . I will survive.'

She went out to find Marcus in the garden.

'I was thinking perhaps we could all go out somewhere,' she said. 'The three of us. Take advantage of the day. Have a walk round Tarn Hows, then maybe have lunch at The Outgate. We haven't done anything like that for ages.' She did not particularly relish the prospect of a day spent playing Happy Families with Sean, but if this was what it took to get Marcus's mind away from moving the stones, then she was prepared to muster a smile and feign enthusiasm.

Marcus agreed with surprising alacrity. He went straight upstairs to rouse Sean, and although it was evident from the snatches of conversation which filtered down the stairs that

Sean, who thought walking anywhere 'a waste of time', was not greatly enamoured of the plan, by eleven o'clock the three of them were climbing into the car in readiness for their outing. As they drove past The Old Forge, Gilda Iceton was also getting into her car. Marcus raised a hand in acknowledgement, but Gilda gave no indication that she had observed the gesture, and a moment later they had rounded the bend and were out of sight.

Jo was driving, and before long she began to catch sight of Gilda's car, travelling at a discreet distance behind them. The hairs began to rise on the back of her neck. Was Gilda following them on purpose, or did she just coincidentally happen to be going the same way? Each time they turned off towards Hawkshead, then Coniston, when the road straightened out Gilda's car duly appeared in the mirror. As soon as they got out of the car at Tarn Hows, she saw Gilda's blue Volvo nosing around the car park, looking for a space to park among the trees.

'Don't look now,' she hissed at Marcus, 'but Gilda – the woman from The Old Forge – has followed us.'

A shadow of anxiety swept over Marcus's expression. 'It's probably just someone with a similar car,' he said. 'It's dry underfoot and there's a made path all the way round, so it won't be muddy. I'm not going to bother with boots. What about you, Sean?'

'Whatever.' Sean lolled against the rear passenger door for all the world as if standing upright was too much effort, let alone walking round the tarn.

'It *is* her,' Jo said in a low, urgent voice. 'Look, she's just getting out of her car.'

'For heaven's sake, so what? It's a beautiful day. The woman's decided to go for a walk.'

'I think she's following us.'

'*I* think you're being silly. You see? She's getting a pair of walking boots out of the car. If she had been following us, how could she have anticipated where we were going and known to bring her boots?'

'Maybe she leaves them in the car, the same as we often do.'

'Really, Jo, this is like having a conversation with an eight-year-old. Let's go, shall we?'

Jo was already fervently wishing that she had chosen somewhere other than Tarn Hows, which happened to be the first place that had come into her head. During the season its tranquillity was marred by a rash of picnics, metal folding chairs, giant cool boxes and the inevitable family who cannot see an expanse of grass without feeling the need to hoof a football across it – all of which she knew Marcus would hate. The place was at its best in the winter, when the trees were reflected in the water as faithfully as a photograph and everywhere was silent and still. On days like that you might glimpse a red squirrel in the trees, or hear the mew of a buzzard: today it would be noisy families with double buggies all the way round.

In fact, Marcus had been happy enough to accept the choice of venue, but now they were here he found that all his efforts to lighten the mood fell on stony ground. Attempts at conversation foundered because Sean – who had not really wanted to accompany them at all – was particularly monosyllabic, while Jo became increasingly distracted, continually looking over her shoulder to keep an eye on the woman from across the road. Inwardly Marcus cursed his neighbour for choosing this particular place and time, because while she clearly wasn't following them, and indeed showed not the slightest awareness of them, Jo in her present state was capable of imagining anything. ('Why would she want to follow us?' Marcus asked at one point. 'To make me feel uncomfortable, of course,' his wife retorted, as if it should have been obvious.) Unfortunately the woman appeared to walk at the same pace as they did, so she neither overtook them nor ever dropped too far behind. Lunch at The Outgate was not a success either. By then Marcus had run out of pleasantries with which he hoped to start a conversation, so they awaited their food in silence. At least there was no question of anyone following them there, but he could tell that Jo would not be dissuaded from the reality of the morning's pursuit.

Unbeknown to his wife, he too had recently been to see Dr Hillier, but it was a complicated situation. Patient confidentiality precluded them from having any real discussion about Jo, who until officially declared otherwise was deemed competent to make her own decisions. Thus, Dr Hillier had explained, it was entirely her choice whether or not she consulted a doctor. The best he could advise was that Marcus continue in his attempts to persuade her to make another appointment. 'If she is happy for you to come along with her, so much the better. And of course, if she is exhibiting signs which give you real cause for concern, you can always call the out-of-hours service.'

'What sort of signs?'

'Well, I think it would be fairly obvious. If she claims to hear voices, for example, or starts talking to people you cannot see, or behaving violently towards other people or self-harming.'

'It's not like that,' Marcus said. 'She doesn't – I mean, she isn't crazy, but she does need help.'

'Crazy isn't a word we really use.'

'No – of course not.'

Their conversation had ended soon afterwards, leaving Marcus feeling, if anything, more perturbed than before.

CHAPTER SIXTEEN

The 'barbecue summer' was short-lived. Within a fortnight the rain had returned and Jo reverted back to jeans and long sleeves again. *Lucky you*, she typed, in response to Nerys's latest message saying how wonderful the weather was (she had now reached California), *it has rained here every single day this week*. She told Nerys about the film she and Marcus had been to see at the cinema, and their overnight trip to Alton Towers with Sean, where she had won brownie points by accompanying him on the scarier rides eschewed by Marcus. She made the whole thing sound so upbeat that Nerys wrote in reply: *I said you would win him over in the end*.

In the meantime, Jo watched and waited anxiously for a response to her message on the lawn. Her hopes were raised one morning at the sight of a small hooded figure in waterproofs, hurrying up the drive with an envelope in its hand, but it was only Maisie Perry coming to drop off an invitation for her garden party, an event to be held the following Saturday in aid of Marie Curie Nurses, complete with strawberries-and-cream teas, the obligatory raffle and plants for sale. The missive ended on the rather down-to-earth note: 'to be held indoors if wet'.

Jo did not want to attend Maisie's fund-raiser, whether it was inside or out. All the permanent residents were sure to have been invited, which obviously included Brian, to whom she had made such a fool of herself, and Shelley, whose Pre-Raphaelite reference books she had yet to return, having steered clear of the gallery since her overly emphatic rejection of Brian's art classes. Then there was Gilda, with whom she had had no direct contact since the episode in the lane. She had seen Gilda a few times from a distance, once narrowly avoiding her by taking evasive action, when Gilda happened to be walking up from the bridge. Jo had ducked into the house and waited for the other woman to pass, covertly observing Gilda as she went by, singing to herself and carrying what appeared to be a bunch of weeds, which Jo presumed to be of artistic or botanical interest.

Marcus had accused her of being obsessed with Gilda, but that was a gross exaggeration. Had she really mentioned Gilda to Marcus all that often? Surely not. It was true that there was still a small part of her which wondered whether Gilda could be behind the shells and the postcards: she had even ruminated on the possibility that Gilda's daughter was Lauren, but a more realistic, sensible voice told her that was fantastical. Apart from anything else, the girl was too old to be Lauren. Thirteen or fourteen, Maisie Perry said, and you could count on Maisie to have all the gen. Gilda's outside light had been on, the night of the third shell's appearance, but outside lights got left on all the time, and surely a guilty person would have made sure that it was off, rather than drawing attention to themselves. Even her certainty that Gilda had been following them round Tarn Hows that day now seemed ridiculous. Marcus had insisted all along that it was no more than a coincidence. She stopped short of speculating that Gilda's regular forays into the wood might be undertaken in order to spy on the occupants of The Hideaway. Plenty of people used the footpath to explore the woods, and there was no reason why Gilda should not go there to watch birds, gather wild grasses, or whatever else it was that took her fancy.

If only Gilda had given her a chance to explain about what had happened in the lane that morning. Not that explanations were particularly easy. Would a third party be able to understand how, after Lauren's disappearance, she had constructed something akin to a steel shutter in her mind – brought down a barrier to avoid confronting her darkest imaginings – those ideas which were just too much to bear? Or, that although the barrier worked well inasmuch that she could never be sure what her thoughts were getting up to behind it, at the same time it seemed to be mounted on a freewheeling roller mechanism which did not have a brake, so that unless she was vigilant it was liable to slide up an inch or two when she wasn't looking – which was when the dangerous ideas slipped out and the trouble began?

Jo considered making an excuse for non-attendance at the garden party, but a convincing invention which would have sufficed for just about anyone else simply would not do when it came to Maisie. The actual subterfuge of absenting one's self from Easter Bridge for the afternoon would probably be required, which was a lot of effort when all she really needed to do was avoid being there at the same time as Brian, Shelley or Gilda. She reasoned that if she simply managed to be there at a different time, it would appear as if she had accidentally missed them, rather than deliberately avoided them – and if an event was running from 2.30 p.m. until 5 p.m., wouldn't most people opt for the middle ground and not come until at least 3 p.m., so that if she turned up at 2.30 p.m. on the dot and made an excuse about not being able to stay long, she ought to be able to make her getaway before the others got there?

Jo was surprised when she arrived outside the Perrys'

bungalow at 2.30 p.m. and found two cars already parked on the drive and Fred directing a third, windmilling his arms in the fashion beloved of elderly men who imagine that women need a dumb show from an experienced male driver in order to park a car.

The weather had necessitated holding the gathering indoors, but in spite of this, two hardy souls were padding round the garden exclaiming over the Perrys' roses, while tilting a golf umbrella against the periodic drifts of rain. For her own part, Jo willingly accepted Fred's exhortation to 'go straight in' without making any pretence of interest in horticulture.

The Perrys had pushed their furniture back and placed as many chairs as they could fit around the sides of the room. There were only three people seated inside: a couple who had positioned themselves near the fireplace, and Gilda Iceton, who was sitting alone at the opposite end of the room. Gilda's appearance was very much that of the woman one does not readily sit next to. Her hair was drawn back into an elastic band, and she was wearing a shapeless pale blue sweatshirt which had the shadow of an old stain on the front. Her brown trousers appeared to have been designed for someone shorter and exposed wide expanses of pale unshaven leg, which vanished none too soon into ankle socks and bus-conductress shoes.

As Jo stood hesitating in the doorway Maisie breezed in from the kitchen, bearing a tray of tea. 'Jo, lovely to see you. Why don't you sit here, next to Gilda, as you already know each other?'

With no obvious means of escape, Jo took the chair Maisie had indicated. It was one of a quartet of dining chairs which had been pushed so close together that only her denim jeans and Gilda's polyester trousers separated their flesh. When Jo shifted to one side, Gilda's thighs merely seemed to overflow further on to her chair.

The trio of ladies whose car had been the subject of Fred's needless arm-waving bobbed in out of the rain, so Maisie made some introductions – the three ladies were friends from the WI, while the couple by the fireplace were fellow members of the Lakeland Horticultural Society. 'And this is Gilda,' Maisie was saying, 'our newest resident in Easter Bridge, who has very kindly said we can use her yard for overflow car-parking if we need it. Excuse me while I go and get some tea.'

Jo said hopefully, 'Can I come and help you carry things through, Maisie?'

'No, no. There's only room for one at a time in my little kitchen. You stay here and get to know our new neighbour a bit better.'

Jo reddened. She had been caught off guard by the presence of Gilda, and could not bring herself to look at the woman, let alone initiate a conversation with her. After Maisie had futtered out there was an awkward silence, while everyone else waited for Jo to say something. It was eventually broken by one of the WI ladies, who addressed Gilda: 'So, you're a newcomer to the Easter Bridge. Where were you living before you moved here?'

'I spent the past few years in Essex, but I've moved about a lot.'

'And what brought you to Cumbria?' Another of the ladies helped the interrogation along.

'I wanted to move nearer to my daughter's school. She's a boarder at St Aelfric's.'

'How old is your daughter?' asked the first WI lady.

'She was twelve in April.'

Jo swivelled round to stare at the woman beside her.

Maisie had told her that Gilda's daughter was thirteen or fourteen.

'The same age as your daughter would have been.' Gilda turned to look her full in the face. 'There was only a couple of months difference between them.'

Jo winced as if she had been slapped. Maisie chose that moment to reappear, evidently having only half heard what had been said. 'Oh, no – Jo hasn't got a daughter,' she put in, clearly thinking to correct a newcomer's minor gaffe. 'Just a stepson, Sean.'

'I'm sorry, I thought everyone would have known . . .' Gilda left the words hanging in the air, pregnant with the implication that there was more to be said.

Jo stood up so suddenly that she almost upset a nearby pot plant. 'I'm sorry, Maisie, but I have to go. Here –' she fumbled in her purse and withdrew a five pound note '– please put this in the kitty.'

'Jo, dear . . .' Maisie was caught on the hop, encumbered with another laden tray.

As Jo all but ran down the hall she could hear Gilda saying, 'I'm so sorry, I assumed that everyone knew.' Outside, she ignored the curious glances of the people in the garden and Fred's attempt to speak to her, not pausing until she had crashed in through her own front door. She knew she had made a dreadful fool of herself in taking flight. Gilda would have told them by now. Maisie Perry would know that she was the Joanne Ashton whose child had disappeared and whose husband had jumped off a cliff – and Maisie knowing was as good as taking out a full-page advertisement in the *Evening News*. You might as well hire a megaphone and tour the district.

She saw the car keys lying on the hall table and grabbed them, glimpsing Sean's surprised face coming downstairs just as she headed back out of the door. 'I won't be long,' she shouted, although she had no idea whether he heard her or not. Worse and worse, she thought as she climbed into the car, Gilda knew about her mother. Everyone from her schooldays knew about it, but by the time of Lauren's disappearance she had been living in a different part of the country and had acquired a new name: it had been almost a decade since the death of her father briefly made the headlines, so no one had made the connection. She had been extremely lucky in that although a lot of people from her past must have recognized her in the papers and on TV, none of them had gone to the press. What happened in 1998 had been bad enough – the thinly veiled suggestions that she had made away with Lauren herself. If the wider public had known about her mother . . .

A car came at her as she rounded the bend below the bridge, forcing her to swerve into the side of the road, only narrowly avoiding a collision. Thank goodness there happened to be a verge just here, rather than a solid stone wall. The near miss shook her, because although the other driver had been travelling too fast, she knew that she had not been concentrating. As she steered the car back on to the road, she had to grip the wheel harder to stop her hands from shaking.

Gilda would tell them everything – she would take a malicious pleasure in it. *Oh, I'm sorry . . . I thought everyone knew.*

Well, they did now.

She had managed to create a wide gulf between herself and her childhood, but Gilda would span the gap in the space of a few short minutes. If only Marcus could be persuaded to move away, start again somewhere; but then there was the postcard, the shells, Lauren . . . She had answered 'yes' to the card, and it was only a question of sticking it out until the next message came.

She realized that she was driving without any purpose. When she reached the main road, she turned east towards Newby Bridge. The A590 was busy with holiday traffic – Saturday was changeover day. She felt sorry for these newcomers, trying to put a brave face on it as they switched on their wipers and scanned the sky above the estuary, hoping in vain to spot a break in the clouds.

This time next week the school holidays would have begun. Sean would be at home all day, every day, lying in bed or closeted in his room with his computer games. Of course Harry would probably be around – his family generally came up in the school holidays – and then it occurred to her that Gilda's daughter would be back too.

Was it really so outrageous – the idea that Gilda might have abducted Lauren?

'Stop it,' she said aloud. She knew it was her own voice, but it could have been Marcus, travelling alongside her like an extra conscience. She could almost hear him talking about doctors again – or maybe actually talking *to* a doctor. 'My wife has developed an obsession with a woman who lives nearby. There's a history of animosity between them, and my wife has become convinced not only that this woman is watching and following her, but even that the woman has her missing daughter.'

She drove in the direction of Bowness, but that was a mistake. The roads around Windermere crawled with holiday traffic, and there were no free parking spaces to be had. The mountain tops were hidden by low cloud. Everywhere you looked there were figures shuffling along in damp cagoules, probably wishing they were somewhere else. Café windows were misted by a combination of hot drinks and tourists'

212

breath, while the colourful window boxes outside bed-and-breakfasts drooped in the rain. From Windermere she drove to Ambleside, and from Ambleside back to Grizedale. The pointlessness of the excursion made her slam her hands on the steering wheel in frustration. What was the point of running away, and where did she imagine she was running to? No doubt Sean would be reporting her abrupt departure to Marcus when he arrived home, and then Marcus would want to know where she had been. She would either have to invent some lame-sounding excuse, or else admit that she had been upset, both courses leading inexorably to another episode being filed under 'irrational behaviour'.

The car clock reminded her that it was after 4.30 p.m., which meant that Marcus should be home fairly soon. He was calling in to see his mother, but that didn't usually delay him too much. She half expected to find his car on the drive when she reached the house, but it was not there, and when she got inside, her eye was immediately caught by the blinking light on the answering machine. She pressed the button and waited while the nasal voice of the machine informed her, 'You have one new message. Message one.' The voice turned into Marcus: 'I'm calling to say I won't be coming home tonight. My mother's taken a turn for the worse, so I'm staying here with Sandra.'

She tried to call him on his mobile but it was switched off.

'Sean,' she shouted up the stairs. 'Didn't you hear the phone earlier?'

'Yeah. The machine got it.'

'Why didn't you take it?'

'It's never for me – and the machine has always cut in by the time I get there, anyway.'

Jo let out a small scream of exasperation. If Marcus was staying over, that must mean his mother was finally dying.

213

For once there had been an opportunity for her to be supportive, but she had not been there for him. He had reached the answering machine instead . . . 'because you were needlessly driving halfway round the South Lakes,' an inner voice chided her. She slammed her hand down hard on the telephone table to quiet the voice, then ran up the stairs.

'Sean,' she said angrily, accompanying his name with a brisk rat-tat on the door.

'Don't come in. I'm getting changed.'

Something in his voice told her that this was not true. 'Why?' she called.

'Why what?'

She could tell from his voice that he was moving across the room. 'Why are you getting changed?'

'I felt like it. I was trying something on.'

She knew he was lying. She had been planning to remonstrate with him about ignoring the phone, but this now became secondary to wondering what he was up to behind the bedroom door. She reached for the handle, then hesitated. There had probably been enough time for him to hide whatever it was by now. No point in provoking a scene.

'In future, can you please answer the phone instead of letting the machine get it. That was your dad to say that your grandmother is very poorly and he won't be able to come home tonight, so it would have been nice if he had been able to speak to one of us.'

'Oh – OK – sorry.' From his position behind the door, Sean listened as the stairs creaked beneath her descent. His heart was still thumping, as it had been ever since that banshee shriek from downstairs had sent him diving for his knife. Now he wondered if he would have had the guts to use it – if she had burst into the room, as he thought she was going to. He replaced it carefully in its latest hiding place, behind the box sets of *Star Wars* and *Lost*. He was a lot more careful about hiding places since that time she had almost caught him out.

It got to supper time, and she had still heard nothing further from Marcus. She made a special effort with Sean – whose grandmother was dying, after all – encouraging him to have a second helping of the chorizo and sweet potato bake, which she knew he liked.

Sean seemed willing to meet her halfway, complimenting the meal and remarking a propos of nothing in particular, 'Some people stopped to look at your sculpture today.'

'Really? Did they? Who?' She tried to keep the excitement out of her voice.

'Just some family who were out walking.'

'With children?'

'Yeah.'

'Boys or girls?'

Sean eyed her a little uneasily. 'I didn't really notice. They'd all got waterproofs on, so you could hardly tell. I saw some scouts looking at it once, too. One of them took a picture over the wall with his digital camera.'

'Oh.' Marcus had been right, of course. It would attract random interest from all sorts of people, not just the ones it was meant for. Sean had almost finished his second helping. She tried a different line. 'Summer holidays next week. Do you know if Harry and his family are coming up?'

'I think so.'

'And now there's that new girl, too. The one across the road, who's at boarding school.'

'She's only twelve,' said Sean dismissively. 'Charlie might want to hang around with her.'

Sean had known her age all along. For the first time it occurred to Jo that Sean might be a valuable source of information. 'Did you meet her when she was home last holidays?'

'Yeah, a couple of times.'

'How about her mother? She's a bit weird-looking, isn't she?'

'Who – the woman you thought was following us that day?'

Jo flushed. Sometimes she forgot that Sean was neither blind nor deaf. 'I'm sure she wasn't really following us. But she does look a bit odd, don't you think?'

'Don't know. She looks a bit old to have a daughter.'

'That's only because she doesn't do anything with her hair, and the way she dresses. She's actually the same age as me.'

'How do you know?'

'Oh – it came up.'

He left the table soon afterwards. She had been so enthused by this burst of communication that she wanted to prolong it, to say, 'Don't go upstairs – let's watch a DVD together or something. You can choose,' but she knew her offer would be rejected. It was only a partial thaw, not the coming of spring.

She was clearing the table when the phone rang again. She raced to pick it up, but it was a recorded message, offering her no-win, no-fee representation in the event that she had had an accident. As she was replacing the receiver it occurred to her that she could ring the hospital. That would show she cared. She had to go into the office to root out the ward number. She tried the back of the telephone book, where they usually kept numbers acquired on loose bits of paper, but then she saw that both the ward and telephone number had been pinned to the cork notice board next to the big wall chart which showed with coloured stickers who was out on tour at any given time. Her eye fell on the chart, where her little yellow stars had all been annotated with the initials of

216

whichever guide had been deputed to pick up her tours while she was 'taking a break'. Marcus's green dots and Melissa's red triangles sat smug and unsullied while the defaced stars mocked her. A red triangle and a green dot were snuggled up next to one another in the box marked with today's date, but there were no symbols at all in tomorrow's square. Marcus's and Melissa's tours had both finished that morning. She flopped into the leather office chair and continued to stare at the two little symbols. They had been stuck on at the beginning of the year – she could not even remember who had done the chart this year – but instead of keeping a decent distance, the green dot and the red triangle were almost touching: you couldn't have got the edge of a ten-pence piece between them.

She reached for the telephone and keyed in the direct line for the ward. It rang for quite a long time before being answered by a young female voice.

'I'm ringing about Mrs Handley,' Jo said. 'I'm her daughter-in-law. I was wondering how she is.'

'She's comfortable.'

'Well, yes . . . but has she got any worse?'

'She's about the same. I'm sorry, who did you say you were again?'

'I'm Mrs Handley, too. I'm her daughter-in-law. My husband is there now. Could you let him know that I rang, please?'

'I will if I see him.'

'He's there now,' Jo said, a touch crossly. 'He's sitting by the bed.'

'There's no one by the bed at the moment. I can see it from here.'

'Oh . . . thank you.' Jo put the phone down. It had become quite dark in the office. No one looking at the rain-streaked windows would have guessed that it was July. Her eyes were irresistibly drawn back to the wall chart. It was too dark now to make out the initials etched on to each of her yellow stars; the symbols representing Marcus and Melissa were turning an identical shade of muddy brown in the dusk, becoming no more than a series of dark blots against the shiny white background. His mobile was switched off, and he was not at the hospital. She picked up the phone again and pressed the speed-dial code for Melissa's home number. The phone rang out half a dozen times, before Melissa's 'Hello?' sounded at the other end of the line. Jo instantly cut the call off.

A minute went by and then the phone began to ring. The caller display lit up with Melissa's name. Jo let the machine take it. 'Hello – I think you just called me. Is everything OK, Jo? Call me if you need anything, otherwise I'll just assume you hit my number by mistake. Byeee.' The line went dead.

Jo stepped into the hall and replayed the message, turning up the volume in a vain attempt to detect any sounds in the background. Then she rewound the tape and listened twice more. *Jo*. How had Melissa known that it must be herself and not Marcus on the end of the phone? She grabbed her fleece from the peg in the hall and yelled up the stairs as she pushed her arms into the sleeves, 'Sean – I'm going out.' She picked up her bag and ran to the door without bothering to wait for his reply. By way of an afterthought, she turned back to the kitchen and grabbed the largest knife out of the block.

As she gunned the engine into life her fury increased. How many times had they contrived to be away together this year already? Joint tours and nights off which coincided . . . She worked through the coming confrontation in her mind; what she would say to them, what they might say to her and what she would do. She had to force herself to focus on the road. The rain was driving down in straight lines, a million tiny silver javelins in the headlights. It was not yet nine o'clock, but already dark as an autumn night.

She had not gone very far before she saw the loom of an undulating blue light above the walls and hedges. She quickly realized that it was static – a police car or an ambulance, pulled up some little way ahead. Then she rounded a bend in the lane and was waved to a halt by a policeman in a dayglo yellow waterproof coat. As he approached the car, she experienced a momentary wave of panic. Did he know what she was thinking, and why she was heading for Melissa's house? Without taking her eyes off the approaching officer, she tried to see whether the knife was visible in the passenger foot well. She lowered the window as he reached the car, noticing the way water cascaded from the peak of his cap as he bent down to talk to her, holding her breath – but he had merely come to tell her that the road ahead was closed due to an accident.

'But I have to get through.'

'Sorry love, but the road's completely blocked. Are you local? Yes? Well if you take the Oak Bank turn, then do a right at Coxley Beck Farm; that'll bring you down to the main road. Best thing is to reverse a couple of yards and turn round in that gateway. Plenty of room back there, and it's solid concrete in front of the gate.'

From within her bag, her mobile trilled.

'Shouldn't have that switched on when you're driving,' he said.

'I didn't know it was switched on. I wouldn't have answered it.'

'Better pull in on that side if you're going to see who it is – and mind you turn your engine off first.'

'Right – yes – thank you.'

She turned the car on to the wrong side of the lane as the

policeman had indicated, so that she wouldn't be blocking any other vehicles which happened to come along and needed to turn round. The phone had stopped ringing by the time she silenced the engine, but she saw that the missed call was Marcus's mobile. With trembling fingers she returned the call.

He answered right away. 'Jo, is everything all right? They gave me the message when I got back to the ward, but when I called home I got the answering machine again. Where are you?'

'I'm out in the car.' She felt so sick that she could hardly speak. She thought of arriving on Melissa's doorstep, demanding to be let in, insisting that Marcus was inside . . . when all the time he had been at the hospital in Manchester.

'Why are you out? What's happened?'

'Nothing's happened. I rang to see how your mum is. I thought you'd be with her, but they said you weren't there.'

'Sandra and I slipped out for a bite to eat. But why aren't you at home?'

'We'd run out . . . of something. I was going to Booths, but there's a road block. There's been an accident, so I'm going back home.'

'Are you sure you're OK? You sound very shaken. You weren't involved, were you?'

'No. I don't even know what's happened. A policeman was standing in the road, making people turn back.'

'Booths won't be open, will they? Don't they close at eight on a Saturday?'

'I'd forgotten,' she said. 'Is your mum much worse?'

'It's difficult to say. Sandra seemed to think this might be it, but you know the hospital won't ever commit themselves. I'm staying to please Sandra, really. I don't believe Mum knows whether we're here or not.'

As they talked she felt colder and colder. It was as if the car had turned into a deep freeze, and the blood in her veins was slowing, turning to ice. The flickering lights of the police car made everything seem unreal: they might not have belonged to a police car at all, because her own car could have been anywhere, the windows obscured by streams of rain and every other external sound eliminated by pellets of water crashing into the metal a thousand times a minute. The policeman must still be out there keeping a lonely vigil against oncoming motorists, but she could not see him. The thought that there was someone standing unseen in the darkness, someone who could be right up beside the car for all she knew – even if he was a policeman – gave her a shivery feeling. Even the interior of the car had become a place of uncertainty in the undulating blue light, which illuminated now the dashboard, now a section of her thighs, now a pale hand, resting against the sill of the window. It might almost have been someone else's hand because in the transient fragmentary light she could not see where and how it joined up with the rest of her. To prove whose hand it was, she made the fingers move, but they seemed to mock her, each of them tapping in turn, forwards and backwards like someone playing a scale on an invisible piano

When she made the fingers stop, she fancied that they carried on wriggling a while longer, just to let her know that she was not entirely in control. It was the same hand which had drawn the pictures of Melissa in her sketch book.

CHAPTER SEVENTEEN

Marcus's mother did not die on Saturday night, contriving to expire instead at a moment on Sunday afternoon when neither Marcus nor his sister were at her bedside. Sandra wanted to arrange the funeral for a week on Monday, but Marcus persuaded her to put it back two days so that it would fit better with his work schedule. It seemed to Jo that every detail of the arrangements became the subject of a spat between brother and sister, with Sandra insisting that the service include 'The Lord's My Shepherd', while Marcus protested that his mother had never really liked it and complaining that Sandra had vetoed his idea of including a Rossetti poem among the readings.

Jo tried to be supportive, but found it difficult to relate to any of their disagreements. Her own mother's funeral had been arranged by the authorities. There were people in 'secure facilities' whose job it was to register deaths and make the appropriate arrangements. They had contacted her and asked if she wanted to attend, but she had replied that there was no point. Her mother had not wanted to see her in life, so it was hardly likely that she would have wanted her around at the funeral. The details of her father's funeral had become obscured among those tangled memories of his death: a blur of uncomfortable silences and shuffling feet, people in dark clothes; herself in the front pew flanked by Aunty Joan and Grandma Molesly, with her father's family keeping separate from her mother's. Two families previously bound together by a marriage, now abruptly disunited because one of their number had destroyed another, a chasm opening up between the two sides and herself being swallowed by it.

Marcus insisted on driving them down for the funeral himself. It was a predominantly silent journey, with Sean in the back seat, wearing his school trousers, white school shirt and a black tie specially purchased for the occasion. Jo half wondered whether Sean's mother would put in an appearance, but she did not come. Sandra wept openly during the service, but Marcus looked straight ahead. Jo squeezed his elbow when the coffin slid away, but he gave no sign that he was aware of her. *That's the trouble*, she thought. *I can never be there for him, because he's self-contained and doesn't actually need me.*

She offered to drive back, but Marcus preferred to take the wheel himself. As they approached the motorway, Marcus began to outline the relationships of the various mourners to Sean, who listened politely while his father explained that the old lady wearing the hat with black net across the top was Aunty Kate, who had been married to Uncle Tom, who was wounded at Monte Cassino, while Uncle Derek was the son of Tom's long-deceased brother Kenneth . . .

Jo let it roll over her. She reflected that this was the second funeral she had attended in a matter of weeks. Grandma Molesly always said deaths came in threes. In the old days, when families were much larger and people didn't live so long, that prophecy had probably been more easily fulfilled, but now that Marcus's mother was gone, she could not think of anyone she knew of who was particularly old or ailing.

At least Marcus would not have to be forever paying duty visits to Manchester any more – or staying overnight there.

She shuddered at the recollection of how close she had come to doing something very foolish. If only she and Marcus were not apart so often. That was the root of the problem – a lack of quality time together – although when they were together these days, she could rarely think of much to say to him, while his own attempts at communication seemed forced or superficial and their sex life was non-existent. There had been a period in their relationship when sex had been joyful and abandoned. Not at the beginning, when Marcus had assiduously avoided putting any pressure on her, preferring to become first a friend and confidant, wooing her gently with romantic gestures, so that sex, when it happened, was a wonderful confirmation of what they already knew. Marcus had put so much effort into making her happy. Her happiness and well-being had been the most important thing in his life – he had actually said that to her once. The thought crossed her mind that perhaps she had been his project of the moment. Marcus had put his heart and soul into turning her life around, but once he believed that he had made her happy, his main focus had transferred elsewhere. Maybe he had intended for Sean to become a project too, but the trouble was, Marcus could only devote himself to one big thing at a time: he might want to be the good son, the good father, the good husband, but his number-one priority now was the business.

Two days after the funeral, he set off to guide the inaugural Daphne du Maurier tour. Jo watched his meticulous preparations with renewed interest. Maybe he wasn't cheating on her with Melissa, so much as disregarding her in favour of Daphne and a host of other dead literary folk, long-departed generals, kings and queens. She waved him away with a pang of envy. She had once been as enthusiastic about it all as he was.

Sean rose late, and after eating a large bowl of Shreddies,

ambled down to Harry's. Soon afterwards she happened to be looking out of an upstairs window and saw Harry's sister emerging from the gateway of The Old Forge, walking side by side with Gilda's daughter, the two of them also heading in the direction of The Hollies. Mindful of recent near-catastrophic events, Jo no longer allowed herself to entertain any speculations about this coincidental child. She and Gilda were the same age, and therefore it was quite likely that they would be producing children at around the same time. Whatever happened, she must not allow her imagination to run away with her again. She moved back from the window and resumed stripping the bed.

By coincidence, Suzanne Wheaton also happened to be changing the beds down at The Hollies. When she and John originally bought the place, they had been determined to buck the stereotype of second-home ownership. Not for them the Friday-night arrival, complete with bags of groceries brought from home, all too swiftly followed by the Sunday night departure with nary a word to their country neighbours in between. On the contrary, they told one another that they would make every effort to be part of the community, using the local shops and fraternizing to a degree which guaranteed their acceptance. When conjuring up this idyllic vision of chatting over the gate with a pipe-chewing farmer, or buying a jar or two of homemade marmalade from his apple-cheeked wife, they had reckoned without the nature of a hamlet like Easter Bridge, where the only emporium was an expensive gallery, and even regular residents like the Handleys were, as often as not, working away for days at a stretch.

Part of the picture had undoubtedly been the prospect of their own children rubbing shoulders with the local kids: children who would be interested in the world around them, conversant with the names of birds and the tracks of badgers – uncomplicated kids who would warm to their townie friends and invite them to come and help with lambing. The complete absence of children in the immediate area had undoubtedly put a damper on this in their previous years at The Hollies, but then Sean had arrived like the answer to a prayer, appearing at just the right time, when Harry was becoming increasingly resistant to the idea of family time spent up in the Lakes. At a stroke Harry's complaints had been cut back to token whining, and within less than a year came the sale of The Old Forge, bringing with it the prospect of a possible friend for Charlotte too.

Alas, the reality of these friendships fell well short of the dream. Harry and his country-dwelling friend, far from disappearing to hunt for badger tracks or climb trees, spent most of their time playing computer games, just as Harry would have done if he had been at home with his friends in Heswall; while Charlotte's new friend, Rebecca, turned out to be a pupil at a fee-paying school. As a good middle-class liberal, Suzanne Wheaton disapproved of private education, preferring to 'support' her excellent local comprehensive – having taken the precaution of moving into its catchment area as soon as Harry was expected. This reservation aside, Suzanne could not help being somewhat intrigued by Rebecca's mother, a woman who, in spite of inhabiting the scruffiest dwelling for miles around, could evidently afford a private education for her daughter. And although Suzanne told herself that she had hoped her children would form friendships with rough-and-tumbling rural children, products of a threatened village school, and parented by the local salt of the earth, she was not unaware of the advantages of making 'good' connections, either. John was an architect, after all, and she could not imagine Rebecca's mother would leave that house unaltered for very long. Even so, she baulked at the idea of inviting the woman round for a drink. On the handful of occasions when the two women had spoken, Suzanne had derived the impression that there was something a bit odd about Gilda Iceton. 'Just nervy,' John had said, but it wasn't that – in fact, she came across to Suzanne as a fairly confident person. It was something she could not quite put her finger on, which went beyond the way the woman's voice was a bit too loud, her laugh off-key.

At least Rebecca herself – unlike her mother – always looked nicely turned out. In fact, she seemed to be a thoroughly pleasant girl all round, who had lovely manners and was very well spoken. Suzanne was not so sure about Sean, who had blotted his copybook with the episode of the unsuitable DVD and the dreadful stories he had told Harry about his stepmother. John had been inclined to take a more charitable view than she had. 'Kids make things up all the time, just to make themselves seem more interesting,' he said. 'Harry's probably told Sean that we're axe murderers.'

'I sincerely hope not!'

Sean's stepmother certainly didn't look like a murderess. If anything, she looked more like a victim, Suzanne thought. A nervous little woman, who all but scurried past the house with her head down, never seeming to want to meet your eye. She hadn't always been like that – she had appeared quite friendly when they first came, but now she looked as if she was afraid of her own shadow. Suzanne wondered if she might be ill. She never seemed to be away working with their tour company any more.

Her uneasiness about Sean was tempered by the difficulties of actively discouraging Harry from seeing him. Having originally encouraged the friendship, it was difficult suddenly to take the opposite line, and anyway, active prohibition seemed too extreme. It was not as if there were any other young people in whose direction Harry could be pointed. Moreover, she knew that the combined presence of Sean and Rebecca had probably been the single factor which had prevented her own two from killing each other this holiday. She was starting to feel the effects of cabin fever herself, as the rain kept them penned indoors day after day.

The weather was the subject of conversation in the sitting room of The Hollies at that precise moment. The youth of Easter Bridge normally segregated itself by gender, but the whole quartet had been temporarily forced into one another's company when Mrs Wheaton ordered everyone out of the bedrooms so that she could change the beds.

'I can't believe Dad has gone walking in this weather,' Charlotte was saying.

'Dad'll walk in anything,' said Harry.

'There's no point. You can't see anything.'

'What's the deal with walking, anyway?' This from Sean. 'Unless you actually need to get somewhere and you haven't got a car, it's just putting one foot in front of the other – a complete waste of time.'

There was a brief silence while the others tried to decide if Sean had just uttered something profound.

'Does it *always* rain like this here?' asked Rebecca.

'Not always,' said Charlotte. 'It was really nice one year. We ate our dinner outside nearly every night.'

'Since I've been home from school it's rained nearly every day. It's like winter all the time.'

'Where did you live before?'

'Oh, loads of places, mostly in Devon and Essex. My grandad used to own lots of property, so when I was little we lived in one of his houses, and when he died, my mum liquefied some of it and bought houses of her own.'

'Oh.' Charlotte was impressed, in spite of being unclear on what liquefying actually involved. 'We've only got two houses, this one and our proper house in Heswall.'

'This is a proper house, too, dummy,' said her brother.

'It's not our real house, though. It's not where we live most of the time.'

'I'm at school most of the time,' said Rebecca.

'Do you mind?'

'No, I like it. And sometimes I go to stay with friends, and some of the time I go to stay with my Aunty Carole in Yorkshire. I really love it there. There are some stables just down the road from her house, where I can go riding. Are there any stables round here? I asked Mum, but she didn't know. She said she'd look into it. I've never seen anyone out hacking, have you?'

'I don't think so,' said Harry, who guessed that hacking must be something to do with horses, although the term conjured up a man going at a hedge with a scythe.

'We're going to the Algarve for the last two weeks of the holidays, to stay in my uncle's villa,' Charlotte announced. 'You can ride horses there. I've seen a picture in the brochure.'

'I've hardly ever been abroad,' Rebecca said. 'My mum doesn't like flying. We've been to Euro Disney on the train. Aunty Carole took us. She was going to take me to France again last year, but then I got a virus and couldn't go.'

'Is she your dad's sister?' asked Sean, who wasn't really interested in familial details, but was fed up with the subject of holidays, conscious that his father and stepmother had no plans to take him away anywhere, so that the best he could hope for was a few days in Manchester with his mother, pretending to admire the new baby. He supposed his father never thought about organizing a holiday for him, because he was always too busy organizing holidays for other people.

'She's not really my aunty. She's my mother's cousin, but I call her aunty because I don't have any real ones. My mum's an only child, and so was my dad.'

'Are your parents divorced?'

'No, my dad died in a plane crash. I think that's why my mum is dead against flying.' She leaned forward and flicked a biscuit crumb across the coffee table. Harry flicked it back, so Rebecca flicked it again, but this time it landed nearest to Sean, who sent the crumb skidding across to Charlotte, whose heavy-handed attempt scattered fragments of biscuit all over the table.

'There's always some reason for not doing stuff,' Rebecca continued. 'We can't go abroad because she doesn't like flying, or we can't have pets because she's allergic.'

'That's why you have Timmy, the stone cat by the fire,' Charlotte put in.

'Yeah,' said Sean, 'cos, like, a stone cat and a real cat are exactly the same thing.'

'Anyway, I'm going to Aunty Carole's for a week, starting next Thursday. She's got a dog and three cats.'

Down at The Hideaway, Jo heard the postman's van while she was separating the duvet from its cover, and her heart quickened as it did every morning at the prospect of another message. She had stopped rushing to get the post because that almost guaranteed that nothing would happen. She knew the pattern by now: something worthwhile only arrived when you did not expect it.

She descended the stairs with her arms full of bedding, giving a little cry when she had almost gained the lower floor. There was a postcard on the mat. She dropped the laundry and ran to pick it up. The communication was instantly recognizable, even from a distance of several feet, as a 'Lauren card'. The picture was the same as always, but there was a new message printed below it: *Claife Station. Saturday midnight. Tell no one. Come alone.*

Tears sprang into her eyes. Her legs almost gave way, so that she had to sit down on the bottom stair. This was it. Lauren would be restored to her – within days. All she had to do was follow the instructions, just as she had when answering the previous card, and this would be easier because no one need know. Saturday night was excellent from that point of view, because Marcus would still be away and Sean was so used to her coming and going that he would ask no questions. What would they say, the pair of them, when she came home with Lauren?

CHAPTER EIGHTEEN

Shelley had managed to avoid Maisie's strawberries-and-cream event by being unavoidably on duty at the gallery, but had promised a donation in lieu of attendance, which she planned to hand over the gate next time she spotted Maisie out in the garden. (A foray as far as the front door was never a good idea, since a swift escape from such an advanced position was extremely unlikely.) Having correctly anticipated that the first dry day would bring the Perrys forth, Shelley strolled down the lane and found Maisie dead-heading in the border alongside the drive, a fortuitous situation which put her within easy eye-catching distance of the garden gate.

After thanking Shelley for her donation, Maisie naturally took the opportunity to go into all the whys and wherefores of who had turned up on the day, and how much money had been raised. 'You haven't seen anything of Jo lately?' she asked. 'I know the two of you are quite friendly.'

Shelley was surprised by the abrupt change of topic. 'No. I haven't seen her for a while. Why?'

'Well, there was a little bit of an upset – I just thought she might have said something to you about it. Tell the truth, I've been wondering whether to pop along and have a chat with her, but it's rather awkward – one doesn't know quite what to say.'

The concept of Maisie ever being at a loss for words was

novel enough to arouse Shelley's curiosity. 'Did something happen at the strawberry tea?'

'Well, yes. I felt awfully sorry for her, but of course if we had known – and with the anniversary coming up . . .'

'I'm sorry, Maisie, but I don't know what you're getting at.'

'Ah – then you're just as much in the dark as the rest of us.' Maisie looked disappointed. 'I thought Jo might have confided in you, with your being friendly. It was Gilda, you see. You can't blame her, of course – she wasn't to know.'

'Wasn't to know what?' Shelley struggled to conceal her mounting impatience.

'That our Jo Handley is also Joanne Ashton . . .' She paused to see if Shelley would register anything, but when she received no more than a puzzled look, she continued: 'The woman whose child was abducted at Barleycombe in Devon. You must remember the case: it was all over the papers at the time, and every so often they drag it up again. Jo is the mother of that little girl.'

'Not really.'

'Oh, there's no doubt about it. Gilda just happened to say something about having a daughter who is virtually the same age as the little girl who was kidnapped, and Jo got upset and ran out. Normally I would have gone straight after her, but I didn't understand what the matter was at first. I assumed she must have been feeling unwell, and what with a houseful of people and more arriving. Then when Gilda explained . . . she was mortified, as you can imagine, she had no idea that we didn't know about it already – well, how could she have done? Not her fault, I said. Not her fault at all. I did walk down to The Hideaway later on to try to have a word with Jo, but her car wasn't outside so I knew she must be out. And if she had been at home, I don't really know what I would

233

have said to her. One doesn't want to make things worse by going on about it because she obviously can't face talking about it, poor girl, and who can blame her?'

Shelley could not help thinking that if Jo had created some sort of scene, then perhaps it should be her rather than Maisie who offered the apology, but her sympathy was tempered by a strong suspicion that Maisie's unsuccessful attempt at commiseration might well have been a front for a fact-finding mission. 'I'm not sure that I really understand,' she began. 'How come Gilda knows about all this? She's only lived here for ten minutes.'

'It seems that Gilda knew Jo years and years ago, when they were both at the same school together; so when Gilda saw the kidnapping case in the papers, she knew who it was, even though she hadn't seen Jo for quite a few years. Then of course she bought The Old Forge, never thinking for a minute that she would be living nearly opposite someone she had been at school with. She recognized Jo straight away, although apparently Jo couldn't remember her. It's such a small world, isn't it? Remind me to tell you in a minute about a very similar coincidence someone told Fred and me about, when we were wardening the other day at Holehird.'

Shelley didn't want to get diverted into funny coincidences at Holehird, so she interposed quickly: 'You're sure Gilda had the right person?'

'Oh, absolutely no doubt about it . . . You don't forget the people you were at school with, do you? I once bumped into one of our old head girls, I don't know how many years after I'd left. She was much older than me, but I still recognized her. And you know, when I thought about it, I could see that Gilda was right about Jo being the woman whose little girl disappeared. She does her hair differently now, but apart from that she hasn't changed very much.'

234

Shelley nodded. While Maisie had been talking, she too had reached back into her memory and plucked out an image, half remembered from newspapers and television.

'I can't imagine why she never told any of us,' Maisie continued.

'I suppose she wanted to put it all behind her – make a fresh start.'

'I don't see how you ever could – not a thing like that. They never found out what happened to the little girl, did they?'

'No.' Shelley's voice was thoughtful. 'Didn't the husband disappear, too?'

'Well it certainly wasn't Marcus who was involved,' said Maisie. 'I don't know about the husband. It's the little girl I remember. She looked such a sweet little thing.'

Shelley delved further into the recesses of half-forgotten headlines. 'He fell off a cliff – that was it. The police decided he'd committed suicide; a lot of people at the time wondered if it was guilty conscience.'

'People will say anything.' Maisie shook her head. 'Anyway, it must have been awful for her to be reminded of it, and coming completely out of the blue like that. Of course, if we had known about it already, then it wouldn't have been so bad. If only she had told us . . . Well, any damage is done now. You know Jo better than I do. Should I have a word with her, do you think? Tell her I'm sorry about what happened, and reassure her that we're not all talking about it?'

But we are, Shelley thought. Out loud she said, 'It's difficult to know how to approach it. I would just leave it, if I were you. Let it all blow over – she obviously doesn't want to talk about it, so I'd say least said, soonest mended. I have to get back – I promised Brian I would only be five minutes.

There's some bookkeeping I'm supposed to be helping him with.'

As she walked away, Shelley wondered what Brian would make of it all, and come to that, what she made of it herself. Was there something a bit strange about keeping such a big thing a secret – or would that be the natural thing to do? She had almost reached her own gate when she encountered the two little girls from The Hollies and The Old Forge, coming the opposite way. They both said 'hello' to her, but a second later she heard the younger one instructing the older one in a low, urgent voice: 'Look out. Mrs Perry's in her garden. Stay on this side of the road and don't let her see us or she'll keep us talking for ages.' Shelley smiled to herself. How quickly the young catch on. As she opened the front door of Ingledene, she glanced back and saw that they had managed to evade Maisie and were just going out of sight round the bend.

Charlotte thought there were distinct advantages to hanging out at Rebecca's house. It not only got them away from Harry and Sean, but also brought them into the orbit of Mrs Iceton's catering, which meant lunches of pizzas and microwave chips, rather than her mother's healthy summer salads. In spite of these advantages, however, Charlotte could not quite decide whether she liked it at The Old Forge or not. The house both attracted and repelled her. It was rather gloomy inside and had a funny smell, although this was partly compensated for by the contents. The Hollies was furnished in the minimalist style of a holiday let – an arrangement intended to reduce the amount of housework her mum needed to do in order to keep everything pristine – whereas Mrs Iceton did not seem to worry about housework, so clutter was scarcely an issue. The living room looked as if someone had taken up residence in a little-frequented junk shop, scattering their discarded newspapers, clothes and coffee cups among the furniture and bric-a-brac while the owner of the business was otherwise engaged.

Charlotte had never seen anything quite like it. There were objects of all kinds just lying about, and all these things seemed to have a story attached. The artificial flowers under a glass dome had belonged to Mrs Iceton's grandmother, while an enormous plant in a crazed china bowl whose dust-laden, leathery leaves flopped haphazardly across a menagerie of dulled bronze miniature animals, was known as 'Esmeralda' and revered as the oldest living thing in the house. She learned that what appeared to be a tiny ancient pair of binoculars were something called opera glasses, and that the ancient photo album on which they rested, a volume covered in dusty grey silk, from which a plaited brown and green tassel drooped over the edge of the table, contained black and white photographs of Rebecca's grandparents' wedding day. The wedding dress in the photographs was kept in a trunk upstairs, from which she and Becky had been allowed not only to remove it for examination, but also to try it on. Everywhere was a confusion of old and new. A plastic mug full of pens sat between an apparently random collection of pebbles and a china pierrot which could have been won at the fair. The pierrot wore a permanent expression of mild surprise, which could have been induced by finding himself in the range of a precariously balanced pile of books. There were books everywhere, and they all looked to Charlotte as though they belonged in a second-hand shop. Even the paperbacks were brown and faded. Her own mother sometimes bought second-hand paperbacks from the Oxfam shop, but these books all looked much, much older than any of them.

Rebecca's bedroom was almost as much of a muddle as the rooms downstairs. There seemed to be just as many books here too, some of them still to be unpacked from the cardboard boxes in which they had arrived at The Old Forge months ago. Charlotte had offered to help with them, partly because she liked reading and partly because she liked Rebecca, who, even though she was nearly as old as Harry, never patronized her.

'I'm glad you came to live here,' Charlotte declared as she knelt in front of a carton of books, passing out the contents volume by volume to Rebecca, who was stacking them spines outwards in a pile on the floor, now that they had filled all the available shelving in the room. 'It means there will always be someone to hang around with when we come up in the holidays.'

'And I'm glad you'll be here.' Rebecca readily returned the compliment. 'It's really nice to have a friend in the holidays, because all the girls of my age who lived near our last house already had their own friends, because they all went to the local schools.'

Basking in the implied compliment of 'my age', Charlotte asked: 'But don't you have friends at your school?'

'I've got lots of friends at school, and sometimes I get asked to stay with them, but I can never invite them to stay with us because Mum always says she needs to get straight first, and somehow she never does. You couldn't put anyone in the spare room here – the bed's all dismantled up against the wall and you'd have to climb over loads of boxes and other furniture to get at it.'

'Why have you got so much stuff?' asked Charlotte.

'It mostly came from my grandparents. They never threw anything away, Mum says. In fact, I think some of it belonged to my great-grandparents. There are some boxes that haven't been unpacked in years – they just move with us. Mum's got a lock-up unit down in Essex which is stuffed full as well.'

'What's in all the boxes?'

'I haven't got a clue.'

'There might be something really valuable.'

'Mum wouldn't care if it was. I don't think she's all that interested in money.'

'But you must be quite rich, if you go to boarding school?'

'I suppose. I don't really know. Mum never talks about money. She wanted me to go to boarding school because she went herself. She thinks it's better.'

'How about your dad? Did he go to boarding school?'

Rebecca hesitated in the act of balancing a book. 'I think that's high enough; I'd better start a new pile.' She glanced towards the door, put a finger to her lips and slipped across to check that the coast was clear before she spoke again. 'You can't shut these doors,' she said. 'None of the latches work properly. You know what I told you before – about my dad?'

Charlotte nodded, eager for confidences.

'Well, it sort of wasn't exactly true. That's just what we tell people, because Mum says it's easier to pretend to be a widow.'

Charlotte's eyes widened. It was outside her sphere of experience for adults to invite children to be a party to shared deceptions. 'How do you mean – it isn't exactly true?'

'It is true and it isn't. It all depends which dad you're talking about.'

'How many dads have you got?'

'The thing is, Gilda isn't my real mother. My real mother died of cancer when I was a little baby.'

'Your birth mother,' Charlotte put in helpfully. Being an aficionado of daytime television was a great help when it came to defining familial relationships.

'Right. She was my mum's – that's Gilda's – best friend, and when she knew she was dying she asked Gilda and her husband to adopt me because they couldn't have any children of their own. Only, she didn't know Gilda's husband all that well, and she didn't realize that he wasn't really very nice. He used to drink too much.'

'So what happened to him?'

'Gilda threw him out. So she isn't a widow at all; she just tells people that because it sounds better than admitting you've got a drunken husband somewhere.'

'What about your real dad?'

'He's the one who really is dead. He was killed in a plane crash before I was born. It's no secret that I'm adopted, but it's easier for Gilda if we mix my adopted dad and my real dad into the same person – which makes her a widow.'

'It sounds more complicated to me. How long have you known about all this?'

'As long as I can remember. Mum says you have to tell adopted people that they are adopted, and she has kept my real name because my actual mother wanted that. A couple of years ago she took me to see the outside of the hospital where I was born, and the house where my parents used to live, and she's shown me photos of my real mum and dad, although she hasn't got many, just a couple of when they were on holiday – stuff like that.'

'And you can't remember your real mum at all?'

'Of course not. I told you, I was only a baby. I can't remember my father or my stepfather, either.'

'Your parents might have been really rich – there might be a big inheritance or something,' suggested the materialistic Charlotte.

'I shouldn't think so. The house where they lived was pretty tiny.'

'It's a really romantic story. A friendship between your two mothers, going on beyond the grave.'

'I suppose so. Come on, don't stop.'

Charlotte obediently reached into the box for the next volume. '*Anne of Green Gables*,' she read. 'How funny – she was an orphan, too.'

'It's not exactly funny being an orphan,' Rebecca chided. 'You don't get comedians going out on stage, saying, "Hey, I'm an orphan", and getting a huge laugh.'

'Sorry.'

'It's OK. It's not a big deal.'

'Becky! Charlotte!' It was Gilda's voice, from the bottom of the stairs. 'Harry is here, wanting to know if you're going home for lunch.'

In response to an imploring look, Rebecca shouted back, 'Can't Charlie stay here for lunch?'

'Of course – if she wants to.'

'Yes pleeeease,' Charlotte shrilled.

'I'll go and tell him.' They heard a door shutting somewhere below.

Charlotte leaned across the almost empty box and gave her friend a hug. 'I don't know what I'm going to do when you go to stay at your aunty's. Why don't you ask if you can stay here?'

'But I like it with Aunty Carole. I go to stay with her every holidays.'

'Don't you like being at home with your mum?'

'It's all right.'

'At least she doesn't nag all the time, like mine does.'

'No-o. But Aunty Carole's . . . well, better at knowing the sort of things I like to do and helping me choose the right sort of clothes. Mum tries, but she's too old-fashioned. She knows she isn't any good at it, so these days she gives me the money and Aunty Carole takes me – she knows the right shops. And plus it's sometimes difficult – it's a big pressure, you know, being adopted.'

'How do you mean?'

'Well, I feel like I have to be, sort of . . . grateful, because you know . . . Mum has given me a home and a good education and everything *and* she's a single parent.'

Rebecca spoke as if she had given the matter a great deal of thought. Charlotte was impressed: that was one of the things she liked about Becky – you could have really grown-up conversations with her.

'Plus, Mum is what Aunty Carole calls overprotective. I know it's only because I'm precious to her – Aunty Carole says I'm all Mum's got – but that makes her a bit weird and freaky about stuff. I often feel like she's watching me, and she asks me all kinds of things, strange things sometimes. Like this one time she kept asking if the girls at school laughed at me? When I said they didn't, I used to feel as if she didn't really believe me. I know it's only because she loves me, but it's a bit intense sometimes.'

'My mother's always asking about scores in tests,' said Charlotte. 'How many did you get, and how many did Tamsin Dyer get, and how many did Aaron Wilkins get. Honestly, it drives me mad. Parents are all a bit hyper, if you ask me.'

CHAPTER NINETEEN

The arrival of the postcard thrust Jo into a helter-skelter of emotions. Euphoria, disbelief, panic; a series of confused ideas which hurtled by faster than she could keep up with them. Among them were thoughts which she could scarcely bear to entertain. To lose a child is the most terrible thing in the world, but to regain that child might be no less terrifying. Suppose the idealized Lauren in her head turned out to be completely different from the flesh-and-blood reality? Suppose the girl she brought home in the early hours of Sunday morning was not Lauren at all? How would she know? In all her fantasy reunions she had known and recognized her daughter as a matter of course; but these scenes had invariably been conducted in well-lit, well-populated settings, with the identity of the child already verified beyond doubt. She had never envisaged a clandestine meeting at midnight, halfway to the middle of nowhere.

What a place to choose – Claife Station – an old viewpoint situated high above Windermere on Claife Heights, the supposed haunt of the Crier of Claife, Windermere's most famous spectre. She wasn't too clear on the ghost story, but she had certainly derived the general impression that you should avoid Claife Heights on your own at night. She assumed the venue had been chosen because it could only be accessed on foot, thereby making any kind of police trap or surveillance that much more difficult.

Jo had never been to Claife Station, but she knew of it from magazines and walk books. She checked it out on Google, and found the good news was that it lay on a well-defined path not too far from a car park, but an accompanying photograph of the place was less encouraging. The text explained that Claife Station – which had nothing to do with railway lines – was a roofless, late-eighteenth-century ruin, built to enable the original tourists to view Windermere in all its scenic splendour, through specially designed stained-glass windows. In its heyday the viewing station had been a popular place for picnics and parties, but subsequent generations had allowed the building to fall into disrepair, preferring to find their own views from greater or more secluded heights; or else to eschew any views which were not visible from the windows of a moving coach or a tea shop window.

As Jo considered the location on an OS map a new thought struck her – suppose it was a trap? What if the abductor wanted to lure her there and kill her? But why? To stop her searching for Lauren? It was not as if she was getting any closer.

Then again, why should anyone want to give Lauren back now, after all these years? Maybe she was ill. Something which couldn't be handled in captivity. Childhood leukaemia? The last and cruellest joke – to have your child restored to you, only to watch her suffer and die.

Anything was possible because once the worst of your fears has been realized – your child snatched – nothing is ever entirely beyond the realms of your reality again.

Three days to go. Three days to think about it. Three days to plan. Three days to wonder. Unable to be still for a moment, Jo matched frenzied activity to frenzied thought. She cleaned the house from top to bottom, made up the spare bedroom, placed a jug of fresh flowers on the window sill, bought a cuddly Dalmatian dog (was twelve too old for stuffed toys?) and placed it in the centre of the bed. Time enough to personalize the room later. She was not sure what a girl of Lauren's age would like in her room. She might be a pink princess or a thoroughgoing tomboy. She removed, then replaced, the Dalmatian half a dozen times a day. Lauren might be bringing things of her own – although a significant amount of luggage did not appear to be indicated by a rendezvous at Claife Station.

Jo could neither eat nor sleep. She was aware of Sean watching her with more than usual circumspection. At times the urge to tell somebody – even Sean – almost overwhelmed her. The knowledge filled her so that she thought she might explode with it, yet she had to keep swallowing it back. *Tell no one*, the postcard had instructed. It did not matter whether Sean could be trusted to keep a secret. Telling anyone at all could be enough to break the spell. Even an email to Nerys was out of the question. She had to stay silent for Lauren's sake.

One of their Lakeland walk books included a route along Claife Heights which passed the old viewing station. The sketch map which accompanied it implied that the building was easy to find and only a short walk from the road, but Jo decided that the wisest course would be an advance visit to ensure that she could find her way there after dark. She had hoped for a dry day, but it rained steadily through Thursday and she set out on Friday in intermittent drizzle. She took a cross-country route, driving through little-used lanes until she emerged alongside Graythwaite Hall, then headed towards Sawrey and the ferry road. The National Trust car park was described in her book as an old quarry, but any quarrying must have ceased decades ago because the small parking area

245

was surrounded by mature trees. There were already a number of cars and two large camper vans in there, but Jo managed to squeeze her car into the last remaining space, then sat on the back bumper while she changed her shoes for walking boots.

Judging from the number of vehicles the weather did not seem to have deterred walkers, who all presumably subscribed to the theory that there is no wrong sort of weather in Cumbria, only the wrong sort of clothing. The only other human beings in the car park were a foursome, who talked to one another in strident Yorkshire accents while they got kitted up for a forthcoming exploration. They seemed to take an age in sorting themselves out, so Jo slowed up too, tying and retying her bootlaces because she was reluctant to set off at the same time as they did. The idea of falling into step and then into conversation with anyone else made her nervous, lest she inadvertently give something away and jeopardize the rendezvous. She knew it was irrational, but their voices – indeed their very presence – began to grate on her. She was just thinking that she would have to give them a long start when they finally departed, clumping in single file along the road rather than up the muddy track which led through the trees towards Claife Station.

There were signs of recent forestry operations in the wood, and these had left a quagmire scarred by the repeated passage of heavily shod feet and even heavier vehicles. Jo had barely been sloshing her way through the mud for a minute before she glimpsed the side of a stone building, standing high above her among the trees. She had not been expecting to see anything so soon, but only seconds later she came in sight of the stone stairs which ascended to the old viewing station. The approach had been constructed to resemble a grand curving staircase built into the side of the hill, but its glory years were long past and now the steps were irregular, sharp-edged and sloping, partly covered in last year's leaves which had melded into a solid mass, looking for all the world like a rust-coloured carpet which had once been thick and expensive, but was now so badly worn that in places the treads showed through. The patches of bare rock were slippery with rain and the jagged edges unforgiving, so that Jo had to ascend with care and was unable to give the viewing station her full attention until she reached the top.

The remains of the building presented a dismal prospect: a roofless ruin surrounded by temporary metal fencing, which had been erected because of safety concerns according to the National Trust sign attached to it. *Dangerous Building. Please Keep Out* requested a separate notice. A small information panel had also been wired to the fence, which included an artist's impression showing how the place must have looked in its prime: a miniature turret from a Hollywood-style medieval castle, complete with battlemented top and even a couple of arrow slits. The huge windows which had once afforded views in every direction were now either bricked up, or else gaped like eye sockets in a skull. It might still have been possible to enjoy some of the famous views if access to the building had been permitted, but from where Jo stood behind the wire fence there was little to see except a surrounding canopy of trees.

The commentary from a passing lake steamer was just audible, a disembodied voice which floated up from the boat as it moved along the opposite shore of the lake. She glimpsed its blue and white hull briefly as it crossed a gap in the leaves. Otherwise there was no sound except for the birds, noisy now that there was a lull in the rain, their song only interrupted by the occasional car heading along the road to join the queue for the ferry.

Jo began to assess the place from the point of view of a midnight rendezvous. Anything which took place here could not be seen from the car park, or even the bottom of the steps. After mounting the steps, the public footpath vanished through an arch in the wall which linked the main turret of the viewing house to the remnants of what had once been a smaller chamber built into the rocky hillside, although little of this secondary structure remained except a knee-high outline showing where the walls had once been and a rather splendid window which matched the main archway. She followed the path through the archway and found that it disappeared behind an outcrop of rock, thereafter becoming a narrow track which headed steeply downhill then steeply up again, like a muddy single-file roller coaster, which vanished into the trees after about a hundred yards. It presented neither a good hiding place nor the means for a swift getaway.

It seemed to Jo that whoever planned to meet her would naturally expect her to come from the direction of the car park, and that by taking up a vantage point close to the top of the steps, it would be simple enough for them to be sure that she had come alone. It would also be virtually impossible for anyone to spy on a transaction undertaken here: even if someone with very strong binoculars was standing over on the eastern shore, the small plateau in front of the ruin was almost entirely masked by the surrounding trees.

If it was raining tomorrow night, then anyone waiting here would get pretty wet because there was no shelter at all. But perhaps the viewing station was merely a first meeting place. Maybe she would be taken on from there, or would find some instructions which would lead her somewhere else. On reflection, that seemed a far more likely scenario than someone bringing Lauren up here to meet her.

Another shower began to patter against the leaves, silencing the birdsong. She put up her hood and began to pick her way carefully down the steps. There was a narrow terrace at the bottom of the flight which curved round the side of the hill. Jo followed it, squelching through the mud, until she found herself looking down towards the southern end of the lake, but the aspect was greenish-grey and disappointing. The mountains to the north were hidden completely by the tree-covered Ferry House promontory.

The rain had eased again by the time she retraced her steps to the car park. A different quartet of walkers had returned to their car, where they were in the process of removing outdoor gear. 'Let's try the Sun at Hawkshead,' said one. 'They might have Bluebird bitter, there.'

Their cheerful conversation conjured a faint echo of carefree days, when all that mattered was what you were going to eat or drink – trivial things that didn't matter at all now. On the drive home she found that she couldn't recall whether she had eaten that day or not. It was impossible to think of anything but midnight on Saturday. At times she almost had to remind herself to breathe.

She checked that she had her maps, boots, torch and anorak in the car a dozen times. Ought she to take a flask, with a hot drink for Lauren? Maybe she should leave a note for Sean, telling him where she had gone . . . just in case she did not come back. *Tell no one*, the card had said. She must not breach the instructions. There could be no leaving of notes.

She set out far too early – even to allow for going the long way round. It was easier to stick to the main roads at night, because the narrow lanes were such a pain if you met anything and had to reverse in the dark. Not that you ever did meet much this late, not even in the middle of the season.

Reaching the car park too early was as problematical as reaching it late. Whatever happened, she must not deviate from the instructions to the slightest degree. It would be terrible to get this far, only to make a wrong move which put the kidnapper off, so after passing Graythwaite she pulled into the side of the road to kill some time. She was well out of sight of any human habitation, and had not seen another vehicle for some minutes, but she switched off the lights and stilled the engine, the better not to draw attention to herself. With the engine silenced she could hear the wind in the trees. The rain had ceased a couple of hours before, but when she eased the window open a crack she could smell autumnal damp, rather than high summer. It made her think of funerals and death. She tried to tell herself that she would always remember this moment – the wind in the trees and the smell of wet bracken – in a positive way, *because this is the night I got Lauren back*. It did not work. The darkness around her seemed to bristle with hostility. A sharper gust gathered up a posse of raindrops which had been clinging to the trees, and flung them on to the roof. The unexpected impact made Jo jump in her seat. She had to fight the urge to start the engine and drive on. She must – *must* – see it through for Lauren. But growing in her mind was the thought that if sitting here in the darkness, safely locked inside the car where no one was watching or waiting, where no one even knew she was there, induced something approaching terror, then how on earth would she bring herself to get out of the car and face up to the actual rendezvous at Claife Heights?

'You can do it, because Lauren is up there waiting for you,' she told herself – but all the time she could hear that other voice, telling her that Lauren was not there. Lauren was far, far away, and the viewing station at Claife was no more than an awful trap, set by someone who had no intention of handing Lauren over. Someone cruel who walked in the shadows: a figure which came tantalizingly close, before receding into the darkness again and taking Lauren with it.

When she resumed her journey she made herself drive very slowly, as if by keeping the car in low gear she could do likewise with her emotions. In the dark she nearly missed the turning for Near Sawrey. There were still lights burning in one of the guest houses here, but when she reached Far Sawrey everyone appeared to have gone to bed. Driving down the hill towards the ferry, Jo glimpsed other comforting signs of life; pinpricks of light on the far side of the lake marked the position of houses in Bowness and Storrs, but when she turned into the little car park it was black dark. She was surprised to find it completely empty – not even the obligatory camper van, whose owners assumed that a prohibition on overnight stays did not apply to them.

She checked her watch. Eleven minutes to midnight. Still time for another vehicle to arrive. Or maybe they were coming on foot. Perhaps they were here already, watching from somewhere nearby to check that she had come alone. She opened the driver's door, edging around in her seat and extending one foot gingerly towards the ground, as if testing thin ice. As well as the rustle and creak of the trees, she could hear the faint *clop, clop* of the lake, as wind-driven wavelets hit the shore on the other side of the road. It came to her then that the proximity of the water was dangerous. Windermere was extremely deep; there were places along the shore where the bottom fell away immediately. An unwary bather could step as if off a cliff edge into cold water, sixty feet deep.

She forced herself to walk round to the rear of the car, put on her anorak and change her shoes, tying the laces by the light of the small lamp which illuminated the open boot. All the time inwardly flinching, expecting every moment that some attack would come out of the darkness, although none did.

Seven minutes to midnight. It was very hard to think positively of her errand, to have faith that Lauren was waiting for her just up the hill. She tried to spur herself on with this hope, but it was difficult to believe in it. Suppose it was a trap. Did the kidnapper perceive some kind of added safety in disposing of her? If he did, then he had chosen an excellent spot to bring his scheme to fruition. There was no one to see or hear anything. It was miles to the nearest habitation – or if not miles, then at least too far away to summon aid by running or screaming. And there was the lake, deep, dark and cold, big enough to swallow a multitude of evidence. The sound of the water seemed to grow louder when she thought of it in that way, turning into a greedy gulping monster which awaited its prey, far removed from the glittering place of enchantment which was Windermere on a sunny day.

She glanced down at her watch again. The moment had come when she must leave the comparatively safe vicinity of the car and walk up the path. She closed the door and switched on her torch as the courtesy light went out. When she pressed the button on the key fob, the car's locking mechanism made a dull clunk while the hazard lights sent out a flash of orange, which briefly illuminated the surrounding area before fading slowly until the car became just another lump in the darkness. She stood listening for a moment, but the effects of wind on land and water were producing more than enough noise to camouflage the movements of any stalker.

Jo picked her way along the path, her feet sliding in the mud. There was no other sign of life, nothing to give away whoever watched and waited above or behind her. She reached the stone staircase and began to climb it, step by cautious step. Was she being watched, or were they yet to arrive? Perhaps they were timing it for midnight precisely. She didn't risk shining her torch on her watch again. That would have meant pausing on the steps, and if she stopped she could not be sure that her legs would obey her and recommence the climb. She had to do it. She reminded herself of how often she had said that she would lay down her life if she could only rescue Lauren. Well, maybe that time had come. Maybe this was the test.

When she reached the top she had to stop and get her breath back. The surrounding darkness seemed to pulse with menace, but she gradually realized that it was no more than her own blood pumping in her ears. The place was deserted. She could feel the emptiness, without even having to shine her torch behind the mock castle wall or through the gaping voids in the stonework. She checked her watch again. Two minutes to midnight. Would it be better to wait out here in the open, or maybe go through the arch and sit on the flat sill of the window, where the little anteroom had once been? She remained rooted to the spot.

One minute to midnight. For a moment she thought she heard someone coming along the narrow path from Claife Heights, but it was only the wind stirring small branches. She was shaking like a leaf herself. Wherever she shone the torch it wavered like a will-o'-the-wisp. She put her wrist within the arc of light again, but the second hand was crawling at only a fraction of its normal speed. She must not keep looking at her watch. She had to stay alert for any other movements, anything at all which might indicate the presence of another human being, but as each second passed, the weight of disbelief became heavier. No one was going to come.

She gave in to the impulse and checked again. One minute past midnight. 'Lauren,' she called softly. 'Lauren.' She raised her voice slightly. As if in response, the rain began to fall again, the sound of it approaching through the treetops like the advance of a phantom army, reaching and enveloping her as it headed north up the lake. Spots clinging to her eyelashes, blurring the bright pinprick which denoted a single light still burning in Storrs Park. With the rain came a denser sensation of cold and despair. There must be a message – some clue as to what she was expected to do next. She began to search frantically, shining her torch everywhere, kneeling on the wet ground and scrabbling among the loose stones and last year's dead leaves, but in the end she had to give in. There was no sign, cryptic or otherwise. Someone must be coming in person, they must be. She waited in the rain for more than an hour, but in her heart she had always known that no one would come.

Only when she eventually began her descent did Jo allow herself to acknowledge the depth of her fear. The wind was whipping into an angry frenzy now. If a branch came down in the dark she would have no warning. She almost missed her footing on the steps, slipping and hurting the hand she put out to save herself when it encountered a razor-sharp lip of rock. Emerging at last on to the car park, she was so disorientated that for a moment she shone her torch in completely the wrong direction and failed to spot her car. When the pale beam found the vehicle's outline she ran towards it with a sob, scrambling into the driver's seat without stopping to change out of her boots. The thought of staying there a moment longer was unendurable.

She normally never drove in her hiking boots. The soles were too thick to get a proper feel on the pedals. The car shot backwards when she put it into reverse, made uncertain progress into the road, then scraped along the stone wall as she misjudged the weight of her foot on the gas at the first

254

bend. Sod it, sod it! She would never make it home in one piece if she carried on like this. She pulled into the first turning and stopped to change her footwear. There was hardly going to be a problem about blocking the junction at this time of night.

The drive home seemed to take much longer than the outward journey had done. She became disorientated and lost confidence in her route. The lanes all looked the same, twisting and turning between dry-stone walls which were unfamiliar in the loom of her headlamps, meandering on for ever. When she crossed Easter Bridge and saw The Hideaway's outside lights glimmering among the trees, she began to cry with relief. As she turned into her own drive, she noticed that on the opposite side of the lane a single lamp was also burning above the front door of The Old Forge.

CHAPTER TWENTY

'I won't be around next week,' Sean informed Harry, as he deftly controlled his joypad so that his onscreen character leaped from one rooftop to another.

'Why not?' Harry's eyes never left the screen.

'I'm going down to stay at my mum's for a few days.'

Harry grunted in response, still concentrating on the game.

'Will you look after my knife while I'm away? I don't want to leave it here, in case *she* starts looking for it again, but I don't want to take it in my bag in case my mum starts mucking about in there, looking for washing and stuff.'

'Yeah, OK.' Harry tried to sound casual, although he was dubious about where he might hide a large knife at The Hollies, which would guarantee that *his* mother did not come across it. He had been uneasy about the knife, ever since Sean had shown it to him at the beginning of the summer holidays. His parents would have an absolute fit if they thought he was messing around with knives.

'I'll get it down to yours just before I go. She's been so bad lately that I'm sleeping with it under my pillow.'

'Why? What's been going down?'

'She's been, like, totally weird and jumpy, and last night she went out somewhere in the car and didn't come back for hours. When she finally did come back around two o'clock, I heard her running up the stairs and crying in her room, like she was hysterical. She's a fruitcake, there's no doubt about it. She's been worked up about something for days now. It's scaring the shit out of me.'

'Would you really go for her? With the knife?'

'Survival of the fittest. One false move and I'll have her. I figure I've got to get in first.' Sean paused to concentrate while his character fought of a trio of zombies. 'Otherwise I'm dead – game over.'

While this conversation was going on upstairs, Jo was out on the drive surveying the damage to her car. Marcus would be back tomorrow, so there was no chance of getting it fixed before he noticed. She would have to explain it somehow or other, but she was determined not to tell him about the post-card or her abortive trip to Claife Station. Although the rendezvous had not turned out as she had hoped, she could not be certain that it was *over*. Yes, she was safely back home, but had she been released from the embargo on com-municating the facts of the visit to anyone else? She thought not. The important thing was to wait and watch in readiness for the next sign. The abductor *would* make contact again, she was convinced of it, and the next communication would surely be as confidential as the last, so she did not want to have Marcus on the alert and looking out for things. At least her being at home all the time considerably reduced the chances of Marcus intercepting any communication when it arrived.

It had been something of a shock to realize that she no longer perceived Marcus as being on the same side. Where once he had given her confidence, now he undermined her with his constant hints about seeing the doctor and his refusal to let her return to work. She knew she could not trust him to go along with what she wanted, or do what was best for Lauren. He might well have insisted on informing the police about the Claife Station excursion. She was just considering this when a footfall on the drive startled her. It was Gilda, approaching with something in an outstretched hand. For a split second she thought it was a postcard, with the photo of Lauren uppermost, but then she saw it was a leaflet about the Liberal Democrats, and managed to stifle the cry which had risen to her lips.

'I'm sorry – did I startle you?' When Jo did not immediately respond Gilda added, 'Would you prefer me to pop this through the door, or can you take it now?'

Jo made a supreme effort and pulled herself together. 'I'll take it,' she said firmly, holding her hand out so that Gilda was obliged to step forward and hand it over. 'Although I'm afraid I probably won't read it. I'm not really interested in politics.'

'Oh, we should all be interested,' said Gilda. 'Especially women. My mother drummed it into me that women died campaigning to get us the vote – we ought never to take it for granted. She had a spinster aunt who was a suffragette. Of course your mother probably didn't have time for politics.'

Jo thought that if Gilda had actually said 'because she was too busy murdering your father', she could scarcely have made her meaning plainer.

'Had a bit of a prang?' Gilda continued. 'I suppose it's easily done. Especially round these narrow lanes.' Jo had the leaflet in her hand now, but Gilda appeared in no hurry to leave, inclining her head to take a better look at the damaged car. 'How did you do it?'

'My foot slipped on the pedal and the road was wet.'

'Dearie, dearie me. Was this last night? I happened to be up late, so I saw you coming home.'

'Why were you up so late?'

'I sat up watching a film and fell asleep in the chair. I'd just gone upstairs and was drawing my bedroom curtains when I saw your car turning on to the drive. I wonder where

258

Jo has been at this time of night, I said to myself.'

Jo said nothing. She transferred the Lib Dem leaflet from one hand to the other and back.

'That business at Mrs Perry's . . .' Gilda paused.

'Yes?'

'I'm sorry about that. It didn't occur to me that they wouldn't have known about your little girl – what was her name?'

'Lauren.'

'Lauren,' Gilda repeated as if trying it out on her tongue. 'I assumed everyone would know. You would think at the very least that they would have recognized you from the papers. The story comes back round again every so often when other children go missing.'

'Well, they know now.'

'I'm sure it would have come out. You can't keep things quiet in a little place like this.'

Jo considered retorting that she had managed to keep it quiet until then, but she reined herself in, saying instead, 'Gilda . . . how much did you tell them?'

'How do you mean?'

'About me?'

'I don't know that much about you to tell them. I didn't tell them what you did to me at school, if that's what you're asking.' Gilda's expression had hardened and her voice grown cold.

'I didn't meant that.'

'I don't suppose you did.'

'I'm sorry about all that. I was very young and stupid, and I should never have got involved.'

Gilda's face twisted into an expression which suggested that she had just eaten something unpleasant and was trying not to vomit it back. She stood for a moment, gripping her

259

leaflets, before turning abruptly and walking away.

Jo watched her go before she too turned away, pausing briefly on her way back to the house in order to consign Gilda's leaflet to the paper recycling bin. Why had Gilda been up so late? Had it been to observe her returning from Claife Station? After a moment or two she called up the stairs, 'Lunch in about twenty minutes – fish fingers, beans and chips. Are you staying, Harry?'

When Harry shouted back an affirmative, she set about preparing the meal, laying everything out for them to sit and eat at the kitchen table, something she insisted on when Sean subsequently wanted to carry their food upstairs.

'So,' she said brightly, affecting to be busy at the sink while they settled down to eat, 'are you seeing much of that new girl – Becky – who's moved in across the road?'

'Not much.'

'I think she plays with your sister, doesn't she, Harry?' Jo pursued.

'Yeah. Most days.'

'I wonder what happened to her father.' When neither boy responded, Jo put it more directly. 'Has she ever mentioned what happened to him?'

'He was killed in a car accident,' Harry volunteered. 'Or maybe a plane crash.'

'Why are you so interested in her anyway?' asked Sean.

'Oh – no reason. Just making conversation. Her mother came here just now, delivering leaflets.'

'Then why didn't you ask her?'

By the time Marcus returned next day, she had fabricated a story about the car close enough to the truth, but altering the time of the accident by several hours, and saying nothing about her real reason for being in the vicinity.

'That's a nasty bend above the ferry,' was his only comment. 'It's lucky there was no one close behind, or they might have gone into the back of you.'

A little later he asked, 'You haven't been to the doctor, have you?'

'No. What for?'

'I thought, you know, maybe you had hurt yourself when the car went into the wall.'

'No, I was fine. The only damage was to the car.'

'You haven't been to see him about your nerves? He hasn't given you anything to take?'

'No. Now what are you saying? That you think I went into the wall because I'm on something?'

'Of course not.' He laughed and quickly turned his attention to the TV guide, remarking a moment or two later that BBC4 were showing a documentary about elephants that evening. 'It sounds interesting,' he said. 'I think I'd like to have a look at it.' In fact he had been wondering if she was on something. Her eyes seemed unusually bright, and she was so restless, scarcely able to sit still. Maybe it was just that she *needed* to be on something. The situation was getting away from him. At one time Jo would have accepted his advice without question: he had been mentor, lover, friend. But looking back, he could see now that he had only been in the driving seat because she had been a willing passenger. Now it was not just that she was travelling separately; they weren't even going in the same direction any more. Sooner or later there was going to be a collision.

He scarcely liked to admit to himself how glad he was that Sean was going to stay with his ex-wife for a few days. He was very conscious that Sean was uncomfortable with Jo's increasingly erratic behaviour, and it troubled him that, having agreed to take Sean on with the best of intentions, he might have let his boy down. There never seemed to be enough time to get to know him properly, particularly now that he, Marcus, was away more often than he was at home. In a real partnership these absences would not matter. Twelve months ago he had been encouraged by Jo's assertions that she welcomed the arrival of his son, and would do her best to make a good home for him, but the reality was that her relationship with Sean had never progressed much beyond the uneasy provision of meals and a laundry service. Marcus was forced to acknowledge to himself that it might have been better for Sean in the long run if, rather than actively encouraging him to come and live up here, he had persuaded him to try and make a go of it with his mother, stepfather and the new baby. Had he encouraged Sean for selfish reasons? Of course he had wanted to spend more time with him, to do the lads-and-dads things which his divorce had mostly denied them. But could it also have been to score a point against the ex-wife, who had hurt him and yet managed to keep their child?

He half wondered whether losing Sean to his first wife, while nothing like so traumatic or painful as the loss which Jo had sustained, had been among the factors which forged the original bond between them. Maybe his getting Sean back – a resolution which, if he was being realistic, was never going to happen for her with Lauren – had helped to fuel her breakdown. Breakdown: the word which so accurately described the condition towards which both Jo's mental state and their own relationship was teetering.

Without the tours – and heaven knows, she couldn't be trusted with them at the moment – he was aware that she had very little in her life. He tried to suggest things she could do, because he knew that she was in perpetual need of distraction from the tragedy she carried with her every day, but at the moment there seemed to be nothing much she was prepared to interest herself in apart from perhaps her drawing. His eye fell on her sketch book, which had been left lying on a chair near the sitting-room door. She never liked him to look at her work, but since she was out of the room for a moment, it could not do any harm. He reached across and began to flick through the book.

Jo's offer to make some coffee had been motivated by an urgent need to escape from the sitting room, where she had been finding it almost impossible to concentrate on what Marcus was saying. Why had there been no one to meet her at Claife Station? Had she failed in some way? Or maybe she was looking at it from the wrong angle. Maybe she had passed the test: after all, she had made it to the rendezvous alone, without telling anyone. The abductor would not want to risk capture by the police, so perhaps the idea had been to see if she would follow instructions to the letter. Claife Station might be just the first of many tests. Only when trust had been established could a real meeting be set up and Lauren handed over.

Or it could have been a cruel, pointless hoax? That had always been the line taken by the Marcus and the police. But why send someone on a wild goose chase, unless you intended to be there to spring a nasty surprise at their destination? How would you even have the satisfaction of knowing whether or not the target had taken the bait . . . unless you watched them leave and waited up to see them return home?

As she poured hot water into the cafetière, she saw in her mind's eye the light glowing above the door of The Old Forge. Gilda certainly could not have followed her, then got back to Easter Bridge before she did without being seen; but she would not have needed to. She could have sat comfortably inside The Old Forge, observing Jo's departure and return.

She tried to recall exactly what Gilda had said: 'I was just drawing my bedroom curtains when I saw your car turning on to the drive. I wonder where Jo has been at this time of night, I said to myself.' Was there something wrong with that statement? How had she known who was in the car? No – there was no mileage in that. Gilda had been living in Easter Bridge long enough to differentiate her car from Marcus's.

She put the cafetière, milk jug and two mugs on a tray, then carried them through to the sitting room while artlessly humming a tune, trying to frame a smile as she entered the room. It died instantly on her lips when she saw the look on Marcus's face and what he had in his hands. The sketch book was open and his face was almost as white as its pages. She stopped dead, a pace into the room.

'What the hell is this?'

Jo could feel the tray shaking in her hands. The mugs chinked like chattering teeth as she walked across and placed her burden unsteadily on the coffee table.

'Why are you looking at my drawings?'

'Is there any reason why I shouldn't? I wasn't aware that they were really a secret – not until now, anyway.'

'Those should have been rubbed out. I should have got rid of them ages ago, put them in the fire.'

Marcus's voice was taut. 'It's Melissa, isn't it?'

'No. It isn't meant to be.'

'Come off it, Jo. They don't just look like her, you've even drawn in her bloody necklace – the one with the "M" on it.'

Jo was unable to say anything. She sank into a chair before her legs gave way on her.

Marcus glanced down again, sparing the page only the briefest moment of attention, as if he could scarcely bear to let his eyes linger on it. 'I had no idea,' he said, slowly. 'I didn't imagine you were capable of this kind of – of stuff.'

264

In a moment of madness she half considered saying, 'No, they're pretty amazing, aren't they? I didn't think I could achieve such a good likeness, but maybe portraiture's my thing.' She knew it was not funny.

'This is sick.' He stood up and strode across the room, shoving the book in front of her face. 'Look at this one – it's bordering on porn, sadistic porn.'

She tried to draw back, but he shoved the book closer to her face, then abruptly withdrew it and flung it across the room. Jo gave a wail of distress as it landed at an angle against the book case, its pages crushed and askew.

'Are those the only drawings like that, or are there others somewhere, showing what tortures you imagine subjecting the rest of us to?'

'It isn't like that . . .'

'Are there any more?' Marcus thundered.

'No.' Jo cowered back in the chair. Marcus hardly ever really lost his temper. He had never spoken to her like this before. 'There are no others. I didn't draw them deliberately.'

'You don't draw something by accident. They don't just appear in the book by themselves.'

'But they do. That's the thing. They're like doodles – the sort of thing your pen does when you're on the phone and you're not thinking.'

'Don't be so bloody ridiculous.'

'I'm not. Everyone doodles. You do it.'

'No one doodles like that. No one who's this side of the gates of Broadmoor, anyway.'

'Marcus, you must believe me. I did them without thinking. I didn't sit down and draw them on purpose. I don't really think about Melissa in that way. I'm not even agreeing that they *are* of Melissa – they're just doodles.'

'Of a woman who is being tortured or murdered.'

265

'I didn't do them on purpose.' Her voice had sunk to a whisper.

He returned to his chair, sat down, drew in a long breath, then said more calmly, 'OK, if it isn't a deliberate, conscious thing, then it must be something that's going on in your subconscious mind – am I right?'

'I'll get rid of them,' she began. 'I'll do it now. We can light a fire and burn them, if you like. If I had only destroyed them, when I first saw them . . .'

'Then I wouldn't have seen them. But I have seen them, and you have seen them, and we both know that this is not something a normal person –' he corrected himself quickly, 'an *untroubled* person – would have done. If these are the kinds of images in your subconscious, then you need –'

'No, Marcus! Don't start all that. I am not going to see any damn psychiatrists or –' She stopped short, catching sight of Sean standing in the doorway.

'Sorry,' he said. 'I think there's a problem with the broadband. Can you come and have a look, Dad?'

'Of course.' Marcus collected himself and rose from his chair.

'It could wait until later,' Sean said; but Marcus was all for attending to it there and then. As he crossed the room he scooped up the sketch book in a swift movement, ignoring the crushed pages as he compressed it closed under his arm and carried it from the room.

Jo watched him go without a word, her possessions confiscated like a child found reading an unsuitable book in class, and instinctively knowing that the volume will never be restored to her. Marcus no doubt intended to keep it, she thought. Not destroying, but rather preserving the page of tormented Melissa lookalikes, to use as evidence against her in the future.

CHAPTER TWENTY-ONE

The three days before Marcus left to take charge of Battlefields of York and Lancaster was an uneasy period of silences and rows, all of them turning on the question of the disputed sketches.

'I want my drawings back,' she demanded.

'That's not possible, I'm afraid.'

'But it's my book.'

'You can buy another one.'

'I want that one.'

'Agree to come and see the doctor and we'll see what he says about it.'

'No. I don't need to see a doctor.'

She tried hunting for the book, but he had either found a very good hiding place or else taken it off the premises altogether.

'You didn't take my book into the office, did you, when you went to Kirkby Lonsdale, yesterday?'

'No.'

'You haven't shown the drawings to Melissa?'

'Don't be ridiculous.'

'Then what have you done with them?'

'Make an appointment with the doctor.'

She did not buy another drawing book. It was mostly too wet for sketching outdoors, anyway – the worst summer anyone could remember in years. Damp, miserable days slid one into another. The garden dripped, perpetually damp underfoot, with any short-lived blooms starved of sunshine and battered by wind and rain. The view from the kitchen window was like a watercolour done in greens and browns, which had run to deleterious effect.

Sean's week with his mother turned into a fortnight, after which Marcus took the unprecedented step of taking Sean with him on one of the tours. Jo tried not to think that he was frightened to leave Sean alone with her.

In spite of having plenty of time on her hands, it was hard to get anything done. Emails from Nerys sat on the machine for days, awaiting her reply. What was there to say?

Every day she waited for another sign – a postcard bearing fresh instructions, another seashell, anything to indicate that the abductor was still in contact – but nothing came. Thin strands of grass crept up between the stones which formed her message of compliance on the lawn, and since it was impossible to mow around the edges, the letters began to look untidy. By the end of August buttercups and cranesbill had woven insidious patterns across the stones, transforming their positive message into no more than an overgrown rockery.

Whenever Marcus came home she expected him to start harping on about the doctor again, and although he did not often raise the issue directly, she knew it was continually in his mind. They were mutually watchful. She was aware of his scrutiny, and felt that he was forever on the lookout for signs of instability, storing up a lot of little clues to use against her, yet more leverage with which to persuade her that she needed professional help. One morning when they were both in the office, she rummaged in a drawer to find a highlighter pen and came up with a pack of blank white postcards she had not known were there. It was one of those forgotten stationery purchases, like the bundle of coloured treasury tags which were never used for anything but no one ever got round to throwing away; except that when she looked up she saw that Marcus was watching her, and knew what he was thinking. The cards were burning her fingers, but she did not know what to do with them – returning them to the drawer or consigning them to the bin both seemed suspect. At one time, she might have said, 'What on earth did we buy these for?' but now the words remained unuttered. The last thing she wanted to do was invite comment, give him an opening.

The constant sense of being under observation made her nervous, so that she forgot things, became confused, lost her thread in the middle of sentences, offered him only garbled accounts of what she had been doing with her time.

There was a lot she did not tell him now. She had returned several times to Claife Station, half hoping that a visit by daylight might provide a clue. She wondered if Lauren had ever been there. Certainly the abductor must know the place, otherwise why choose it? The abductor must be somewhere near – which meant that Lauren was too. She changed the bedding in the spare room regularly and replenished the flowers. Soon Lauren would be coming home. That would change everything. Then she would show Marcus that she could be a real mother. She would be vindicated, and they could remake themselves into a real family. There would be fun and laughter in their lives again.

September finally brought another postcard. Jo had been surreptitiously lying in wait for the postman as usual, and seized on the card almost as soon as it hit the mat, clutching it to her chest and hurriedly retreating upstairs, so that Marcus, who happened to be at home that day, would be unaware of its arrival. She did not turn it over to read the message until she was safely behind the closed bedroom door. *I still have her.*

'No, no.' She wanted to beat her fists against the door. This was going backwards. It was hopeless. She had to take a few minutes to compose herself. Marcus must not find out about the postcard. At least it was some form of contact to hold on to. Maybe it was meant to reassure her, and presaged something more positive to arrive soon.

'Why?' she whispered. 'Why are you torturing me? Why won't you just give her back?'

When she returned downstairs, she felt Marcus watching her. Where once his glance might have been admiring, now he was just keeping her under surveillance. *He loved me so much*, she thought, *and I loved him – as much as I could give. But now we just circle around one another. Both our lives have become about something else.*

When Marcus and Sean were not there, her footsteps seemed to echo more loudly around the house. It reminded her of walking through rooms stripped of their furniture and ready for the decorators. The house had acquired that same hollow chill she associated with curtainless windows and bared floorboards. Everything in The Hideaway was still in its place, but it had faded, become insubstantial. She waited for the postman to arrive each day, then drove somewhere to escape the emptiness of her disappointment. She no longer began and ended her walks in Easter Bridge, since that opened up the possibility of having to stop and speak with neighbours. Often she just drove to a lay-by or a car park, where she sat watching people come and go, killing time until she felt obliged to return to the empty house, where the tune of 'The Laughing Policeman' sometimes crept into her head, as if it were being sung by some unseen maniac in another room.

Shelley's books on the Pre-Raphaelites sat reproachfully on a chair in the hall. She had neither read them nor returned them. Shelley came to the house and rang the doorbell once, but Jo had seen her coming and hid in the office until she had gone. Groups came to stay in the old farmhouse for a week or a fortnight, but the weather kept all but the hardiest of them indoors. There were no incursions into the garden of The Hideaway, by dogs, Frisbees or nosey temporary neighbours exercising their 'right to roam'. The stinky barbecue sat unused, dripping in the rain.

She occasionally saw the inhabitants of The Old Forge from a distance, usually passing in their car, occasionally out on foot. Once Rebecca had gone back to school, Gilda Iceton appeared to be as solitary as she was herself. Gilda, who had never managed to make any friends at school, ever the loner, footling about on her own, just as she appeared to be now. She had stood by while the other kids taunted Gilda for her differences, but maybe she and Gilda had not been so different as she had liked to believe. Maybe the real difference had been that Gilda would not sell her soul in exchange for cheap popularity. She had joined in when the others laughed at Gilda and mocked her for being 'touched' and 'soft in the head', although Gilda was clearly neither. Now it was not Gilda but herself whose faculties were being called into question – a sort of ironic justice, if you like. It had always been there, of course. Like mother, like daughter. If your mother is crazy, why not you? *Bad blood*. It didn't always follow, of course. Insanity did not have to run in families. *No*, said a voice in her head. *It doesn't need to run; it just creeps and crawls, but it gets there in the end.*

Jo tried to retreat from the memories of what they had put Gilda through – the name-calling, and worse. There were so many things she did not want to remember – and some she could not. Ever since the day of Aunty Joan's funeral, she had been forced to question the reliability of her own recall.

271

What was truth and what was fiction? If she had been incorrect about her father's death, then maybe other mistakes had crept into the transcript of her life. Lately she had taken to waking suddenly in the early hours, desperately trying to remember something to do with Lauren's disappearance. Something significant that she had noticed that day. Something important that had been overlooked.

The transition from summer to autumn occurred without any noticeable change in the level of precipitation. Green leaves which had been shiny with water for weeks and weeks lost their colour, faded and fell sodden to the ground. With Harry and Charlotte long since departed for Heswall, and Rebecca Iceton gone back to her boarding school, Sean was again the only person in Easter Bridge who was not old enough to vote. He continued to tread warily around his stepmother, who seemed ever more withdrawn. She had developed a habit of occupying a particular chair in the sitting room, maintaining the same position for up to an hour or more in an attitude of concentration, her eyes focused on a patch of carpet just beyond her feet. The first time he saw her like that he assumed she must be watching something – a woodlouse or a spider, perhaps. But in the weeks that followed, he encountered her sitting in the same position again and again. In spite of his better judgement, his curiosity was aroused.

One evening when supper was long over and his father was away as usual, Sean had ventured downstairs to organize a snack. On his way back to his room, he paused in the doorway of the sitting room and stood watching her. He had been there for about a minute before she became aware of him and looked up.

'Sorry. I didn't mean to distract you if you were meditating or something.'

'I was – sort of meditating – but it's OK.'

'I didn't mean to disturb you.' He edged away into the hall.

'It's OK,' she repeated. 'Did you want something?'

'No. I just thought it was a bit funny, you sitting there like that. I wondered if you were ill.'

'It's OK,' she said again. 'I was trying to remember something, that's all. It's a technique I read about – on the internet.' She would have elaborated, but Sean was already moving further in the direction of the stairs.

'Whatever,' he said.

Jo shrugged. A few months ago she might have been elated at the hint of a breakthrough – Sean pausing to see if she was OK – but now it hardly seemed to matter. She resumed her position. The trick was to be comfortable, relaxed – but not overly so – to keep your eyes open, but try not to concentrate too hard on what was in front of you, *leaving the way open for internal visualizations* was what the instructions said, the idea being that you *reconfigure the scene, detail by detail, until what you were seeing then, you are seeing in the here and now*. It was called The Doctor Heinsel Method. According to Dr Heinsel, everything you had ever seen or experienced was locked away in your mind, so that if you only went about it the right way you could remember everywhere you had ever been and everything that had ever happened to you – or at least, some people could. Dr Heinsel claimed that with appropriate training, everyone had the capacity to do this, providing they were prepared to put enough time into achieving what he called Dynamic Cognitive Memory State.

Jo had been following his Beginner's Programme religiously. Dr Heinsel said that a trainee should not begin on troubling or traumatic episodes. According to his theories, the reason you had difficulty recalling them was because the mind invariably shied away from memories like these: so you had to start with happy memories, which the mind would *more willingly embrace*, working your way up to the scary stuff only when you and your mind had got to grips with the Heinsel Method. Thus Jo had started off with a very happy memory indeed – her first honeymoon, spent on the Isle of Wight in 1995. Saving for their deposit had not left them with sufficient funds for anywhere more exotic, but as Dom had said, 'Who needs the Caribbean, when they have palm trees here?'

Dr Heinsel was big on working through things in chronological order. Apparently the untrained mind liked to jump about, flicking from one memory to another, thereby missing important bits out, so you had to find a starting point which was a recognizable beginning, then work forward from it. Jo had chosen the ferry crossing from Lynmouth, and been surprised to find that she could piece together quite a lot. The amount she could recall about their small hotel in Shanklin astonished her. There had been a china shepherdess on the dressing table in their bedroom, a room which they had reached by climbing the steep stairs lined with an odd mixture of cheap prints, everything from Millais's *Boyhood of Raleigh* to dogs playing snooker. The hotelier had walked around at breakfast time, offering extra triangles of toast from a wicker basket lined with red paper napkins. Dominic had always accepted at least one extra slice.

On the first morning they had descended to the beach before breakfast, via a steeply sloping road which curved back on itself. The tide had left a band of flat wet sand where no one else had walked, so that their two sets of footprints might have marked new arrivals on a desert island. At night the stars had been astonishingly bright, and sometimes you could see the lights of big liners or cross-channel ferries, proceeding from left to right down the channel.

Each time you revisited the memory, you had to start right back at the beginning again, and try to recall a little more, *pausing to take in the scene*, Dr Heinsel called it, filling in the gaps. There had been stainless-steel dishes, one containing strawberry jam and one orange marmalade, on each of the breakfast tables. The chairs and tables had been made of dark wood, and each chair had a thin red cushion tied loosely on to it, which didn't quite match the red paper napkins. If you opened the bedroom door too wide it bounced back off the side of the bed. She tried to picture the host with his basket in one hand and the stainless-steel tongs with which he distributed the toast in the other, but it was very hard to put a face to people you had not known well, or with whom you'd had only brief contact, such a long time ago.

Dom she could picture perfectly. If only he had not given up on her. Life could have been so different. They could have found Lauren together – Marcus had tried to be kind but he did not really understand. No one did.

In October Maisie held another fund-raiser, but Jo waited until she knew the Perrys were out – they always gardened at Holehird on Wednesdays – before slipping an envelope containing a scribbled apology and a ten-pound note through their letterbox. It was weeks since she had spoken to Shelley, whose books lay gathering dust on a chair in the office, where they had been placed in readiness for the short journey back along the lane which she somehow never got round to making.

Sean had been invited to spend half-term with his mother, the visit in summer having been a modest success. Marcus was away in Cornwall on the last Daphne du Maurier tour of the year, and with no reason to keep regular hours, Jo's days lost any semblance of rhythm. The Hideaway again developed that sense of emptiness, through which Jo flitted like an insubstantial phantom.

One night she sat up until 3 a.m., concentrating on Dr Heinsel's Method, working her way through the Isle of Wight trip, followed by Lauren's first birthday. There had been a cake in the shape of a big number one, covered in white icing edged all round in pink. Lauren had blown out the candle and clapped her hands: little stubby fingers, each with a knuckle that went in like a dimple, instead of out in the bony pattern of ridges and furrows found on an adult's hand. There had been cupcakes in spotted paper cases which peeled away to leave a sharp zigzag pattern in the icing, chocolate finger biscuits which disintegrated in small pink hands and dishes of ice cream and jelly. Later she had washed the chocolate off those little hands with a flannel, feeling each delicate digit as it wriggled and resisted the damp cloth.

By the time she went to bed her mind was bustling with memories and did not want to shut down. Was this the moment to move forward? *There will come a time*, Dr Heinsel advised, *when your memory is so well attuned to the process that you can take things to the next level, forcing your memory to recognize and bring forward the things it has been trying to suppress.*

She switched on the bedside light and propped her pillows up against the bedhead. It felt cold in the bedroom. The sun had been absent without leave for so long that a constant chill permeated everything. Marcus claimed that she felt the cold more lately because she was not eating properly – which might be true, but she simply wasn't hungry. Food did not interest her, and while Marcus and Sean were away, it did not seem worth the bother of cooking. It occurred to her that she *had* eaten very little during the day. Perhaps if she heated that half-tin of rice pudding in the microwave, it might warm her up a bit – but the thought of it made her feel sick. She had eaten the first half earlier in the day, realizing as she consumed it that she did not really like tinned rice pudding, the illustration on the tin being much more attractive than the reality. Instead she slipped out of bed and gathered up a pashmina which was draped over the back of a chair. When she had wrapped it around her shoulders, she slid back under the duvet, which she pulled right up to her chin.

She had never tried the Heinsel Method anywhere but her regular chair (Dr Heinsel advised that trainees should work to establish a routine in the beginning, so that the mind would learn to recognize what was expected of it), but tonight she was feeling so receptive that it did not seem to matter – and besides which, it would be even colder downstairs without the duvet.

She would begin with the moment of waking up in their bed and breakfast: that would be her starting point for this new excursion into the past. They had been allocated a large, irregular-shaped room, which had odd angles and alcoves: a family room with a double bed, a single and a cot. Mrs Potter (yes – Potter – that had been her name) had let them have the family room at no extra charge because she said her double room was a squash with the cot. The wallpaper had been a very old-fashioned design: big blue flowers and purple grapes in a diagonal pattern, the same sequence going off in all directions. There were three different configurations of the blue flowers and two different bunches of grapes, and the pattern had repeated itself, again and again, up, down, left, right, sideways, backways, diagonal garlands of grapes and flowers, woven together with dark green ivy, which she would remember to her dying day, particularly at the place where the pattern met the empty cot and partially disappeared behind the bars. It had been an old-fashioned cot with pictures

277

on the ends: a fluffy yellow duck at the head and a bounding lamb at the foot. She remembered sitting on the edge of the double bed much later, staring at the empty cot, unable to comprehend the enormity of what had happened.

No, no – this was not the way to do it. Go back to the beginning of the day. Start with waking up, getting Lauren ready to go down to breakfast . . . putting on the bright red T-shirt and the sky-blue dungarees, fastening the buttons on the royal-blue canvas shoes.

Breakfast – what had they had for breakfast? The high chair was rather tatty, with a half-moon white plastic tray which had seen better days. Lauren eating cereal, making a bit of a mess, although she was generally pretty good. Deciding to give the beach a miss that day. Strapping Lauren into her car seat . . . jumping ahead there, lots of things must have happened between the cornflakes and the car seat . . . Lauren flexing her legs and resisting the process. She hadn't wanted to go in the car. It was almost as if she knew something bad was going to happen – no, that was silly – she always stuck her legs out rigid when you tried to strap her in.

'Stop it, Lauren. Sit nicely.' How sharp her voice sounded. If only she had known. If she had realized this was their last morning – their very last morning together – she would have gathered Lauren in her arms and run far, far away with her.

Concentrate – don't get distracted. The car is going along the lanes, Dominic is driving – quite fast, as tended to be his style. Occasionally there are glimpses of the sea, flashing silver where it caught the sunbeams, but mostly it's just farmland glimpsed between high Devon hedges. There's a tape playing . . . maybe REM. Focus now – try to hold that moment, there in the car – can you hear what's playing? Can you see the cover of the cassette?

Sod the cassette. The car is warm inside and the interior

278

rather grubby, even when viewed from behind sunglasses. There are crumbs and crushed-up drink cartons, the remnants of holiday picnics. It's going to need a good clean-out when we get home.

The car park fills up early at Barleycombe. The only spaces left are right at the far side. There's a caravan taking up two spaces. Caravans are a bête noire of Dom's. Statics are just about OK, but he thinks tourers are an invention of the devil. He gets the pushchair out of the boot while she leans into the car to unfasten the clasp of Lauren's harness and lift her out of the car seat. In the background 'The Laughing Policeman' is guffawing fit to bust, rocking back and forth on his heels and pointing at her as she straps Lauren into her Mothercare buggy this one last time . . . no, that's not right.

There are seagulls, always seagulls at the coast, raucous, strident, the predominant noise against a background hum of cars arriving, people getting out, slamming doors, talking and laughing. Dominic buys a ticket at the machine and sticks it on the inside of the driver's window. The instructions say 'display on windscreen', but Dom takes no notice.

There's a little newsagent's next to the car park. Lauren gestures up at the window display of faded Airfix kits and old-fashioned sweet jars. 'Weeties,' she says, hopefully. They debate whether or not to buy a paper – decide not to bother. They are just moving on from the shop when she notices a woman across the road; a woman who has in the same instant seen her, and who pauses for a moment but then hurries on, as if she has been mistaken in thinking that there is mutual recognition, but she is not mistaken – it is Gilda – that girl she was once at school with.

As they proceed down the road people have to step off the narrow pavement to make way for Lauren's buggy. Lauren is kicking her feet up and down, lifting each leg in turn, as if they are pistons powering the buggy along. They get stuck behind an older couple, who are walking arm in arm, not quite fast enough, so that Jo is afraid the buggy will catch their heels. The man's brown overcoat is somehow familiar: it's an old-fashioned garment, unseasonably warm, quite unsuited to the day. Typical of her mother, too, to be inappropriately dressed, in a faded gingham check number, which looks like part of a cowgirl fancy dress. It's a wonder she hasn't gone the whole hog and worn the hat as well – and as for her father's burgundy Crimplene trousers . . . but her father cannot have been there. She has got it wrong, wrong, wrong.

Rewind and start again: that was Dr Heinsel's advice. Start at the beginning and take each scene, one detail at a time, linger on everything, don't try too hard, don't rush.

She began again in the bedroom of the blue flowers and purple grapes. Dominic beside her in the double bed, enjoying the soft warmth of one naked limb against another, both of them staying quiet, not wanting to alert Lauren, because once she realized they were awake she would be clamouring to come out, toddling around the room, getting into everything. Lauren who is sitting up in the cot, burbling cheerfully to her pet cat Puddy, a grey and white soft toy which always looked grubby because it went with her everywhere.

Work through the movements of the day again: everything . . . the cornflakes, the high chair, Lauren dropping Puddy as they were going out so that he nearly got left behind, the crumbs in the car – she still couldn't remember what had been playing on the tape deck – but when she reached the village street there was Gilda again, staring at her from the opposite pavement before turning abruptly away.

CHAPTER TWENTY-TWO

'What are you doing in here?' Marcus had spoken quietly but the sound of his voice made her jump.

'Nothing. I'm just reading my book.'

'Why are you reading in the spare bedroom?'

'I like it in here. I often sit in here to read when you're away. There's a good light from this window.'

'You're not watching The Old Forge, are you?'

'Of course not. What on earth would I want to do that for? Anyway, it's raining so hard, you can't see across the road.'

'It's so dark in here, it's a wonder you can see to read at all.'

'I'm OK.'

'I'm going now,' he said.

There was very nearly an awkward pause, but she gathered herself in time, put the book on the bedside table and crossed the room to facilitate the obligatory farewell embrace.

'Take care,' she said. 'The roads are going to be bad.'

'I know – flood warnings out all over the place, and more rain forecast.'

'Rain yesterday, rain today, rain tomorrow,' she said, wearily. 'I can't remember the last time it wasn't raining.'

She allowed herself to be pressed against his shirt, receiving a kiss on the cheek. She could feel the warmth of him through the shirt. The first time he ever held her had been like an awakening on a spring morning, when the flowers open up and the birds begin to sing. It had signalled the end of a long, cold winter, that quickening of her heart. When he made love to her they had basked in the heat from the summer sun; but it was autumn now. At first she had just said she was tired, a touch unwell or merely not in the mood; lately there had been no need to say anything at all. This fundamental absence in their relationship had never been discussed. She was grateful for his silence on the matter, relieved when he did not ask her to explain the way in which desire had died; how she was always cold now, always huddled under layers of t-shirts and outsize cardigans. How she felt as if her body was held together by a skeleton of dried-up twigs which would snap into a thousand pieces if he tried to hold her too tightly, or thrust into her as he had been wont to do before.

Even these perfunctory gestures of farewell had begun to feel dangerous, so she was alarmed when, with the customary hug and peck accomplished, he did not immediately release her, only allowing her to withdraw an inch or two so that his face remained close to hers. She hated it when that anxious look came into his eyes because it made her feel guilty. She did not want him to worry about her, still less to start seeking solutions, formulating plans which involved counsellors, doctors, or taking some quality time out together. Why couldn't he just go off and sleep with Melissa, complaining that his wife did not understand him, like any normal, red-blooded male would do? She managed to exert enough gentle resistance that he let his arms fall away and she was able to take a couple of steps backwards.

'You will try to eat sensibly while I'm away, won't you?'

'Of course.' She noticed in an abstract sort of way that Marcus's hair was going grey. When had that happened?

'Because Sean told me you hardly ate anything at all last week.'

'You shouldn't listen to what Sean says. He doesn't like me, and anyway it's wrong to use a fourteen-year-old as your spy.'

'I'm not using him as my spy. He just happened to mention it. And he's had his fifteenth birthday now.'

'What does he know, anyway? He's out at school all day, then he locks himself away in his bedroom the rest of the time.'

'You're losing weight . . .'

She pulled away from him. 'I thought you had to go now.'

'Jo, darling, don't let's part on a quarrel.'

'Well, don't badger me about my weight then. I'm fine. I don't need to eat any more than I am doing. I don't need to see a doctor. I don't need a referral to a psychiatrist –'

'Who said anything about a psychiatrist?'

'No one.'

They stood looking at one another. He forced a smile and held his arms out to her. When she did not move, he stepped forward and enveloped her in another hug. 'Come on, Jo,' he said. 'We're going to get through this.'

'Of course,' she said. 'Of course we are.' *Just as soon as I get Lauren back.*

'I have to go now.'

'I'll come to the door with you.'

'No need. You stay warm and dry. Shall I put the light on, so you can go on reading your book?'

'No – I'm coming downstairs now.'

She followed him down to the hall. He shrugged himself into his jacket, picked up his laptop bag which was waiting by the door, then paused to give her hand a parting squeeze.

'Goodbye, Marcus.'

'Goodbye, darling. Take care of yourself.'

The rain continued to fall steadily. When she switched on the television it was dominated by reports of flooding, with Cumbria seemingly bearing the brunt. The ground was saturated, of course. There was simply nowhere for the water to go.

When Sean came in from school his trousers were soaked to the knees. 'It's right up over the road at the bridge,' he said. 'I had to wade through it to get here – it was really dodgy.'

'God, Sean! You should have rung me.'

'You wouldn't have got through it in the car. There's water rushing down the lane as if it was a river. I had to walk up using the verge. If this keeps up I won't be able to go to school tomorrow because we'll be cut off.' It was impossible to tell whether he was more enthused by the drama of the situation, or the possibility of an unscheduled day's holiday.

She could hardly believe it. Even when the beck was in spate after heavy rain, it never got anywhere near as high as the bridge. Driven by doubt and curiosity, she put on her over-trousers, wellingtons and cagoule, rustled her way to the kitchen door and set out into the downpour. The first thing she noticed was the noise of running water. On windless days you could hear the musical note of the beck in the distance, but she could never recall its being audible over the sound of heavy rainfall before. The sight and sound of running water was everywhere, pouring down drainpipes, overflowing from gutterings, but in the background she could also hear a muted roar of the kind she normally associated with large waterfalls. When she reached the lane a surreal sight met her eyes. A circular drain cover opposite their gateway, a hitherto seldom-noticed object over which one walked or drove without a second thought, had turned into a fountain with a perfect circle of jets each firing to a height of several inches, while a complimentary circle of water oozed up around its rim, all of it merging into the tide of water which was flowing steadily down the lane towards the bridge.

Although the water was no more than an inch deep, it was flowing fast, and Jo decided to follow Sean's example, picking her way along the verge, until she got within sight of the bridge. He was absolutely right about that, too. Only a fool would attempt to negotiate it in an ordinary vehicle. The beck had overflowed the bridge on either side, spreading itself across the tarmac for several feet in either direction and out on to the bridge itself, where the two channels from each side almost met in the centre. The water was moving at speed, rippling across the stones and other debris which had accumulated in the road. The boulders around which the beck normally picked its way had entirely vanished beneath the dirty brown torrent which was roaring down the gulley. It crashed against the old stone archway, throwing up a spray which was unnaturally white against the gloomy backdrop of wet tree trunks and drooping ferns.

Jo decided not to venture any nearer. When she had retraced her steps to the gates of The Hideaway, she decided to test the strength of the flow by placing one foot cautiously on to the tarmac. This caused the water to surge angrily over the toe of her boot, creating a bow wave from verge to verge. A shout made her look up. Shelley was hurrying towards her, clad in a dripping anorak and pastel-coloured wellington boots. The thought of that pile of unreturned books flickered momentarily, but Jo could tell from the urgency of Shelley's approach that the Pre-Raphaelite Movement was probably the last thing on her mind.

'Is Marcus at home?' Shelley called out, when she was still some yards away.

'No. He left about four hours ago.'

'Damn. I was coming to see if he would help.'

'Why? What's wrong?'

'You know the little stream that runs through the field at the back of us? It's normally just a trickle but there's masses of water coming down it. It goes through a sort of culvert under the track up to High Gilpin and the culvert's almost blocked, so the water's starting to find other places to go, and if we don't do something it's going to be into the Perrys' bungalow soon and maybe Honeysuckle Cottage and The Old Forge as well. There's some big stuff blocking the culvert that we urgently need to shift. I rang Mr Tyson to see if he could bring his tractor, but he's already out helping some motorist who's in trouble. Brian reckons we could do it between us if we had a bit more help – he's down there now, with Fred Perry.'

Jo did not hesitate. 'We'll come. I'll get Sean.'

It took her only moments to explain the situation to Sean, who appeared to relish the idea of action and could scarcely be restrained long enough to don suitable clothing. They splashed along the road together, turning in through the gap in the stone wall where the track went up to High Gilpin. From here they could appreciate the problem at once. Just as was happening with the main artery down at the bridge, so this normally insignificant vein of water had trebled or quadrupled in volume, and was haemorrhaging across the field towards the dry-stone wall which marked the perimeter of the Perrys' back garden. The channel which marked the stream's passage was deep enough to contain the water until it reached the culvert, where the blockage was starting to divert it elsewhere. Not only Brian and Fred, but also Shelley, Maisie and Gilda were labouring up to their ankles in water, prodding and poking at the edges of the obstruction with various implements brought out for the purpose. Brian was using his weight to lever a crowbar against something. His hood had fallen off to reveal a red knitted hat, which had taken on the appearance of a tea cosy fresh out of the washing machine and ready to peg on the line. When Sean and Jo reached the water's edge, the source of the problem became apparent. A large section of branch – perhaps six feet long and half the circumference of a pillar box – was lying within inches of the culvert, where an ever-growing accumulation of smaller debris was forming a dam against it.

'I still think the only answer may be to get my chainsaw,' Fred was saying. 'If we could reduce the size of the log, it would be easier to pull it away.'

'It'll take a long time to saw through it,' said Brian. 'And I'm not sure how it could be done, with the water level as it is. It certainly wouldn't do your chainsaw much good. Let's try to shift as much of the other stuff as we can, so that we're not pulling against that as well; then we'll have another go at shifting it.'

During this pause to discuss strategy, Jo could see that a climbing rope had been tied around the rogue branch where one end protruded from the water and some of the smaller branches and stones had already been dragged clear.

'The trouble is, there's more debris coming down all the time,' said Shelley.

'We need to get as much away as we can if we're going to have any chance of dragging that big branch out of the way,' Brian said.

'If we all work together, I believe we can do it.' It was the first time Gilda had spoken since Jo's arrival. She sounded brisk and sensible.

A variety of implements, rakes, a draw hoe, a crowbar and a mattock had already been assembled, but when all seven of them set to with a will, it immediately became clear that if serious injury was to be avoided, some degree of organization was required. Brian divided the process into three stages with himself, Fred and Sean standing in the water to drag the debris loose and shunt it in the direction of Maisie and Gilda, who then pulled it to the edge of the shallows where the two smallest women shifted everything right back from the water, so that there was no possibility of its being swept back against the log. They worked mostly in silence, with Brian grunting occasional instructions and Maisie reminding Fred to be careful on account of his dodgy hip.

'It's working,' said Shelley. 'There's less water coming across here than there was a few minutes ago.'

'It's only temporary,' said Brian. 'Unless we can get this big bugger shifted, it will all build up again in next to no time.' He leaned on the crowbar for a minute then said, 'Let's have another go at it, shall we?'

Brian organized them along the rope, making everyone stand well apart. 'We don't want to step straight back into one another,' he said. 'We'll have the men at the front, where there's more chance of losing your footing.'

Jo experienced an unexpected stab of pride as Sean took a place between Brian and Fred. He had worked as keenly as any of them – in fact, if she had not known any better, she would have thought he was enjoying himself. She found herself immediately behind Gilda, looking straight at her broad shoulders and back. Gilda's wet cagoule shone like newly laid tar: she was in black from head to foot, cagoule, waterproof trousers and, singularly among the women, old-fashioned black wellingtons. (Jo and Maisie had country-dweller green, while Shelley's were pink with pictures of sheep on them.) Although they had exchanged no words directly, Jo knew that for the moment at least there was no animosity between herself and Gilda. All that mattered was curbing that rushing water before it got too far across the field and invaded people's homes and gardens.

'Take up the slack,' Brian instructed, sounding for all the world like the captain of a tug o' war team. Jo sensed that, in an odd sort of way, Brian was enjoying himself too. His voice echoed across the open ground, reducing the rain to a whisper, putting the beck on notice that it might not be having things all its own way for very long. 'On three. One, two, threeee . . .'

'I wonder if it's worth trying Mr Tyson again,' mused Maisie, not really loud enough for anyone but Jo and Shelley, who were nearest, to hear.

'One, two, threeee . . .'

'I don't think we're going to do it without the tractor.' Maisie's voice was much louder this time, and carried more conviction.

'Rubbish,' Brian bawled back. 'How do you think people managed before there were telephones and tractors? Really put your backs into it this time.' His voice rose to a roar. 'One, two, *THREEEE* . . .'

Whether it was a collective determination not to be outdone by pre-industrial man, or fear of Brian on the warpath, there was a different feeling on the rope and all of them – even Shelley, who was right at the rear – felt a movement on the end of the line.

'That's it,' yelled Brian. 'We've got it moving now. OK, Sean, me lad? You all right Fred? Ready? Again – one two, *threeee* . . .'

'That's got it this time,' cried Gilda, who, unlike Jo, could see the end of the obstructing branch. 'We must have moved it a good six inches with that last pull.'

'Everyone move round. Change the angle.' Brian shouted, waving an arm to indicate the direction in which they needed to move. 'We've got the bugger. Now we need to shift it sideways, so that it starts to swing round this way, right out of the beck. We've already freed up a lot of the channel. Come on, let's have another big effort . . .'

It took perhaps fifteen minutes of steady work before the huge branch was dragged into a satisfactory position. The Easter Bridge tug o' war team had been victorious in its first and only contest, and with the task accomplished there was almost a reluctance to abandon the site of battle. They nodded to one another in the near darkness, sharing their moment of triumph.

Jo's back and shoulders ached horribly, but in spite of this she felt renewed. The task seemed to have galvanized those brittle twigs inside her into sinew and solid bone. Looking round at the faces of the others, she knew that whatever mysterious energy had seized her, they were gripped by it too. Fred had forgotten that he was seventy-two; Shelley was grinning in spite of the rain trickling down her face and neck; Sean looked shyly pleased with himself and at least an inch taller.

'You must all come inside and have something to warm you up,' said Maisie.

Everyone began to protest, saying they were close to home and far too wet, but Maisie was having none of it. 'You've saved our home today. Another hour or maybe less, and the water would have been inside. No one is going anywhere until we've had a chance to say thank you properly. Our fire will still be lit, and it won't take a minute to get it going properly again. So what if you're wet? Our veranda is always full of wet gear; just leave your outside stuff in there and get warmed up. I can soon rustle up some hot drinks.'

'I've got a nice drop of scotch in the sideboard.' Fred winked at Brian. 'Just the job on a day like this.'

Jo's first instinct was to decline and beat a hasty retreat back to the safety of The Hideaway, but she knew that it would appear churlish if everyone else accepted. Then she caught sight of Sean's face, and realized how mean-spirited it would be to drag him away from what was taking on the semblance of a celebration: the victory of the Easter Bridge Irregulars over the Elements. So she fell into step with the others, following Maisie back to Throstles, where everyone peeled off their soaking outer garments in the veranda as instructed, before hesitantly entering the sitting room in their stockinged feet.

While Fred switched on the lights and stoked up the fire, Maisie conjured up a pile of towels, which she handed round for people to mop their faces or rub down their hair. The towels were followed in remarkably short order by plates of biscuits and fruitcake, mugs of tea and hot chocolate and optional tots of whisky. Catching Jo's eye, Fred said that he was sure it would be OK for Sean to have some, provided it was diluted with a drop of water. 'He's done a man's work today, haven't you, lad?' Fred said, in that hearty way which childless septuagenarians think the ideal tone to address a teenage boy. Sean accepted the glass and mumbled, 'Thanks,' blushing to the roots of his hair.

'I don't understand how that tree got swept down in the first place,' said Jo. 'It's such a weight: you would never think a little stream like that would be enough to shift it, not even with the amount of water coming down today.'

'It wasn't swept down today,' Shelley explained. 'It came down ages ago when we had that big blow, this time last year. Mr Tyson did say he was going to cut it up, but I suppose he never got round to it. It wouldn't have mattered normally, because the way it was lying across the beck, the water usually passes right under it with loads of room to spare. But with the beck running four or five times higher than normal, smaller stuff started to catch on it and build up, so that before you know where you are there's a blockage. Then of course, the water starts finding itself another route.'

'We've been so lucky,' Maisie put in. 'If Gilda hadn't spotted what was happening and alerted everyone, the first thing we would have known about it was when water started coming into the house. We're in a little dip here, and once it came down the steps at the back, that would have been it.'

'It was pure chance,' Gilda said. 'I happened to go upstairs for something, looked out of my bedroom window and saw the way the water was spreading out across the field. If I had gone up just a little bit later it would have been too dark to notice.'

'Well, we've Gilda's sharp eyes to thank – and of course all of you, for turning out to help. That's what's saved our bacon,' said Fred.

'To good neighbours,' said Maisie, raising her glass.

'To good neighbours,' everyone repeated.

CHAPTER TWENTY-THREE

The scale of the flooding which overtook Cumbria that night emerged gradually via the television news, the internet and word of mouth. Towns in the north of the county captured the majority of the headlines, for here the devastation had been most marked, with bridges collapsed and loss of life. The inundation left its mark further south, too, where lakes rose dramatically, rivers burst their banks and water found its way into hundreds of homes, businesses and vehicles, spreading across roads to a depth which turned normally landlocked communities into islands, enforcing the closure of shops, schools and offices, which, if not entirely cut off, were deficient in stock, pupils or staff.

Marcus telephoned, alarmed by what he was hearing on the news, only to be reassured that all was well. Jo made a point of emphasizing to him Sean's part in the work of defeating the rising water. Credit where it was due.

In places where no real damage had been sustained, life swiftly returned to normal. It even stopped raining for a few days, and when Marcus was at home he began to talk enthusiastically about Christmas. His last tour of 2009 was scheduled to finish on 22 December, after which he would be at home for almost a fortnight. 'We'll get some walking done,' he said. 'Maybe we could have a look at some of your suggestions for the Artists in the Lakes tour.' His heartiness struck an artificial note. They both knew that she had done nothing about the idea for months, and the deadline for inclusion in their 2011 programme would soon have come and gone.

Jo knew that Marcus genuinely liked Christmas, and in previous years she had endeavoured to make a great deal of it. Not just for Marcus, but also because she was ever mindful of the possibility – however faint – that Lauren might be there to share it with them. Wasn't Christmas the time of triumphant homecoming? The arrival of the long-lost relative, the erstwhile lover and returning prodigal sons – the time of family unity, reunion and forgiveness? Imagine if Lauren were to come home at Christmas, and find instead of fairy lights and tinsel, an undecorated house without so much as a mince pie in the larder to herald the festive season. So, this year, as she had done every year, Jo decorated the Christmas tree in mid-December, wound garlands of expensive artificial greenery around the uprights which supported the banisters and stocked up the cupboards with everything from brandy snaps to pickled gherkins. It seemed to take her longer than usual, and all her efforts felt hollow, not least because she was unable to summon up much optimism that this year would be the one when she was finally able to lay that longed-for extra place at the Christmas table.

There had been no more postcards, seashells, or any other signs and portents. Nor was she getting any further with Dr Heinsel's Method. She had relived their final day with Lauren again and again, but her memory was treacherous, forever introducing someone or something alien to the scene, some cunningly contrived distraction which prevented her from seeing what had really happened.

As the number of unopened windows on the advent calendar decreased, the Met Office began to forecast heavy snow. There was already snow on the tops, of course. They had been iced white since mid-October, but the valleys remained green save for the spun-sugar frosts which settled across everything on clear nights. Jo had very little faith in the Met Office. They seemed to get it wrong as often as they got it right, and changed their forecast from hour to hour. The most reliable indicator was still a glance through the window, and on the Sunday morning before Christmas any fool who had risen early and looked out into the grey half-light could tell that snow was imminent. Sure enough, a curtain of white flakes began to descend at breakfast time, steady and persistent, the kind of snow which an experienced Lakeland dweller recognizes as here to stay: picture-postcard pretty, but creating havoc on the roads. Easter Bridge was well off the route of any gritting lorry, and there was never enough passing traffic to keep the lane clear. Not that passing traffic would be a match for this stuff, which had soon fallen to a depth which could be measured in inches.

Jo watched the garden transform itself into an illustration from a children's story – *Winter Holiday* perhaps, or *The Lion, the Witch and the Wardrobe*. At around eleven o'clock the sound of feet stamping beside the front door alerted her to Shelley's arrival. She had come to deliver their Christmas card, and at Jo's invitation was easily persuaded to divest herself of coat and wellingtons while Jo located their card and made some tea to have with mince pies. The November floods had drifted her back into the orbit of her neighbours. She had returned Shelley's books, and even exchanged an uneasy greeting with Gilda when they passed one another in the lane.

'Is Sean out, enjoying the snow?' Shelley asked, cupping her hands round the warm mug.

'He's still in bed. I expect he'll want to take the sledge out when he gets up. Harry's family are supposed to be coming

295

up for Christmas, so if this carries on the kids will have a whale of a time.'

'Do you think they'll still come, if the weather's like this?'

'I suppose so. They've got a four-wheel drive. More fun for Sean if Harry's here.'

'Isn't Gilda's daughter home? I bet she'd like to go out sledging.'

'Sean thinks younger girls are beneath his attention.'

Shelley shrugged. 'I would have thought he'd be glad to have someone to throw snowballs at. And I bet he'll be interested enough in a couple of years' time. That girl is going to be absolutely stunning. I don't mean to be rude, but she doesn't get it from her mother, does she?' Shelley took a dainty bite of mince pie and masticated thoughtfully, before saying: 'This is nice. Did you buy them at Booths? My mum used to make her own and you could have paved the streets with them – they were all pastry and no mincemeat.'

'Mine used to buy them,' said Jo, 'when she remembered.'

There was a short silence.

'We're supposed to be going down to my parents for Christmas.' Shelley paused for another mouthful of pie. 'Although I don't think we will if this weather keeps up. Brian won't be broken-hearted, I can tell you. My dad's driving us all crazy with his family tree. He started with the online census, but now he's going off all over the place, looking at old gravestones and heaven knows what. You can hardly get in the door these days before he's producing a huge long chart and going on about great-uncles no one has ever heard of, and people emigrating to Canada in 1850. I can't keep up with it, and Brian isn't interested at all.'

'I don't suppose it is very interesting unless it's your own family.'

'And believe me, not always then.'

After Shelley had gone, it occurred to Jo that she could have asked her to pop their card for the Perrys through the door of Throstles as she passed, although asking someone else to deliver your Christmas card was a bit lazy, surely. And anyway, trudging along the lane in the snow to deliver them yourself was very traditional, very *A Christmas Carol*. That was the proper way to do it. What had Brian said about people managing before things had been mechanized? Not that the tradition of exchanging cards went back all that far, but never mind.

The card destined for the Perrys was propped up on the back of her desk in the office, where it had been left with Shelley and Brian's when she took all the others to the post office. It struck her that she could not walk to the Perrys without passing The Old Forge. She had never so much as considered adding Gilda to her Christmas-card list, but there was something very pointed about walking straight past the woman's gate with a card in her hand which was obviously destined for the only other permanent residents. Gilda was part of their tiny community, too. She thought of the way Gilda had saved the day when she spotted the overflowing beck in the nick of time; Gilda tugging on the rope, while the rain beat down on her shiny, black-clad shoulders . . . Gilda always being the last person to be picked for teams, the only Christmas cards to appear on her desk coming from one or two of the kinder girls who pitied her – although not enough to make her their friend. It was Christmas, after all, and Gilda was her neighbour. Peace on earth and goodwill to all men.

She rooted out the box of unused cards and selected a snow scene (nicely appropriate) for Gilda, writing inside *With best wishes from Jo, Marcus and Sean.* Then she addressed the envelope to *Mrs G. Iceton & Miss R. Iceton*, pushed the card inside, sealed it down and propped it against the one she had written a couple of weeks before for Maisie and Fred.

It was still snowing hard, so before leaving the house she wrapped the two envelopes inside a plastic bag to keep them dry. The snow on the drive was pristine except for Shelley's footprints, which had already been partially obscured. Strange how heavy snowfall brought its own special intensity to everything, that special hush, the acute brightness, in spite of poor visibility and a leaden sky. She avoided Shelley's tracks, preferring to scrunch into the virgin snow, sinking almost to her ankles at every step before the compressed snow beneath her feet brought her up short. If this went on they would need Mr Tyson with his snowplough, never mind a four-wheel drive.

Even after a heavy snowfall The Old Forge did not manage to look picturesque. Gilda had been in residence for nearly a year now, but there had been no sign of any improvements. No builder's vans parked outside or planning permission notices tied to the gate. Perhaps Gilda was doing it up herself, from the inside out.

Either Jo's approach had been observed or else coincidence was in play, because just as she reached the front door it was opened by Gilda's daughter. Shelley was certainly right about Rebecca Iceton – she was extremely pretty. It must make Gilda so proud to have a daughter who had turned out like this.

'I brought your Christmas card,' Jo said, fumbling with her plastic bag, while the girl stood just inside the door, regarding her with an uncertainty which might have been no more than shyness. 'What do you think of this weather?' Jo groped for something suitable to fill the silence. She had to get her glove off in order to separate the two cards, and the glove was proving stubborn. 'Will you be out sledging, later on?'

'I don't have a sledge.'

'We've got at least two,' Jo said. 'I'm sure Sean will be out later – when he gets up. I'll tell him to call for you, if you like.'

'Thank you.' The girl continued to look uncomfortable. Jo wondered if she was remembering their first encounter in the lane; or perhaps Gilda had actually instructed her to steer clear of the strange woman who lived at The Hideaway. When she handed the card over, Rebecca said 'Thank you' again. As she was shutting the front door, Gilda's voice came from somewhere at the back of the house. 'Is there someone there, Becky?' Jo was still on the front step, taking a moment to replace her glove and reorganize the plastic bag around the Perrys' card, and in the stillness of the snowy hamlet she heard the girl's voice clearly through the closed door. 'It was the woman from across the road, bringing a Christmas card. Shall I open it? It's addressed to both of us – although she's got my name wrong, as usual.' The voice was growing fainter as the speaker retreated down the hall and any reply was inaudible.

Jo froze on the spot. In what way was the name wrong? Why would Rebecca's name not be Iceton, the same as her mother's? It was not as if Gilda had kept her maiden name, which might have explained it. What other reason but that this was not Gilda's daughter at all? She set off almost at a run towards Gilda's perpetually open gate, nearly forgetting in her hurry that she still had the Perrys' card in her hand. She almost turned back towards The Hideaway, but stopped herself just in time. She must walk calmly and quietly to Throstles and deliver the other card. She must not let Gilda – if she was watching – realize that she had overheard.

And Gilda might be watching. Gilda was always watching – she had been watching from her bedroom window that night when Jo had returned from Claife Station, and again from her bedroom window when the beck flooded – except that one of those events could only be seen from the front of Gilda's house and the other from the back. No wonder she had been turning things over and over in her mind, because subconsciously she had known all along that Gilda was lying when she said that she just happened to be drawing her bedroom curtains that night. Gilda's bedroom was not at the front but at the back – she had given herself away the night of the floods. Of course, Gilda could have moved from one bedroom to another, said the devil's advocate in her mind, but Jo was not really listening.

How would it work, exactly? Supposing you saw someone you really hated, had always hated and longed to get back at: someone who had something which you had not got but badly wanted. What would you have to do, if you had taken the ultimate revenge and stolen their baby? She swung the Perrys' gate open so violently that snow sprayed off it in all directions, plastering itself against her jeans and cagoule, some of it dropping in icy dollops down her boots, but she scarcely noticed. You would have to pretend to everyone that the child was yours. It would be much easier to pull it off if you had money to take you to different places, plenty of cash to set yourself up with an instant kit of cot and pram and so on. Difficult to explain to friends and relations how this child had suddenly appeared in your life – but if you didn't actually have that many close relatives . . . or friends . . . Gilda was an only child, and her parents had been getting on when they had her. They might have been dead by 1998. What about the husband she claimed to have had? (Ouch, the Perrys' letterbox was vicious.) Maybe the husband was just a figment of Gilda's imagination, or maybe the marriage had been short-lived, so that he was off the scene by the time she took Lauren.

'Hell-o-oo.' Maisie had been alerted by the snap of the letterbox and was standing on the step, waving aloft the envelope Jo had just delivered.

'Hello, Maisie. Can't stop.' She had already made it to the gate. It was a bit rude, but she didn't look back. Provided you didn't look back, you would neither be turned into a pillar of salt, nor snared by Maisie's invitation to join her for a festive sherry.

But why call the child something different? Surely that just drew attention to the fact that she wasn't yours. It was because you would sooner or later need documents. Children only had their birth certificate. You would have to apply for someone else's birth certificate, then come up with some plausible reason why the details didn't fit properly – could you make that work, or was the whole thing just plain crazy?

By now she was passing The Old Forge again. She forced herself not to look up at the place, concentrating instead on where she was putting her feet. The falling snow had softened the set of prints she had made coming the other way. The outlines were there, but the imprints left by the soles of her boots in the bottom of each hole were already gone. It would be impossible to get a car along the lane now.

When she opened her own front door, Sean was just coming downstairs. She took a deep breath. 'I've just dropped a card off with the neighbours,' she said as casually as she could. 'Becky at The Old Forge is home, but she can't go out sledging because she doesn't have a sledge. I guessed you'd be going out later, and we've got the wooden sledge and at least one of those cheap plastic ones in the garage, so I said you would call for her on your way out. I hope you don't mind.'

Sean didn't look exactly pleased, but he didn't argue. 'I want something to eat first' he said.

'Of course. You'll need something warm before you go out. What would you like? A bacon sandwich, maybe? I'll make some porridge, if you like.'

'A bacon sandwich, please.' He regarded her suspiciously, noticing the way her eyes looked glittery and overexcited – although he supposed that might be because she had just been out in the cold.

Jo often took herself off somewhere else while he ate whatever food she had prepared, but today she hovered around in the kitchen, humming snatches of a tune, opening and shutting cupboard doors in a vain search for nothing in particular. Sean regarded her warily, wolfing down his sandwich as quickly as he could. He would have taken it upstairs, but she had very pointedly put out a knife and table mat, along with the ketchup which was de rigueur for the consumption of bacon butties.

'You won't forget to call for Becky – is that what you call her, Becky?'

'I won't forget.'

'You don't happen to know what her other name is?'

'Becky Iceton, I suppose.'

'No, it isn't Iceton; it's something else.'

'Oh.' Sean sounded disinterested.

She sat down at the table in the chair opposite him. Sean still had at least two or three mouthfuls of sandwich to deal with. He began to fiddle uneasily with the ketchup bottle.

'Sean, will you do something for me?'

He didn't make eye contact. 'What?'

'Will you find out what Becky's other name is? Just ask her – casually – don't make a big thing of it, and don't tell her that it's me who wants to know.'

Sean hesitated, uncomfortable beneath the weight of her full attention. 'OK. But what's the big deal?'

302

'It's not a big deal. It's just something I want to know. OK?'

'OK.' He stuffed the remaining lump of bread and bacon into his mouth and stood up to make his escape.

'You won't forget?'

His mouth was too full to attempt an answer. A trickle of ketchup was escaping from the corner of his mouth, like a cheap effect in a vampire movie. He flapped his hand up and down a couple of times in a gesture she was intended to read as, 'All right, calm down.'

Jo watched Sean cross the lane, dragging a sledge from each hand. The snow had eased now, as if in blocking the lane and turning the garden into a Fred Swan painting its work was done. As he was on the point of leaving she had called out casually, as if by way of an afterthought, 'Bring Lauren back when you're finished. I'll do some hot chocolate and mince pies.'

'Becky,' he said impatiently. 'Her name is Becky.'

'Yes, of course. I meant Becky.'

He didn't bring her back with him, of course. He had probably forgotten, or else she had declined. Jo did not bother to ask which. They had played out in the snow for more than two hours, and Sean needed to change out of his wet clothes before he was ready for the promised hot chocolate. When he reappeared, she only managed to contain herself for as long as it took to place his mug on the breakfast bar and put a couple of mince pies into the microwave. 'Did you find out what Becky's last name is?'

'Yeah. It's Ford.'

'She didn't ask why you wanted to know?'

'No.' Sean's voice was contemptuous. 'I said, like it was just conversation, that I was glad I wasn't at the very beginning or the very end of the alphabet, because that way you're never first or last when you get called out to do stuff at school, and she said she wasn't at the very beginning either. Then I said, I'm H for Handley, and she said she's F for Ford.'

'That was clever.' He had just gone up several notches in her estimation.

'I'm not a complete amateur. So why do you want to know?'

Jo was ready for the question and embarked on a convoluted, but entirely untrue story about Gilda's having been married to someone who might have been an old school friend of someone else, but not wanting to ask a direct question in case she put her foot in it. She could see that this was working just as she had intended, with Sean obviously wishing he had never asked, and breaking in at the first possible opportunity to say, 'Yeah – whatever.'

She left him in the kitchen finishing his hot chocolate. She had not been idle during his absence. If Shelley's father had begun his family researches via the computer, that must mean there was a way of accessing people's birth certificates. She had found a site where, by registering herself and paying a fee by credit card, she could search the official indices of births, deaths and marriages online. You could not see an actual birth certificate without applying by post, but by looking up Lauren's entry, she had established that the basic information shown in the index included mothers' maiden names. Now all she had to do was check the birth of Rebecca Ford.

Her hands shook as she brought up the site and keyed in her search. There were two pages of Rebecca Fords, but none of them had a mother whose maiden name had been Stafford. She kept staring at the screen, going back from one page to another to double-check. And all the time the blood pounded in her head, making her feel giddy, setting up a pain behind her eyes. A combination of shock and rage coursed through her. She had long suspected that Gilda's so-called daughter was one and the same as her own, but it was a very different thing to have proof of it.

And now she had her proof, what next? Should she ring the police? It was a Sunday afternoon and they were cut off by the snow. What would happen if she told the police? She knew enough about red tape not to imagine that a friendly constable would simply take her word for it, tell Lauren to pack her bags and move across to The Hideaway. Any delay at all would afford Gilda the opportunity to make a run for it, taking Lauren with her. They could be out of the country within hours.

Alternatively, the authorities might arrange to take Lauren into care while they made up their minds about whose daughter she was. She thought of Ma and Pa Allisson, who were probably dead by now. Foster-parents, or a children's home. She thought of Lauren, with her boarding-school accent and nice clothes, thrown into a lion's den shared with the kids of criminals, drug addicts and various other inadequates. She remembered the smell of cabbage and wee in the hall, the scuffed furniture in common rooms decorated with posters of pop stars and cartoon characters, always torn at the edges and missing their Blu-tack from one corner. The bits of last year's tinsel trapped under yellowing Sellotape in the corners near the ceiling, faded duvet covers on the beds with washed-out Barbie dolls or Ninja Turtles on them – things which people thought kids liked, but which you would never have chosen for yourself. None of this must be allowed to happen.

There must be some other way. She could not simply spirit Lauren away as Gilda had done, so many years ago. Apart from anything else, the girl would not come with her. The prospect of Lauren rejecting her was akin to having a bucket of icy water tipped over her head – but Lauren had grown up believing she was Gilda's daughter and that her name was Rebecca. What would her reaction be when she found out the truth? Would she want to stay with Gilda? Well, that wasn't an option, because Gilda would go to prison, of course . . . but how would Lauren take that? Would she blame Jo for Gilda's incarceration? Children did not invariably react in the most logical of ways.

It probably wasn't a bed of roses having Gilda for a mother. Jo knew what it was like, being trailed everywhere by someone wearing a mustard-coloured number from a jumble sale, with a purple chiffon scarf wrapped around their head. Having a mother who was persistently out of touch with the way the rest of the world worked, but bridled at any suggestion of falling in line. Then again, what sort of alternative to Gilda would Lauren see in her – someone she only knew as the weird woman who had jumped out at her one day in the lane?

And there was her schooling – she and Marcus could not afford school fees. Lauren would have to attend the local comp, like Sean. She might like having a stepbrother – they had not exactly been the best of friends so far, but at least they'd been out sledging together – that surely counted for something.

She remembered the various bargains she had tried to strike with God. She wanted what was best for Lauren. She wanted Lauren to be safe, well and happy: those things were more important than anything else. If she knew that Lauren was all those things, wasn't that better than actively making her unhappy? It was not as if she knew whether Lauren was happy or not. But if she was happy, and being forced to return to her natural mother would make her less so . . .

No, no, no. That would mean Gilda had won. A person should not be allowed to profit from their crime – that could not possibly be right. From somewhere at the back of her mind a memory of a social worker emerged, a woman having a bad hair day, pontificating on television: 'When making a custody decision, the interests of the child are paramount.' Suppose they decided that Lauren should stay with Gilda, irrespective of her crime. Would Gilda even get a custodial sentence? Only the other day a man had been given a suspended sentence for poisoning his ex-wife – as if permanently disabling her in the process was a matter of small account. These days the courts seemed capable of anything. No doubt the usual psychiatrist would be wheeled in to explain that it wasn't really Gilda's fault – she'd had a tough time as a kid, which meant that she had been temporarily suffering from some kind of compulsive disorder and was now full of genuine remorse for what she had done. Rather than punishing her, a judge was just as likely to decide that since Gilda had taken good care of Lauren, it was a first offence and she posed no obvious threat to any other children, a bit of litter-picking on Saturday afternoons for the next six months by way of community service would put everything right.

Jo thought about the cuddly dog waiting patiently on the spare-room bed. She pictured baby Lauren in her pyjamas, still pink from the bath, as she was carried upstairs and laid sleeping in her cot. Tears splashed on to the desk, narrowly missing the keyboard. She had never quite managed a happy ending for herself, but perhaps she could engineer one for Lauren. They would have to let Lauren decide. It must be done between themselves – no police, no social services, no tawdry children's homes, or well-meaning foster-parents. Lauren should not suffer as she had done. Sometimes, if you really love someone, you have to let them go.

She went upstairs to change her clothes. She would have to put her big coat and wellingtons on top, but she wanted to look smart for the moment when Lauren understood that she was looking at her real mother. It took her some time to decide, practicalities weighing heavily in favour of most other considerations, so that she eventually ended up wearing her best jeans and a cheerful multicoloured sweater, bought on a visit to Bowness three years before and hardly worn since.

An early dusk was falling. When she opened the front door she was immediately aware of that heightened quiet brought by the snow. The temperature was already well below freezing, and the snow creaked in protest as it compressed beneath her boots. There was a light on above the front door of The Old Forge, just as if she was expected. And all the time that sense that this could not really be happening.

It was Gilda who answered the door on this occasion.

'I need to talk to you. Can I come in?'

'Of course,' Gilda said, stepping back in a stance of invitation, although her expression was wary. Jo dragged off her boots and stood them upright on the front step before following Gilda along the hall, which was dimly lit with a single energy-saver and had a roll of carpet lying along one side of it, which had to be stepped over in order to access the sitting room at the back of the house. There was a fire blazing in the grate, but to Jo's eyes this was about the only cheerful thing in the room, which suggested not so much someone's living accommodation, as an abandoned stage set into which disparate props from half a dozen other plays had been randomly dumped for storage.

'Sit down.' Gilda indicated a chair from which she had removed a copy of a TV guide in passing. Jo sat. She was half disappointed and half relieved not to find Lauren in the room. Gilda tossed the TV guide on to a miscellanea of magazines and newspapers which stood several feet high on top of what might have been an old-fashioned needlework box, then lowered herself into the chair she had obviously been occupying before her visitor's arrival, so that she faced Jo across the hearth rug.

Now that she was here, Jo found that it was not easy to know how to begin. She had effected no rehearsals, simply hoping that the right words would come when she needed them – which they did not. She cast about the room helplessly for a moment until her attention fell on a life-size stone cat which was sitting on the hearth.

Gilda saw what she was looking at. 'We call him Timmy,' she said. 'Becky would like a real cat, but cat hair and I don't get on.'

'Lauren had a cat.' Jo spoke so quietly that the last word was almost drowned by a crack from the fire. Gilda automatically extended her foot to rub out the spark which had leaped on to the rug. 'She called him Puddy,' Jo continued. 'She had him with her on the day she was taken.'

Gilda frowned momentarily before saying, 'Oh yes – Lauren was your daughter, wasn't she?'

'Is. She *is* my daughter. Does she still have Puddy?'

Gilda frowned again – harder this time, so that her eyes narrowed to shadows beneath a deeply puckered forehead. 'I'm sorry, but I don't understand. What cat are you talking about? Do you mean this cat – Timmy?'

'No, I mean Puddy. Does Lauren still have Puddy?'

'I'm sorry,' Gilda repeated, 'but I'm afraid you've lost me. What is it you've come to see me about, exactly?'

'Where is Becky at the moment? Can she hear what we are saying?'

'I doubt it. She's up in her bedroom, listening to something on her iPod, I think.'

'I know the truth, Gilda. I know that Becky is Lauren.'

'Dear God – you're mad! Absolutely mad!'

'No, I'm not. Becky isn't your daughter. I've checked up. Her name is Rebecca Heidi Ford, and her mother's maiden name was Parsons, not Stafford.'

'Well, that's no secret. Rebecca Ford is my adopted daughter, and her mother, Heidi Ford née Parsons, was my friend. I adopted Rebecca when my friend and her husband died. As it happens, I can't have children myself.'

'You're just saying that,' said Jo, but her voice wavered.

'I cannot believe that you have come over here to confront me with such a half-baked tale. Imagine how upset Becky would have been if she had heard what you said. And how dare you obtain a copy of my daughter's birth certificate! Whatever possessed you? It's horrible to think that you must have been checking up on us, watching and spying . . .' Gilda appeared to be gripped by a mounting sense of outrage. She stood up and took a few steps towards the window, before returning to grip the back of her chair as if she could hardly contain herself.

'I didn't get a copy of her birth certificate. I looked it up on the internet.'

'I don't believe you. I don't believe people's birth certificates are on the internet.'

'Not exactly – not the whole certificate.'

'I should think not.'

'She's the same age,' Jo said. 'She's got blonde hair—'

'So has half the population.'

'And – and I didn't believe you'd been married.'

'I suppose you tried to check that up, too.'

'No.'

'I suppose you just took that as read. It would be like you to assume that I couldn't get a husband if I wanted one.' A

310

strange smile crossed Gilda's face. Bitter, while at the same time knowing and in control. The smile of one who knows their adversary, and is capable of inflicting great damage. It was the sort of look which made Jo instinctively want to flinch away.

'I thought I saw you there – in Barleycombe – that day she was taken. And then you were watching the night when I went to the rendezvous on the postcard.' Jo's voice shook. She knew that at any minute she would succumb to tears.

'What postcard? What on earth are you talking about? You know what the trouble with you is, Joanne Savage? You're as barmy as your mother. When I first knew you it just manifested itself in your being a nasty little piece of work, but now you've gone completely over the edge – just like she did. Look at yourself. You're a wreck, a laughing stock. Oh, you thought you'd got it made, with your nice little business showing rich tourists where Wordsworth ate his supper, but it's all gone wrong again now, hasn't it? Of course they're still at the stage of being sorry for you, Maisie and Shelley and the others, but they don't know the half of it, do they? Did your first husband see it coming, when you pushed him over the cliff? You got away with it, too, didn't you? Not like your mother. Still locked up in Broadmoor, is she? And how about Marcus, is he watching his back? Because he certainly ought to be.'

'Stop it!' Jo stumbled to her feet. 'Stop it. My mother's dead – and I'm not Joanne Savage any more. That's all behind me now, all those terrible things.'

'I don't think so,' Gilda spat. 'I don't think anyone forgets that easily. I don't. Remember that time you all got me in the toilets, shoved my head down and flushed the chain? Or burning my homework with Colleen's cigarette lighter, so I'd get into trouble for not handing in my assignment?

311

Remember the names you called me? That way you all had of sticking out a foot, so that I tripped over it? You see, I don't forget things, either.'

'But that wasn't me. It really wasn't. I didn't do any of those things – it was the others. I should have stopped them, I know I should, but I was afraid of them, too.'

'It wasn't *me*,' Gilda jeered. 'Oh, yes – it's always someone else, isn't it? You picked on me at school and you think you can do the same now.'

'I don't. I'm not. I'm truly sorry about what happened to you at school,' Jo sobbed. 'But my child – someone took my child.'

'Well, maybe that was your punishment. Maybe that's how life works: what goes around, comes around. You give someone hell, and it comes back at you in a hotter form. And being the victim is still your trump card, isn't it? It kept you out of trouble at school – *poor* Joanne, we have to make allowances because she's had *such* a rough time – and now you think you can come here and make accusations, and then when someone calls your bluff, you turn on the tears and start to bleat. *Someone took my child*,' Gilda mimicked cruelly. 'How dare you come into my home, trying to upset me and my daughter, pushing your particular brand of lunacy into our lives.'

Jo stood up and made her way unsteadily into the hall, almost falling over the roll of carpet on the way. 'I'm sorry. I can see that it was wrong . . . I just thought . . .'

'I don't want to hear any more. Get out of my house.' Gilda marched down the hall behind her, a threatening presence before which Jo cowered at the front door, where it took her an age to fumble her feet into her wellingtons, while tears cascaded on to her hands, blurring her vision, muffling her voice, as she repeated over and over again that she was sorry, that she should not have come.

The cold outside took her breath away. Gilda had shut the door at her back, but the outside light was enough to see by. Her own footprints were mixed up with the tracks made by Sean and Rebecca earlier in the day, all of them now frozen into a lethal skid pan. She picked her way around this bumpy patch of ice, seeking the relative safety of the virgin snow. Shame lashed her as she trod a wavering path across the lane. How had she reached such a dark place? How could she not have foreseen this obvious flaw in her perverted logic? Gilda's daughter was *adopted*. She had followed a false trail, wrought of her own imagination and despair. If Gilda was right, then she should end it now, before she did something really terrible. If she walked the other way along the lane, turned up the footpath through the woods and carried on until she reached the moor, she would only have to sit down among the cluster of rocks in her drawing place and she would surely be dead by morning. She had once read that hypothermia was not a painful death. Strangely, it was not the thought of death that deterred her, so much as the thought of the darkness among the trees. It reminded her of the night when she had gone to Claife Station, not knowing what unseen horror might be waiting for her there. And if she killed herself, who would be left for Lauren? *Unless*, said a voice in her head, *Lauren is already dead. Maybe Lauren wants you to do it. Maybe she is waiting for you on the other side. Perhaps that is what lies just out of sight, those shadowy watchers that you are afraid to confront . . . maybe it's Lauren and Dom, hand in hand, waiting for you.*

But it was already too late. She had reached the house and was stamping the snow from her boots. When she got inside she ran upstairs, buried her face in the duvet and wept hysterically.

CHAPTER TWENTY-FOUR

Sean had not realized that his stepmother had left the house, but he was aware of her return because he heard the front door slam and her feet on the stairs, followed by the sound of her bedroom door closing. When she had not emerged by eight o'clock, he put a frozen pizza in the oven, then went around the ground-floor rooms, switching on lights and closing the curtains and blinds. He did not like uncurtained windows after dark, with their ever-present sense that some-one might be on the opposite side of the glass, looking in. Not that there was ever anyone around, but it felt spooky – even on nights like this when the combination of moonlight and heavy snowfall made it easy to see into the garden without switching on the outside lights. It occurred to him that it would be pretty neat to go sledging by moonlight. Maybe it was something they could do when Harry came.

He looked forward to Harry's visits. He sometimes talked to his old mates online, but it wasn't like being able to hang out with them. The kids at school were OK, but they already had their own friends, who they seemed to have known for ever. They didn't deliberately exclude him, but they didn't bother to include him either. He missed his old mates, and the comfortable familiarity of a mother who could be relied upon not to take off without telling anyone where she was going, who would always provide meals at predictable times and who could yell at him with impunity because she didn't have to be seen to be making a serious effort to like him all the time.

He remembered the artificial jollity of his first Christmas at The Hideaway – in less than a week they would be playing out the same farce again – except that *she* was getting worse and worse at managing to play her part. You never knew where you were with her. Only that morning she had appeared to be in a fairly reasonable mood, but there was something up with her again now. At one time she had seemed quite scary (he still had the knife, currently slipped into an old box which had once housed *Buffy the Vampire Slayer Season Seven*), but lately she just seemed pathetic. He wondered what she was doing now. Just sitting on her own, staring at the carpet, probably.

He couldn't imagine why she was so interested in Becky. He had not minded being asked to find out her last name. In fact, he was pretty pleased with the way he had managed it. Nor had he really minded taking Becky out sledging, because things like that were more fun when there was someone else to have a laugh with and he had sort of said he would call for her again tomorrow.

Jo lay on her bed for a long time. She tried to empty her mind completely; not to facilitate remembrance, but in order to forget. Imagine if the accusations she had levelled at Gilda travelled beyond the four walls of The Old Forge. Gilda could easily tell other people what she had said – she might even go to the police and make a complaint of some kind. Harassment. It might constitute harassment. Suppose Gilda did something spiteful, like sell the story to the papers. Tell them how she, Jo, went about accusing innocent widows of having stolen her child. That awful excoriating shame of publicity. Everyone would know who she was. Marcus and the business would get dragged in; he and Melissa would be furious.

She crawled under the duvet without bothering to remove her clothes, then lay there trying not to think. If only she could blot everything out by falling into a deep, dreamless sleep.

After a long time she sensed that the room was becoming lighter. It was an uneasy feeling, as if an unseen hand was turning up the dimmer switch millimetre by millimetre, the better to spy on her. It took her a while to realize that it must be the moon, moving around the house until it shone in at the window.

The moon made her think of the path along the cliff top at Shanklin; she and Dominic, hand in hand on their honeymoon, looking at the stars while the moon reflected silvery patterns on the sea. Happy – so very, very happy. Not caring that they could not afford a Caribbean island. She had the strangest feeling that if she turned to look out of the window he would be floating just outside, beckoning her to come away with him, out into the cold pale moonlight and away to the dark places where there is no more feeling, no more pain, no more doubting what is real and what is true because there you know everything.

The feeling was so overwhelming that she rolled over to look, but there was nothing to be seen except the skeletons of the trees, the uppermost edge of each shiny black branch highlighted by a coating of snow. Ransoms grew among those trees in springtime, and beautiful carpets of bluebells, but that was a long way off. Maybe she would not be here by then.

She slept for a while, then woke suddenly in the darkness, crying out in confusion. The air felt cold against her face. For a minute she thought she must be in a sleeping bag, camping

316

out on the fellside – not that she had ever done so. Then she remembered that the heating would have gone off for the night, and with the weather being so bitter, she should have set it to override the timer. *Cold as the grave*, said a voice in her head. She had once driven through a part of the municipal cemetery set aside for the interment of children. A terrible place of soft toys and withered balloons. She had not wanted that for Lauren. She would have done anything – anything at all to give Lauren the chance to live and have a happy life. After a time she fell asleep again. In her new dream Lauren was riding a pony. The pony kept breaking into a trot, and although she could hear Lauren laughing and encouraging it to go faster, she was afraid for her. Surely Lauren was too small to be on the pony by herself, without someone there to hold the reins. She tried to catch them up but the pony was always a bit too fast for her and full of cunning tricks, getting itself on the far side of a hedge or the opposite bank of a stream. The girl in the saddle seemed to have grown – she turned to look over her shoulder, and Jo saw that it was Gilda's daughter after all. The girl pressed her knees into the pony's sides and the animal galloped away.

When she next awoke it was to broad daylight, and Sean's voice was coming from the other side of the bedroom door. 'I'm going out,' he shouted. 'I'm taking the sledge.'

'OK.' Her first attempt to respond was just a croak. She tried again, and her response emerged more clearly, although she was uncertain whether Sean had waited for an answer.

She rolled over and looked at the clock. It was approaching eleven in the morning. She dragged away the duvet and stood up, straightening one sleeve of her jumper which had become twisted around her arm, dragging up her socks before they completely parted company with her feet. She went downstairs slowly, reaching the sitting room just in time to

317

see Sean dragging two sledges into the gateway of The Old Forge. She ought to have warned him that he might not be welcome. She waited anxiously at the window, but it appeared that whatever animosity Gilda might entertain towards Jo, she was not taking it out on her stepson, because after what seemed like an age Sean and Rebecca emerged from between the gateposts, he pulling the larger wooden sledge, she the cheap plastic job. As they turned away down the lane, she saw them both raise a hand in acknowledgement of someone she could not see.

While she was waiting for Sean to reappear, she saw a large green Jeep drive slowly along the lane. The world was waking up and moving along without her. The world, in fact, did not need her. She went into the kitchen, which bore evidence of both Sean's breakfast and supper. He had actually remembered to put his cereal bowl into the dishwasher, although the crumbs from his toast lay forgotten on the worktop.

She imagined him now with Becky. That singular exhilaration of travelling fast downhill on a sledge. Happy, laughing, their whole lives ahead of them. Her life had never really been like that. It was true that there had been moments of exhilaration, but it seemed to her now that they had always been tempered by shadows. She remembered once holding Lauren up in front of a mirror. Lauren had been laughing and trying to touch the glass with her stubby fingers, but Jo had not let her get close enough to put smudges on it. As she watched their reflections looking back at her – mother and daughter together – from nowhere had come the thought that one day she would have to explain to Lauren about *her* mother and what she had done; after which Lauren, too, would have to bear the burden, wonder what it might mean for her own mother and for herself. Always that past which you could not escape from – and whenever you thought you

318

had got away, someone sent a postcard, dropped a pebble in a pool, left a paperclip on the carpet, or a penny down the back of the settee. The only way you could escape your family history was by not knowing about it in the first place. She thought of Shelley's father, digging away so eagerly, wanting to find it all out. Well, her advice to anyone would be: run away, run as fast as you can in the opposite direction and don't look back.

She found that she was standing at the foot of the stairs. What should she do now? Clean your teeth and have a shower, suggested an inner rationale. Then have some breakfast. That's what a normal person would do. Ah, but I'm not normal, said a second voice which sounded suspiciously like her mother.

Jo gripped the knob at the end of the banister, feeling the artificial greenery of the Christmas garland prickling against the back of her hand. She *would not* hear her mother's voice, she told herself angrily. Her mother was dead.

That was it . . . Dead.

She ran into the office, threw herself down into the big leather chair and scrabbled the mouse to and fro on its mat, impatient for the computer to wake into life. It had been left on all night, the screen saver weaving never-ending patterns against its own version of the night sky, but now it sprang to life as if eager to do her bidding. She keyed in the website address from memory, logged into her account with the password she had acquired the day before, then typed in the search. Deaths – Ford – Rebecca. There were only three results for the relevant period, and the last one was 'Rebecca Heidi Ford, born 13 Mar 1998, death registered Dec 1998.'

She logged out and almost ran into the kitchen. She pulled a knife out of the block so violently that all the other knives jumped and clattered, as if unnerved by this unaccustomed rough usage. She took the one with the six-inch blade, which she normally used for vegetables.

She pushed her feet into a pair of flat black ankle boots which were lying near the front door, then flung on her old gardening coat, which she did not bother to button. She strode down the drive and across the lane, entirely careless of slipping on the snow and ice. When she got to Gilda's gate, she found the other woman in the act of kicking snow off her boots, alongside the open front door. Jo instinctively hid the knife behind her back like a guilty child.

Gilda had been clearing away the snow between her parked car and the road, so she was evidently planning to drive somewhere, either now or later. At the sound of Jo's approach she looked up in surprise. 'If you've come for Sean . . .' she began.

'No,' said Jo. 'I have come to see you.'

'I really don't think –' Gilda began, but Jo walked forward so purposefully that Gilda broke off and darted into the house. Jo was too quick for her and got there before she had time to get the door even part way closed.

'If you don't leave', said Gilda, retreating up the hall, 'I am going to call the police.'

'Oh, I don't think so.' Jo continued to advance, not bothering to close the door behind her, never taking her eyes off Gilda, who had backed into the sitting room, taking an elaborately large backward step over the roll of carpet, unable to look down for fear of taking her eyes off the knife, now clearly visible in Jo's right hand.

'Rebecca Heidi Ford died in December 1998,' said Jo.

Gilda said nothing.

'You were there, weren't you? That day in Barleycombe. You saw me with my husband and my baby, you followed us and when I went into the shop, you took her. Out of spite

320

and revenge and jealousy. And if that wasn't enough, you tormented me all these years, sending those bloody postcards. You even came to live opposite me, so you could *see* what you were doing to me. You hated me so much that you wanted to destroy my life.'

Now that they had reached the living room, Gilda stood her ground, taking up a position alongside the armchair in which she had sat the day before, resting one hand on its back. 'This isn't going to do you any good,' Gilda's voice was remarkably calm. 'If you harm me in any way, do you think for a moment that they will give Becky back to you?'

'She's not Becky. Her name is Lauren, and I am her mother. A DNA test will prove it.'

'She answers to Becky. Has it occurred to you that she may not want to be with you? I am her mother, you see. She loves me – even though she knows I'm not her real mother. I'm the person who brought her up, cared for her when she was ill, taught her to read before she ever went to school. You're just a stranger. An unstable woman who careers around the village, acting strangely and threatening other people with knives.'

'She won't love you when she finds out what you did.'

'Love isn't switched on and off like a tap. Becky loves me – she doesn't even know you. You're going to tell her that nothing she has ever believed about herself is true; that her birthday happened two months after she thinks it did; that her real father threw himself off a cliff; and that her maternal grandmother finished up in Broadmoor. And then you're going to tell her that she's got to live with the village loony and a stepfather who's more concerned with what happened on a medieval battlefield than what's going to happen next week. Do you think she's going to fall into your arms in an ecstasy of delight?'

321

'She'll grow to love me, once she gets to know me.'

'Look at yourself. You're a wreck – see the way your hand is shaking? That knife is wobbling like a jelly. Why don't you put it down, before you do yourself an injury?' As Jo glanced down in spite of herself, Gilda asked, 'Are you going to destroy that girl's life by making her come and live with you?'

'She's my daughter. I love her.'

'Love her? You don't even know her! She's just an idea to you – an obsession.'

'That's not true. You don't know what it is to be a mother.'

'I *have* been a mother – a good mother. What kind of a mother do you think you would ever have made?' Gilda's eyes abruptly focused on something beyond Jo's right shoulder. 'Becky!' she shouted.

Even as Jo turned to register the empty doorway, Gilda was on her, flinging her whole weight against Jo's left side so that she tumbled face down on to the sofa, with the knife trapped and useless beneath her. Gilda was by far the larger and heavier woman, and she used her weight to crushing effect, pinning Jo down and pushing her face into the cushions so that she could hardly breathe. When Jo managed to twist her face aside, Gilda grabbed the hood of the old gardening coat and forced it over Jo's head, holding it over her mouth with one hand while she used the other to quest between Jo's body and the upholstery, seeking the buried weapon. Although half suffocated, Jo mounted a frenzied defence, thrusting her free hand over her head and clawing blindly at her adversary, until Gilda was forced to let go of the hood in order to defend herself, grabbing Jo's wrist and snapping it back so that the other woman screamed.

In spite of Gilda's determined assault, the sheer unreality of what was happening and the knowledge that her wrist was probably broken, Jo was still thinking clearly. She knew what she needed to do – it was just a question of timing. When Gilda's fist slammed into the back of her head, even in the midst of blinding pain, she guessed that Gilda would repeat the action and knew it represented an opportunity. As the second blow fell, she gave a loud moan and let her body go limp. Gilda's momentary hesitation was enough: Jo pushed up with all her might, throwing her entire body backwards in a twisting movement which tumbled them both off the sofa.

Jo's 180-degree turn had taken Gilda completely by surprise, but as they hit the floor with a crash that reverberated through the house, it was Gilda who managed to wrestle herself into a position of superiority with Jo still trapped underneath her, although Jo was now facing her assailant with her right hand freed. She stabbed the knife wildly in Gilda's direction, but Gilda saw it coming and grabbed Jo's wrist, forcing it away. Using one hand to keep Jo's arm at bay, Gilda used the other to claw at her fingers, hoping to prize them from the handle.

With her left arm now useless, Jo focused everything she had on retaining her weapon. She tried holding the knife at full stretch above her head, but the other woman's reach was longer. She flexed her legs, but it was impossible to gain much purchase against the carpet, which seemed to slide away from her like quicksand. She attempted to buck Gilda off, but nothing was working – and all the time Gilda's full weight bore down on her ribs, pressing the breath out of her.

Gilda too had sustained damage. Jo had scratched and bitten her, and her right knee throbbed agonizingly where it had taken the brunt of the impact when they hit the floor. She had the greater bulk, but Jo was fitter – and had managed against all odds to keep hold of the knife, so that while Gilda laboured for breath and struggled to keep her adversary

323

pinned down, she could not afford to lessen her grip on Jo's wrist for a second – because a second was all it would take.

Jo's attempts to unseat her assailant had gradually moved them across the floor. Inch by inch, they were getting nearer to the hearth, where Gilda knew that the poker was resting upright against the fireplace, but still well out of reach. Then she became aware of something else appearing at the very periphery of her vision: a dark shape at ground level, which she recognized as Timmy the stone cat. She dared not take her eye off the knife, but in spite of this she judged the distance perfectly: a lunge to her right, and within a single arc of movement she had grabbed Timmy from his usual place on the hearth and smashed him against the side of the other woman's head.

The hand holding the knife drooped in her grasp, then relaxed until the handle slid out of Jo's grip on to the carpet. Gilda instantly grabbed it. For some moments after gaining the knife she stayed where she was, alert for another trick, watching and waiting while her own breath came in ragged gasps – but Jo was not faking. Her eyes were closed, her body limp.

Gilda's overriding emotion was one of relief. Like the drowning woman who has been swept away in the floods but unexpectedly fetches up in an isolated tree top, her immediate thoughts did not extend to how she was going to escape from her new predicament. As she sat astride her neighbour, dishevelled from recent combat and clutching a kitchen knife, she was abruptly reminded of the moment when, striding along the cliff path clutching someone else's baby to her chest, she suddenly realized that she had gone too far to turn back.

She stood up slowly and looked around the room. Remarkably little had been disarranged. She was uncertain whether or not Jo was still alive, but shied away from close investigation. Blood had begun to appear in Jo's hair, at the place where the stone cat had impacted with her head, but the thick hood of her coat had fortuitously fallen in such a way that, as it began to drip out of her hair, it found the coat rather than the carpet. She could not have Jo's blood on her carpet. Somehow she had to get rid of the woman and quickly. No one must ever know that she had been here, and there was no time to waste because Becky might be back at any time, walking in on the scene, needing answers.

Still clutching the knife, she hurried into the hall, where she dragged on her coat and thrust her feet into outdoor shoes. She returned to the doorway of the sitting room, where she made a pig's breakfast of tying the laces because she was trying to do it without looking down, watching all the time for any movement from the form on the floor. Her first thought was to put Jo in the boot of the car, but it was still full of logs she had bought a couple of days before. If she tried to unload them now the delay might prove fatal. She glanced at the figure on the floor again but it gave no sign.

Gilda hurried outside and got into the car. While the demister sprang into action, she manoeuvred the Volvo closer to the front door. With the engine left running, she opened the rear door nearest the house, then set about half lifting, half dragging Jo along the hall, out of the house and into the car, taking care to keep the hood of the coat between herself and the head wound. It did not appear to have bled very much, but she did not want to get blood on her hands or clothes. In fact, she wanted to touch Jo as little as possible, but at the car door she was forced to bend almost double as she manhandled her load on to the back seat, so that Jo's coat hood brushed her face, making her recoil as if she had been stung.

It was difficult to get a proper purchase: tugging at the woman's clothes merely disarranged them without shifting their contents. It was almost as if Jo herself was holding back, trying to extend the operation until someone walked past the gateway, looked in and saw them there. The best she could achieve was to prop Jo half inside, then go round to the offside door and drag her the rest of the way. She began to doubt her own strength. Her breath was coming in gasps, as if she had been running in a race, and Becky might appear at any moment, coming home to her – because she had won. Triumph gave her strength. She heaved the body across the seats and closed the door. Did Jo stir at that moment? Was it just coincidence, or imagination – or maybe the jolt of the door itself? Round the other side she found Jo's feet were still dangling against the sill of the car. Gilda slammed the door against them. When it didn't close first time, she slammed it again – harder.

The knife – she must not forget the knife. She had put it on the table in the living room, when she first attempted to move the body. It must not be left there for Becky to find when she came back from playing in the snow. Gilda carried it into the kitchen and rinsed it under the tap, before dropping it into the drawer where she kept her own kitchen utensils. As she passed through the living room on her way back to the car, she stopped to retrieve Timmy from where she had dropped him, after striking the blow which had ended the contest. He bore no visible sign of his involvement in the fray, but his stone eyes followed her accusingly to the door.

No one was around to see the car creep into the icy lane. The state of the roads was inconvenient, but at least it reduced the likelihood of witnesses. The car slid badly on the descent towards the bridge, and Gilda had to coax it up the incline on the other side, almost by sheer strength of will. She had embarked on the journey with no clear plan in mind, focusing only on the fact that she must get Jo as far away from the house as possible. She wasn't absolutely sure whether Jo was alive or not – she thought not – but she needed to be sure. It was hard to think at all when she had to concentrate on keeping the car moving along the parallel tyre tracks left by earlier vehicles, but now she considered two possibilities. First, that she could dump Jo just as she was, somewhere well out of the way – or as far out of the way as she could manage, given the state of the roads. The sky was pregnant with the promise of more snow, and a fresh fall would obscure any tracks and hasten death by hypothermia – assuming that she wasn't already dead. Jo's head injury might even look like an accident. She was given to wandering off by herself, and probably reckoned daft enough to do it in these conditions. But suppose someone found her, and she *was* still alive? Hill walkers, shepherds, random motorists stopping for a pee. There was always that chance.

On the other hand – Gilda gulped and recovered her steering as the car skidded on a bend – if she made sure of it by hitting Jo with something else, or maybe strangling her, then it would obviously be a case of murder and there would be a big investigation, starting in Easter Bridge where Jo had last been seen alive and where her car was still parked at the front of her house. The police would inevitably take an interest in everyone else in the hamlet. Her own past connections with Jo were common knowledge. Jo had been in her house, and would surely have left some forensic evidence behind – and all of this would have to be explained.

Then she heard a sound from the back of the car. Lower than a moan, but a sound of life. She glanced in the rear-view mirror, but Jo was completely hidden below the level of the front seats. Panic travelled up Gilda's spine, settling in the

327

roots of her hair and radiating down her arms until it tingled in her fingertips. She should have made sure. If Jo came round, she could pull herself into a sitting position and attack from behind. She could signal from the windows to attract attention – even open the door and throw herself out – God knows, they were travelling slowly enough to facilitate it. If they stayed on the main road, it meant driving through Penny Bridge and Greenodd, where there might easily be someone to see.

The fingerpost at the next junction was obscured by snow, but Gilda knew where the lane went and it appeared to be just about passable. She eased the Volvo into the turning. Very few vehicles had attempted to come this way, but if she could just force the car up one more incline, after that it was downhill all the way to the main A590. Once she got that far, the road would be well traversed and gritted. She could get up enough speed to preclude any escape attempts. If she drove to the place where the road ran alongside the estuary, there was a lay-by which was all but invisible from the road once you had pulled into it, with only a low barrier between the verge and the water's edge. She would drown the bitch if necessary.

Another low animal noise came from the back seat as the car crested the hill. She hit a patch of ice at the crest and the car almost spun full circle, before coming to a standstill with its front bumper inches away from a catastrophic encounter with a ditch. Gilda revved the engine desperately, edging the vehicle forward and back to get it going in the right direction again, all the time glancing in the mirror, expecting to see a head or hand emerging into view. As she righted the car and continued down the lane, she became aware that she had made a bad mistake. It was steeper than she had remembered, and the lane was like a sheet of ice. Even in first gear the car was gathering speed. She would have to brake, otherwise their own momentum would take them straight out into the main carriageway, but if she applied the brakes she was sure to skid.

She sensed the movement behind her before she saw the face in the rear-view mirror. Even as she tried to focus on the road, she was mesmerized by the look in Jo's eyes. The end of the lane came into view below them, and she could see the vehicles flashing by at normal speed, sending up showers of dirty brown slush. The 'give way' sign was partly obscured by dimpled snow. She pressed the brakes and nothing happened. She put her foot down harder just as Jo reached for her. The car skidded sideways into the path of the tanker and the noise of metal on metal obscured her screams.

CHAPTER TWENTY-FIVE

Shelley answered a knock at the door to find Maisie waiting on the front steps of Ingledene.

'I was thinking', the older woman said without any preamble, 'that perhaps we ought to do something in the way of flowers – now that the dates for the funerals have been set.'

'Yes,' said Shelley. 'Yes, of course. Come in while I get my purse . . . although on second thoughts, I think it will have to be a cheque – will that be all right?'

Maisie acquiesced to the cheque, while following Shelley into the hall and wondering how on earth anyone could live amid such confusion. All those piles of books and papers on the stairs, for example. Hardly enough room to walk up and down.

'We hadn't really got to know Gilda,' Maisie said. 'She was here less than a year, poor thing, but as I said to Fred, I don't feel that you can do something for one and not the other – and naturally we should make some sort of gesture for Marcus's sake. Poor man, it must have been a terrible shock for him.'

'From what little I've seen of him, Marcus seems to be coping remarkably well,' Shelley said. 'Of course, having Melissa has been a great support.'

'And an awful thing for young Sean, too,' Maisie went on, either failing to catch Shelley's meaning, or choosing not to pursue it. 'An accident out of the blue like that. I understand he's going back south to live with his mother.'

'So I've heard. Do you know what's going to happen to Gilda's daughter?' (If anyone knew, Shelley thought, it would be Maisie.)

'She's going to live with a cousin of Gilda's. I met her, in fact – the cousin, I mean. She seems a very nice woman. I happened to be passing the house when she came to collect some of Rebecca's things.' Shelley had to turn away so that Maisie did not catch the expression on her face. 'Rebecca calls her Aunty, apparently, and it seems they've always been close, so hopefully it will all work out. Such a terrible shock for everyone,' she repeated. 'And as Fred keeps saying, it was an avoidable tragedy. So silly to risk a shortcut like that, with the roads so bad.'

'Marcus said he couldn't understand what they were doing together in the car at all. They weren't exactly good friends, and he's never known the two of them to go anywhere before. In fact, Marcus told me that Jo must have gone out in a hurry, because she hadn't taken her purse or her credit cards or even locked the front door, although she was very scatty about things like that.'

'Perhaps Jo had hurt herself, or been taken poorly, and Gilda offered to run her to a doctor,' Maisie suggested. 'There would have been no way of knowing, afterwards, because I heard the bodies were almost unrecognizable.'

'It was probably something quite mundane,' mused Shelley. 'But I suppose none of us will ever know now.'

ACKNOWLEDGEMENTS

I would like to record my thanks to all those who have helped and encouraged me as I wrote this book, in particular Erica Woolley, Emma Dickens, Jane Conway-Gordon, Krystyna Green and all at Constable & Robinson. Last but not least I want to thank my husband Bill for his unfailing love and support . . . and the real Timmy for keeping my feet firmly on the ground.